FORT WORTH LIBRARY

3 1668 05886 7059

P9-DBW-306

LARGE PRINT MYSTERY JANCE
2014
Jance, Judith A.
Moving target /

03/11/14

MOVING TARGET

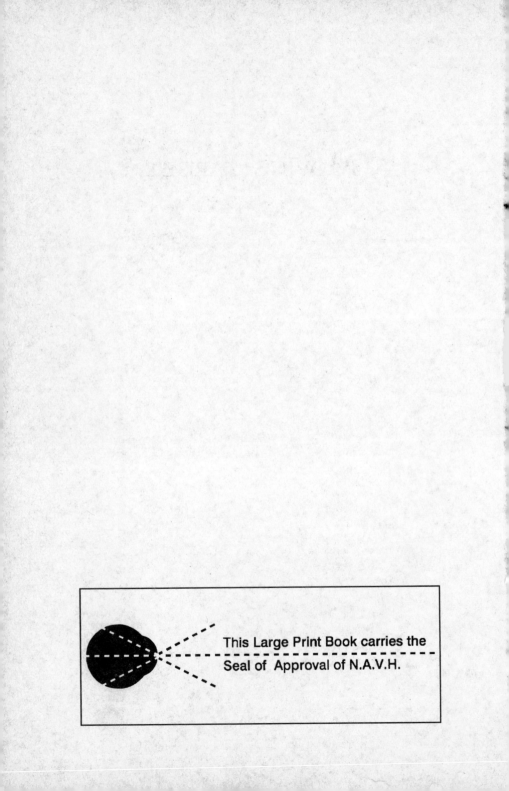

This Large Print Book carries the
Seal of Approval of N.A.V.H.

MOVING TARGET

J.A. JANCE

THORNDIKE PRESS
A part of Gale, Cengage Learning

GALE
CENGAGE Learning®

Detroit • New York • San Francisco • New Haven, Conn • Waterville, Maine • London

GALE
CENGAGE Learning®

Copyright © 2014 by J. A. Jance.
Thorndike Press, a part of Gale, Cengage Learning.

ALL RIGHTS RESERVED
This book is a work of fiction. Any references to historical events, real people, or real places are used fictitiously. Other names, characters, places, and events are products of the author's imagination, and any resemblance to actual events or places or persons, living or dead, is entirely coincidental.
Thorndike Press® Large Print Basic.
The text of this Large Print edition is unabridged.
Other aspects of the book may vary from the original edition.
Set in 16 pt. Plantin.

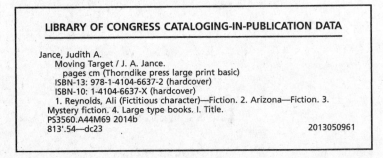

LIBRARY OF CONGRESS CATALOGING-IN-PUBLICATION DATA

Jance, Judith A.
    Moving Target / J. A. Jance.
        pages cm (Thorndike press large print basic)
    ISBN-13: 978-1-4104-6637-2 (hardcover)
    ISBN-10: 1-4104-6637-X (hardcover)
        1. Reynolds, Ali (Fictitious character)—Fiction. 2. Arizona—Fiction. 3. Mystery fiction. 4. Large type books. I. Title.
PS3560.A44M69 2014b
813'.54—dc23   2013050961

Published in 2014 by arrangement with Touchstone, a division of Simon & Schuster, Inc.

Printed in the United States of America
1 2 3 4 5 6 7 18 17 16 15 14

For Michael Reagan and his Fallen Heroes Project, and for doing what he does so faithfully and so well.

PROLOGUE

Lance Tucker had always hated ladders, but between climbing up and down a ladder in the recreation hall and sitting through another one of Mrs. Stone's endless GED classes, there was no contest. Climbing the rickety ladder to decorate the nine-foot Christmas tree was definitely the lesser of two evils.

Lance was five months into a six-month sentence at the San Leandro County Juvenile Justice Center facility in the Hill Country some fifty miles northwest of Austin. All his life he had hated having a December birthday — hated having whatever he was getting for his birthday and Christmas lumped into a single gift that never measured up to what other kids got. This year, though, his turning eighteen on December 18 meant that Lance would be out of jail in time for Christmas — out and able to go home. The problem with that, of course, was that he might not have a home to go to.

The last time he'd seen his mother, on visiting day two weeks ago, she had told him that she was probably going to lose the house. She'd finally admitted to him that she'd had to take out a second mortgage in order to pay the king's ransom he owed in court-ordered restitution. Now that her hours had been cut back at work, she wasn't able to keep up the payments on both mortgages. Which meant that, most likely, the house would go into foreclosure.

That was all his fault, too. Ears reddening with shame, Lance climbed down the ladder, moved it a few inches toward the next undecorated section of branches, picked up another tray of decorations, and clambered back up.

Don't think about it, he told himself firmly. What was it the counselor kept saying? Don't waste your time worrying about things you can't change.

This definitely fell into the category of stuff that couldn't be changed. What's done was done.

He heard a burst of laughter from the classroom. It was just off the dining room. The kids were probably giving Mrs. Stone hell again. He felt sorry for her. She seemed like a nice enough person, and he knew she was genuinely trying to help them. But what she was offering — course work leading up to earning a GED — wasn't at all what Lance wanted. It had never been part of what he had envisioned as his own future.

A year ago, just last May, his future had been promising. As a high school junior honor student at San Leandro High, Lance had been enrolled in three Advanced Placement classes and had done well on his SATs, coming in with a respectable 2290. With the help of his beloved math teacher, Mr. Jackson, Lance had been preparing to lead his computer science club team to their third consecutive championship for that year's Longhorn computer science competition.

Now his life had changed, and not for the better. Mr. Jackson was dead. Lance's mother had told him that San Leandro High had won the Longhorn trophy after all, but without Lance's help, because someone else was the team captain now. As for doing his senior year in the top 10 percent of his class and getting to wear whatever he wanted to school? That had changed, too. Now Lance found himself locked up twenty-four hours a day and with nothing to wear but orange jumpsuits. The state of Texas offered college scholarships to kids in the top 10 percent of their respective classes, but he wouldn't be able to take advantage of that, either. Lance was now officially considered to be a high school dropout with an institution-earned GED as his best possible educational outcome. No matter what his SAT score said, trying to get into Texas A&M, or any college, with only a lowly GED to his credit wasn't going to work.

The problem was that the GED class was the only one offered inside the facility. Some of the other kids were able to take online classes, but since Lance's sentence stipulated no computer or Internet access, those classes weren't available to him. His court-mandated restrictions made the GED the only route possible. It was also boring as hell.

Lance had looked at the questions on the sample test. He already knew he could ace the thing in a heartbeat without having to sit through another dreary minute of class. Mrs. Stone probably understood that as well as he did. That was why she had let him out of class yesterday and today. That way he got to deal with the Christmas-tree issue, and she got to look after the dummies. Not that his classmates were really dumb, at least not all of them. Several of the guys spoke no English. He suspected that several of them probably had issues with dyslexia. One of those, a fifteen-year-old named Jason who couldn't read at all, filled his books with caricatures of Mrs. Stone. The pencil drawings were realistic enough in that you could tell who it was. They were also unrealistic in that Mrs. Stone was usually pictured nude, and not in a nice way.

All of which left Lance dealing with the Christmas tree. It was big and came in four separate pieces. It was old — ten years, at least, according to Mr. Dunn, the grizzled old black man who was in charge of maintenance at the facility. He was the one who had enlisted Lance's help to drag the tree and the boxes of decorations out of storage.

"No money for a new tree," Mr. Dunn said. "Not in the budget, but at least I got us some new lights. By the time we took the tree down last year, half those old lights had quit working. We'll have to restring it before we put it up."

That part of the project had taken the better part of a day. First they'd removed the old strings of lights. Then they'd taken the new ones out of their boxes and wound them into the branches, carefully positioning the plug-in ends close enough to the

11

tree trunk so that all the lights could be fastened together easily once the pieces were dropped into place. It was time-consuming, tedious work, but Lance liked the careful way Mr. Dunn went about it, his methodical method of testing each new string of lights before letting Lance take them out of the box. "No sense in putting on a defective string that won't light up the first time you plug it in," Mr. Dunn muttered under his breath.

The way Mr. Dunn talked as he worked, more to himself than to anyone else, reminded Lance of Grandpa Frank, his father's father back in Arizona. Lance missed Grandpa Frank, but his grandfather, along with his entire collection of aunts, uncles, and cousins, had disappeared when his parents got a divorce. It wasn't fair. Just because parents couldn't get along shouldn't mean that the poor kids involved had to lose everybody.

Lance's favorite memory of Grandpa Frank was going with him to the state fair in Phoenix, where he ate so much cotton candy that he ended up getting sick on the Ferris wheel. The attendant had given him hell while cleaning up the mess. At the time, Lance had been beyond embarrassed, but Grandpa Frank had laughed it off. "Look," he said. "Crap happens. You clean up your own mess, tell the world to piss off, and get on with your life. You want some more cotton candy?"

Lance had not wanted any more cotton candy. Ever. And he wished he'd been able to talk to Grandpa Frank after he got into trouble. His advice probably would have been a lot like some of the things the counselor said, only more colorful. Unfortunately, sometime between the divorce and now, Grandpa Frank had dropped dead of a heart attack or maybe a stroke. Lance didn't know for sure. If his parents had been able to talk to each other, Lance might have had more information — might even have been able to go back to Phoenix for the funeral — but that didn't happen. Grandpa Frank was gone without Lance even being able to say goodbye.

"You gonna hand me another string of them lights?" Mr. Dunn asked. "Or are you gonna stand there all day staring into space?"

Jarred out of his Grandpa Frank reverie, Lance fumbled another string of lights out of a box and plugged it in to the outlet. The new one lit right up, just as they all had, but as Mr. Dunn said, "Better safe than sorry."

"I didn't know prelit trees could be so much trouble," Lance remarked.

"They are if you think you can keep 'em forever," Mr. Dunn replied, "but with budgets as tight as they are, we're lucky to get the new lights."

When the tree was finally upright and glowing with hundreds of brand-new multicolored lights, Mr. Dunn studied it for a moment and then shook his head. "Tomorrow's my day off. Ms. Stone tells me you're gonna be the one putting on the decorations."

Lance shrugged. "Fine with me," he said.

"Before I take off tonight, I'll leave everything you need in the closet next to my office, and I'll make sure the guy who comes in tomorrow knows what's what. The flocking's looking pretty sorry these days. I got us some glitter and some self-adhesive glue. Before you put on the decorations, spray some glue on the tree and toss some glitter on it. That's supposed to make it look a little better."

"Okay," Lance said. "Will do."

Mr. Dunn turned to him. "You seem like a good kid," he said. "Not like some of them other ornery ones. What the hell are you doing here?"

Lance bit his lip. That was the whole

problem: He was a good kid. He never should have been locked up here, but he didn't want to go into it, not with this old man. "Long story," he said.

Mr. Dunn shook his head sadly. "Aren't they all!" he said.

Which brought Lance to the next day, when he was working on his own. Marvin Cotton, one of the guards, had opened the door to the closet next to Mr. Dunn's office. Had Mr. Dunn been there, he for sure would have helped Lance carry all the stuff into the rec room. Marvin was only a couple of years older than Lance. The guy was thick-necked, stupid, and surly, and he probably didn't have a college degree. He wandered in and out of the rec room from time to time to check on things, without saying a word or even nodding in Lance's direction. But then there were plenty of guards who acted like that — who treated the prisoners as something less than human.

Rather than worry about Marvin, Lance concentrated on the tree. For as long as he could remember, decorating Christmas trees had been high on his list of favorite things to do. Not this time. At home, they always had a live tree, although his mother usually bought them late on Christmas Eve, when they were already marked down and cheap. That meant that the trees they had were the rejects — scrawny, uneven, and downright ugly, but his mom made sure they always did the decorating together: all four of them, Lance, his mom, and his two younger brothers, Connor and Thad. Connor was only six and believed in Santa Claus. Lance and Thad no longer had that option. At home, decorating the tree was a joyous occasion with laughter and joking around and plenty of popcorn and home-made cookies. Here, although it was a solitary chore, it was preferable to suffering through the agonies of Mrs. Stone's class.

A few people besides Marvin had come and gone while Lance worked, so he didn't turn to look when the metal door clicked open behind him. Intent on having lost the wire hanger to one of the Christmas balls, he was staring into the tree branch, trying to find it, when he heard an unexpected hissing from the glue can he had left on the table with the other decorations. Just as quickly, he felt the cold in his legs as the aerosol spray hit, freezing his pant legs to his skin. Lance glanced down then. "Hey!" he demanded. "What the hell do you think you're doing?"

All he could see below him was a hand holding one of the spray cans of glue. Then a second hand came into his line of vision. It took a moment for his brain to register what he was seeing. The second hand held a cigarette lighter. Lance had time enough to register the flash of flame from the lighter, then the very air around him seemed to explode in flame. Writhing in pain, he attempted to lean over and pat out the fire on his legs. That was enough to tip the shaky ladder. The next thing Lance knew, he was falling and burning.

Mercifully, for a long time after that, he remembered nothing.

1

As the British Airways 747 lumbered toward
Heathrow, Ali Reynolds looked out into the
early-afternoon light. The ground gradually
appeared through the gray, the details
obscured by flurries of snowflakes eddying
around in the turbulent air. The previous
day, a Sunday in early December, when she
and Leland Brooks had driven down from
Sedona, Arizona, to Phoenix to board their
evening flight to London, the temperature
at Sky Harbor had been in the low seventies. Obviously, it was a good deal colder
than that in the UK. The full-length leather
coat she had brought along — the one her
flight attendant had delivered to her seat
just as the plane began its descent — would
be most welcome in London's wintertime
weather.

Ali glanced across to the opposite side of
the aircraft to see how Leland Brooks, her
eighty-something traveling companion, was

faring after sleeping in his own private pod, a clone of hers, in the front-most section of the first-class cabin. He sat bolt upright in his seat, staring out the window. She suspected that he was searching for some familiar detail in the hazy landscape. Though he was always exceptionally neat, Leland's usually impeccable white hair was slightly mussed. He'd had fun on the way over and looked a little worse for the wear after sampling a few too many of the comforts of flying first class.

When Leland, her longtime aide-de-camp and majordomo, had learned that B. Simpson, Ali's fiancé, had booked Leland's accommodations in a first-class seat right along with hers, he had strenuously objected. "You shouldn't," he had said. "Surely a coach ticket would be more than sufficient for me."

"For the guy who saved my girl's life by doing battle with a murderous thug in the middle of the desert?" B. had responded. "For you, my dear sir," he added with a grin, "first class is just barely good enough."

It was only a matter of weeks since Leland had put his Korean War–era Royal Marine Commando training to good use by taking down an armed gunman intent on adding Ali's name to his growing list of homicide victims. The drama had taken place on the banks of Lake Mohave, in the northwest corner of the Arizona desert. Although Leland was the one who had landed the vicious blow to the skull that had taken the bad guy down, it had required the combined efforts of several of the men in Ali's life to make that blow possible.

B. Simpson hired the helicopter that had flown her rescuers to a timely rendezvous in that almost fatal corner of the vast Arizona desert. Stuart Ramey, second in command at High Noon Enterprises, B.'s high-tech security company, had found an effective but not exactly legal way to locate Ali's murderous captors. Her friend Dave Holman, a Yavapai County homicide detective, had arranged for the coordinated multiagency law enforcement response that had taken down the remaining bad guys once Leland disabled the one intent on harming Ali. This all-expense-paid trip, Leland's first visit back to the land of his birth in almost sixty years, was B.'s generous way of saying thank you to the man for saving Ali's life. It was also a way to use up some of B.'s ever accumulating stash of frequent-flier miles.

Leland seemed to feel Ali's eyes on him. Glancing in her direction, he reached up and self-consciously smoothed his ruffled hair. He had come on board wearing a suit and tie, looking the part of a dapper, well-traveled gentleman. The first-class flight attendants had been drawn immediately to his still discernible English accent. From the moment the first one helped him stow his hand luggage, he was her favorite. She had fussed and fawned over him the whole trip, plying him first with champagne and single-malt Scotch and later with brandy. Ali suspected that when he fell asleep, he was probably more than slightly tipsy.

Now, though, from the way he kept watching out the window, Ali suspected he was anxious. Why wouldn't he be? After being estranged from his family for decades, Leland Brooks was about to meet up with his long-lost relatives. Anticipating how the reunion would go, Ali and B. had agreed that there most likely would be very little middle ground. It would either be good or it would be bad, without much in between.

Ali knew that a simmering quarrel between Leland and his two older brothers had forced him to leave his homeland all those years earlier. The brothers were deceased now, and one of their grandsons had issued the invitation for Leland to come home for a visit. Those long-dead brothers were also the main reason Ali had decided to accompany Leland on this journey. If the reunion turned out to be a good thing and all was forgiven? Fine. No harm; no foul, and she would leave Leland and his collection of relatives to their own devices. On the other hand, if everything went south, Ali would be on hand to watch Leland's back and lend whatever help was needed, including an immediate escape if that was deemed necessary.

The plane landed on the tarmac with a gentle bump and then went into what seemed to be an endless taxi. Ali took the time to repair her lipstick and check her makeup. She had slept some, too, although not enough. She was glad they had decided to stay in London tonight rather than setting out right away for Leland's old family stomping grounds in the city of Bournemouth in southwestern England. This afternoon they would be meeting up with the first of the relatives. Jeffrey Alan Brooks, the great-nephew who had sent Leland a handwritten olive-branch letter some two months earlier, had agreed to meet their flight and accompany them as far as the London hotel.

When the plane finally swayed to a stop at the gate, Ali stood up and retrieved her carry-on luggage. Leland joined her in the aisle.

"Did you sleep well?" she asked.

"Far better than I expected," he said. "The accommodations on board remind me of home."

By "home" he meant his compact fifth-wheel camper, which was parked on the far side of Ali's garage at her home on Sedona's Manzanita Hills Drive. Before Ali purchased and refurbished the place, Leland had spent most of his adult life working and living in the house, where he served as aide-de-camp for both the previous owners, first Anna Lee Ashcroft and later Anna Lee's troubled daughter, Arabella. When Ali assumed ownership, Leland had offered to stay on long enough to help with the remodeling. That rehab project was now years in the past, and Leland was still very much part of the package.

In the intervening time, he had managed to insinuate himself into the very fabric of Ali's life. He was far beyond what most people regarded as retirement age, but since he lived to work, Ali let him keep on working — up to a point. Out of deference to his age, she hired a crew of gardeners and housecleaners to do the heavy lifting that she considered beyond Leland's physical capability. In her kitchen — a room designed to Leland's own exacting specifications — he continued to reign supreme, cooking delectable meals with a practiced ease that always left her in awe.

"I hope we'll see you again," the flight attendant said, beaming at Leland as he stepped into the Jetway.

"Next week," he said.

"Your father is so sweet," the attendant whispered to Ali as she went past.

Their relationship was far too complicated for Ali to attempt an explanation in passing, so she didn't. "Thank you," she replied, and let it go at that.

Leland paused in the concourse and waited for Ali to catch up. Behind them, a flood of business and coach passengers, rushing to appointments or to make plane connections, came surging past them. Not in a hurry themselves, Ali and Leland stood for a moment like an island in a stream while the flood of hurrying people eddied around them.

"Heathrow seems a lot bigger than Sky Harbor," Leland observed. "And far bigger than I remember."

"It is bigger," Ali agreed with a smile, "and this is only one terminal. Let's get going." They stepped into the moving current of people, among the last of the passengers to come down the concourse. "I know you said Jeffrey will be meeting us here, at Heathrow," she said. "Do you have any idea what he looks like?"

Ali had no doubt that Leland was filled with misgivings about meeting up with a relative who also happened to be a stranger among the crowds who would be clustered in the arrivals lounge. Ali sympathized. The idea of finding the right stranger anywhere was something that gave her fits of anxiety as well.

Leland shook his head. "Jeffrey wasn't born until twenty years after I left home," he said. "So I've no idea what he looks like."

With some effort, Ali bit back a possibly caustic comment. In the age of the Internet, it would have been easy and thoughtful of Jeffrey to forward a photo of himself. Since he hadn't done so, there was no point in agonizing about it. "We'll make it work," she said determinedly.

The immigration line seemed to take forever. Soon another planeload of hurrying and impatient passengers was lined up behind them. When Leland first went to work for Anna Lee Ashcroft, she had sent him back to the UK to attend a butler training school, where he evidently made no effort to be in touch with his friends and relations. Since then, he had done no traveling outside the U.S. When B. had suggested that Leland might want to visit his family sooner than the planned family reunion scheduled for the following summer, his lack of a current passport had seemed like an insurmountable problem; with the aid of some of B.'s connections inside the federal bureaucracy, Leland's brand-new passport had arrived in under a week. This was the document he now handed to the immigration official, who smiled at him when she paged through it and saw there were no previous stamps. "First time here?" she asked.

"First time in a long time," he said.

"Business or pleasure?"

"Pleasure."

"Enjoy, then," she said cheerfully, and handed it back. The woman turned to Ali. "Business or pleasure?"

"Pleasure," Ali told her. "And to buy a wedding dress."

"When's the wedding?"

"A little over three weeks now," Ali answered. "Christmas Eve."

When B. suggested that she squeeze in taking Leland to England in December, under a month before their scheduled Las Vegas wedding, it had seemed like a bad idea. Later, when she saw how much of an emotional tailspin the wedding had created for her parents, she was more than happy to be out of town for part of the intervening time. Her mother, Edie Larson, was in full meltdown mode, frantically sewing matching ring-bearer and flower-girl outfits for Ali's grandchildren, twins Colin and Colleen, who would be part of the wedding party.

Edie was making her own mother-of-the-bride dress while Ali's father, Bob, was in a funk over the prospect of having to show up in a rented tuxedo. The more momentum the planning gained, the happier Ali was to escape some of the pressure, to say nothing of her parents' next "will not wear a tuxedo" battle; as far as Ali was concerned, her father could show up in a pair of OshKosh overalls. The trip had given Ali an excuse to step away from the circus atmosphere, as well as the opportunity to shop for her dress in privacy rather than with a band of too eager assistants, her mother included.

The immigration officer stamped Ali's passport and handed it back. "Enjoy your stay," she said. "And congratulations."

Moments later, Ali and Leland stepped through the glass door and into the terminal at large. Just as she'd anticipated, there was a large crowd assembled in the arrivals area outside immigration. Ali paused, looking around and trying to imagine how they would recognize Jeffrey Brooks in that crush of people. Leland, however, didn't hesitate. He strode forward with his hand outstretched and a broad smile on his face, aiming for a tall, spare young man — a thirtysomething with thinning hair — who stood front and center. Moments later, the two men were clasped in a tight embrace.

Ali arrived on the scene as Leland escaped the hug. He stood staring in wonder at his great-nephew and shaking his head. "I would have recognized you anywhere!" he exclaimed. "You look just like my father as I remember him."

"DNA will out," Jeffrey replied with a grin, "and you're not the first person to mention that. My great-aunties are forever saying the same thing." Noticing Ali's arrival, Jeffrey turned to her. "You must be Ms. Reynolds."

"Call me Ali," she said, holding out her hand and replying before Leland was able to say otherwise. In the departure lounge at Sky Harbor, Ali had elicited Leland's grudging agreement that for the duration of the trip, he would address her by her first name rather than by something more formal.

Jeffrey grinned back at her. "Ali it is, then," he said. "Now, what about your luggage? Shall we go pick it up?"

"We're only here for a week," she said. "We're making do with carry-ons."

"Very good, then," Jeffrey said. "I've hired a car and driver. Shall we go?"

He led the way through the terminal. When they reached the proper transportation door, he went out to locate the vehicle while Ali and Leland took the opportunity to don their coats.

"So Jeffrey looks like your father?" Ali asked.

"Very much so," Leland answered.

"If you'll pardon my saying so, he bears quite a resemblance to you as well."

Leland nodded. "Jeffrey looks the way I remember my father. He wasn't much older than Jeffrey is now when I left home, and I never saw him again after that."

Ali heard the wistfulness in Leland's voice. Only Jeffrey's return, as he was blown back inside with a blast of cold air, caused her to stifle a sympathetic comment that, under the circumstances, she doubted would be welcome.

Jeffrey ushered them out to the curb, where a distinctive London-style cab waited. The driver loaded the luggage in front while the three passengers piled into the back with Jeffrey facing them on the fold-down seat.

"That'll be the Langham?" the cabbie asked, confirming what he'd already been told.

"Yes, please," Ali said.

"So how was your flight?' Jeffrey asked once they were settled. "I hope you were able to get some rest. Since you're here for such a short time, it would be a shame if you lost a whole day to jet lag."

"The flight was quite comfortable," Leland said, "and I was able to sleep on the plane with no difficulty." Since he didn't mention that they had traveled in first class with a full-length flat bed to sleep on, Ali didn't mention it, either.

They left the airport in a whirling shower of snow. It was falling but not sticking.

"Are you sure you want to drive to Bournemouth tomorrow?" Jeffrey asked. "I have a court appearance then; otherwise I'd be more than happy to drive you there. If you take the train, I can come down and fetch you at the weekend."

Ali and Leland had discussed that and come to the conclusion that they wanted their own wheels available so they wouldn't be dependent on anyone to take them where they wanted to go. To that end, Ali had used

B.'s platinum Hertz card to rent a Land Rover that would be delivered to the hotel by ten the next morning. "No, thanks," she said. "We'll be fine on our own."

"You're from Arizona, aren't you?" Jeffrey asked. "If it's still snowing, will you be able to manage the drive?"

Like many people who had never visited Arizona, he most likely envisioned Arizona as a vast, cactus-dotted wasteland. During Ali's years at Northern Arizona University in Flagstaff, where the elevation was close to seven thousand feet, and while she had been living in Chicago and on the East Coast, she had done more than her share of winter driving.

"Don't worry about that," Ali assured him. "I'm fine in snow. I'm more concerned about driving on the left side of the road." She didn't add that she was also concerned about being in the car with Leland in a reversal of roles. At home in a vehicle, Leland was generally at the wheel. Now that he was beyond the age where rental companies would allow him to drive, Ali would be driving him. Leland had almost balked at going on the trip when he learned about that unwelcome bit of age discrimination. It had taken a good deal of cajoling on Ali's part to bring him around.

"Do you have plans for dinner this evening?" Jeffrey asked. "If not, my partner and I would be delighted if you'd come to our place. Charles is the most marvelous chef."

He made that statement tentatively, as though unsure what Leland's or Ali's reaction would be to the telling admission. Ali wasn't privy to all the gory details, but she knew in general that Leland's homosexuality was the reason his older brothers, Langston and Lawrence, had prevailed on their father to disown him. He had been run out of town in disgrace when he returned home to Parkstone after his stint with the Royal Marines during the Korean War. Now, it seemed, his great-nephew was following in Leland's footsteps.

Ali stole a quick glance in Leland's direction. Nothing in his demeanor indicated that he had known anything about Jeffrey's sexual preference in advance of their arrival.

"I'm sure we'd be delighted," Leland replied, "unless . . ." He paused. Ali realized that he was struggling to resist calling her Madame Reynolds. "Unless Ali here isn't feeling up to it," he finished finally.

It was touching that Leland was concerned about Ali's welfare while she, in turn, worried about his. "How far is it from the hotel?"

"We're just in Knightsbridge," Jeffrey said. "Not far at all."

Ali nodded. "As long as it's not too late. I suspect we're going to be ready to bail pretty early."

Jeffrey frowned briefly, struggling with her American usage, and then he brightened. "Oh," he said. "I see. You mean you'll want to make an early night of it. Of course. Time zones and all that. Perfectly understandable." He pulled out his mobile phone and punched in a number, then spoke into it. "It's a go. They'll come to dinner. As long as it's early. Seven?" He raised one eyebrow questioningly in Ali's direction.

As far as she was concerned, six would have been better, but she wanted to get off on a good foot with all these folks. Earlier she had e-mailed the hotel with a request for an early check-in. The staff had not yet responded, but if they could get into their rooms, perhaps there would be time for a quick nap before dinner. She nodded. "Seven will be fine."

She glanced down at her watch. Ali had switched it to local time when the flight attendants made the time announcement on the plane. Once they got to the hotel, she'd try to be in touch with the important people in her life. She thought it was most likely late at night in Tokyo, where B. would be for the next three days, and it was sometime in the early morning back home in Sedona, where wedding planning was no doubt going on apace. On her iPhone, Ali had a world-clock application that would translate London time to Tokyo time or Phoenix time. The problem was that until she had a chance to exchange the SIM card for the one B. had given her to use on the trip, the phone was virtually useless.

Jeffrey interrupted her thought process. "Charles needs to know if either of you has any food allergies or objections to Chinese food. That's his specialty, you see, and it's also what he serves in his restaurants — Charlie Chan's. He has three restaurants scattered around London. He also owns a catering company that specializes in hosting those campy murder-mystery dinners, complete with trunks full of fabulous period costumes. They're great fun."

When Ali looked at Leland, she saw that he had dozed off with his chin resting on his perfectly knotted tie. Consequently, she answered for both of them. "No food allergies at all," Ali replied. "Chinese food will be perfect."

Jeffrey heaved a relieved sigh before passing along her message. When he ended the call, he turned back to Ali. "So glad you said yes," he said. "Charles makes the most marvelous Peking duck. He was already cooking up a storm — a busman's holiday, as it were — with the expectation that you'd come to dinner, but we had agreed in advance that if it turned out you hated Chinese, we'd eat the duck as leftovers and take you somewhere else."

Ali looked fondly at Leland, who was still dozing. If the other relatives turned out to be this pleasant, this trip would be a walk in the park.

2

Traffic was barely moving, and it took a
long time to reach the Langham. As Ali and
Leland stepped out of the cab, Jeffrey joined
them in the driveway while they unloaded
their bags. "Do you want me to come back
for you this evening?" he asked.

"No," Ali said. "That's not necessary. Just
give me the address. We'll call a cab."

She ended up walking away with a handwritten note that the doorman jotted on a
pad he pulled out of his pocket. Their early
check-in arrangements still held, although
the slow trip through traffic had rendered
them unnecessary. Once they'd been delivered to their adjoining rooms, Ali stripped
out of her clothes and took a leisurely
shower. Then she put on the pair of loung-
ing pajamas handed out by the flight attendants to passengers in the first-class
cabin.

Ali was about to address the SIM card issue when the landline phone rang on the writing desk. When she answered, she was surprised to hear B.'s voice. "What are you doing still up?" she asked, glancing reflexively at her watch. "Isn't it the middle of the night there?"

"Good call," B. admitted. "It is the middle of the night. I can't sleep, so I thought I'd see if you and Leland got checked in to your rooms all right."

That was unusual. B. was someone whose work took him across multiple time zones and the international date line with wild abandon. Most of the time, he did so seamlessly and without seeming to suffer from jet lag or sleep-related problems on either end of his travels.

"My room is great, and I'm sure Leland's is, too," Ali told him. "Leland's great-nephew Jeffrey met our plane and rode in the cab with us as far as the hotel. We'll be joining him and his partner for dinner at their place a little later this evening. But what's going on? Why can't you sleep? You usually fall asleep the moment your head hits the pillow. Pre-wedding jitters got you down?"

"It's not about the wedding," B. said gloomily. "I'm not worried about that at all. I'm upset about a kid named Lance Tucker."

Ali had to think for a moment before she remembered hearing B. mention the name previously. Lance was some kind of juvenile computer wunderkind who had gotten himself into major difficulties when he managed to hack into his school system's server. High Noon had been called in by the school district's systems manager to consult on tracking down the culprit and plugging the resulting security breach. Ali knew that B. had come away from the incident with a more than grudging respect for the kid's computer abilities.

"I remember," Ali said as the pieces slipped into her mind. "Wasn't he the kid from Texas who broke into the local school district's computer system?"

"That's the one," B. answered. "He shut down the school district's server as a protest because they were instituting a program that would require everyone in the school district — students, teachers, and employees — to wear tracking chips that would allow them to be located on or off campus. Lance was part of a group of activists who claimed their constitutional rights were being violated. When the courts found against them, Lance took it upon himself to shut down the district's server."

"All that happened months ago," Ali

observed. "Why are you worrying about it now?"

She heard B. sigh into the phone. "Because Lance Tucker is in Austin Memorial Hospital with two severely broken legs and second- and third-degree burns over half his body."

Ali knew something about burn injuries. They were ugly and terrifically painful, and recovery was a long and difficult process. "That's terrible," she said. "How did it happen?"

"The local sheriff's department has been investigating the incident," B. replied. "At first it was assumed this was an inmate-on-inmate attack, and the facility was put on lockdown. Yesterday afternoon investigators released a report saying they've determined that Lance's injuries were self-inflicted. They claim Lance sprayed himself with some kind of aerosol and then used a cigarette lighter to set himself on fire."

"Why on earth would he do that?" Ali murmured.

"Why indeed?" B. replied. "What I've been told is they think he did it as a way of getting released early, but that makes no sense, none at all. His eighteenth birthday is less than a month away, at which time he would have been released automatically. I've met Lance. He's a smart kid. I can't imagine that he'd do something this stupid."

"What are you saying?" Ali asked.

"I think someone inside the facility — either a fellow inmate, a visitor, or one of the guards — managed to set him on fire."

"You think the sheriff's department is involved in some kind of cover-up?"

"It's possible," B. said, "and since I was involved in helping put him behind bars, I'm feeling like what's happened is all my fault and that maybe I should do something to fix it."

"Wait a minute," Ali said. "I remember High Noon was involved in finding the kid and in gathering some of the evidence used against him, but that doesn't mean you're in any way responsible for what happened."

"I still feel responsible," B. countered bleakly. "High Noon was part of the investigation. We're the ones who helped track the intrusion back to Lance's computer. I was even called to give evidence in the case. The problem is, it was a first offense and a one-time thing. There was no reason to go after the kid as though he were the second coming of Al Capone, but the school superintendent went absolutely ballistic and insisted on having Lance prosecuted to the full extent of the law."

"Was he the only one involved?" Ali asked.

"There were other people who made public objections to the tagging system, but Lance was the only one who was charged with disrupting the server. Shortly after Lance was convicted, his computer science teacher — a man who was also publicly opposed to the proposed tagging system — committed suicide."

"Was the teacher ever charged?"

"As far as I know, the teacher, Everett Jackson, was never officially mentioned in any of the court proceedings, and his involvement was never proved one way or the other. If he was in on it, Lance never ratted him out. There were people who speculated that he must have been involved, because they didn't think Lance was smart enough to do it on his own. I know better. The kid is brilliant."

"A brilliant kid wouldn't set his own pants on fire."

"That's my take on the situation."

"What about the hospital bills?"

"I think that's a big part of why the investigation came back as self-inflicted. This way, the facility dodges that liability, and the hospital bills — which will be huge — will be on the family's nickel. In the meantime, someone else is getting away with assault, at least, and maybe with attempted murder."

"Wait a minute," Ali said. "This whole thing happened on the inside. Every juvenile detention facility I ever heard of has security cameras everywhere. Doesn't this one?"

"It does," B. agreed, "but it turns out the cameras in one whole section of the building, including the room where Lance was putting up Christmas decorations, went on the fritz the night before the incident took place. A work order was issued that morning, prior to the fire, requesting the facility's security contractor to send technicians to either fix the malfunctioning system or replace it. The repair appointment was scheduled to take place the following day — the day after Lance was burned."

"So what part of the system was offline?" Ali asked.

"The part that included the classrooms, the rec room, and the cafeteria. The rest of the system seems to be functioning properly."

"That seems suspicious right there, doesn't it?" Ali asked.

"It does as far as I'm concerned," B. agreed. "That's why I'm thinking there may be a lot more to this than meets the eye."

Ali didn't bother asking how B. knew

about the malfunctioning security system or the request for service, all of which were things he could have gained access to only with help from Stuart Ramey, the guy manning a High Noon keyboard back home in Sedona. Since B. shouldn't have known, in terms of plausible deniability, it was probably better that she not know too much about them, either.

"Let's say the kid's injuries weren't self-inflicted," Ali said. "What does that mean?"

"It means that someone inside the facility — someone with access to the security camera system — is involved in what happened."

"A guard?" Ali asked.

"Or maybe a guard and an inmate, two people working in conjunction. One to take out the security system and the other one to set the fire."

"So the real question is, why would Lance be targeted? Is it due to something that was going on inside the facility, or does it have something to do with why he got sent there in the first place?"

"What got him sent there," B. replied, "is something that could have been treated as a kid's prank and wasn't. I keep thinking about the stunts that I pulled when I was his age. The thing is, I got away with them.

Lance didn't."

That was when Ali finally tumbled. B. was taking this personally because he was seeing his own history reflected in what was going on with Lance Tucker. As a child, B. had been teased unmercifully by the other kids for his name — Bart Simpson. When other kids were out playing Little League and Pop Warner football, an outcast B., who had already shed his given name, had taken refuge in technology. Hidden away in the family garage, he had cut his computer science teeth by taking old computers apart and putting them back together. By the time he was in junior high, he had taught himself how to write code.

A high school dropout without a trace of a college degree, B. had moved to Seattle in his late teens and made both a name for himself and a fortune in the computer game industry. Because he was a natural at computer hacking, he was also a natural at designing computer security measures. And that was the business B. was in now. His company, High Noon Enterprises, based in Sedona, counted among its clients a collection of Fortune 500 companies from all over the world. Even so, Ali knew that the guy she loved was still a rogue hacker at heart.

"When did all this happen?" Ali asked.

"And how did you hear about it in the first place?"

"The incident occurred over a week ago. Since computer security breaches are my bread and butter, I subscribe to Internet Security News. ISN is a news aggregator that's been following the story from the beginning. Once the burn victim's name was leaked to the media, someone made the connection back to the school district hacking job. That's how the story made it into one of today's ISN postings. As soon as I read it, I felt sick to my stomach. I feel as though I ought to do something about it, but I don't know what."

"You have meetings scheduled in the morning?" Ali asked.

"Of course," B. said. "All-day meetings, starting at eight A.M. That's my life for the next three days."

"I'm going to have plenty of spare time while Leland is dealing with his relatives," Ali offered. "Why don't I do some digging so that by the time you're on your way home, you'll have a better idea of what the situation is there?"

"I'd like that, but there's a small problem," B. said.

"What kind of problem?"

"This needs to be very discreet," he said.

"I can't go into all the details right now, but let's just say no one can find out that we're involved with helping Lance Tucker." He waited while Ali filled in the blanks.

"In other words," she said, "no searches that could be traced back to High Noon."

"Exactly," B. agreed. There was a slight pause before he added, "Your mom just sent me a photo. She wanted me to see it, and you should see it, too. I'll forward it to you. In the meantime, I'd better try to hit the hay. I'm going to be a wreck in the morning."

"Good night," she said. "I love you."

It took Ali a few minutes to get her computer out of her bag and hooked up to the hotel's Wi-Fi system. By the time she did so, B.'s e-mail with her mother's forwarded photo was already in her mailbox. Except Ali knew from the address that the e-mail had nothing to do with her mother. The address, elarson@highnoon.com, was a decoy mailbox that B. and Stu Ramey used to exchange encrypted messages that they didn't want to surface in the light of day.

When she opened the e-mail, there was a photo of Colin and Colleen, standing side by side with Ali's lush English garden blooming in the background. She sent an immediate reply to B: "Great photo. What cute kids. No wonder Mom likes it. Thanks. Good night."

After responding, she pulled a tiny thumb drive out of the bottom of her purse, inserted it into her computer, and logged on using a complex nine-digit code. The next time she opened the e-mail, she used her steganographic program. The photo disappeared, leaving behind a long list of files. Hunkering down on the bed, Ali began to read the collection of articles and reports Stu Ramey had encrypted into the pixels.

In her previous life, before her curtailed career as a news anchor, Ali had worked as a journalist. She knew how to pull a story together. So did Stuart Ramey. It was just that much of what he'd included contained information that no legitimate reporter would have been able to touch. She started with the most recent, a dry-as-dust public information officer briefing from the San Leandro County Sheriff's Department.

An exhaustive investigation by detectives from the San Leandro Sheriff's Department has concluded that last week's incident, in which an inmate of the San Leandro Juvenile Detention Center was severely burned, was either accidentally or intentionally self-inflicted.

The unnamed juvenile was working alone in a recreation area when his clothing caught fire. Examination of physical evidence found at the scene revealed the presence of no one else at the scene.

DNA and fingerprint evidence on both the aerosol spray and on the cigarette lighter used to ignite the fire have been found to belong to the victim himself.

The victim, whose name is being withheld because he is a juvenile, is currently being treated at Austin Memorial Hospital for second- and third-degree burns over much of his body. He also suffered several broken bones in a fall from a ladder that happened in conjunction with the fire. He is currently in critical condition.

This individual, who was sentenced to a six-month confinement, was serving time on a computer hacking charge. He was due to be released in less than a month, upon attaining his eighteenth birthday. As of this morning, the county prosecuting attorney has forwarded a formal request to the governor's office asking that his sentence be commuted to time served.

Ali leaned back and stared at her computer screen. Commuting Lance's sentence to time served was almost as convenient as having the pertinent cameras out of working order when the incident happened. If and when his condition improved, there would be no need to post any kind of guard outside Lance's hospital room. In his current condition, the kid was an unlikely flight risk, and since the party line was that he had done this to himself, there was no reason for the authorities to consider him in any additional danger.

Ali didn't have to read further to realize that both B. and Stuart were convinced otherwise. This was not an accident. Lance hadn't done this to himself in a misguided attempt to gain access to a health-related get-out-of-jail-free card. No, someone had tried to murder Lance Tucker. Since they hadn't succeeded the first time, what were the chances that they would try again?

Ali chose another file and opened it. This one came with an admonition, printed in bright red letters: PROPERTY OF AUSTIN MEMORIAL HOSPITAL. CONTAINS CONFIDENTIAL DATA. NOT FOR TRANSMISSION TO UNAUTHORIZED PERSONNEL.

And that would be me, Ali told herself, but that didn't keep her from reading. Ali's first husband had lost his battle with glioblastoma decades earlier, but during the time she spent at his hospital bedside, she had learned to navigate the complex narratives doctors and nurses wrote in the charts and had taught herself to read through the bland words to unlock the much darker meanings hidden underneath. She did the same thing here.

Yes, the burns were serious, but the last notation on the chart indicated that his primary doctor was seriously concerned that wounds to Lance's legs, caused by compound fractures to both tibias, were showing signs of serious infection. If the infection couldn't be controlled in a hurry, there was a chance that the patient would lose one leg, both legs, or even, perhaps, his life.

Ali leaned back on the pillow and thought about that. No doubt this was the part of Stuart's report that had left B. sick at heart and sleepless in Tokyo. It wasn't just that B.'s company and testimony had played a part in sending the kid to prison; his very life was on the line, and so was at least one of his legs.

Ali was sitting there thinking about it when jet lag made its presence known and sleep overtook her. She dozed off with the computer open on her lap. She was startled awake sometime later by a faint knock on her door. She looked up from her computer and was shocked to see that it was almost six-thirty. When she went to the door, Leland Brooks, looking rested and well turned out for their upcoming dinner, stood waiting in the hallway. "Just wanted to let you know that I'm on my way to the lobby," he said.

"Great," she told him. "I'll be right down."

Removing the thumb drive, she hid it away in her purse and then closed both the file and the computer. Her hair was slightly damp from the shower, but there was no time for a blow dry. Quickly she pulled her blond hair into a French twist and fastened it in place with a silver and jade hair comb that B. had brought back from one of his many trips to China. After hurriedly applying makeup, she slipped into the little black dress she had brought for upscale dining. Standing in front of the room's full-length mirror, she pulled on the jade silk brocade jacket, another gift from B. After pronouncing herself ready, she headed downstairs.

A bare ten minutes after Leland's discreet wake-up knock, Ali hurried out of the elevator and into the spacious lobby. She found Leland standing by the concierge's counter, chatting away. "Ready?" she said.

He nodded.

"Let's go find ourselves a cab."

3

It was cold outside, but snow was no longer falling as they stepped into the waiting cab. The address on the doorman's handwritten note was a ten-minute cab ride away, in Brompton square. From the Langham, that would have been within easy walking distance, but not in this weather.

"That'll be Harrods," the cabbie said helpfully, pointing at the easily recognizable facade, brightly lit with Christmas decorations. "In case you Yanks would fancy a bit of shopping."

Ali glanced in Leland's direction, wondering if he would be offended by being referred to as a Yank. He appeared to be too busy taking in the sights to pay any attention. When the cab stopped in front of the building, Leland stepped outside and waited as Ali finished paying; then he handed her out onto the sidewalk, looking up at the Edwardian building before them as he did so.

"It's a bit grander than I would have expected," he observed.

"Well then," Ali said, smiling and taking his arm, "let's see about making a good impression."

Nothing in Jeffrey's manner during their ride from the airport had indicated that his and Charlie's place would be in any way exceptional. Ali revised that idea the moment they stepped into the polished wood lobby. They rode up to the sixth-floor penthouse in an elevator that was smooth and utterly silent. A beaming Jeffrey was waiting outside the elevator when the doors slid open. "Welcome, welcome," he said. "Do come inside."

He ushered them into a room that could have been taken straight from the pages of *House Beautiful.* A gas log fireplace, complete with a massive marble mantel and hearth, burned cheerily in front of a seating area made up of two immense chintz couches large enough to hold four people each. Shaded lamps on end tables and occasional tables bathed the room in a golden light that barely illuminated the subtle floral pattern that overlaid the striped wallpaper. In front of the wall of windows stood a beautifully decorated Christmas tree whose freshly cut scent filled the room. At the end of the room was a formal dining area where a linen-covered table was laid for four. A low red and white chrysanthemum centerpiece punctuated with lit taper candles set the scene for an intimate dinner. From behind a swinging door came the complex aroma of some kind of sophisticated cooking.

"Charlie's out in the kitchen," Jeffrey explained, leading them to the couches and directing them to take a seat. "He's in heaven. You'd think with three restaurants to run that he'd be sick to death of cooking at the end of the day. He's not. This is the kind of entertaining he loves to do, but I'll let you in on a secret. He borrowed one of the sous chefs and a server from the catering company to come over and help out for the day. That way he could dodge some of the prep work, all the serving, and a lot of the cleanup. Now, what can I get you to drink?" Jeffrey went to a small and almost invisible wet bar that was tucked into an alcove by the dining room.

"Scotch," Leland said at once.

"Single-malt or blended?"

"Definitely single-malt. Neat."

"And you?" Jeffrey asked, turning to Ali.

"I'll have mine blended," she said, "and if you'll excuse the impropriety, I prefer lots of rocks."

He smiled at her. "Very well," he said. "I have some Famous Grouse 18 that should be just the ticket. I understand it's Prince Philip's favorite, you know, and I'll join Uncle Leland here in a dram of Glenmorangie." Once the drinks were poured into cut crystal Waterford glasses, he brought them back to the sofas and settled down opposite his guests, raising his glass in a toast. "Welcome."

"Glad to be here," Ali said.

Jeffrey beamed at his great-uncle. "And I'm so proud to be the instrument that has brought you back to us."

"How exactly did that happen?" Ali asked.

"I found one of my Great-grandmother Adele's letters among my father's papers after he died. In it she said something to the effect that she had already lost one son, and she would not lose another. That piqued my curiosity, because I didn't remember anyone mentioning that my grandfather had any other brother besides Lawrence. No one ever spoke about the existence of a third brother. I asked Aunt Maisie about it. She won't let anyone call her Great-aunt Maisie because she says being called great anything makes her feel ancient. She's the one who told me that the missing brother's name was

Leland and that he had run off to join the Royal Marines."

He turned his attention to Leland. "When I heard that, my first thought was that you had died in the war, but Aunt Maisie insisted that you had returned unharmed from wherever you were posted. That bit of information is what sent me searching through the Mathison family papers in the library in Cheltenham. That's where I saw the letters you wrote home to Great-grandmother Adele from Korea. Armed with that, including the fact that you were with the Royal Marines, I then used their veterans' organization to track you down, and here you are."

"Yes, we are," Leland agreed, looking around the beautifully appointed room and deftly changing the subject. "You have a lovely place."

Jeffrey nodded and smiled. "It's lovely now," he agreed, "but you're seeing it after the construction project. I didn't think it was ever going to end. It's been nonstop for the better part of two years. We bought two flats, you see, this one and the one directly below us, both in desperate need of refurbishing. We kept this one as our primary living space so we'd be able to take full advantage of the view. When it isn't the dead of winter, we have a fabulous view of the park. Putting in the staircase was a nightmare, but we've converted the flat downstairs into what we like to call our bedroom wing. That way, if we have wild parties — which Charlie and I have been known to do on occasion — there's no one directly below us to be bothered."

Looking back toward the entryway, Ali realized that she had been so focused on the rest of the room that she had failed to see the polished wood banister leading to the lower unit. Prior to the trip, she had spent a little time cruising the pricey world of London real estate, so she had some idea of the going rate for single units in the area. The fact that Jeffrey and Charlie had purchased two units — fixer-uppers or not — left Ali duly impressed. In view of her hosts' upscale circumstances, Ali was glad she had insisted that she and Leland stay at the Langham. She didn't want anyone looking down their proper British noses at Leland as some kind of poor relation.

The door from what was evidently the kitchen swung open into the dining room. A dark-haired man several years younger than Jeffrey hurried into the room, smiling as he came. He was of Asian ancestry, with handsome good looks that were at odds with the studied plainness of Jeffrey, who was still dressed in a suit and tie. There was an intensity about Charles that wasn't softened by the colorful Hawaiian shirt he wore. Several inches shorter than Jeffrey, he moved with a peculiar catlike grace.

So maybe opposites do attract, Ali thought, taking Charlie's proffered hand.

"I think it's all under control now," Charles Chan said. "You must be Ali. I'm Charlie." Once the introductions were complete, Charlie sat down on the other couch while Jeffrey hurried back to the bar, then returned with a glass of white wine that he handed over to Charlie. "What have I missed?" the new arrival asked. When Charlie spoke, Ali thought she detected a hint of an accent that wasn't British, although it wasn't one she was immediately able to identify.

"Not much," Jeffrey answered with a laugh. "I was just giving them a blow-by-blow description of our two-year construction war."

"Oh, that," Charlie said, taking a small sip. "It's not over a moment too soon. They've only just finished painting the nursery, and the baby's due in less than a month."

Leland blinked at that bit of news. He

took a quick sip of his drink, leaving Ali to field the ball Charlie had casually whacked into the air. "You're having a baby?" she asked. Looking around that elegant room, she wondered how the gorgeous furniture and the exquisite wallpaper would survive assaults from an active toddler, but neither Jeffrey nor Charlie seemed dismayed in the slightest by the prospect of raising a kid who might turn out to be your basic human wrecking ball.

"Not us, of course," Jeffrey interjected. "We're using a surrogate. It's a boy. We're naming him Jonah, after your father," he added in Leland's direction. "We haven't broken the news to all the relatives yet, especially the aunties. We're planning to unveil him officially at the family reunion in Cheltenham next summer."

"The aunties?" Ali asked.

"That would be Leland's cousins, the twins — Maisie and Daisy, Adele's sister's daughters. You've yet to meet them," Charlie said to Ali. "They're the family's self-appointed resident busybodies. Rather than telling them about Jonah in advance and letting them get all hot and bothered about it, we decided we'd spring him on them as a fait accompli this summer and count on the baby to provide enough charm to win them over."

"The twins," Leland repeated, shaking his head. "I had almost managed to forget about those two. Whatever became of them?"

Jeffrey turned to Ali. "Are you familiar with the family tree?" he asked.

"Not really."

"Maisie and Daisy Jordan," Leland explained. "My mother, Adele Mathison Brooks, and theirs, Beatrice Mathison Jordan, were sisters. The twins were about ten when I left home. Their family was somewhat better off than ours. Whatever became of them?"

"They both married," Jeffrey said, picking up the thread of the story. "Maisie is Maisie Longmoor now, and Daisy's married name is Phipps. Their younger brother, Billy, was never quite right in the head. He was a late-in-life baby with Down syndrome. He lived at home with his parents his whole life and died of pneumonia in his twenties."

"I didn't know there was a brother," Leland said.

Jeffrey nodded. "It was a tragedy. He was never able to look after himself, and taking care of him was a terrible burden on his parents. They died just a few years after he did, in their late sixties, and within a few

61

months of each other. When their parents died, both twins happened to be at loose ends. Maisie had recently divorced her husband, and Daisy was widowed. When they inherited their folks' place in Bournemouth, they decided to pool their resources. They changed the place into a B and B — using the term loosely — and call it Jordan's-by-the-Sea. Guests stay in the main house, while the two sisters live in the carriage house out back and oversee the running of the place."

"What a shame," Leland said. "I believe we're booked into the Highcliff up on the bluff. If we'd known about this, we could have stayed there."

Charlie laughed aloud. "Don't give that idea a moment's thought," he said. "To hear the aunties tell it, Jordan's is everything in luxury, but don't be fooled. It's not. I've read some of the online reviews. Dreadful is more like it. That's one of the reasons we're having next summer's family reunion in Cheltenham, home to the Mathisons, rather than in Bournemouth. We didn't want having to stick visiting guests in Jordan's-by-the-Sea."

"And we didn't want to have to explain to the aunties why no one wanted to stay there," Jeffrey added.

Charlie looked down at his watch. "It's probably about time," he said. "I'll go check on things in the kitchen while you open some wine."

"White or red?" Jeffrey asked.

"Let's live dangerously," Charlie told him. "Open a bottle of each."

The wine they served was divine, and dinner was nothing short of delectable. It was impeccably served by a dark-haired young woman who brought dishes in and out, poured wine, and then cleared the table, all without saying a word to anyone. Although silverware was available, so were chopsticks, which Ali and Leland managed to maneuver properly without embarrassing themselves. The centerpiece of the meal was Peking duck, but there were any number of side dishes — spicy noodles topped with grilled shrimp; saffron fried rice flecked with bits of chicken and pork; tangy barbecued ribs; and a batch of spicy bits of beef that would have been welcome at any Mexican food joint on the planet.

Conversation was easy. When Jeffrey and Charlie questioned Leland about what he did for a living, Ali jumped into the breach, explaining that he was the property manager for both her home and her fiancé's. That took them off into a discussion about B.'s business and into a discussion about B. and Ali's upcoming wedding. For a dress, Jeffrey recommended the name of a small but exclusive shop on the main square in Bournemouth, Anne's Fine Apparel. "Bournemouth's not the best place for world-class shopping, but Anne's the wife of an old school chum of mine, and her place might just fill the bill."

It was during the following brief pause when Ali asked Jeffrey how long he and Charlie had been together. The question was casual, the kind of thing strangers ask strangers when they're trying to get the lay of the land. As a pall fell over the table, silencing what had previously been a care-free conversation, Ali would have done anything to take it back.

"Not quite ten years," Jeffrey said quietly. This time there was no hint of a smile in his voice or in his face. "We met in Thailand. In Ao Nang on the day of the tsunami."

While Ali sat wishing to disappear under the highly polished parquet floor, Jeffrey continued, his voice flat and his eyes etched with pain. "We were both there with other people," he said. "Other partners. We didn't know each other then, but it happened that we were all four staying on the sixth floor of a beachfront hotel. Charlie and Michael had flown in the day before after visiting Charlie's grandmother in Hong Kong. I was there with Philip; we'd been together ten years. We had already been there for the better part of a week, and we were due to come home the following day.

"That morning Philip and I were scheduled to do a climbing expedition on Railay. Unfortunately, Philip and I quarreled that morning. He decided to stay in Ao Nang and maybe do some scuba diving. That's where Charlie and I met, on the climb at Railay. We were up on the cliffs over the water when we saw the water recede.

"I had never been around a tsunami, so at first I really didn't understand what was happening. Charlie did. He got on his cell phone immediately, trying to warn Michael and tell him to get to higher ground. The call didn't go through. We were still up on the cliff when we saw the first huge wave crash ashore. From where we were, there was no way to grasp the size of it or to understand what had happened."

"By the time we got back down, all hell had broken loose," Charlie said, taking up the story. "There were six of us in the group — Jeffrey and me and four guys from Sweden, all of us from the same hotel. The guides were too concerned about what had happened to their families to worry about us, so they took off. The rest of us all stuck together. We spent the better part of twenty-four hours making our way back to Ao Nang. The devastation was unbelievable. Cell phones didn't work. There was no way to contact anyone. When we finally made it back to town, the hotel was standing, but everything on the first three floors had been washed away. Up on the sixth floor, where our rooms were located, everything was just the way it was when we left. The beds were even made. We never found any trace of Michael or Philip. They were just gone. Two of the Swedes were eventually reunited with their wives. The other two weren't so lucky."

For a long moment, no one said a word. There was nothing to say.

Charlie took a deep breath. "Because of the restaurants, I had to come back home as soon as I could catch a flight. Jeffrey stayed on for two more weeks, searching for Michael and Philip. He called me with daily reports, but he never found a trace of either one. When he came back home, we were both in the same boat. No one really understood what we'd been through or what we'd lost."

Jeffrey nodded. "When you're gay and your partner dies, it's not like you're a widow and all the old family and friends rally round and pitch in, bringing you hot dishes and sympathy. It was more like Charlie and I were stuck together on a deserted island. By the time it was over, we were . . ." He stopped and shrugged.

Charlie looked at him, smiled sadly, and came to the rescue. "We were a couple," he finished. "It was a year or so later when we moved in together. We've been here a little over two years. Doing a live-in remodel may be easier than surviving a tsunami, but don't quote me on that. The jury's still out.

"Come on," he added. "Let's go back into the living room so Sari can finish clearing up."

Back in the living room over snifters of Courvoisier, Ali tried to get the evening back on a somewhat sounder footing. "So tell me about your restaurants," she said to Charlie.

"There are three," he said. "One's up the street here on Sloane; one's near Whitehall; the third is just off Covent Garden. I'm happy to say business is booming in all three. The catering business is in a warehouse district out near Heathrow, where the rents are lower."

"It sounds as though you're very successful," Ali offered.

Charlie nodded. "I have to be," he said. "I have a very demanding silent partner — my grandmother."

"The one you were visiting in Hong Kong?"

"My parents left Hong Kong in the mid-eighties. They were worried about what would happen when Hong Kong went back to China. The truth is, nothing much happened. They thought they could come here and turn me into a perfect English school-boy and gentleman. That didn't work out very well, because from the time I cooked my first batch of chow mein when I was eight, I knew that's what I wanted to be: a cook; a chef. My parents kept trying to fit a square peg in a round hole. That didn't work, either. When I had my gap year, they sent me back to China to see my grand-mother. They thought she'd be able to shape me up, and they were right. She just didn't do it the way they wanted. They wanted me to go to university. She paid my way to Cor-don Bleu.

"That wasn't at all what my parents expected. The first thing they did was disown me. The second thing that happened is that my grandmother disowned them. My parents didn't expect that, either."

"You know what they say," Ali said. "Turn-

68

about's fair play."

"Indeed. When I wanted to start my first restaurant at age twenty-six, my grandmother was the one who provided the capital. She's also the one who made the purchase of these flats possible. She's Jeffrey's and my silent partner. After payroll and rent, she's our biggest creditor. We pay her money every month. We're also giving her the one thing she's always wanted and didn't think she'd ever live to see — her first great-grandchild." He sent a fond glance in Jeffrey's direction.

"I'm the contracts guy," Jeffrey put in. "I chase after the accountants and the bankers and the lease agreements and keep track of the income and outgo. By mutual agreement, I don't do any of the cooking. Eventually, we'll have a nanny, but we're thinking I'll do the majority of the child care. I've worked out of an office in the past, but there's an office downstairs now, and I should be able to use that."

"Sounds great," Ali said, hoping to sound supportive. The problem was, she remembered all too well how, when her son and daughter-in-law, Chris and Athena, were expecting, they had voiced similar intentions, anticipating that Chris would be able to stay home and do artwork while looking after what had turned out to be two babies. In their case, the services of a nanny had been required sooner than later.

Glancing in Leland's direction, Ali could see that he was at the end of his endurance. "I hate to eat and run," she said. "But it's been a difficult day, and we have a long drive tomorrow. Would you mind calling a cab?"

"Not at all," Charlie said. Whipping out his cell phone, he dialed the number from his contact list. While he gave directions, Jeffrey took another shot at trying to talk Ali out of driving to Bournemouth.

"They're still predicting snow," he objected. "Wouldn't you be better off taking a train?"

"No," Ali said. "I have experience driving in snow, and we'll have a Land Rover. Besides," she added with a smile, "from what you've told me about the aunties, if they're too tough to handle, I don't want to be stranded in Bournemouth without our having a way to get out of town under our own steam."

"Now that you put it that way," Jeffrey said, "driving yourself is probably the best idea."

As the cabbie drove them back to the hotel, Leland fell into a somber mood.

"What's wrong?" Ali asked.

He shook his head before he answered. "Parents," he said quietly. "How can they be like that? I thought times had changed between then and now, but it turns out they haven't, not really. My father chucked me out like so much trash because he couldn't accept me for who I was. Charlie's parents evidently don't mind that he's gay, but they dumped him because he wanted to be a chef instead of going to university. It makes no sense."

Reaching over, Ali laid a comforting hand on the back of Leland's bony wrist. "I agree," she said. "It makes no sense to me, either, but I can tell you this. In both cases, it's the parents' loss."

4

Ali's first thought was that she'd try reading once she got back to her room, but the moment she was out of her shoes and dress and into her jammies, she disabused herself of that notion. The nap she'd had before dinner hadn't done enough to counteract her jet lag, to say nothing of the cocktails and wine. She fell into bed and slept straight through until morning, rising just in time to dress and go down to the buffet for breakfast before their car was due to be delivered at ten.

Leland was in the dining room, sipping coffee when she arrived.

"I suppose you're already packed," she said.

He nodded. "I left my bag with the bell-man."

Ali grabbed a bite of breakfast and then hurried back to her room to finish her own packing. By the time the Land Rover showed up at ten on the dot, she and Leland were checked out and ready to go. The GPS in the rental car said the trip down the A3 from London southwest to Bournemouth would take two hours and one minute. Maybe on a regular day, but not on a day when the drive was punctuated by intermittent snow showers followed by what came close to whiteout conditions. Grateful for the extra traction in the four-wheel-drive Land Rover, Ali kept both hands on the wheel. Occasionally, she glanced in Leland's direction. "You don't look like you're having much fun at the moment," she offered.

"I'm not," he admitted with a shake of his head. "I can't imagine that the rest of my family will be nearly as welcoming or as understanding as Jeffrey and Charlie were. It's going to be a disaster."

"No, it won't," Ali countered. "It doesn't matter if they are welcoming or not. That's why I'm here — to have your back. If they prove too difficult or too obnoxious, we shake the dust off our heels and decamp for somewhere better." She paused. "I realize you've never told me the whole story. I can certainly understand why, and you don't have to tell me now, if you don't want to. But I'm here to help, Leland. It might give me more of an insight if I knew some of the details."

"All of it?" he asked, peering at her sideways.

Ali slowed and turned the wipers on high as they plowed into yet another swirling mass of snow. "All of it," she replied.

Leland sighed. For several long moments he was silent. "I knew I was different from other boys from a very early age, although I spent years of my life trying to convince myself otherwise. Langston and Lawrence teased me relentlessly, calling me names I'd rather not remember. Langston, Jeffrey's grandfather, was always the ringleader. He'd turn over in his grave if he knew he had a pouf for a grandson."

"It's probably just as well he doesn't," Ali said.

That garnered the faintest of smiles from Leland, but it disappeared as quickly as it appeared. "That was one of the reasons I joined the Royal Marines. Lawrence and Langston both tried to get in and didn't make it. I not only got in, I served with honor. While I was there — including the whole time I was in that hellhole called Korea — I never said or did anything that would have dishonored my family or my fellow marines. You believe me when I say that, right?"

"Of course," Ali replied.

"The problem is, when I came home from the war, I was the same person I had always been. My brothers were the same, too. They ragged on me constantly. Never in front of our parents, always behind their backs."

Leland fell silent as if struggling to find a way to go on. Ali was tempted to interject something, but ultimately she waited him out.

"Then I met someone," he said at last. "It isn't like now, when you can go out to a gay club and meet other people who are in the same situation. His name was Thomas. He was a teacher — a new teacher — at a nearby preparatory school, Kembry Park Academy. During the midsummer holidays, I went to the cricket grounds in Bournemouth to watch a match, and there he was, out on the field. From the time I was little, Langston always said I ran like a girl. Some rough fellows in the Royal Marines said the same thing, but since I could run faster than any of them, what they said didn't bother me the way it did when Langston said it.

"So there was this one young batsman out there playing — a handsome lad about my age — who seemed to run the same way I did, and he was fast. After the match was over, I ran into him in a pub. I raised a glass to him and said, 'Hey, you run like a girl.' He looked like he was getting ready to punch me. Then I said, 'So do I,' and we both laughed. That was it. As I said, his name was Thomas — Thomas Blackfield. Never a Tom; always a Thomas."

Wistfulness had come into Leland's voice. Silence enveloped the car as the Land Rover moved slowly through the snow. As close as they were to the sea, Ali understood that this had to be a powerful storm. Even with all the traffic, snow was accumulating on the highway. As long as people didn't drive too fast for the conditions, everything would be fine.

She was about to prod Leland to continue, but Leland resumed his tale without further urging. "Thomas and I were both young and inexperienced. We didn't want to rush into anything, and with his position as a teacher at stake, it was important that we be discreet. It was summer. We spent a good deal of time just walking and talking, getting to know each other. Late in August we were down in the gardens by the promenade. We were looking for a little privacy when we literally stumbled over Langston and his then girlfriend, Frances, Jeffrey's grandmother. Let's just say we found them in a rather compromising position. Langston was furious. He told me that if I breathed a word of what I had seen, he would tell our parents what he called the 'truth' about me. He also threatened to go to the school authorities and tell them about Thomas.

"I didn't want to do anything to jeopardize Thomas's livelihood, so I did the only thing I could think of. I shagged off to London. With the help of an American soldier, a marine whose life I had saved, I managed to emigrate to the U.S., where I found employment with Anna Lee Ashcroft." He paused and shrugged. "The rest you know."

Ali did know the rest, not all of it, but a good deal. She was aware of Leland's failed romance with a judge from Prescott. It had been a long-term relationship begun while the judge's wife faded into the lost world of Alzheimer's. Leland's hopes of establishing something more permanent had been dashed when, after the wife's death, the judge's children had nixed any kind of involvement between their father and Leland Brooks. As for the heartache with Thomas that predated the judge? Although Ali hadn't known the details, she had guessed most of it.

They were much closer to Bournemouth now. The snow had lightened to mere flurries, the road was reasonably clear, and traffic had sped up.

"You never saw your parents again?" Ali ventured at last.

"No," Leland replied. "After I got to the States, I contacted Langston to let him know where I was and to inquire after our parents' health. He told me that our father had died after a fall and that our mother had returned to Cheltenham. He said that when Father discovered the reason for my abrupt departure, he had disowned me for bringing such dishonor on our family and had written me out of his will. Somehow I had expected better of my father, but there you are. Langston also said that our mother was so ashamed by my behavior that she never wanted to hear from me again. I simply abided by her wishes. It wasn't until I began corresponding with Jeffrey that I learned she had died of a stroke sometime in the late sixties.

"And now here I am, the grand old man of the family, where it evidently no longer matters if I'm gay, but where Charles can be cast aside by his parents for following his dream of wanting to be a chef and own restaurants. It makes no sense."

"No, it doesn't," Ali agreed. "Whatever became of Thomas?"

"I have no idea," Leland replied. "I never made any effort to contact him again. As I said, back in those days, any hint of that kind of scandal could well have cost him his position. For all I know, he may have died in the AIDS epidemic in the eighties. I lost a lot of friends back then. I did go online and Google the Kembry Park Academy. Turns out it closed years ago. Now there's an industrial park where the school used to be."

The snow had stopped completely by the time they passed Southampton. As the GPS began issuing clipped orders for exiting the freeway and entering Bournemouth, a few bits of pale blue sky appeared in the gloom. Ali noticed that Leland was sitting forward in his seat, searching for familiar landmarks, and she caught the fleeting smile on his lips when he first glimpsed the sea. Yes, this long-delayed homecoming was difficult for him, but there was no disguising the pleasure in his sightseeing commentary as Ali negotiated the three roundabouts that put them on the B3066, also known as Bath Road, toward West Cliff Road. When they reached the hotel, she was more than happy to turn the keys to the Land Rover over to the valet and let someone else put it in the car park.

Ali had booked a suite with two bedrooms on either side of a connecting sitting room, to give them privacy from each other and also from the hotel's public areas, in case things with the expected onslaught of relatives became dicey. The first of those, Leland's cousins — the ones Jeffrey and Charlie had referred to as "the aunties" — were due for tea that very afternoon.

Ali and Leland made their way through the check-in process and up to their suite. The sitting room was spacious, with expansive windows that overlooked the sea. B.'s frequent guest points were paying the bill here, and his membership status was high enough that a bottle of chilled champagne and an enormous basket of fresh fruit awaited them. Walking over to look down at the view of the seaside promenade and the shoreline far below, Leland grew quiet again. "This hotel's been here for a very long time," he said. "I never would have thought I'd be staying here as an overnight guest."

Ali grabbed a pear from the fruit basket and joined Leland at the window. "Didn't you ever come here as a boy?"

A shadow fell across his face. "Not as a boy," he said. "My father was a thrifty man, and he maintained that the place was far too grand for us when I was growing up, although my parents did bring me here once. We came to Sunday-afternoon tea after I joined the Royal Marines and before I shipped out for Korea."

"Oh, my," Ali said. "If I had known that, I could have booked us somewhere else."

"No," Leland said. "This is an excellent choice. I can see that parts of this trip will mean facing down some of my own personal demons, including Daisy and Maisie."

"We can go down for lunch if you like," Ali offered.

"No," he said. "If afternoon tea now is anything like it was then, we won't find ourselves starving. If you don't mind, I think I'll grab a short nap before that. I didn't sleep well last night, and I want to be at my best."

Ali smiled at that. "You do that," she said. "I'm going to order a pot of coffee from room service. I ended up on the short end of the coffee stick this morning. Then I have some work to do."

Once the coffee arrived, Ali settled at the desk in her own room and pulled out her computer. Her e-mail account was chock-full of the usual spam. Even on the far side of the Atlantic, a Canadian pharmacy wanted to sell her Viagra. Hidden away in all the junk were two real messages. One, from her mother, contained a photo of Colleen looking darling in her finished flower-girl dress. The other was from B., saying his meetings were going well, but that he was beat and would be hitting the sack early. She replied to both. Then she extracted her thumb drive from the bottom of her purse and returned to the files Stuart had sent in the encrypted photo. This time she went to the opposite end of the string of files and started at the beginning with articles, all of them culled from what was evidently a local newspaper, the *San Leandro Lariat.*

Ali soon realized that in order to keep track of the whole story, she would need to take notes. Not wanting them to be readily accessible, she used the same steganography program to create a separate file on the thumb drive, one she'd be able to put into another photo to send back to Stuart and B.

There was a whole collection of articles dealing with school board meetings, in which the pros and cons of the proposed SFLS — student/faculty location system — were discussed in mind-numbing detail. Ali had reported on enough meetings like that to know how opposing sides had most likely lined up behind a standing microphone to take public potshots at each other. Either the reporter was incredibly evenhanded or the townsfolk had been evenly divided for and against the system, which would allow school administrators to know at all times where each person — visitors included — could be found on the various school campuses.

The program required that everyone involved would be issued a bracelet that contained a GPS tracking device associated with that person's name, which would allow administrative personnel to instantly locate the targeted individual. The school superintendent, Dr. Richard Garfield, was a huge proponent of instituting the system, which seemed incredibly expensive. For the amount the district would be paying to install and maintain it, they could have hired two to three beginning teachers. From Ali's point of view, paying teachers to teach was far more important than being able to monitor where everyone was.

People in favor of the system, the ones who spoke out in public about it, sang its praises from a student-safety point of view. Outspoken opponents, including some students and faculty members, compared it to putting ID chips in dogs or the Nazis requiring every Jew to wear a Star of David sewn on his or her clothing. They objected to the tagging on constitutional grounds as a violation of prohibitions against unlawful searches and seizures. It was from one of those quotes, namely in the dog-ID-chip comparison, where Ali first encountered the name of Everett Jackson, identified as a longtime San Leandro High School faculty member and computer science club adviser. The article mentioned that several club members had been in attendance at the meeting and had applauded Jackson's statement of objection.

The files dealing with school board meetings were grouped together, so this article was not the only one dealing with the topic; over several months, SFLS was listed under old business in the meeting agendas. In April of the previous year, the school board had approved the purchase at a rancorous meeting where no further provision for public comment was allowed. The next meeting after that, the one in May, dealt with the unauthorized intrusion and interruption of service, by person or persons unknown, of the school district's server.

Ali made a note in her file. The server disruption had happened in April. When the school board met in May, the culprit, Lance Tucker, had not yet been identified. Between the articles about the April meeting and the one that followed, Stuart had inserted another article, this one from the *Los Angeles Times,* which featured a profile of an up-and-coming businessman named Daniel Crutcher. Ali had to read through the article before she understood his relevance. Mr. Crutcher was United Tracking Incorporated's ace salesman in the U.S. He spoke enthusiastically about the importance of San Leandro's pilot use of the program as a model for schools all over the U.S. "Before long," Crutcher was quoted as saying, "these systems will become a basic part of the country's educational system, as necessary as pencils." In another part of the article, he said, "That way, in case of a serious emergency such as a school shooting or an earthquake or flood, school officials will be able to tell anxious parents exactly where they will be able to find their children."

Ali stared at the man's photo for a long time. Was this guy on the moon or what? Did he know any actual kids? More to the point, did he know any teenagers? Ali did, and she understood there was a good chance that those "anxious parents" would still be unable to find their children. Just because the kids were supposed to wear the bracelets didn't mean they would.

There was a discreet tap on the door to Ali's room. "Time to go forth and meet our guests," Leland announced.

Ali looked up in surprise, shocked to see how much time had slipped through her grasp while she was dealing with the minutiae of the San Leandro school board. "I'll be right there," she said.

She took a minute to change out of her travel clothing and refresh her makeup before joining Leland in the sitting room. He was nattily dressed, with a brightly colored red vest under a blue sport coat and a matching red bow tie properly tied and sitting at a jaunty angle at the base of his scrawny neck. His white hair was properly combed, and a cloud of musky aftershave wafted into the air as he moved. He stood still while Ali examined him. "Well," he asked, sounding uncharacteristically nervous. "What's the verdict?"

"You'll do," she said with a smile. "How many years has it been?"

"Sixty plus," he said.

"Then they'll be so glad to see you that they won't pay any attention to what you look like. Come on. Let's go knock 'em dead."

Out in the corridor, they called for the lift and waited for it to show up. "What can you tell me about these ladies?' " Ali asked.

"They were very young when I saw them last, but the two of them were little demons — always getting into trouble and mean as snakes."

"Charming," Ali said. "I can't tell you how much I'm looking forward to this." From the look on Leland's face, he obviously felt the same way.

When she was making reservations, Ali had expected the Highcliff to be a bit on the dowdy side, and it didn't disappoint. In the conservatory, where afternoon tea was served, they were shown to a pair of brocade-covered sofas facing each other across a low polished wood table. Ali and Leland were comfortably seated on one of the two when the aunties arrived.

As they made their way toward their table, it seemed to Ali that Maisie Longmoor and Daisy Phipps fit right in with their surroundings: They were a bit on the dowdy side as well, women of a certain age, several years north of seventy. Ali had the momentary sensation that the two of them had just walked off the set of the old PBS sitcom *Keeping Up Appearances.* The twins were not dressed alike, but their brightly hennaed hair, tinted to the same shade, indicated that they utilized the services of the same colorist.

As soon as Leland stood to greet them, they dodged away from the hostess and made a mad dash for him, shrieking with joy. "Lee! Lee! Lee! How good to see you again!"

It took a moment for them to stop smothering him with kisses before they turned to Ali so Leland could make the introductions. Ali noted that Daisy was slightly more heavyset, while Maisie was the more outspoken. She was the one who immediately went to work to set the record straight. "I'm Leland's cousin," she announced formally. "I'm Maisie Jordan Longmoor, and this is my sister, Daisy Jordan Phipps."

"I'm Ali," she replied, holding out her hand in greeting but offering no further explanation of her presence.

Maisie instantly lived up to the advance billing. Remaining standing, she turned back to Leland and went on the attack. "I know there was all that unfortunate business. Still, we could never understand why you took off like that with never a word to anyone. Isn't that right?" Maisie shot a questioning look in her sister's direction. "It broke poor Aunt Adele's heart, I can tell you that."

Ali noticed the shadow that flitted briefly

across Leland's face. Clearly, he didn't appreciate having his youthful transgressions bandied about in casual conversation so many years later.

Daisy nodded in vehement agreement to everything her sister said. "Indeed," she added. "The poor woman was completely devastated."

"She cried constantly after you left, wept her heart out for weeks and weeks," Maisie continued, blissfully unaware that her tasteless remarks might be hurtful to Leland. "She was inconsolable, and of course, that was before your father died a few weeks later. That additional awful blow was just too much."

Daisy nodded again. "Aunt Adele was utterly inconsolable."

That seemed to be the way the pair of them worked, double-teaming as they went along, with Maisie doing the bulk of the talking and Daisy adding the occasional adverb as the conversation warranted.

They were still standing. From the way Maisie and Daisy goggled at their surroundings, Ali understood that the Highcliff Hotel wasn't the sort of place the two women visited often, if at all. Maisie and Daisy were here as Ali's guests, but Ali's reaction was something less than hospitable. With introductions barely out of the way, she was ready to strangle them both.

Once they finally took their seats on the far side of the coffee table, Maisie turned her laserlike attention on Ali. "I'm so sorry. What was your name again?"

"Ali. Short for Alison."

"Is this your daughter, then?" Maisie asked Leland.

Despite Maisie's earlier reference to Leland's tarnished past, it seemed that she had failed to get the memo about his supposedly being gay. If the secret of Leland's homosexuality had been kept for all these years, Ali saw no point in arming Maisie with any added ammunition. Ali answered the question without giving Leland an opportunity to speak. "We're just good friends," she said with a smile.

"I understand we owe a debt of gratitude to Jeffrey for bringing you back into the family fold," Maisie said to Leland.

The words were bland enough, but the underlying hint of disapproval in their delivery suggested that Maisie felt Leland's "cousin" had any number of things to answer for.

"Yes," Leland said smoothly. "He was the one who initiated the contact. The original idea was for me to come for the family reunion he's planning for next summer. This opportunity came up, so I decided to drop in somewhat sooner than that."

The server came to take their order, high tea all around.

"We won't be going to the reunion, of course," Maisie said when the waitress went on her way. "Summer is our busy season. Daisy and I run a B and B out of what was once our family home," she explained for Ali's benefit. "It's rather posh — Jordan's-by-the-Sea. You certainly would have been welcome to stay with us rather than coming here. But as I said, we can't afford to go gallivanting all over the place during the summers. That's when someone needs to be here keeping a sharp eye on the business. I'm sure several of the grands will be going. They love the kinds of parties Jeffrey and that partner of his know how to throw. I suppose you know about all that," she added with a sniff, "about his partner, I mean."

"We had dinner with Jeffrey and Charlie just last night," Ali replied with a bright smile. "What a delightful couple."

A spot of color suddenly appeared through the thick layer of white powder on Maisie's pale cheek. "Oh yes," she huffed. "The two of them live together quite openly, but they're in London, of course. That kind of behavior isn't as easily overlooked or as easily tolerated here as it is there."

In a matter of a few minutes, it had become clear that the prejudices that had sent Leland fleeing his homeland years earlier hadn't disappeared. In fact, they were alive and well, as least as far as these particular members of his family were concerned.

Maisie took a delicate sip of tea and made a determined effort to change the subject. "It would appear you've done quite well for yourself, Lee," she said. "Exactly what kind of work did you do? I assume you're retired now, of course."

"He's a property manager," Ali answered in Leland's place. "And no, he's not retired. You love what you do, don't you?" She was tempted to give him a wink. Afraid that one of the twins might intercept it, she refrained.

"Quite right," Leland agreed smoothly. "I don't ever see myself retiring. I expect I'll be more like one of those old dray horses and die in the traces."

"Do you have children? Grandchildren?" Maisie persisted. "You must have photos. Please show us."

"Yes, do," added Daisy. "By all means."

"I lost the love of my life several years

92

ago," Leland answered quietly. "We were never able to have any children."

"Your wife is deceased, then?" Maisie asked.

"It's all too painful and I'd rather not talk about it, if you don't mind." Leland's deft reply left Maisie free to draw her own conclusions. "What about the two of you?" he added. "What all have you been up to while I've been gone?"

For the next twenty minutes, Maisie delivered a monologue with a detailed rundown of how the two sisters had taken ownership of the family home and turned it into a thriving business. As far as Maisie was concerned, she and Daisy were among Bournemouth's finest hoteliers, and Jordan's offered the very best in accommodations.

While Maisie talked, Daisy systematically ate her way through most of the food on the table. It would have been a lot more difficult for Ali to listen to Maisie's brag-o-rama if she hadn't been able to see that Leland was enjoying himself immensely. Eventually, Maisie ran out of steam. When she went looking for food, there was precious little left.

Maisie then returned to grilling Leland about his life in the U.S. Where exactly did he live? Wasn't Arizona terribly hot? Did Indians live anywhere near where he did, and were they dangerous? Had he ever thought about returning to England to live?

That last question Leland answered with a definitive shake of the head. "The U.S. is my home now," he told them. "It's been very kind to me, and there's nothing for me back here, not anymore."

Maisie pursed her thin lips. Ali could almost see the words "But what about us?" running through her hennaed head, but she didn't say them aloud.

"Have you been in touch with that friend of yours? What was his name again? Tom something."

Ali saw Leland's jaw tighten. "Thomas," he said quietly. "Thomas Blackfield."

"That's the one," Maisie said with a nod. "He was quite handsome, wasn't he? Did you know Daisy had a terrible crush on him?"

Leland shook his head.

"That was before I met Roger," Daisy interjected. "My late husband."

"Did you let Thomas know you were coming to visit?" Maisie asked.

"I'm afraid Thomas and I lost touch," Leland said.

"Well," Maisie went on, clearly happy to

fill in the blanks, "he spent his entire career at the Kembry Park Academy, first as a teacher and later as headmaster. He was in charge when they closed it down. People can't afford private schools these days, not the way they used to. He's still around, though. You should be sure to see him while you're here. I understand he's not been doing all that well since his wife died. Sally was such a wonderful person, a local girl, several years younger than we were. One of those people always reaching out to give others a helping hand. You would have loved her." She smiled confidently at Leland.

"I'm sure I would have," Leland murmured.

"I knew them both from church," Daisy said. "Sally was utterly delightful. They were never able to have children. That must have been difficult for her since they spent so much time with other people's children."

"What happened to her?" Ali asked.

Maisie shrugged. "It was at least a year or so ago. First there was an announcement in the paper about celebrating their fiftieth wedding anniversary with some kind of upscale get-together — I believe it was in the ballroom at the Royal Bath. A few weeks later, poor Sally was dead, just like that. Something quite sudden, I believe. A stroke or something on that order. So sad, really. Terribly sad."

It's sad, all right, Ali thought, glancing at Leland's stricken face. And for more than one reason.

At that point, Daisy nudged her sister's arm and glanced pointedly at her watch. Maisie took the hint. "We should be going," she said. "It is getting late. I'd hate to think we overstayed our welcome."

By the time Leland and Ali walked them to the front entrance and said goodbye, Ali was more than ready to be rid of them. "That wasn't so bad, now, was it?" she said to Leland as the glass doors swung shut behind their departing guests.

"Wasn't it?" Leland replied grimly. "The whole thing was their fault, you know. Thomas and I were trying to steer clear of those girls when we ran into Langston and Frances that day. If we hadn't — if Langston hadn't been so outraged at being caught with his pants down — who knows how things would have turned out?"

"Who knows?" Ali agreed. "But here's one good thing. We're staying at the Highcliff as opposed to Jordan's-by-the-Sea. I don't know about you, but I've had quite enough of your relatives for one day. Why don't we go up to the room? If we're hungry later, we can order from room service or raid the rest of the fruit basket."

"I doubt I'll be hungry," Leland said.

Ali studied him as they rode up in the elevator. Some of the light had gone out of that jaunty, nattily dressed gentleman who had ridden down with her in the same elevator only an hour and a half earlier.

"What's wrong?" Ali asked.

"Fifty years," Leland replied dejectedly, shaking his head. "I wondered about Thomas from time to time, but I never would have imagined that — that he would have been married for fifty years. That's a very long time for me to have been so mistaken about who I thought he was. It's as though my entire life was based on a series of erroneous assumptions."

"Maybe you weren't wrong," Ali said. "Back in that era and even now, I have a feeling, there have been more than a few gay people who married and stayed married for camouflage reasons."

Leland shook his head. "Maybe so," he said.

Hoping to brighten his spirits, Ali asked, "What's on the agenda for tomorrow?"

"If the weather's better, I'd like to visit the cemetery and spend some time at my parents' graves. If you don't mind, that is."

So much for brightening spirits, Ali thought. She said cheerfully, "Regardless of the weather, I'm here to do whatever you want to do."

5

"How about some coffee?"

At the sound of her mother's voice, LeAnne Tucker roused herself and sat up on the uncomfortable love seat where she had finally fallen asleep. Sunlight was streaming in through the window on the opposite side of the waiting room in the burn unit at Austin Memorial Hospital. Her mother, Phyllis Rogers, stood in front of her holding out a cardboard-wrapped cup of Starbucks from the lobby coffee bar downstairs.

When LeAnne's son landed in the ICU, her mother had offered to drive down from Eugene to help. At first LeAnne tried to put the kibosh on the whole idea. She hadn't wanted her widowed seventysomething mother to be out on the interstates, driving by herself with only her two yappy pugs as traveling companions, through hazardous winter conditions for the better part of two thousand miles. Phyllis had been adamant, insisting that she was more than capable of taking care of herself and of traveling cross-country. She and her two dogs, Duke and Duchess, had made the trip in her Honda Accord in what Phyllis regarded as a "leisurely" five days; she'd smoked Pall Malls every mile of the way.

Once Phyllis arrived, LeAnne couldn't imagine how she would have coped without her mother's help. She had to admit that having a second vehicle available, even one that reeked of cigarette smoke, was a definite blessing. While LeAnne remained camped out in a hospital waiting room, waiting for Lance to awaken from his drug-induced coma, Phyllis had taken charge of things back home in San Leandro, some fifty miles away, supervising Lance's younger brothers, making sure they had food to eat, and providing transportation as required to and from various school activities.

LeAnne accepted the cup, noticing gratefully that the coffee was far too hot to drink. That was the problem with the tepid stuff that came out of the machine in the vending alcove down the hall. Not only was it barely lukewarm, it was tasteless. LeAnne had complained about the machine, but so far no one had come by to fix it, and no one had returned the two bucks she had fed into it when no coffee came out, either.

Phyllis had arrived in the room carrying a small overnight bag. When she took a seat in the next chair over, a cloud of secondhand-smoke residue wafted in LeAnne's direction. Phyllis set the bag on the floor between them. "How are things this morning?"

"The same. He's still in the drug-induced coma," LeAnne answered. "The doctor hasn't been by so far this morning." She glanced at her watch. "He should be here any minute. Maybe today will be the day they'll bring him around." She paused while tears sprang to her eyes. "Oh, Mom," she groaned. "What am I going to do? I have to be there when they wake him up. I have to be the one who tells him about his leg, but what am I going to say? What can I say?"

Hours earlier, at a few minutes before midnight, Lance had been wheeled into surgery, where doctors, hoping to stop the spread of a raging infection, had amputated his right leg just below the knee.

Phyllis didn't answer immediately. "I think you need to tell him the truth," she said quietly. "Soft-pedaling it isn't going to work."

LeAnne sighed and tried to get a grip on

herself by changing the subject. "How are things at home?"

"Thad has a basketball game after school. I told him I'll pick Connor up from Susan's place and bring him to the game. I know he loves watching his big brother play."

Susan and Les Madigan were LeAnne's next-door neighbors in San Leandro; Susan had willingly pitched in to help look after six-year-old Connor as needed. She had also masterminded a hot-dish brigade that was organized so that one hot dish appeared each day and the previous day's dishes were picked up and returned to their proper homes by whoever brought the next day's meal.

"Thank you," LeAnne said, patting her mother's bony knee. "It's so good of you and Susan to keep some semblance of normal life going on at home for Thad and Connor."

"Speaking of normal life," Phyllis said, passing her daughter a heavily laden grocery bag, "I brought you a change of clothes. There's also shampoo, conditioner, and hair spray in there."

LeAnne managed a tentative smile. "Is that a subtle hint?"

"Not so subtle," Phyllis allowed. "Since they've got that shower room for bicycle-riding employees downstairs, and since they're willing to let you use it, you should. You'll feel better."

"Yes," LeAnne agreed, "but not until I see the doctor."

"Have you had anything to eat?"

"I've had coffee, thanks to you. I'm not hungry."

"Maybe not, but you're going to eat. I'll go down to the cafeteria and get you something. What do you want?"

"One of those wrapped tuna sandwiches and some yogurt."

Phyllis sighed and shook her head. "Not a very nutritious breakfast, if you ask me," she grumbled, "but I suppose it's better than nothing." Grabbing up her purse, she headed for the cafeteria.

As her mother left the waiting room, LeAnne picked up her phone. For the past week, her world had shrunk to endless hours in this waiting room and the few minutes she spent each hour at her son's bedside. During most of that time her only connection to the outside world had been through her cell phone. Flipping it open, she studied the call history. Most were back and forth to her mother's phone, to Thad's cell, or to the landline at home. Several of the incoming calls came from blocked numbers, mostly from media types hoping for interviews, all of which she had declined.

The last blocked call, the one that had come in early this morning, had been from someone who claimed he wasn't a reporter. LeAnne wasn't sure of the name; she hadn't quite caught it. The guy had said he was the father of a kid from Lance's school — the old one — from before their lives had all gone to hell. It had touched her to think that at least some of the kids from San Leandro High still cared about Lance.

All it had taken was that little bit of sympathy from a complete stranger for LeAnne to end up spilling her guts. Now she worried that she had said too much, telling him about the joke of an investigation that had ruled Lance responsible for his own injuries, about the doctors amputating his leg, about the foreclosure situation on the house, and about being held responsible for the hospital bill. She had blabbed about anything and everything. LeAnne was embarrassed to think that she had told someone else — a complete stranger — about Lance losing his leg when her son had yet to be told.

It was at that juncture when LeAnne's mother returned from the cafeteria with a cellophane-wrapped sandwich and a small container of yogurt.

"What's wrong?" Phyllis asked, handing them over. "You look upset. Did the doctor come by while I was gone?"

"No, not yet," LeAnne answered. "Just worried, I guess."

"About what?" Phyllis asked.

Something in LeAnne snapped. "What do you think? I'm worried about everything. About Lance losing his leg; about probably losing the house and my job; about figuring out where we'll live if I do; about paying the hospital bill, which I'm sure will be astronomical. What don't I have to worry about?" The moment the words were out of her mouth, LeAnne was sorry. "Oh, Mom," she said. "Forgive me. I shouldn't take it out on you."

Phyllis sat down next to LeAnne and put a comforting hand on her daughter's thigh. "Don't worry about me," she said. "You have every right to feel overwhelmed right now. You need to vent to someone, and I'm the person who happens to be here. Believe me, I can take it. As for where you and the boys will live? I'm sure we'll manage. I've already told you you're welcome to come live with me. It'll be a tight fit, but it's better than being out on the street or dumped into some kind of Section Eight housing."

LeAnne, concentrating on unwrapping the sandwich, said nothing. What her mother had said was true, but LeAnne didn't want to do that. For one thing, she loved living in the Texas Hill Country, and she knew she'd hate the rain in Oregon. For another, it had taken her months to get her nursing license from Arizona validated so she could work in Texas. If she moved to yet a different state, she'd most likely be out of work for months again, assuming there was any work to be had. In this economy, jobs for qualified LPNs weren't all that plentiful. Then there was Lance. How long would it take for him to recover from his burns or get fitted for a prosthetic leg or learn to walk on it?

LeAnne bit into the sandwich. Though the bread was dry and tasted like cardboard, she knew her mother was right. LeAnne was in this fight for the long haul, and she needed to eat whether she wanted to or not.

"By the way," Phyllis said, "I talked to that nice Detective Hernandez yesterday after basketball practice. He was there picking up his son when I stopped by for Thad. Did you know his son and Thad are on the same junior varsity team?"

LeAnne choked on a chunk of sandwich and spent the better part of the next minute coughing her head off. Nice? LeAnne

couldn't believe that her mother had referred to Detective Richard Hernandez of
the San Leandro Sheriff's Department as
nice. He was the guy who had shown up on
her doorstep some months earlier to place
her son under arrest for what was referred
to at the time as malicious mischief. Of
course, the charges had escalated from
there. Maybe the man had just been doing
his job. Lance had done the crime, and he
had also done his time, but in LeAnne's
book, Richard Hernandez would never
remotely be considered a "nice" man.

"Yes," she said when the coughing fit
subsided. "I was aware of that."

"He said he was sorry to hear about what
had happened, about Lance's accident."
Phyllis shrugged. "That's what it said in the
paper yesterday, by the way — in the San
Leandro paper. That last week's incident in
which an inmate at the San Leandro Juvenile Detention Facility suffered serious
burns had been determined to be an accident."

"It was not an accident," LeAnne hissed
through clenched teeth. "First they said
Lance did it to himself as a ploy to get an
early release. Now they're saying it was an
accident? Someone tried to murder him,
Mother, and no one, not one person, be-

107

lieves it when I try to tell them so. How could they already write what happened off as a so-called accident when Lance is still unconscious and no one has bothered to interview the person it happened to? That makes no sense. It's a cover-up, plain and simple."

Phyllis said nothing aloud, although her silence spoke volumes. For some reason, she seemed to have drawn the same conclusions the investigators had — that Lance was somehow responsible for his own injuries. Angered by her mother's complicit agreement with the rest of the world, LeAnne stood up abruptly, dropped the remainder of her sandwich in the trash, and donned the required paper gown and slippers. "It's time for me to go in," she said.

ICU rules for the burn unit allowed patients to have one visitor per hour for five minutes at a time. LeAnne ducked into Lance's room, wiping away unwelcome tears and hoping her mother hadn't noticed them.

The room was dimly lit, with the blackout curtains pulled shut. The atmosphere hummed and buzzed with quiet noises from the collection of life-sustaining equipment arrayed around Lance's bed. Oblivious to everything but her son's pale face on the pillow, LeAnne stood at his bedside and let the tears course down her cheeks. His face looked fine — well, almost fine, if you could ignore the oxygen tube fastened under his nose or the fact that most of his eyebrows and eyelashes had been singed away. The drugs must have been working. As far as LeAnne could tell from his expression, he was resting comfortably. The problem was, Lance's face didn't tell the whole story. She had seen the awful damage the hospital sheets kept hidden from view — the hideous seeping burns from his chest down, the broken bones, and now the missing leg.

Days earlier, before the surgeon took Lance into surgery to repair the compound fractures, he had warned LeAnne of the dangers of infection from the burns or from the surgical incisions. He had told her that Lance was receiving the very best treatment and that hospital personnel were doing everything they could, but still . . .

LeAnne had heard the momentary hesitation in the doctor's voice. It had taken several days before she had filled in the blanks. The doctor had been trying to prepare her for the possibility that Lance might end up losing one or both of his legs. He hadn't mentioned the other possible outcome, one that was far worse. Standing there, she realized that what had been unthinkable to begin with was now a very real possibility. Lance, her beloved firstborn child, might die.

In the long hours after the orderlies had wheeled him back into his room after the amputation, LeAnne Tucker had forced herself to come to terms with that life-shattering possibility: Lance might die, and that possibility brought another horrifying consideration into LeAnne's life. If Lance died and the cops continued to blame him for what had happened, then whoever was responsible for his death might well get away with it.

LeAnne stood there for several of her paltry five minutes feeling as lost and alone as she had ever felt in her life. When the door swished open, she turned, expecting to see a doctor, since this was about the time of day when the doctors usually did rounds. Instead, a woman, properly paper-gowned for the occasion, entered the room and stood beside LeAnne. The new arrival wasn't someone LeAnne had seen in the hospital before. This was an older woman, far older than any of the other nurses. Her hair, mostly white, was pulled back into a tight bun. She wore gold-framed glasses. On a chain around her neck, she wore a gold crucifix.

"You're Lance's new nurse?" LeAnne asked. "I'm his mother."

The woman shook her head. "I'm not a nurse. My name is Sister Anselm, and I'm happy to meet you. Not happy to meet under such difficult circumstances, of course," she corrected quickly. "Your son must be very important. My bishop made special arrangements for me to come here from Arizona to look after him."

"Your bishop?" LeAnne asked, feeling stupid. "You mean you're a nun?"

"Yes," Sister Anselm answered, smiling. "I'm a Sister of Providence. I'm also what's known in the trade as a patient advocate."

LeAnne noticed something very comforting about that smile, but none of this made sense. Sister Anselm had come because a bishop had sent her? What bishop? And what's a patient advocate?

"I'm sorry," Leanne said finally. "There must be some mistake. Our family isn't Catholic."

"Oh no," Sister Anselm disagreed. "There's no mistake. None at all. What Bishop Gillespie told me on the phone when he was making the transportation arrangements was that one of his friends had called in a marker."

There were two hospital beds in the room, but only one was occupied. Sister Anselm went over to the other bed, retrieved the chair that was sitting there, and dragged it to Lance's side of the room. Once it was in place, she sat down on one chair and motioned for LeAnne to take the second. "Tell me about your son," the nun said.

LeAnne glanced at her watch. "I can't," she said. "My five minutes are up."

"Let's not worry about minutes just now," Sister Anselm said. "I'm here to be of service to your son and to you. To do that, I need to know as much about him as possible."

LeAnne hesitated, but for only a moment, and then she settled gratefully into the offered chair. There, for the second time that morning, she found herself spilling out her tale of woe into the listening ears of a complete stranger.

6

Once Leland disappeared into his room, Ali went to hers, stripped out of her clothing and into her jammies, and then returned to the sitting room. During tea, her phone had vibrated with several incoming-mail announcements, but she hadn't wanted to open any of them while they were dealing with the aunties.

In looking at her mail, she was pleased to see that the first message was from B. When she opened it with her iPhone, she saw a photo of B. smiling back at her. He was one of several businessmen in the photo, all of them wearing suits and smiles while posed in front of a window with a bite-sized view of Tokyo's nighttime skyline showing in the background. Naturally, B. was head and shoulders above his counterparts. The accompanying message said:

Last night's dinner at the Crown restaurant in the Palace Hotel. I guess you can see why I'm standing in the middle of the back row.

Love, B.

The message seemed innocuous enough, but Ali's instincts told her that something else was going on. Retrieving her thumb drive, she reopened the e-mail using her steganography program and password. After unzipping the enclosed file, she used her encryption key to unlock and read B.'s real message.

After I got off the phone with you this morning, I still couldn't sleep. This whole thing stinks. See additional accompanying files from Stuart. My gut tells me someone is after Lance Tucker, and just because he's out of the juvie facility doesn't mean he's out of danger. I'm contacting Bishop Gillespie and asking for reinforcements.

It didn't take an encryption key for Ali to understand what B. meant. He was going to Bishop Francis Gillespie in Phoenix to ask for help from the bishop's traveling patient advocate and emissary, Sister Anselm Becker. The idea that Bishop Gillespie would send Sister Anselm to look after the welfare of a seriously injured burn-unit patient wasn't at all surprising. What was surprising was that he'd send her all the way to Texas.

Years earlier, a burn unit was where Ali first met Sister Anselm, who was now a valued and trusted friend. In that instance, a woman named Madeline Langley Cooper had been seriously injured in an arson fire near Camp Verde in Arizona's Yavapai County. She was initially hospitalized with no identification and no one to intercede on her behalf. Sister Anselm had been dispatched to run interference for her. Because Arizona had then and still has an ongoing problem with undocumented aliens ending up in hospitals under similar circumstances, Father Gillespie, the bishop of the Phoenix archdiocese, had made those unfortunate individuals the focus of his personal ministry, and he had tapped Sister Anselm, a trained nurse, to serve that particular community.

At first Mimi Cooper was thought to be the innocent victim of an accidental fire. When a subsequent investigation revealed the crime to be an attempted and ultimately successful homicide, both Ali and Sister Anselm were drawn into the killer's crosshairs as they attempted to keep the severely injured woman safe. The trauma of that shared experience had turned Ali and Sister Anselm into fast friends. It was also the reason Sister Anselm, who refused to carry a gun, now never went anywhere without her trusty Taser.

In this instance, Ali wondered if Sister Anselm was being transported across state lines due to her abilities as a patient advocate, or did it have more to do with the expectation that she could function as Lance's on-site bodyguard? Either way, Ali understood that if Sister Anselm were there, any number of serious strings had been pulled. The only way to find out why was likely to be found in the new collection of files hidden in the pixels of this latest e-mail. As tempting as it was to go straight to the new files, Ali forced herself to go back to the ones from the day before — the ones she had started reading before going down to tea.

She spent the next two hours reading through the voluminous court proceedings surrounding Lance Tucker's eventual conviction and incarceration. Since Lance was a juvenile at the time, he was never mentioned by name in the *Lariat* articles that reported on the trial. The court transcripts were another matter, and it was easy to see that the deck had been stacked against Lance and his mother.

The cyber evidence, including tracking done by High Noon Security, clearly pointed to Lance as the culprit in the server hacking incident. Not only was the kid found guilty and jailed, his mother was ordered to pay restitution in the amount of one hundred thousand dollars, which his mother had paid by taking a second mortgage on her house, which was now in danger of foreclosure.

As Ali read through the material, it looked like there had been a rush to justice, and Lance's public defender hadn't done him any favors. The defense seemed inadequate all the way along. Lance hadn't been allowed out on bail pending trial, and upon conviction, he had been given the highest possible sentence.

It was an article from the *Lariat* that followed the one reporting on Lance's sentencing hearing that caught Ali's attention:

Longtime San Leandro High School math teacher Everett Jackson, age 58, passed away suddenly in his home on May 23. For the past ten years, the popular teacher has served as faculty adviser to the school's prizewinning computer science club, which has won the statewide Longhorn computer science competition three of the last four years.

He is survived by his former wife and two children, Everett Jr. of Dallas and Linda Gail Thomas (Richard) of San Antonio. He is also survived by his mother, Grace Jackson, of San Leandro.

Services are pending.

The family suggests that in lieu of flowers, donations be made to the San Leandro Suicide Prevention Line.

Ali read through the article twice. What it didn't say was far more revealing than what it did, and it left Ali asking any number of questions. The only clue that the man's death was a suicide had come in the line about suggested donations. So how had this popular and presumably well-respected man killed himself, and if so, why? Had he been in danger of losing his job for some reason? Had he faced some kind of looming health issue, or did he have difficulties with substance abuse? Had he been diagnosed with depression? The article said that Jackson was married with two grown children. Was his suicide the result of some kind of marital discord?

Ali was wondering about that when the

ringing of the room's landline phone interrupted her thought process.

"Hey," she said when she realized it was
B. calling. "I got your photo. You looked
tired."

"I was tired," he admitted, "and I still am.
I just found out the doctors amputated
Lance's right leg last night."

"I'm sorry," Ali said, and she was. She
could tell from the catch in B.'s voice that
he was, too. "Do you think he's in danger
from more than just his injuries?"

"Yes," B. said. "It's in the file. You'll find
it."

It struck Ali as odd that he was being so
circumspect on the phone, as though he
suspected that someone from San Leandro
might be listening in on the conversation.
"You're not going to give me any more clues
than that?"

"Not right now. I've got Stu working on
another aspect of the case. Once he comes
up with something, I'm sure we'll both hear
from him. In the meantime, I wanted someone to be in Austin to keep an eye on
things."

"Sister Anselm, you mean?" Ali asked.

"Yes."

"But B., this is sounding more and more
like it should be a police matter," Ali said.

"It will be eventually, but right now the authorities aren't interested in anything besides what they've already determined," B. replied. "We'll bring them into the picture once we can point them in the right direction without getting in too much trouble ourselves. Pay close attention to the science fair articles. I think what happened to Lance might have something to do with that. Now it's your turn. Tell me about the rest of your day. How was the drive?"

"Snowy most of the way, but it cleared up. We just came back to the room after tea with Leland's cousins, either one of which would have been reason enough for him to run away from home all those years ago."

"And what's on the agenda tomorrow for you and Mr. Brooks?"

"I'm going to look at wedding dresses in a shop here that Jeffrey suggested. Leland wants to go to the cemetery to visit his parents' graves. I'm not sure how to feel about that. When they sent him away all those years ago, they clearly intended for him to stay away, but I think he's still grieving their loss."

"It makes sense to me," B. said. "I went through some of that when I came back to Sedona. I was at war with my parents the whole time I was growing up. By the time I was a success, they were both gone. Leland's a success now, too. He left all of them behind, went to another country, and made a whole new life for himself, but being back where he grew up has to be bringing back some nostalgia for what might have been."

Such as Thomas Blackfield, Ali thought.

"Does he know where his parents are buried?"

"He knows which cemetery — the one at St. Stephens Church. He may even know where the graves are located. His father died in the early fifties, his mother in the sixties, his two brothers in the eighties, and the two sisters-in-law, the brothers' widows, sometime later than that. I looked on the Internet for him. A lot of cemeteries have grave location apps, but not this one."

"Are you going with him?" B. asked.

"He didn't say that he wanted me to. I got the feeling that this is something he needs to do on his own."

"So he's going to the cemetery, and you're going shopping. If you find a dress," B. added, "be sure to send me a photo."

"I'll think about it," she said with a laugh, "but I won't promise."

By the time they hung up, it was long past dark outside. Off to the west, the sea was a fathomless black void. After one more raid on the fruit basket, Ali returned to her files and worked her way through to the most recent batch. The science fair articles from two and three years earlier were interesting, just as B. had said. In both cases, Lance Tucker had walked away with the code-writing honors, leading his school's computer science club to easy victories. In an article dated two years earlier, Everett Jackson had told a reporter from the *San Leandro Lariat* that freshman Lance Tucker had all the makings of becoming the next supernova of the computing world.

Ali had no doubt it was the possible loss of all that potential that had goaded B.'s involvement in Lance's case, but it wasn't until she saw the article about the most recent fair, one in which San Leandro again took first place, that Ali tumbled to what B. had seen.

When the San Leandro Computing Club went looking for their fourth win in the annual Longhorn Science Competition, the idea of coming away with the grand prize, as they had in years past, was seriously in jeopardy. For one thing, the club's faculty adviser, longtime math teacher Everett Jackson, passed away last year. In addition, the talented student who led the charge in the recent past and who had served as team captain in the two previous winning years no longer attends San Leandro High.

Concerns about not winning proved groundless when the San Leandro Saints brought home the grand prize in the competition once again, this time under the leadership of their new team co-captains, Andrew Garfield and Jillian Sosa.

As she had previously, Ali took copious notes. There was something about the name of the first co-captain that hit home. She highlighted it and pressed Find. Immediately, her cursor landed on an earlier note and the name of the San Leandro superintendent of schools — Richard Garfield. Were Andrew Garfield and Richard Garfield related? Garfield wasn't all that common a name.

Ali remembered reading articles about girls' cheerleading competitions getting out of hand when parents saw to it that their daughters made it onto the cheering squad no matter what. Maybe this was a variation on that theme. Maybe this was all about a second-class geeky guy wanting to be captain of the team.

She wrote a brief note to Stuart Ramey

back home in Sedona: "Are Andrew Gar-field and Richard Garfield related?"

Once the note was written and encrypted, she loaded a photo onto her thumb drive from her camera, one she had snapped of Leland boarding the plane in Phoenix, dropped the question into the mix, and sent it off to elarson@highnoon.com. Under the photo, she added the unencrypted caption "Leland Brooks is headed home."

With that, having done as much as she could in one day, Ali turned off the lights in the sitting room and returned to her own part of the suite.

She went to bed, but she didn't sleep. As she lay there, restless and wakeful, Ali had a feeling there was something she was miss-ing — some part of the puzzle that B. hadn't told her or that she had yet to glimpse on her own. She also worried about Sister Anselm. If B. thought Lance Tucker was in danger, then what about Ali's friend? Wasn't she in danger, too?

At last Ali slept. When she awakened, it was late enough that wintery sunshine filled the room. Knowing that a run would do her a world of good, she dredged up the run-ning shoes and tracksuit that she had crammed into the bottom of her suitcase and headed out.

The Highcliff Hotel was just that — on a high cliff overlooking the beaches and promenades for which Bournemouth was famous. She raced down the aging flight of stone steps that led away from the hotel's grounds. First she went west on the footpath along West Cliff Promenade, past the lift, and down the zigzag path that led through the garden, where she turned back east, still on the footpath, this time running next to the sandy beach.

As Ali pounded past the pier, the amusement park and rides and beachside cafés were shuttered for the season, although people were taking full advantage of a small break in the cold weather. The footpath was crowded with people out walking dogs or pushing strollers; the beaches were alive with preschool-aged children chasing after seagulls. Along the way Ali nodded and smiled at her fellow runners, who, like her, were pleased to be doing their wintertime morning workout outside rather than in some overheated gym. When she finished her long circuit, the stairs leading back up to East Overcliff seemed far longer and steeper than they had on her way down.

Ali arrived in their suite to find Leland not only fully dressed but happily enjoying a solitary room-service full English breakfast. There was only one breakfast tray, but Ali noticed that there was a large pot of coffee along with an extra cup and saucer. Unasked, Leland filled the empty cup and passed it to her.

"For decades I somehow resisted the American custom of drinking coffee in the mornings," he said with a smile, "but I believe you and Mr. Simpson have worn me down. I still can't drink the stuff straight the way you two do, however. I much prefer mine with a bit of cream and sugar."

Ali took a sip of coffee. It was weaker than she would have liked, but at least it was coffee. She sat down on the sofa and waited. Leland Brooks had been part of her life long enough that she understood there was more going on than the mere offer of morning coffee. In the old days, when she worked as a journalist, Ali might have pressed for answers at once. Her classes in interrogation at the Arizona Police Academy had taught her that sometimes it was best to simply wait and let the looming silence create its own kind of pressure.

"I thought about it overnight, and I'd like you to come with me," Leland said at length. "To the cemetery, I mean. Yesterday's storm seems to have blown itself out, and today is expected to be unseasonably warm."

"I'll come along on one condition," Ali said.

"What's that?"

"After the cemetery, you come with me to look at wedding dresses."

"Fair enough," Leland agreed.

"Let me shower and change clothes, then," Ali said. She disappeared into her own room. When she emerged half an hour later, Leland's empty breakfast tray had been replaced by a fresh one.

"I took the liberty of ordering for you," he said, pulling out a chair. "I hope you don't mind."

Ali shook her head. "Even on vacation, you can't get out of the habit of looking after me, can you?"

"I suppose not," he said. "It's hard to teach old dogs new tricks."

An hour after Ali returned, she and Leland left the hotel, properly attired and comfortably fed. It would have been easy to catch a cab, but they decided to take advantage of what felt like balmy late morning weather, meandering through the central shopping district and the winter-dead gardens with Leland confidently directing their path as though no time had passed between now and when he had last wandered these same streets. On the way, he pointed out the building on Albert Road where his father's print shop had once been located. The space was now occupied by an Indian restaurant.

A little over half an hour after leaving the hotel, Ali and Leland made their way into the small churchyard cemetery tucked behind St. Stephens Church. Many of the grave markers were so moss-covered that the names engraved on them were unreadable. Some of the stones leaned at odd angles, as though the slightest wind might send them tumbling. Leland led Ali through the collection of assorted grave markers with the same confidence he had used to guide them through the streets of Bournemouth.

"Our family plot was always in the far corner," he said.

Though Leland had said that he wanted Ali to come with him, on the way there, he had maintained an uncharacteristic silence. He walked past the graves of both his brothers and their wives without a word and without giving either a second glance. It wasn't until they stopped in front of two matching headstones that he spoke again. "These were my parents," he said in a flat voice, as if offering an introduction to someone among the living rather than to someone long dead.

Ali studied the words and numbers printed there. Jonah Brooks. Adele Mathison Brooks. According to the dates chiseled into the granite, Jonah Brooks was a relatively young man when he died. When Adele died eighteen years later, she was the same age as Ali's father now. Their outcast son had outlived his father by over three decades, but in that moment, as Leland pulled a white hankie from his pocket and dabbed at his eyes, Ali realized that, for him, the pain of losing his parents was as fresh right then as if their deaths had happened yesterday. They had died while he was gone, and he had never, in all the intervening years, had a chance to pay his respects.

"I'm sorry," Ali said. At first that was all she could think of to say. After a pause, she added, "Your father was only fifty-five when he died."

Leland nodded. "When I was growing up, he always seemed larger than life. I always thought he was a good father. One of the things I respected most about him was that he was always scrupulously fair. Some parents clearly favor one child over another. He was never like that, or at least I never thought he was like that." Leland paused.

"But you're right, of course. He was very young. He died in September 1954, less than a month after I left Bournemouth for the U.S. My father wasn't ill, at least not as far as I knew. It seemed to me he was in the prime of life. When Langston told me he was dead, I had a hard time believing it was even possible. Not only was our father dead, Langston was only too happy to let me know that I had been disowned prior to his death. That was a second blow, one that hit me hard. I wouldn't have expected that of my father. Even now I find it difficult to accept. My decision then was to simply turn my back on all of them — to move forward with my life and not give them another moment's thought. In large part, I succeeded in doing that, but now that I'm here, I find myself wanting to know more, especially after what Jeffrey said the other night."

"What was that?" Ali asked.

"Don't you remember? It was a line from one of my mother's letters. In it, she said that she had already lost one son and she had no intention of losing another. I'm assuming that the lost son was a reference to me, but what I'm wondering is why she thought she might be in jeopardy of losing another. And which one of my two brothers did she mean? Was she referring to Langston or Lawrence?"

Now that Leland reminded Ali, she recalled Jeffrey mentioning something to that effect, though she hadn't paid much attention at the time. Clearly, Leland had been mulling over the matter ever since.

"What are you saying?" Ali asked.

"I'm saying that I'd like you to look into it for me," Leland said. "I'd like to know more about the circumstances surrounding my father's death, and my mother's, too, for that matter. By the time I first communicated with Langston after arriving in the States, my father's death was already months in the past. Given Langston's role in all that went on before I left Bournemouth, I would rather have eaten ground glass than to ask him for any of the details. I refused to give him the satisfaction. At that point in my life, living in what one can only politely call reduced circumstances, I was in no position to mount any kind of independent investigation. The very idea was entirely outside the realm of possibility. Now that I'm here, however, things have changed."

"What do you mean?" Ali asked. "What's changed?"

"For one thing, Langston is dead. For another: you," Leland said, smiling in her direction.

"What about me?" Ali asked.

"I'm fortunate enough to have you in my corner. One thing I've learned over the past several years is that there's very little that you, Mr. Simpson, and that company of his can't suss out once you put your several minds to it or else when you enlist the aid of High Noon's very capable collection of computers and computer operators. No doubt the details I'm missing are out there, hidden in plain sight in some official document or other. The problem is, I lack the ability to know where to go looking. In addition, I have neither the skills nor the mind-set that would enable me to ask the right questions once I get there. You can do all that, and quite handily, too. And it happens that I'm now able to pay whatever costs embarking on such an investigation might entail."

"What difference will it make?" Ali objected. "Your father died sixty years ago, your mother almost twenty years later. After such a long time, what's the point in looking into the death of either of your parents?"

Leland shrugged. "You're right. There's probably very little point. My parents are dead. My brothers are dead, but I can tell you that finally knowing all of what hap-

132

pened will make a difference to me. Let's just say it would put a doddering old man's mind at rest."

That was the one answer — the only one — for which Ali had no comeback. That was, after all, the purpose of the whole trip: allowing Leland Brooks to come to terms with his past.

"You're not doddering," Ali objected, "but if that's what you want, I'll go to work on it as soon as we get back to the hotel. There is, however, one condition."

"What's that?"

"We investigate; you owe nothing."

"But —"

"No buts," Ali insisted. "I mean it. Nothing. Nada. Understand? B. would never agree to your paying us, and neither will I."

After a long pause Leland finally nodded in agreement. "Very well, madam. Thank you. I'm most grateful, but in the meantime, I believe we have one more errand to run. You came to the cemetery, now it's time to look for that dress. Shall we?" he asked.

"Yes," Ali said. "Let's."

As they left the cemetery, Ali noticed that Leland did so without once glancing back over his shoulder toward the family plot. Following his lead, neither did she.

7

Somewhere in the middle of LeAnne's long talk with Sister Anselm, Lance's doctors came into the room, both the surgeon, Dr. Kim, and the burn unit's lead physician, Dr. Walker. LeAnne more than half expected to be chastised by the two doctors for having overstayed her visiting time, but she was not. The doctors nodded politely to the nun and then conferred in low tones before turning to LeAnne.

"Fortunately," Dr. Walker explained, "we're seeing no signs of infection in the other leg. That doesn't mean we're home free, but it's encouraging. Even though Lance lost the one leg, there's a good possibility that we'll be able to save the other one. The problem is, as much as it helps with the pain, we can't allow him to remain sedated for much longer. Overnight, we'll begin reducing the coma-inducing meds. By this time tomorrow, he'll be awake. You need to be prepared for the fact that he'll be enduring severe pain. Agony, actually. When he starts doing rehab — as he must — the accompanying pain of that will be excruciating as well."

LeAnne bit her lip. "I understand," she said.

Dr. Walker gave her an appraising look. "I'm not sure you do," he said gently. "I know you've been here night and day, that you've barely left your son's bedside, but I'm suggesting you might want to give yourself a break starting today, and for the next day or two after that. You have no concept of how bad it will be, and the first few days are by far the worst. Watching a child deal with that kind of suffering is something most mothers can't bear, and they shouldn't have to. I know you have other children at home, Mrs. Tucker. Go look after them for a day or two, and leave us to look after Lance. It'll be better for him and better for you."

"No," LeAnne said stubbornly. "I'm staying. I need to be here when he wakes up. I need to be the one to tell him that his leg is gone."

Dr. Walker studied LeAnne. Then he shook his head and turned to Sister Anselm. "Perhaps you'll be able to convince her otherwise, Sister."

"Perhaps," Sister Anselm agreed.

The doctor left the room, and LeAnne turned on the nun. "I suppose now you're siding with them and ganging up on me?"

"I said 'perhaps,' " Sister Anselm noted. "That isn't the same as saying yes. I think Dr. Walker is absolutely correct to warn you that Lance is going to be in agony. I also think it might be a good idea for you to distance yourself from that, if only for a little while. Besides, coming out of the coma, Lance is likely to be so disoriented that he'll have no remembrance of your being here or not."

"I'm an LPN," LeAnne said. "I'm not someone who's never been inside a hospital, and I know what they can and can't do to manage his pain."

"Being a nurse is one thing," Sister Anselm said. "It's quite another when the suffering patient is your own child. What I will promise you is this: If you take the doctor's advice and give yourself a day or so to let Lance adjust, I'll be here with him."

"He's my son," LeAnne argued. "I'm going to be here no matter what." Angry because it seemed even Sister Anselm had turned on her, LeAnne spun around and fled the room, biting back tears as she went.

Out in the lobby, she swept past her mother, grabbing up the grocery bag of clothing Phyllis had brought to the hospital. "I'm going to go take that shower now," she announced. "I'll be back in a little while."

A woman at the reception desk on the ground floor directed her to a room in the basement area that housed a rack for twenty-five or so chain-locked bicycles. At the far end of the room were doors that led to a pair of compact Jack-and-Jill locker rooms. A stack of laundered towels sat on a wooden bench outside the ladies' shower stall, and the shower was stocked with dispensers for body soap, shampoo, and conditioner. There were even hair dryers on the counter.

Standing under the steaming water and with the luxury of not having to pay for either the water or the water-heating bill, LeAnne let the tears flow. She hadn't needed the doctor to tell her that Lance would be in dreadful pain. She had known that from the moment she saw how badly he was burned. The idea that the doctor thought she would turn and run without telling Lance about his leg was provoking. LeAnne Tucker wasn't a turn-and-run kind of mother. She never had been, and she wouldn't be now.

Forty-five minutes later, showered, dressed, blow-dried, and with a little makeup dabbed on her face, LeAnne felt almost civilized as she made her way back up to the waiting room. There she saw her mother huddled in quiet conversation with a large black man, a hulking bear of a guy with broad shoulders and grizzled gray hair.

"Here she is," Phyllis said when she caught sight of LeAnne. "This is my daughter, Lance's mother, LeAnne."

The man stood up, clutching a Texas Rangers baseball cap in one meaty paw while offering Ali the other one. "Pleased to meet you, ma'am," he said. "My name's Dunn, Lowell Dunn. I'm so sorry about your son."

LeAnne realized that her mother had been right. The shower had put her in a better place. An hour earlier, having someone express that much sympathy toward her and toward Lance's situation probably would have driven her to tears. Now she straightened her back, smiled back at the broad face peering down at her, and shook the proffered hand. "Thank you," she said.

"Mr. Dunn works at that place," Phyllis said quietly. "At the place where Lance was . . ."

"At the detention center?" LeAnne asked.

Lowell Dunn's leathery countenance wrinkled into a deep frown. "Yes. I'm one of the facilities supervisors," he said sadly. "I'm the one who asked Lance to put up that doggone Christmas tree, and I am deeply, deeply saddened to think that, as a result, that fine young man has lost a leg. That's tragic — that's the only thing to be said about the situation — it's tragic. Your mother tells me he's been out the whole time, that he ain't been able to say one way or another what happened or who might've done this."

"That's right," LeAnne said. "The doctors say they're going to try to bring him around tomorrow, but it remains to be seen if he saw who his attacker was. The official position is that he was alone when it happened."

"Your son's a good boy, ma'am," Lowell told her after a pause. "At least compared to some of the disrespectful scumbags that generally turn up in places like that. I can't for the life of me figure out how someone like him got sent to juvenile detention in the first place."

"He did something to the school district's computers," LeAnne said. "They decided to make an example of him."

"They done that, all right," Lowell said.

"But Lance was payin' for his crime, and he was excited about gettin' out. Wanted to be home on his birthday, just a little over a month from now. Said you'd probably make him his favorite cake."

LeAnne nodded. "Devil's food," she said.

"Gettin' back to this Christmas-tree situation. Him and I worked on it together that whole first day. I saw him up on that ladder and working with them lights. Lance is a careful worker. This wasn't no accident, and I can't see why anybody in their right mind would think Lance would be doin' some fool stunt like this on purpose to his own damned self, pardon the expression. After all, the only thing he had to do was wait it out another month, and he'd be home free."

LeAnne stood looking into the wells of compassion in the old man's bleary eyes. Finally, stunned by the idea of having an unlikely ally in this fight, she sank down into a chair. Lowell Dunn sat down beside her.

"You're saying you believe someone else did this?" she asked. "Someone who isn't Lance?"

Lowell Dunn nodded. "That's my take on it."

"Have you mentioned that to anyone?" she asked. "To the investigators, I mean?

Have you told any of them what you just told me?"

"Oh, I've mentioned it, all right, not that anybody's of a mind to listen," Lowell Dunn replied. "Matter of fact, I've talked until I'm blue in the face, if you get my drift, but most of those people's minds are already made up. I know that's the official version of things — that Lance did this to himself, either accidentally or else on purpose. The powers that be are going to cling to that version of the story for dear life. That's what powers that be seem to do best, by the way. My big beef with all this is the thing about the security cameras going on the blink that day."

"Wait," LeAnne said. "You're saying the security camera system wasn't working?"

"Not the whole system, just the cameras in that part of the building," Lowell answered grimly. "I didn't think anyone would bother mentioning that to you. But the whole deal with the cameras is a load of bull. I've got a monitor right there in my office. The cameras were all working fine as frog's hair the day before. If part of the system went down, it's because someone made it go down, and believe me, whoever did that was up to no good."

"So you think someone deliberately targeted Lance?" LeAnne asked.

"Yes, ma'am," Lowell replied. "I most certainly do."

"And do you know who?"

"I've got a good idea, but there's no sense bringing it up to anybody until I have some proof. If Lance can wake up and point a finger at whoever did this, then it's a whole new ball game."

"But why would anybody do this?" LeAnne asked. "Why would someone set my son on fire?"

"Some kids are just plain mean," Lowell answered with a shrug. "If they see somebody else who's smarter than they are or has more privileges or something like that, they go after them for no other reason than to grind the smart kids down to their level. By the way, Ms. Stone, the GED teacher, told me that Lance was far and away the smartest kid she'd ever had in any of her classes."

"You're saying that you think one of the other kids did this?" LeAnne pressed.

"I'm saying I think one of the other kids probably had a hand in it, but there's a problem with that. Ain't none of them other kids smart enough to turn off the cameras."

"It sounds like you're suggesting this was an inside job of some kind."

"Yes, ma'am," Lowell said. "Much as I hate to admit it, I suppose that's exactly what I'm sayin'. And most likely somethin' changed hands in the process. There's a lot of what you call currency in a place like that that's got nothing to do with the United States mint, and I've got me an idea of a guard or two who might not be above gettin' involved in somethin' dirty."

"So what should I do?" LeAnne said.

"If I was you, I'd get myself a lawyer. My guess is that's why they're tryin' to put this whole thing on Lance. If they was supposed to be lookin' after him and didn't, then maybe a good lawyer can see to it that they're liable for what happened to him. And if you get one of them, feel free to give 'em my name. I'll be glad to give 'em my two cents' worth."

LeAnne was overwhelmed with gratitude. "Mr. Dunn," she said, "How can I thank you for this? And what about your job? If you go up against what you call the powers that be, what will happen to you?"

"Don't you worry none about that, Ms. Tucker. I happen to be seventy-two years old, which is a good six years beyond when they all thought I'd retire. My wife died the year before I turned sixty-five. No way was I gonna stay home in that empty house where we lived together for all those years and pine away all by my lonesome. So if somebody looks at me crosswise for what I'm saying, I'll quit faster 'an they can spit in my eye."

"I've been too busy here at the hospital to even think about contacting an attorney," LeAnne said, "but if I do and I need to reach you, do you have an e-mail address?"

"Not at home," Lowell Dunn said. "Never had no need to have a home computer or one of them Facebook thingamajigs, either. But if you need to reach me, you send an e-mail to my grandson, LaVonn, no spaces, no caps. He's at something called AOL. He'll stop by and give me the message on his way home from school."

"Tell me one thing," LeAnne said. "Why was Lance in the rec room in the first place?"

"Me and Ms. Stone, his teacher, we look at things pretty much eye to eye. She's of the same mind I am about Lance — that he's a good boy who got a raw deal and who got a sentence that was way more than what he deserved. She also thought he was too smart to be wastin' time sitting in her class with all those other kids who are dumber than stumps. She was glad to let Lance loose from class to come help me put up that tree. We worked on it one day, stringing lights and putting the sections of the tree together. The next day was my day off, but I made arrangements for Lance to get into the closet by my office to get the rest of the decorations. He was almost done when it happened, so he'd been using that spray can and glitter all morning long without nothin' bad happening. That's why I'm sayin' that whatever went on wasn't no accident."

Having said his piece, Lowell Dunn stood up abruptly. "I best be going, ma'am. My daughter Susannah is waitin' downstairs to give me a ride back to San Leandro. She don't trust me to drive this far on my own. Says I'm too old to be out there on the highway all by myself in case the car breaks down or somethin'. Truth is, I'd be more likely to fix a broke-down car than she would be. All she'd do is to call AAA and get them to send out a wrecker. But you remember what I told you: If you need any backup on this, you call me."

"Backup?" Sister Anselm asked. Unnoticed by the other people in the waiting room, the nun had emerged from Lance's room.

"This is Mr. Dunn," LeAnne explained to Sister Anselm. "From the detention center.

Lance was working with him on the tree decorations when the incident happened. He thinks I should hire an attorney. If we do, he's willing to speak up on Lance's behalf."

"In that case, Mr. Dunn," Sister Anselm said, holding out her hand, "I'm pleased to make your acquaintance."

8

Ali had been back in her room for under half an hour and was putting the finishing touches on an e-mail to B. when he called. "It's about time I got to talk to you," she said. "I'm having a tough time making our new time-zone situation work. I know what time it is when you're there and I'm in Sedona, but now that I'm in England my internal clock isn't working as well. I'm glad to hear your voice for a change."

"What time is it there? I just got back to the hotel from dinner," he said.

"It's two o'clock in the afternoon here."

"What are you doing?"

"I was writing you a long e-mail."

"I thought you were supposed to go out shopping today," he said. "Something about finding a wedding dress."

"That's done," she said.

"Done?" B. echoed. "Already? That didn't take long."

"No, it didn't," Ali agreed with a laugh. "It will probably go down as one of the shortest wedding-dress shopping excursions trips in history. We stopped by the shop Leland's nephew recommended. I was in the fitting room trying a dress on when Leland showed up with another dress, one he'd found on a rack out front. That one turned out to be perfect. It's gorgeous. It's an Amy Childs, an ivory silk sheath covered with exquisite lace that fits like a glove. The wonderful thing is, I already have a pair of shoes that will work with it perfectly."

"Did you send me a picture?" B. asked.

"No, I did not. The groom isn't supposed to see the dress until the wedding, remember?"

"I wouldn't think you'd turn into such a stickler for all those niggling details," B. said.

"They're not niggling details," Ali countered. "They're traditions. I told you when I said yes that if we were going to do this, we were going to do it right, but if you really want to see the dress, you can Google Amy Childs."

"That's okay. I wouldn't want to violate any serious taboos. What else is new?"

"Well," Ali said after a pause, "we have a new client. I just sent Stu a list of what I need him to do."

"A new client? For High Noon? How is that possible? You're supposed to be on vacation with Leland Brooks."

"I am, and Leland Brooks is the new client," Ali replied. "His father died weeks after he left home to come to the States. There was bad blood between Leland and his older brothers, especially one named Langston. When Langston notified Leland of their father's death, he didn't give out any of the details. Years later, when Leland's mother died as well, the estrangement was still in effect. We know when they died — I took photos of both headstones. What Leland wants to know is where they died and why. Since Jonah, the father, was only in his fifties at the time of his death, there could have been some underlying health issue that Leland knew nothing about."

"If you gave Stu their dates of birth and death, he should be able to run with it. Once he gets into the right database, he'll have answers for you in a matter of minutes. But couldn't Leland just ask his nephew, the one who met you at the airport?"

"The problem is Langston, the problem brother, was Jeffrey's grandfather, and Leland doesn't want to step on his toes."

"What was behind this brotherly feud if it still carries weight all these years later, the fact that Leland is gay?"

"Yes," Ali said. "To hear the redoubtable Maisie and Daisy talk, being gay in Bournemouth in the twenty-first century still isn't all that cool. There was a whole lot of tsk-tsking from them about Jeffrey and Charles, and I suspect that'll go into overdrive this summer when the two of them show up with their new baby in tow."

"So having you there to play backup with Leland's relatives is still a good thing?"

"I'll say," Ali answered. "So how are things on your end?"

She heard the buzz of an incoming call. "Oops," he said. "I need to take this."

"Bye," she said to an empty phone, and then lay there on the bed staring at it and wondering what kind of call would be coming in that B. would have to take in the middle of the night and in the middle of a call to her. She was still sitting with her phone in her hand puzzling about that when an e-mail showed up from Stu:

I found what you were looking for. The mother's case is pretty cut-and-dried. Adele Mathison Brooks died in Cheltenham Royal Hospital, July 23, 1968, of a heart attack. The problem is the father. Jonah Andrew Brooks died October 1, 1954, as a result of blunt force trauma. His death was and is considered an unsolved homicide. Records from back then have not been uploaded to any computerized databases. If you want to know more, you'll probably need to pay an in-person visit.

Ali stared at the words as if willing them to dissolve on the screen and turn into something else. Though this was not news that she wanted to give Leland, she didn't give herself a chance to think about dodging the issue. Instead, she hopped off the bed, went straight through the sitting room, and tapped on Leland's door. "Come on out," she said. "We need to talk."

Leland sat bolt upright on the chair, looking out to sea while Ali read Stu's brief e-mail. She glanced up at him when she finished. "You suspected something like this, didn't you?"

Leland closed his eyes for a moment, then he nodded. "At the time I never really considered the idea of homicide. I assumed it was something else — some sudden health issue or else . . ."

"Or else what?" Ali asked.

"You have to take the times into consideration," Leland said with a sigh. "This was a small town back then. I was convinced that the shame of having a homosexual for a son had caused my father to commit suicide."

"But you never asked?"

Leland shook his head. "It wasn't like it is today. You couldn't get news from all over the world with a simple click of a button, and I was so wounded at the idea of having been disowned that I couldn't bring myself to ask any questions. Besides, whom would I ask? My mother had already told me that she wanted nothing more to do with me."

"Your mother told you that herself?"

"Through Langston," Leland said. "He was the messenger."

"Do you recall exactly what was said?"

Instead of answering, Leland stood up and left the room. He returned, carrying an envelope that he handed over to Ali. The ink on the outside had faded away to almost nothing. Ali was able to make out the words: "In care of Anna L." That and the words "California, USA." Inside the envelope she found a piece of simple stationery with a handwritten note. Protected from light damage by the layer of envelope, that ink was completely legible. The note was dated November 1, 1954.

I regret to inform you that our father

passed away suddenly a little over a month after your abrupt departure from Bournemouth. He took the news of your vile behavior very badly. Before his death, he and Mother made arrangements to remove you from their lives as well as from their wills. As you can imagine, this has been a most hurtful process for both of them, and Mother entreats you to make no further attempts to contact her in the future.

Sincerely,
Langston

"Langston was an asshole!" Ali exclaimed. To her surprise, Leland laughed outright at her blurted comment — a regretful laugh rather than a hearty one. "That's certainly calling a spade a spade."

"And what's this about vile behavior?" Ali asked. "You told me you and Thomas hadn't gotten around to doing anything."

Leland nodded. "That's true. We hadn't, but if Langston was carrying tales to our father, as I have no doubt he did, he probably neglected to mention what he and Frances were up to. What they were doing when Thomas and I stumbled across them was a bit more risqué than a bit of snogging."

"Tell me about your brother," Ali said.

Leland looked off into space a moment before he answered. "Langston always thought he was smarter by half than anyone else. He's the only one in our generation who went to university. He always saw himself as something of a gentleman, and he married well. Frances was a plain-looking girl, but she had some money of her own, which, to my way of thinking, made up for her looks and was most likely her main attraction as far as Langston was concerned. My father was an entrepreneur with a farm just north of Bournemouth and a print shop in town. When Father died, the farm went to Langston, and Lawrence got the print shop. With the benefit of Frances's money, I'm sure Langston was able to lark about posing as a gentleman farmer. Years later, he sold the farm so it could be turned into housing estates. I'm sure Langston made a fortune on that."

"When your father died, there were only two sons to take into consideration," Ali observed. "That must have made divvying things up much easier: One got the farm; one got the shop. If you'd been around, dividing the estate would have been more complicated."

"I suppose," Leland agreed.

Ali stood up and reached for her purse. "I think I'm going to go for a ride," she said.

"Where are you going?"

"To pay a surprise visit to Jordan's-by-the-Sea and see if I can wrangle a spot of tea with one or both of your cousins."

Leland started to rise. "I'll get my coat," he said.

"No," Ali told him. "You stay here. I want Maisie Longmoor to dish some dirt. She's a gossip at heart, but your father was murdered, and she didn't mention a word about that yesterday. She may not be willing to talk about it to your face, but behind your back she'll blab to her heart's content. Later, we'll have our debriefing over dinner here at the hotel — fillet of beef with all the trimmings."

"Are you sure about going to Jordan's on your own?" Leland asked. "You've never been there. I could come along and show you the way."

"Not to worry," Ali said. "My GPS knows all."

"Should I call them and let them know you're coming?"

"No. I'm going to practice being an ugly American and drop in unexpectedly. They're more likely to talk freely if I have the element of surprise on my side."

"All right, then," Leland agreed. "It's odd. I know that I've asked you to look into this for me, but I find myself of two minds about it. I want to know and I don't want to know."

"Both reactions are entirely understandable," Ali said, "but I'm coming down on the side of knowing rather than not knowing."

She called for the car and went downstairs. Once she was in it, she used the GPS, but her first destination wasn't Jordan's-by-the-Sea. Instead, she drove the Land Rover through the jumble of curving downtown streets to the Central Police Station at the far end of Stafford Road. The entryway lobby was the same as that of every other police station Ali had ventured into over the years. The space had started out grand and ended up grimy. The granite tiles in the floor were worn down and pitted with long use, and the clerks minding the front desks now did so from behind a wall of bulletproof glass.

Ali approached the part of the window marked RECEPTION, behind which sat a woman wearing a black hijab. Everything about her, including the frown on her face, indicated that she was there to rebuff casual visitors rather than welcome them.

"May I help you?" she asked.

Ali had already determined that her best course of action was to simply brazen it out. "Is there a homicide investigator on duty?"

"You're here to report a homicide?" the woman asked.

"No, I wish to speak to a homicide investigator."

"About a current case?"

"No," Ali answered, pulling out one of the High Noon business cards B. had given her to carry in her purse. "It's about a very old case here in Bournemouth, one from almost sixty years ago."

"Do you have specific information about this case?" the clerk asked.

Intent on wearing the clerk down, Ali kept a cheerful smile on her face and made sure her tone of voice was pleasant rather than confrontational. She expected that the clerk was used to sending people packing after one or two questions. Ali was prepared to ask as many as it took to get past the gate-keeper.

"No," she said. "What I have are specific questions about the case. So let me ask this another way: Does the Bournemouth police department have a cold-case unit or else someone who would be able to look up the pertinent records from a case back then?"

"This isn't the U.S.," the woman answered shortly. "We don't do cold-case files."

"But I'm sure you have detectives," Ali continued, smiling. "The city of Bournemouth must have at least one of those."

"Wait here," the clerk said, giving up. Taking one of Ali's business cards with her, she huffed off.

Five minutes or so elapsed before a door from the interior of the building opened, and a woman walked into the lobby, peering around. She was a decade or so younger than Ali. She wore glasses and her hair was pulled straight back into a bun. She was a plain-looking woman, and the way she dressed was all business. When her searching gaze finally landed on Ali, she came forward briskly, offering a hand and a disarmingly bucktoothed smile.

"I'm Detective Sergeant Elkins," she said. "Marjorie. I understand you're inquiring about one of our cold cases. Are you a journalist, by any chance? If you are, you should be working with our media relations people."

"I'm here on behalf of a client, the son of a homicide victim," Ali said. "My client's name is Leland Brooks. His father's name was Jonah Brooks. He died on the tenth of

October 1954. My understanding is that the case was never solved, and the son, my Mr. Brooks, would like to know what progress, if any, was ever made toward closing the case."

Marjorie Elkins smiled. "Nineteen fifty-four? That's a bit before my time, but if you'll come with me, let's see what we can find."

Marjorie led Ali through a maze of dingy intersecting corridors before taking her into an office space that would have reasonably handled the presence of four cubicles but was far too small for the eight gunmetal-gray desks that had been crammed inside it. The room was lit by a series of long overhead fluorescent tubes, one of which was winking in preparation for going out entirely.

Ali knew that back in Prescott, Arizona, at the Yavapai County Sheriff's Department, this kind of homicide group-grope office arrangement was called the bull pen. She had no idea what it was called in Bournemouth, but the result was the same: too many people, too little space, and zero privacy.

There were four guys, all of them in shirtsleeves, chatting around the desk closest to a windowed interior office from which their commanding officer no doubt held

159

forth. The casual chitchat ended as Ali and Marjorie Elkins entered. Ali would have had to be blind and deaf not to notice the air of hostility suddenly loose in the air. Unfortunately, that kind of toxic atmosphere was something Ali recognized all too well: Before Marjorie Elkins's unwelcome arrival on the scene, this room had most likely been an all-male preserve. The four guys watched the new arrivals in that obnoxiously assessing way that some men do when women, strangers or not, walk past them. Ali wouldn't have been surprised if one of them had cut loose with a wolf whistle.

Marjorie's desk was in the far corner of the room, pushed up against a wall with a window. At some point in the dim past, the glass had been painted over in a vile shade of green. In a room that was decorated with industrial-strength testosterone, her desk was the only one with a few softening elements, including a tiny lit Christmas tree and a collection of framed photos that featured a boy whose bucktoothed smile clearly pronounced him his mother's son. Some of the pictures were official school photos; others featured him in a series of soccer uniforms. It was like seeing him age in fast-framed photography from a pre-schooler to a confident-looking young man.

"My son, Aiden," Marjorie explained, motioning Ali into a side chair. "You know the drill," she added. "Single mum and all that. He's a good lad, though. Off to university next year."

Ali nodded. "I do know the drill," she said. "I put in some time as a single mother myself."

"Which means you work at a crap job to keep body and soul together, but you get to go home to your kids at night, right?"

Ali nodded. Nothing more was said, but that small exchange was enough to put both women at ease, an outcome that was most likely not the one the clerk out front had expected.

Marjorie took a seat on a grungy rolling chair that was probably several decades old and frowned in concentration while studying Ali's business card. "What's High Noon?" she asked. "I mean, besides that old Gary Cooper/Grace Kelly movie? My grandfather loved that movie. He had it on video. After my grandmother died, he watched it day in and day out. That song, you know." She hummed a few bars of "Do Not Forsake Me, Oh, My Darlin'." "That one always made him tear up."

"This High Noon takes after that one," Ali explained. "It's sort of like the movie: It started out as a single good guy taking on a collection of bad guys. Now he deals mostly with with cyber bad guys."

"Cyber security?" Marjorie asked.

Ali nodded. "The man who founded it, B. Simpson, is my fiancé."

"What exactly does High Noon and cyber security have to do with Mr. Jonah Brooks, who died here in Bournemouth in 1954?"

"His death has nothing to do with cyber security. Our interest in Mr. Brooks is a private inquiry we've undertaken on behalf of a longtime family friend, your homicide victim's son Leland. He emigrated to the U.S. after a family quarrel and shortly before his father's death. After that, he was estranged from his family until recently. He's only just now learned of the homicide, and we're trying to glean whatever details we can."

"Let's give it a try," Marjorie said. Turning to the surprisingly old-fashioned computer terminal on her desk, she logged in and sat with her fingers poised over the keyboard. "What was the victim's name again?"

"Jonah," Ali told her. "Jonah Andrew Brooks. His date of death was October tenth, 1954."

Marjorie typed, waited a few moments,

162

then looked up at Ali, shaking her head. "I was afraid of that," she said, standing up. "No results. What that means is that none of the information has been uploaded to the computer." At first Ali thought she was being dismissed, but she was wrong. "That means we'll have to do this the hard way," Marjorie added.

"What does that mean?"

"We go down into the dungeon and dig through the boxes." Marjorie cast a critical look at the black knit pantsuit Ali had worn on the plane and to visit the cemetery earlier that morning.

"It's quite musty down there," she cautioned. "You might want to change into something a little more workmanlike."

Ali was worried that any delay might cause her to miss the opportunity to visit the evidence locker. "I'll be fine," she said. "The Highcliff is a name-brand hotel. I'm sure they have adequate laundry facilities."

The two women rode downstairs in a rickety elevator. When they reached the basement, Marjorie showed her credentials to a clerk seated just outside the folding grille. After signing Ali in, they entered an immense room where an eerie light was cast by a series of naked bulbs that hung on aged cords and cast small halos of light on rank upon rank of heavily laden metal shelving.

"This is the central storage facility for all of Dorset, not just Bournemouth," Marjorie explained. "It never was an actual dungeon; we just call it that. In this climate, it takes a lot of work to keep things dry enough so whatever's stored in the boxes doesn't get ruined. Most everything from the early seventies on has been digitized. Cases earlier than that are digitized as the time and monies become available. These records go all the way back to the 1880s. There's been talk of transferring some of these earlier records to an interested museum, but so far, no one has been able to figure out how to make that happen."

Obviously, Marjorie had known in advance that the lighting would be several levels below adequate. Leading the way unerringly through the maze of shelving, she pulled a small flashlight out of her pocket and used that to illuminate the labels on the astonishing array of boxes. "Here we are," she said at last, looking around. "Now that we're in the fifties, it should be right around here somewhere." Moments later, she located the applicable box. The one labeled Jonah Andrew Brooks was in the middle section of a bottommost shelf. "Got it!" she exclaimed. "Amazingly enough, it wasn't misfiled."

Marjorie pulled the cardboard container out, leaving an empty-toothed gap behind on the shelf, then she hefted the box to her shoulder. "There are some library tables over there on the side," she said. "Believe it or not, they come equipped with better lighting. Let's go have a look."

Seated side by side like a pair of schoolgirls, Ali and Marjorie sorted through the contents of the box, starting with the murder book. According to that, the victim, Jonah Brooks, age fifty-five, had been reported missing by his wife, Adele, on Saturday morning, October second, after he failed to come home from a business meeting on Friday evening. He had met with a Mr. Alexander Harrison, at Mr. Brooks's print shop in Bournemouth, to discuss engraved invitations for Mr. Harrison's daughter's upcoming wedding. After finishing their business, the two men had stopped off at a pub on Yelverton Road for dinner.

According to the barman, the two men left at about eight-thirty in the evening. That was the last time Jonah Brooks was seen alive. Two children playing on the beach found his body washed up under the pier in Bournemouth on Sunday afternoon. At first he was thought to be a drowning victim, but an autopsy showed that he had died of blunt force trauma to the head prior to going into the water. There were defensive wounds on his arms, hands, and chest that indicated Jonah had tried to fight off his attacker. Three days later, his bloodstained Jaguar sedan was found abandoned miles away on a street in Southampton.

At the time, the incident was thought to be a simple robbery gone bad. The victim's Bulova watch and his wallet, thought to contain a considerable amount of cash, were both missing and never located. No suspect was ever identified.

Jonah had been a well-respected local businessman. The case remained unsolved, but it wasn't for lack of trying. Family members, including Jonah's two sons, were routinely questioned, but when their alibis checked out, they were taken off the suspect list. There was some mention of a family squabble with a third son who had left home under a dark cloud of some kind. One of the detectives, after noting that the quarrel had resulted in a change in Jonah's will, had attempted to track down Leland. Later, it was learned that at the time of the murder Leland had already embarked on his transatlantic crossing. As a result, his name was removed from the list of possible suspects.

There were notations in the murder book all through the last few months of 1954 and into 1955. By the end of 1955, the notations became far more sporadic, mostly on the anniversary dates of the homicide. The last notation by a detective was dated 1961.

Having skimmed through the murder book, Ali and Marjorie turned their joint attention to the other items in the evidence box. Sealed in clear plastic was the tab from the King's Arms for Friday, October 1. The bill was for two roast beef dinners and four pints of ale. Jonah Brooks evidently paid for both himself and Mr. Harrison.

In the bottom of the box, neatly folded, was a collection of clothing: an old-fashioned three-piece suit of lightweight brown wool. Two of what had been six pearl-colored buttons were missing from the vest. There was a white shirt with what appeared to be bloodstains on the back of the collar and the French cuffs, one of which held a monogrammed cuff link. Other items of interest included a brown-and-yellow-striped silk tie, a white undershirt and a pair of briefs, a pair of brown socks with one toe carefully repaired by a darning needle, and a single brown loafer. It was assumed that the other shoe had been washed out to sea.

Ali picked up the shirt, unfolded it, and

examined the bloodstains. Then she glanced in Marjorie's direction. "What if the bloodstains on the cuffs and on the collar aren't from the same person?" Ali asked. "The autopsy noted there were defensive wounds on Jonah's body. What if some of this spatter is from the killer rather than the victim?"

Marjorie Elkins shrugged. "It's possible," she said. "Back then, blood was blood. It says in the report that the blood in both places was of the same type — A-positive — but that's all it says. Without the benefit of DNA technology, there was no way to know much more than that."

"Has any of this evidence ever been subjected to DNA analysis?"

"Not that I know of," Marjorie said. "If it had, there'd be some kind of notation in the book. For one thing, the case is sixty years old; so are the samples. They've sat in the box all this time, but they haven't been refrigerated. There's no telling how degraded they are. Furthermore, the kind of testing you're talking about is expensive, prohibitively so. Believe me, no one in my department is going to be willing to pay for it."

"What if High Noon agrees to pay?" Ali asked. "If I signed a document agreeing that we would be responsible for any costs incurred and gave you my Amex card, do you think you could walk the request through your department?"

"I could try," Marjorie said, "but I'm not making any promises. How do I get back to you once I have an answer?"

"I'm staying at the Highcliff," Ali said. "Room 501."

Marjorie handed over a business card with her name and e-mail address as well as a series of phone numbers. "Here's how you can reach me as well."

After returning the evidence box to its designated spot on the shelves, Ali and Marjorie made their way back upstairs. As Ali walked through the lobby toward the front entrance, she was careful to keep her face averted from the watchful clerk. Ali knew she was grinning from ear to ear. It was probably just as well that the clerk couldn't see it.

9

By the time Ali stepped back outside and into the fading afternoon sunlight, it was almost four o'clock. Out of courtesy, Ali had turned off her phone while working with Marjorie. She had felt several vibrations about incoming messages that she was sure were from B. Still a little miffed at him for dropping his call to her so abruptly, she wasn't in any great hurry to respond. As soon as she read his message, she felt guilty.

Big DoS problem is slowing down the Internet all over Europe. Some of our clients are adversely affected. I'm on my way to the airport. Have booked a seat on the first flight I can get from Tokyo to Zurich by way of Helsinki. More later. B.

Ali was savvy enough to know that "DoS" was nerd-speak for "denial of service." She also knew that if the attack was serious enough that it was hamstringing internet connections across an entire continent, then it was a huge problem. No wonder B. had hung up on her almost in midsentence. The second message came from Ali's mother — Edie's real e-mail account as opposed to the fake one at High noon. This one showed a picture of Colin looking cute as a button in the pint-sized tuxedo his great-grandmother had made for him. The third was another photo of a Sedona red-rock sunset and did come from the fake address. The caption said, "Thought you'd want to see this. Dad took it from the back porch. Mom."

Ali recognized the photo. It wasn't from her parents' current back porch in Sedona Shadows, the active-adult community where Bob and Edie Larson now made their home. This was one her father had taken years ago, from their old front porch, with a corner of the Sugarloaf Café's roof visible between the camera lens and the setting sun. Ali knew it was an encrypted message from Stuart. In order to read it, she would need access to both her thumb drive and her computer. The thumb drive wasn't a problem — it was safely in the bottom of her purse — but the computer was back in the hotel.

In other words, the message from Stu would have to wait until after tea. She sent B. a message telling him to travel safely, then she went looking for Jordan's-by-the-Sea. It was at the other end of Bournemouth, at the far southern tip of East Overcliff Drive. Jordan's was at about the same elevation as the Marriott, but the way to the beach was a steep footpath that meandered down the bluff through a forest of brambles and bracken. The place may have had a view of the sea, but anyone who came thinking they had fallen into a seaside resort was in for a rude awakening. As for Jordan's current crop of guests? From the six or seven motorcycles parked in the gravel lot, it looked as though the clientele might be a bit on the rough side.

As Ali stepped out of the Land Rover, she was surprised to realize that the weather was still almost balmy, due to the proximity to the water at the bottom of the bluff. She walked through an iron gate and up a paved front walk through a ragged winter garden badly in need of some TLC. The house was a tall and narrow two-story brick affair with a small front stoop. When Ali rang the bell, she was surprised when Daisy herself — at least she was reasonably sure it was Daisy

— answered the door.

"We're completely booked," she began, then stopped abruptly and stepped back in surprise when she realized Ali wasn't some stray traveler ringing the bell in search of a room.

"Who is it?" Maisie called from some other room. "Tell them we're full."

Ali took advantage of Daisy's momentary surprise to horn her way into the entry. "I hope you'll forgive my dropping by this way, but Leland is back at the hotel, and I wanted to speak to you both in private."

Maisie bustled into the dining room from what was evidently the kitchen wearing a full-length apron covered with a dusting of flour. Her dour expression was anything but welcoming. "I wish you had called," she said shortly. "We're baking for tomorrow morning's breakfast."

"This won't take long," Ali assured her. "I wanted to ask a few questions, and you're probably the only people who might be able to provide the answers."

A subtle shift washed across the contours of Maisie's face, and Ali knew she had called the right shot. Maisie Longmoor was a gossip to the bone, and talking behind Leland's back was more of a temptation than she could resist.

"Well, all right, then," Maisie said, feigning reluctance. "Come through to the sitting room." Speaking over her shoulder, she told her sister, "Do see if you can come up with a bit of something for tea."

"That's not necessary," Ali said. "Really. I'm not hungry."

"Go," Maisie growled at Daisy, and her twin scurried away. That appeared to be the pecking order in this family. Maisie was the commanding officer who issued the orders, and Daisy was the grunt who carried them out.

The sitting room was crowded with furniture far too large for the available floor space. Maisie motioned for Ali to take a seat on an antique sofa that was scratchy enough to be genuine horsehair. The room was dimly lit by a series of faux Tiffany lamps whose yellowish-orange light did nothing for the maroon upholstery.

"What questions?" Maisie asked, taking a seat and making zero pretense of pleasantry.

Since her hostess was being only one step under rude, Ali responded in kind, and her first question was nothing short of accusatory. "Were you aware that until this morning Leland had no idea that his father was murdered?"

"I had no idea," Maisie said. It was an

obvious lie.

"I'm surprised neither you nor your sister made no mention of it when you came to tea."

Maisie shrugged. "It's a painful subject," she said primly. "Having someone in the family murdered isn't something one goes about mentioning to complete strangers."

"I may be a stranger," Ali countered, "but Leland is not. Jonah Brooks was his father."

"Yes," Maisie replied, "but he's been away for a very long time. We weren't sure how he'd react to seeing us, let alone to discussing something as difficult as his father's death."

"You didn't look unsure," Ali replied. "From what I saw, you both seemed overjoyed to see him again."

"All right," Maisie admitted. "Maybe I was glad to see him, but more out of curiosity than anything else. It's been a long, long time since he was here last. Even so, I'm surprised he could come back and not be concerned about showing his face to all and sundry, especially after everything that happened."

"After what happened?" Ali prompted.

Maisie paused. Ali expected her to launch off into a discussion of Leland's illicit relationship with Thomas Blackfield. She didn't.

"The war and all that," Maisie said.

"The war?"

"Yes, dear girl. The Korean War," she said. "That one's ours, Daisy's and mine. We were all too young for the previous one."

"What about the war?" Ali asked.

Daisy came in from the kitchen, carrying a tray laden with a teapot, cups and saucers, and some tired store-bought cookies. Whatever baked goods were being made in-house were reserved for paying guests.

They're biscuits here, Ali reminded herself. Not cookies.

Maisie turned to Daisy, who was busy pouring tea. "She's asking about Leland and what he did doing the war."

"Oh, that," Daisy said, nodding.

"What?" Ali asked.

Maisie turned toward her, eyes blazing. "Leland Brooks was a traitor, if you must know. That's what he did. He may have signed up for the Royal Marines, but the whole time he was over there, he was really selling secrets to the enemy."

The charge was so outrageous, Ali wanted to laugh outright. "What secrets could he possibly know?" she asked. "He was a cook."

"That may well be, but Langston had a

friend at the War Office," Maisie said archly. "An old chum from his university days. He's the one who told Langston about it. The authorities were about to pick Leland up and charge him with being a double agent when he dodged out of town in the dark of night, never to be heard from again. He never once tried to get back in touch with Aunt Adele. Not once."

"He emigrated to the States," Ali said. "If there had been some kind of charge like that hanging over his head, he wouldn't have been allowed to leave this country, to say nothing of being given citizenship in the U.S. And he was heard from again. He wrote to Langston to let him know where he was. Langston told him their father was deceased and that his mother wanted nothing more to do with him."

"That's his story," Maisie said with an audible disbelieving snort. "No one went after him because there was a cover-up. No one wanted to have the fact that a Royal Marine had gone bad bandied about in the newspapers. Once Jonah heard about it, I'll tell you the man was livid."

"Absolutely furious," Daisy offered.

"He was humiliated beyond words to think that one of his very own sons would betray Queen and country. He went straightaway to the family solicitor and had a new will drawn up."

"To disown his own son," Ali murmured.

"Yes, and why not?" Maisie demanded. "Jonah was so shamed by what had happened, he could barely hold up his head in public. If he hadn't been murdered, I believe the poor man would have died of a broken heart. I remember our mother saying that his dying right then was probably a blessing in disguise. At least it put him out of his misery."

"What kind of a father would disown his own son without hearing the son's side of the story?" Ali asked. "How could Jonah take that kind of drastic action on Langston's word alone?"

"Wait a minute," Maisie objected, waggling a finger in Ali's direction. "Don't you speak ill of Langston. He was a good man; a decent man."

"Entirely trustworthy," Daisy added. "We never would have been able to turn this place into a B and B if he hadn't offered us some financial backing."

"What you're telling me is that you believed every lie Langston ever told about Leland."

"You could take what he said to the bank," Maisie offered.

"It sounds like you did just that," Ali observed.

If Maisie noticed Ali's ungenerous comment, she paid it no mind. "The whole town believed it, why wouldn't we? And Aunt Adele believed it, too. If you had seen how Leland dodged out of here like a criminal, under the dark of night and without a single word to anyone, maybe you'd understand."

As though a light had been switched on, Ali suddenly did understand. Leland had left town in the dark of night not because he was a traitor but because he was hoping to keep Thomas Blackfield's damning secret. All these years later, that bit of subterfuge was still working as far as Maisie and Daisy were concerned.

"What can you tell me about Jonah's murder?" Ali asked.

Maisie shrugged. "Nothing much. I do know it was never solved. We were told that someone wanted his car. Uncle Jonah and Aunt Adele had a fairly new car — a Jaguar, I think. After Jonah died, Aunt Adele went back home to live in Cheltenham with her parents. She just couldn't stand being here without her Jonah."

"And without Leland," Daisy added quietly. "He was her baby, you see. When he and his brothers were growing up, I think

Lee was always Aunt Adele's favorite."

Maisie glowered at her sister as if willing the woman to shut up. Ali took that moment to set down her teacup and reach for her purse. "I need to be going," she said. "Thank you for your hospitality."

Daisy hurried to open the door. As Ali walked back down the front path, she heard loud laughter and boisterous voices coming over the laurel hedge that separated the yard from the parking area. A group of leather-wearing motorcycle riders stood clumped around their bikes, drinking beer and smoking cigarettes. They gave Ali the same ogling looks as she walked to the Land Rover that Marjorie Elkins's officemates had dished out an hour or so earlier.

Inside her vehicle with the door shut and locked, Ali Reynolds realized Jeffrey Brooks and Charlie Chan were both right. Jordan's-by-the-Sea was exactly the wrong place for a family reunion.

10

The one thing that LeAnne Tucker had learned in the days her son was hospitalized was that out in the waiting room, time stood still. Far inside the building, with only a single window to help mark the changing of morning to afternoon or afternoon to evening, she had few clues to help her gauge the passage of time. Yes, she wore a watch, but the hands seemed to move so slowly that there were times when she held it up to her ear to make sure it was still ticking.

Sometime after Mr. Dunn left, Sister Anselm and LeAnne returned to Lance's room to maintain what was now a mostly silent vigil. LeAnne noticed that Sister Anselm often clutched her rosary, passing the beads through her fingers one by one. LeAnne supposed the woman was praying, which made her think guiltily that she should be praying, too, but she couldn't bring herself to do it. Her needs right then were so overwhelming — to have Lance live; to be able to keep the house; to not lose her job — that praying seemed like dropping empty words into a bottomless pit.

She was grateful to Lowell Dunn for coming by and being willing to take Lance's part, even against his own employers. She was grateful for his advice, too, though she had no idea how to put it into action. She'd had only two dealings with attorneys in her whole life. One had been the sleazy guy she'd found on the Internet to help get her divorce; that had been mercifully cheap because her ex made no effort to contest it. The other had been the guy who was Lance's public defender. Everyone knew how that had turned out. All of which meant that as far as hiring attorneys went, LeAnne Tucker had no idea where to start.

Now that Sister Anselm had appeared on the scene, the hospital's five-minute visiting restriction seemed to have been lifted, but when the nurses came in to deal with Lance's dressings sometime in the afternoon, Sister Anselm advised LeAnne to go elsewhere.

Out in the waiting room, LeAnne looked around, more than half expecting that her mother would be there. Then, glancing at her watch — the hands had moved this time

— she realized it was early afternoon. Phyllis would be on her way back to San Leandro to pick Connor up from school and go to Thad's basketball game. It was easy to sit in Austin and feel guilty about missing the game, but the truth was, even if Lance hadn't been in the hospital, it was unlikely that LeAnne could have made it to an afternoon game. She was usually at work.

She was sitting there waiting when a man walked into the room. The guy was dressed in a finely tailored blue suit that fit him well enough that LeAnne wondered if it had been custom-tailored. Her first instinct was that the man was an attorney. It was only as he came closer that LeAnne realized he looked oddly familiar.

"You wouldn't happen to be Mrs. Tucker, would you?" he asked.

Oops, LeAnne thought. Another reporter. How'd he get up here? "And who might you be?" she asked.

He gave her an ingratiating smile. "I don't believe we've ever officially met," he said, ignoring her off-putting tone. "My name is Crutcher. Daniel Crutcher."

It came back to LeAnne in a rush: This was the guy who had been selling the student locating system, the tagging system. She had never met him in person, and he hadn't been called to testify during Lance's trial, but she had seen him being interviewed on TV; she knew he worked for some big multinational company.

"I have nothing to say to you," she said coldly. "Get out. Leave me alone."

"Please, Mrs. Tucker. I wish you no harm. I'm here at my company's behest, with only your best interests and those of your son in mind. I came by to see how he's doing and to give you this." He reached into the pocket of his suit coat, pulled out an oblong piece of paper, and handed it to LeAnne. "You might want to take a look at it."

She looked, and then she looked again. It was a cashier's check made out in her name in the amount of fifty thousand dollars. "What's this?" she demanded. "Is it some kind of joke?"

"I can assure you, it's no joke," Crutcher said. "I work for United Tracking Incorporated. We make the SFLS — the student/faculty location system — the use of which your son adamantly opposed, by the way. UTI wants you to know that what happened after Lance took the actions he did to protest the system had nothing to do with us. Bringing charges was the prosecutor's decision, not ours. When I heard about last week's unfortunate incident, I let higher-ups in UTI know what had happened. The check you are holding in your hands is their response. This is my company's way of showing how much United Tracking International and all of its subsidiaries regret any part we may have played, however indirectly, in the terrible calamity that has befallen your family."

Tears blurred LeAnne's vision, causing the numbers on the paper to swim out of focus. It was an impossibly large amount of money. Enough to catch up her back mortgage payments; enough to get them out of hock.

Just then a shadow fell over her shoulder. "What's this?" Sister Anselm asked.

"It's a check from United Tracking International, the people who made the tracking system that got Lance in so much trouble in the first place," LeAnne explained, holding the paper up so Sister Anselm could see it. "That's what Lance was doing when he broke in to the school district's server: protesting the student locater system. UTI executives heard about what happened to Lance last week, and they sent Mr. Crutcher to give me this."

The nun turned to Daniel Crutcher and gave him a stern look. "They did this out of the kindness of their hearts? How very

Christian of them!"

"It's a matter of public relations," Daniel Crutcher began. "The boy and his family have already been punished enough. Now, with this unfortunate accident —"

Sister Anselm deftly removed the check from LeAnne's trembling fingers. She studied it and then handed it back to Daniel Crutcher. "I suggest you take this back to wherever it came from."

Daniel Crutcher and LeAnne both gaped at Sister Anselm. "Wait," LeAnne objected. "You can't do that. He gave it to me."

"I know he did," Sister Anselm said calmly. "You do not want to take this man's money or his corporation's money, at least not right away. If this was their first offer, you can expect that there's a lot more where that came from. Now, let's go back into Lance's room and see how he's doing."

With that, Sister Anselm took LeAnne's hand, bodily lifted her up, and led her away. LeAnne was still protesting as they walked through the door into Lance's room. Looking back, she saw Crutcher glance quickly around the room, as if checking to see whether anyone else had witnessed his humiliation at Sister Anselm's hands. Then he stood up, tucked the check back into his inside coat pocket, and strode out of the room. LeAnne Tucker read the thunderous expression on Daniel Crutcher's face. She had lived with her ex-husband long enough to recognize fury when she saw it.

LeAnne turned on Sister Anselm. "Why did you do that?" she demanded. "Why did you make me give the money back?"

"Because there are a number of counter-vailing forces at work here," Sister Anselm explained. "That includes someone who was prepared to murder your son rather than see him released from jail. Lance is still alive but that doesn't mean whoever wanted him dead has given up. Maybe the UTI people were behind it and this is their way of try-ing to get close enough to you to try again. On the other hand, what Mr. Crutcher said might be true — that the UTI people feel guilty about what happened to Lance and they're trying to salve their consciences. In any event, that was only their first offer. Trust me, it won't be their last."

"But what's this all about?" LeAnne asked. "I don't understand."

"Let's say that good and evil exist in the world," Sister Anselm answered. "I have it on good authority that your son — your brilliant son — has come up with something that could help tip the balance of power one way or the other. With something like that

187

at stake, there are some people who hope to tap into the brilliance while others want to shut it down. The latter would be the people who tried to kill Lance and didn't quite succeed. The former would include the folks who just offered you that enormous check, and that's probably only a drop in the bucket of what Lance's prototype is really worth. What was that company's name again?"

"UTI. United Tracking International."

"Had you accepted the check, you would have felt beholden to them, right?"

LeAnne nodded. "I suppose."

"And that would lead them to believe that once Lance is released from the hospital, they'd have both you and him in their back pocket. My bishop sent me here to help look after your son's medical interests, LeAnne, but I'm also here to look out for your entire family. There are plenty of underhanded folk in the world who are hoping to take undue advantage of your current situation, Mr. Crutcher and his misguided check being a case in point."

LeAnne wasn't sure she could believe any of this. "You're saying that my not quite eighteen-year-old son has created something that's worth more than fifty thousand dollars in the open market?"

"That's my understanding."

"So what should I do?"

"It means you must be very careful," Sister Anselm cautioned. "It means that we have to protect Lance from all comers, because in this instance, the first bidder as well as the highest bidder may turn out to be the kind of people with whom your son won't want to do business. Come to think of it, it's probably time to give some serious thought to Mr. Dunn's suggestion."

"What suggestion is that?"

"Get an attorney on board."

"I don't know any attorneys," LeAnne said.

"I don't, either," replied Sister Anselm, "at least not here in Texas, but I do know someone we can ask."

11

When Ali arrived back at the Highcliff, Leland was sitting in the lobby bar with an almost untouched glass of scotch on the table in front of him. He stood up as she entered. "You were gone for a long time," he said.

"I made more than one stop," she answered. "I paid a visit to the local cop shop before I went calling on your cousins. Are you aware that some of your nearest and dearest, most notably your cousins, are under the impression that you spied for the North Koreans during the war?"

Leland's jaw dropped. "They think I was a spy? That's preposterous. I was a cook."

"That's what I told them," Ali replied, "but apparently, that's the story Langston spread about you after you left town. It appears that a lot of people believed him, including both your parents."

Leland went back to his chair and sat

down heavily, as though his knees would no longer support his weight. "My parents believed I was a spy?" he asked. "How could they?"

"Langston was evidently very convincing. He used a pal of his, a friend from his university days, to sell the story. The legend goes that the authorities let you trot off to the States unencumbered by charges to keep things quiet. They didn't want any kind of unpleasantness that might have reflected badly on the Royal Marines."

"They thought I was a spy?" Leland demanded. "How could they? I never would have done such a thing!"

Ali sat down next to him and placed a hand on his knee. "I know that," she said. "So does anyone with a brain who knows anything about you. What struck me as odd yesterday, with Maisie and Daisy going on about your friend Thomas and his dead wife, is that it seems as though they knew nothing at all about what was going on between you and Thomas, and that's the good news in all this. Thomas's part of your leaving town went completely under their radar and most likely everybody else's, too. So I'm asking: Do you want to see Thomas while we're here? I found his phone number. I have it."

"No," Leland said without hesitation. "What's done is done. Let's leave that in the past, where it belongs. As for my father? When you left, you said you were going to visit the police. Did you learn anything about my father?"

While Ali and Marjorie Elkins had been going through the evidence file, Ali had used her iPad to make a series of notes. Pulling out the device, she consulted the notes as she gave Leland an overview. "The assumption was and still is that your father's death was a robbery gone bad. This was back before credit cards came into use. Your father was thought to be carrying a small sum of money. His watch and wallet disappeared along with the money. His blood-stained vehicle was found abandoned in Southampton a few days later. I looked at the crime scene photos, Leland. The blood in the car was definitely smear rather than spatter. The supposition is that he was killed elsewhere and then the body was placed in the vehicle and driven to a dump site."

"No one knows where it happened?"

"No crime scene other than the vehicle was ever established. The evidence suggests your father was already dead or else badly injured when he was loaded into the car. He went missing after a Friday-afternoon business meeting here in town that stretched into dinner at a local pub. His body was found two days later, washed up in the sand under the pier here in Bournemouth, but with no sign of drowning. He was already dead at the time he went into the water."

"He was found under this pier?" Leland asked.

Ali nodded. "Do you remember when it was that you left town?"

"Toward the end of August," Leland answered. "I managed to get hired on with a tramp steamer leaving Liverpool. I jumped ship in San Francisco."

"You were an illegal immigrant?" Ali asked.

"I was to begin with," he admitted. "I was very fortunate in that Anna Lee took me under her wing and helped me formalize my status. I expect she pulled a few strings to make that happen."

Ali nodded. "I expect she did, too, but here's the thing that bothers me: Your father's death occurred only six weeks or so after you left town. By the time he died, he had already rewritten his will to exclude you. Why would he have done that so soon without even bothering to hear your side of the story?"

"Langston must have made an excellent

case against me," Leland said. "If my father truly believed I was a spy, then his reaction is entirely understandable. As far as my father was concerned, honor was everything. His father died at the Battle of Verdun in World War I. Father was too old to join up for World War II, but he served here at home with the Civil Defense. Having a suspected traitor in the family is something he wouldn't have tolerated."

"Still," Ali said, "to cast you out without any kind of formal charges ever being brought against you? And to do so simply on your brother's word . . ."

"Langston was a bully," Leland said with a shrug. "He could be amazingly charming when he put his mind to it, and amazingly persuasive as well."

"Lucky, too," Ali added. "With you gone, he got the farm, which he eventually sold for a tidy profit while Lawrence got the print shop and probably not nearly as good a deal."

"Are you saying what I think you're saying?" Leland asked. "You suspect Langston had something to do with Father's death?"

"It's possible," Ali said. "The last entry in the murder book dated from 1961. That means that in all this time, there's been no effort to subject any of the remaining evidence to modern forensic technology. The autopsy showed defensive wounds on your father's hands and body as well as bloodstains on his shirt. Those samples have never undergone DNA testing."

"Could they be?" Leland asked dubiously. "Even after all this time?"

"It's not a slam dunk," Ali told him, "it's possible. A few years ago samples like that would have been useless, but they're doing some pretty miraculous things with DNA these days. If the guy who did this was a juvenile delinquent who went on to a life of crime, his DNA may be in the UK's national criminal database."

"Except you don't really believe that the perpetrator was some kind of common criminal," Leland said. "You think he was my brother."

Ali nodded. "Yes, I do," she agreed. "Nothing I've heard about Langston Brooks causes me to have a good feeling about him. If he did do it, DNA testing would most likely be the only way to prove it. Unfortunately, at this point, we don't know if those sixty-year-old samples can be tested, and we don't know if Marjorie Elkins can even obtain permission to send the evidence out for testing."

"That's expensive, isn't it?"

"I told her High Noon would cover any expenses the local authorities won't handle."

"That's not fair."

"We'll cover it, Leland," Ali insisted. "No argument. Now how about if we go into the dining room and have some dinner. I'm starved."

"How was tea at Jordan's-by-the-Sea?" Leland asked.

"Believe me," Ali said with a laugh, "it was nothing to write home about. We're far better off here than there."

They were given a seaside view table, but there wasn't much to see. The vast seascape had turned inky black, with only the occasional lights of a seagoing vessel to indicate there was life of any kind out there. Ali satisfied her longing for beef with a well-aged bone-in fillet accompanied by duck-fat fries and the best Brussels sprouts that had ever passed her lips. Leland settled on the sole but didn't attack his food with much enthusiasm. He seemed lost in thought throughout the meal. The unwelcome possibility that Langston might have been responsible for their father's death was clearly weighing heavily on his mind. Having been the bearer of that news, Ali didn't push it.

They were perusing the dessert menu

when the maître d' approached the table with a frown. "Excuse me, Ms. Reynolds. I hate to interrupt your meal, but there's a visitor here who needs to see you. She says it's a matter of some urgency."

Ali looked back toward the entrance and was surprised to see Marjorie Elkins standing in the doorway. "Invite her to come join us," Ali said. "Perhaps she'll have a bite to eat."

Marjorie apologized as she approached the table. "I didn't mean to interrupt your dinner," she said. "I could always come back later."

"We were about to have dessert," Ali said after making the introductions. "You're welcome to join us for that or to have something else, if you'd like."

"A glass of wine would be appreciated," Marjorie said. "It's been an interesting afternoon."

The strained look on her face indicated that it hadn't been interesting in a good way. When the waiter appeared, Marjorie ordered a glass of merlot while Ali and Leland chose their dessert course — Dorset apple cake with clotted cream.

Marjorie waited until the waiter left before she leaned down, pulled an envelope out of her purse, and laid it on the table. "I had to see you and do this tonight," she said. "I was afraid if I gave myself time to sleep on it, I'd back out."

"Back out of what?" Ali said.

Marjorie met her eye. "I don't like being laughed at," she said quietly.

"By your fellow detectives at the station I presume?" Ali asked.

Marjorie's lips curled into something that didn't remotely resemble a smile. "Indeed," she said.

She started to say more but then waited to speak until after the waiter delivered both the wine and the cake.

"If you'd been passed along to one of the detective superintendent's fair-haired boys when you stopped by today, it might not have come to this," she said. "If one of them had initiated the request for DNA testing, it might have been approved."

"But yours wasn't?" Ali asked.

"No," Marjorie said glumly. "It was not."

"Don't worry about it," Ali said. "None of those other yokels would have given me the time of day. You at least listened."

"Yokels," Marjorie said, savoring the word and a sip of wine. "How apt, but that's why I came. The official answer may be no, but the unofficial answer is yes. I went back down to the evidence room and used my scissors to remove a strip of bloodstained material from the victim's shirt collar and from the shirt cuffs as well. You'll find both samples in here." With that she pushed the envelope across the table.

Ali stared at it in slack-jawed amazement. "Are you kidding? If you deliberately removed or destroyed evidence, you could be fired."

"True," Marjorie said grimly. "I could be, but I won't. When I went into the detective superintendent's office with your request, I received a very public dressing-down for my trouble. I was told in no uncertain terms that I had absolutely no business bringing up a sixty-year-old case that nobody, with the possible exception of Mr. Brooks here, gives a damn about anyway." She paused and sent a small nod in Leland's direction. "I was told that this case is so far beyond cold that it's frozen solid, and the only way there'd be any testing done on those blood-stains was over the detective superintendent's dead body." She gave a dismissive shrug. "Since no one in authority is going to make use of any of that evidence, I decided to bring some of it to you. I can tell you, no one else has any intention of going back through that evidence box. If the DNA testing works on the samples and we end up identifying a possible suspect, which I think is highly unlikely, I'll deal with the evidence-box problem then. Cross that bridge when I get to it, as they say."

Not wanting to give Marjorie an opportunity to change her mind, Ali snatched up the envelope and tucked it into her own purse. "Thank you," she said.

Marjorie nodded. "There's a place just outside Oxford, a private DNA lab, that I know about. It's an NGO. A secondary-school chum of mine, Kate Benchley, runs it. I don't remember what it was called when her uncle started it years ago. After he died, Kate was left in charge. She renamed it after she took over. Now it's called the Banshee Group."

"As in screaming banshees?" Ali asked.

"Something like that," Marjorie said with a nod. "The name comes from an Irish legend about the Angel of Death. Kate was responsible for changing the company name because they specialize in DNA testing on the remains of war crime victims."

In the past, Ali's friend Sister Anselm was sometimes called the Angel of Death due to her service as patient advocate to badly injured patients. Kate Benchley, it seemed, had taken that theme one step further.

"Katie was still in her teens when she cut

her good-deeds teeth working with her uncle on the skeletal remains found in mass graves in Kosovo back in the nineties. Banshee Group's goal was then and still is to return the bodies of war crime victims to surviving family members so they can receive a proper burial. I already called Kate and told her about you, by the way. She says she can make time to see you late tomorrow morning. Here's the address." Marjorie handed Ali a slip of paper with a phone number and address that included the town of Littlemore.

"Where's this?" Ali asked.

"Just outside Oxford, a little south of the Oxford Ring Road. Banshee Group is located in the Danby Building in the Oxford Science Park."

"How long will it take to get there?"

"If the weather stays like this, a couple of hours. The problem is, there's a new arctic front pushing down through the Midlands. Bournemouth should be spared, but weather in the central part of England is going to be bad again over the next several days. If I were you, I'd come and go as early as possible, starting early in the morning rather than later in the day."

"Does your friend understand that this is all slightly irregular?"

"One thing you should know about Kate," Marjorie said with a fond smile. "The more irregular things are, the better she likes them. The two of us got in our share of scrapes growing up, before she went back to the U.S. for college and I went off to the University of Portsmouth. According to our teachers, we were both considered less than exemplary students."

"In other words, most unlikely to succeed?" Ali asked.

"That's it," Marjorie responded. "Considering what I've just done, maybe that assessment isn't far from wrong." With that, Marjorie polished off the last of her wine, set down her glass, and stood up. "And now that I've shoved it to those 'yokels,' as you call them, I believe I'll head home and pick up some tandoori chicken for my son and me on the way."

"Thank you for doing this, Inspector Elkins," Leland said, rising formally and holding out his hand.

"Glad to," Marjorie said with a smile. "Especially now that I can see quite clearly that you're not one of the yokels."

She left. Leland sat back down. "It seems to me that Inspector Elkins is putting rather a lot of faith in someone she just met."

"You should see how her fellow officers

treat her," Ali said. "Compared to them, we must feel like a breath of fresh air. I have a feeling your brother Langston would have been right at home with those guys."

"Bullies?" Leland asked.

Ali nodded. "Every last one of them."

"Do you want me to accompany you to Oxford tomorrow morning?" Leland asked. "If so, I'll be glad to go along. After all, it's my problem."

"Is there something you'd rather do?"

"Mostly, I want to walk and woolgather," he said. "It's odd being someplace I know so well where I'm also a complete stranger."

"You do that, then," Ali said. "I'll take care of the DNA testing."

They rose and started toward the door to the dining room. Out in the lobby, Ali turned back. "Oh wait," she said. "I forgot something. I'll catch up with you at the lift." She got back to the table just as a busboy was starting to clear it. "Sorry," she said, gathering up Leland's empty coffee cup. "I'll just take this up to the room, if you don't mind. We still have some coffee, but they took the cups away."

On her way to the lobby, she slipped the cup into her purse. If Banshee Group needed a sample to use as a comparison, Ali wanted to be prepared. Better to have it and not need it than to miss the boat.

Back in the suite, Ali shut herself away in her room and tried to dive into her computer. The hotel Wi-Fi was exceptionally slow, and she wondered if that had anything to do with the situation that had put B. on that last-minute flight from Japan to Zurich. When she was finally able to access her e-mail, she found an encrypted file from Stu that confirmed that Sister Anselm had been posted to Austin to help look after Lance Tucker. She was relieved to see, however, that the information about his medical condition, including the amputation of his right leg, continued to come from patient files Stu had hacked from the hospital records department rather than from the nun. B., with the assistance of Bishop Gillespie, may have asked the good sister to provide patient advocacy for Lance Tucker, but Ali knew her friend well enough to understand that she would never divulge a patient's private information to anyone, including both B. Simpson and Stuart Ramey.

Ali sent B. a brief e-mail letting him know that she would be off to Oxford bright and early in the morning. Once she was able to get her recalcitrant search engine to cough up the information, she settled in to learn what she could about Kate Benchley and the Banshee Group.

According to Wikipedia, Kate Benchley, now forty-four, had been born in the U.S. and left an orphan at age eleven when her parents, Clyde and Roxanna Benchley, were killed in a car crash. She had been sent to England to live with her father's brother, Arnold, an eccentric millionaire and Oxford-trained medical researcher, who had chosen to specialize in DNA analysis. When he was asked to come to Kosovo to examine the mass graves of war crime victims, he took his new ward with him. He had made use of much of his own money to create the initial funding for DNAAA: DNA Atrocity Analysts.

When it came time for Kate to attend university, she had returned to the U.S. and enrolled in UCLA's microbiology program. After receiving her Ph.D., she returned to Oxford to help out after her uncle was diagnosed with Parkinson's. She renamed the company Banshee Group in honor of the mythic Irish fairy who was thought to wail her song of mourning at the death of important personages.

"My uncle started this organization, but I am honored to carry it forward," she was quoted as saying. "Banshee Group takes the position that all people are important. Rather than simply keening over dead bodies, we help them find their way home to their loved ones."

Or in this case, Ali thought, closing her computer, you may unmask a killer who's gotten away with murder for sixty-odd years.

12

Unable to face the prospect of another cardboard sandwich from the cafeteria, LeAnne let herself out through the lobby entrance. Setting off into the brisk evening air, she went in search of the taco truck Sister Anselm had located a few hours earlier when she went on a similar food-chasing expedition. A chill wind was blowing in from the west. According to the weatherman droning away on the television set in the burn unit waiting room, there was a possibility of a dusting of snow.

Cold as it was, the taco truck was doing land-office business, with diners carrying their paper plates of food and cups of hot coffee to folding tables strategically placed around a series of propane heaters. LeAnne had taken a single bite of her taco when her phone rang. Her mother was on the line with the welcome news that Thad's basketball team had won the game when Thad scored the winning basket in overtime. Once Phyllis put Connor on the phone, he rattled on about having lost another tooth and wondering if the tooth fairy would put in an appearance. He also wanted to know when his mommy was coming home.

"Soon," LeAnne said with a catch in her throat. "As soon as Lance is well enough for me to leave him alone."

"Will he have one of those blade feet, like that guy who ran in the Olympics?"

"I don't know what kind of prosthetic he'll have," she answered, "and he won't be fitted with one until the burns are healed."

Connor's innocent conversation was enough to break LeAnne's heart because Connor already knew about the amputation; Lance did not. Yes, Lance needed her at the hospital, but clearly she was missing important milestones with her other two sons, too. What she really needed was time-travel capability.

"Why would someone hurt him like that?" Connor asked. "It has to be someone really mean — a bully."

"Yes," LeAnne agreed. "It was someone really mean."

"Will you tell Lance I miss him and want him to come home? Thad and I were talking. I'll move into Thad and Lance's room so he can have mine."

That one took LeAnne's breath away. She thought again about the check, the one Sister Anselm had insisted she give back. Had she accepted it, they'd still have a house to live in. "That's very generous of you, Connor," she said.

"Grandma says I have to go shower now. Do you want to talk to her?"

When Phyllis came on the phone, LeAnne gave her tooth fairy instructions. By the time she got off the phone, her tacos were cold, and so was her coffee. Even cold, the tacos tasted better than the food available in the hospital cafeteria. Taking a deep breath, and feeling somewhat recharged, she headed back to the hospital.

Approaching the waiting room Leanne saw Sister Anselm talking to a visitor. To LeAnne's surprise, the visitor turned out to be Andrew Garfield. Lance and Andrew had once been pals who shared an obsession with computers. Andrew also happened to be the son of the superintendent of schools. Their friendship had suffered due to Lance's legal problems with the school district. With Lance out of the computer science club, Andrew had become co-captain of the team. Just seeing Andrew there, seemingly healthy and happy, made LeAnne furious. "What are you doing here?" she demanded.

Taken aback by both her tone and visible anger, Andrew said nothing at first. Sister Anselm answered on his behalf. "Andrew came all the way down here from San Leandro, hoping to see Lance. I've explained that at this point no nonfamily visitors are permitted."

Andrew finally found his voice. "My folks are at a conference in Phoenix. That's why I came today. I wanted to tell Lance I'm sorry about everything that's happened to him. We all hate the tagging system. I tried to tell my dad that half the kids in the computer club could have broken in to his stupid server. He told me if they did, he'd see to it that they'd all go to jail, me included. He also said that I couldn't be friends with Lance anymore."

His words rang true. LeAnne softened, but only a little. "Which is why you're sneaking around to come see him?" she asked.

Andrew nodded. "For right now," he said. "Once I leave home, my father won't be able to dictate who my friends are, but I wanted to bring Lance this."

A blue and gold San Leandro High School athletic bag sat at his feet. He reached down into it, pulled out something, and handed it to LeAnne. It was the plaque awarded to that year's winning team in the Longhorn computer science competition.

"After our team won," Andrew explained, "we took a vote on the way back home and decided that when he got out, we'd give the plaque to Lance because he's the reason we won. We based what we did on one of his old codes, and the judges said it was brilliant. You'll give it to him?"

LeAnne looked down at the plaque and bit her lip before she answered. "Yes," she said. "I'll see that he gets it."

"And tell him that when he gets better, I hope he'll let me work on his GHOST project with him."

"Ghost?" LeAnne asked. "What kind of ghost?"

"That's what Lance called it: go hide on server technology. It's a cool app for browsing the dark Web," Andrew said. "He and Mr. Jackson were working on it together. When Lance got arrested and sent to jail, Mr. Jackson . . . well, you know."

"He committed suicide," LeAnne supplied.

Andrew nodded.

"Are you saying you think what Mr. Jackson and Lance were working on, this dark Web thing, might have had something to do with Mr. Jackson taking his own life?"

"No," Andrew said. "GHOST had nothing to do with that. Mr. Jackson's suicide is my dad's fault, too. On the day the judge sentenced Lance to juvie, my dad called Mr. Jackson and told him he was next. Dad was going to see to it that Mr. Jackson lost his job and would never again work as a teacher. My dad's a real classy guy, blaming Mr. Jackson and firing him for something one of his students did."

"I know a good deal about computers," Sister Anselm said, "but what exactly is this dark Web thing? I've never heard of it."

"You wouldn't," Andrew said with a sigh. "It's full of stuff you wouldn't put on Facebook or Google. It's a place where people can buy and sell all kinds of things you can't buy in a store."

"Illegal things, you mean?" LeAnne asked. "Like drugs?"

"And other stuff, too. It's also a place where people can hook up for money."

"So both drugs and prostitution," LeAnne surmised.

"Among other things."

"Does Lance use this dark Web?"

"He used to," Andrew admitted. "I'm sure that's what he was on when he hacked into the school district server. The problem is, the guys brought in by the school district to investigate were able to track him down anyway."

"What's the GHOST thing all about?"

"People count on being anonymous on the dark Web. Lance was working on a way to find out and trace whoever was there without anyone knowing he was there."

"Was this on his computer when the cops showed up with a warrant and took it in for evidence?"

"Probably not," Andrew said. "If Lance had any warning the cops were coming, he would have overwritten everything on his hard drive. I know I would have. Mr. Jackson probably did, too. I hide files from my folks all the time, but if I thought some cyber security guru would be going through my computer, overwriting is the only way to get rid of something permanently. If Lance and Mr. Jackson did any e-mailing about it, the cops might have found traces in some of the messages on their servers, but that's it."

"You're saying that whatever they were doing is lost?" LeAnne asked. "There's no way to get it back?"

"It may be encrypted and stored on a cloud where they both would have had access to it." Andrew looked at his watch and jumped to his feet. "I need to go," he said. "It's a seventy-mile drive, and I've got school in the morning. You'll give Lance my message?"

LeAnne nodded. "I will."

She and Sister Anselm sat side by side as Andrew walked away. By the time he entered the elevator, Sister Anselm had her iPad out and was logging on. She scrolled through several pages before she spoke again. "It's not hard to find," she said, "and I think we may have just discovered why your son was attacked. The kind of people who would frequent a place like this would be unsavory at best."

"You're thinking what Andrew referred to as GHOST might have something to do with what happened to Lance?"

"Exactly," Sister Anselm said. "According to Andrew, only two people knew what he was trying to do. One of them is dead, and the other one nearly so. I'm sure the kind of application Andrew mentioned would be very valuable to some people. Maybe that's why the gentleman from United Tracking International made you such a generous offer today. If Lance has come up with something truly innovative, they'd like to be in on the ground floor."

"But then who set Lance on fire and tried

to kill him?" LeAnne argued. "If he had created something that valuable, why would they try to get rid of him?"

"It depends on who's responsible," Sister Anselm said thoughtfully. "If someone besides the late Mr. Jackson and your son knew about GHOST, maybe this third party wants it all to himself. The other possibility is just the opposite: Someone operating on the dark Web wants to make sure GHOST is gone for good."

"Should we go to the police?" LeAnne asked. "Given what went on before, I doubt they'd be receptive, but still."

"No," Sister Anselm cautioned. "Not yet. All we have so far are unfounded suspicions. I'd like to know more about Mr. Jackson's suicide before we say anything to the authorities."

"How do you propose to find out about that?"

Sister Anselm smiled. "It pays to have friends in high places," she said. "I was a little puzzled when I was asked to come here. Usually, my patients need me to speak for them because they don't speak the language or have no one to run interference with the medical establishment. When I was told that my patient wasn't out of danger, I assumed Bishop Gillespie was referring to

Lance's precarious health situation. I'm beginning to think he meant something else."

"That whoever did this to Lance might try again?" LeAnne asked.

Sister Anselm nodded. "With that in mind, one of us needs to be either in with your son or out here in the waiting room, at all times. By the way, do you happen to carry a weapon?"

"A weapon?" LeAnne asked faintly. "Are you kidding? I have a six-year-old at home."

Sister Anselm reached into the capacious pocket of her skirt and pulled out something that wasn't much larger than a cell phone.

"What's that?" LeAnne asked.

"My Taser," Sister Anselm answered. "I generally don't leave home without it, especially if I'm going to be traveling long stretches of lonely highway by myself. You should probably look into getting one. Now, if you'll go see to Lance, I should make some calls."

Puzzling over what kind of nun would advise her to carry a weapon, LeAnne returned to Lance's room. Inside nothing had changed. The machines still hummed; the lights were still dimmed. As she slipped into the chair, however, Lance opened his eyes. "Mom?" he croaked. "What hap-

pened? Where am I? And why does it hurt
so much?"

13

On the way back to San Leandro from Austin with her father in the passenger seat, Susannah Bissell had insisted on stopping off at Denny's to have some dinner. Ever since her mother died, Susannah had nagged him constantly, worrying about his living alone and whether he was getting enough to eat.

"No warmed-up canned soup for you tonight," she said as she turned in to the restaurant parking lot. "You're having real food for a change."

He did, ordering the senior-plate roast beef special from the pictured menu. It was dark when Lowell Dunn made his way into the small wood-frame bungalow he called home. The neighborhood, not far from San Leandro's Old Town, was gradually being gentrified, but it had once been part of the barrio and the only part of town where a mixed-race couple — a black man married to a Hispanic woman — could buy a house back in the bad old days.

With both him and his wife working — Lowell as a janitor at the juvenile detention center and Juanita as a cook in the high school cafeteria — they had qualified to buy the place. It was the first and last house the couple purchased. It was the house where they welcomed and raised their two daughters, and it was where Juanita died after a long battle with diabetes.

Most of the other houses on the block dating from the same era were in a state of disrepair. This one was perfect. The paint was fresh. The roof had been recently replaced. Inside there were no squeaky floorboards or leaky faucets. Lowell had replaced or repaired them all. The neighboring lots might be weed-choked wastelands, but Lowell Dunn's tiny yard, surrounded by a sturdy wire-mesh fence, was a smooth carpet of wintering-over yellow Bermuda grass where not so much as a single dead dandelion dared show its scrawny neck.

The yard and the house constituted Lowell's private domain. He knew its every inch and every nuance. As soon as he stepped inside and switched on the lights, he felt that something was wrong, as though someone had been there in his absence. He went from room to room, checking, but nothing seemed to be missing or out of place. Neither the front nor the back door showed signs of having been jimmied or forced. The windows were properly closed and latched. The television sets in the living room and the bedroom were where they belonged. The microwave, two years old but unused, sat untouched on the kitchen counter. Two weeks earlier, Susannah had taken him to Costco and used her card for him to buy cigarettes. The half-used carton of Camels — expensive enough to merit being stolen — was still in the fridge. The thumbprint-operated gun safe in the bedside table was where it belonged and showed no evidence of tampering.

"You been livin' by yourself so long, you're turning into a girl," Lowell chided himself sternly. Back in the living room, he settled into his recliner. First he lit a cigarette — Susannah didn't allow smoking in her minivan — and reached for the television remote. He scrolled through the channels, looking for something he hadn't seen before. Had Lowell Dunn been able to read, he would have been able to use the guide to see what was on as well as which programs were new and which were reruns, but that was his big secret: Lowell Dunn couldn't read.

He could work with his hands. If something was broken, he could look at it and figure out how to fix it. That was how he had made his way up through the janitorial ranks at the detention facility: by being the best handyman there was and by making himself indispensable, but reading was beyond him. That was why he had never used the microwave his daughters gave him for Christmas two years ago. He couldn't read the instructions. That was why he liked Denny's — because the menus had pictures instead of words.

After clicking through the channels, he realized that the episode of *Criminal Minds* looked to be new, but he didn't stay with it. He knew too much about the bad things some people did to others. As uneasy as he felt right then, he didn't need any further reminders. Instead, he switched off the TV and sat alone in his silent house, smoking three cigarettes in rapid succession and thinking about who on the staff might have been behind what happened to Lance Tucker.

All his life, Lowell Dunn had been early to bed and early to rise. Eventually, weariness got the better of him. When he felt himself starting to snooze a little after eleven, he dumped the long-extinguished contents of his ashtray into the trash can beside his chair. Then he got up, switched off the lights, and went into the bedroom.

Once undressed, he sat on the side of the bed and considered what it meant to be an old man alone in the house. He remembered all too well that after Juanita died, the girls had suggested that he get a dog to keep him company, and a telephone so he could call for help if the need arose, but Lowell Dunn had implacably resisted both. Now, still unsettled by the thought that some stranger might have gained entry to his house, he wished he hadn't been so stubborn. He was tempted to try sleeping without removing his hearing aids, but as soon as he put his head down on the pillow, the ungodly screeching in his ear made him rethink. He sat back up and removed both hearing aids, putting them on his bedside table as a cloud of cottony silence descended around him.

He was restless. He tossed and turned for some time before he fell asleep. The last time he looked at the clock, it was after one. He knew that, in a few hours, when the alarm went off at five, it would be tough to drag his weary body out of bed.

At last he drifted into a sleep so sound that he never heard the tiny click of the front door as someone used a key to gain entry to the living room. He didn't notice the brief flare of a cigarette lighter as someone moved the tail of the living room curtain into the trash can by his chair and set it on fire. After that, there was another small click as someone went back out the front door and used the key again to lock the deadbolt.

Had the smoke alarm installed by his son-in-law two years earlier been operational, the din might have been enough to awaken Lowell Dunn. Oddly enough, the batteries had been removed. The silenced smoke alarm gave out no warning at all.

By the time a passing motorist saw the flames an hour or so later, the house was fully engulfed. Unable to go in through the front door, firefighters broke down the back one. They had hoped to find someone alive, but it was too late. The house was a total loss, and Lowell Dunn, evidently overcome by smoke, never managed to get out of bed.

The fire trucks were putting out hot spots when LaVonn Bissell came by on his bicycle on his way to school. The poor kid came running into the yard, screaming for his grandfather. So much for making a proper notification to the next of kin. As for the guys investigating the incident? Once the fire cooled off enough so they could work, the cause was readily apparent. The fire had obviously started in a trash can next to the remains of a leather recliner. When they pulled the crushed trash can out from under the collapsed roof and ceiling, they found the telltale remains of dozens of cigarette filters. One of the investigators held one up for his partner to see.

"Is that what I think it is," the second one asked, "a cigarette butt?" The first guy nodded. "The trash can is full of them."

"Figures."

They examined the house for residue of accelerants and found only the track where the blazing curtain had run up the wall, setting fire to first the ceiling and then the rafters. They found the melted remains of a smoke alarm from which the batteries had been removed.

As far as the investigators were concerned, the story was clear: The fire, although accidental, was neither unexpected nor inexplicable. Another careless smoker bites the dust. What else is new?

14

Watching the news in her hotel room the next morning, Ali learned that the Internet was still being disrupted throughout Europe. It was provoking to realize that some kids in Shanghai with too much time on their hands could inconvenience people half the world away. Knowing that, she didn't bother trying to log on to the hotel's system. Instead, she stopped in the dining room for the breakfast buffet and then headed out. Without Leland along, she programmed Banshee Group's address into the Land Rover's GPS.

By the time she had negotiated her third roundabout in under a mile, she was grateful to have the chirpy female voice keeping her on the right path. The balmy weather was gone on this cold and frosty morning. The predicted storm, complete with another round of snow, was heading south, but it wasn't due to hit Bournemouth until late in the afternoon. There were patches of fog here and there on the roadway as she headed north, but that was all. She wondered where B. was in his ten-hour flight from Tokyo to Helsinki. When the phone rang, Ali was surprised to hear Sister Anselm's voice.

"I understand you're in Texas," Ali said. "Will you be home in time for the wedding? You're not calling to back out on being matron of honor, are you?"

"Certainly not," Sister Anselm replied. "I fully expect to be back home by then. I wouldn't want to miss the wedding. I take it you know why I'm here?"

"I'm assuming you were dispatched by Bishop Gillespie at B.'s request, right?"

"That's the general idea."

"It must be late at night there."

"Yes, it is," Sister Anselm replied. "The witching hour. Someone needs to be with the patient around the clock, and I volunteered for the night shift. Since my charge's mother hasn't slept in a real bed for days, I gave her the key to my hotel room at the Omni and told her to get a good night's sleep. In the meantime, I wanted to run something past you. Do you know anything at all about this case?"

"Some," Ali admitted. More than I should,

she thought.

"For some reason, Bishop Gillespie directed me not to contact B. about any of this directly, so I decided to work through you instead. If I'm not mistaken, people at High Noon are able to gain access to information that might be problematic for other people."

"What do you need?" Ali asked.

"A couple of things happened today that I think B. needs to know about. For instance, you know about the tagging situation at the school, that landed my patient, Lance Tucker, in jail?"

"Yes."

"B. should know that a representative from that company, United Tracking Incorporated, sent a smarmy guy named Crutcher to the hospital today. He offered Lance's mother a check for fifty thousand dollars."

"Fifty thousand?" Ali repeated.

"That's right. Crutcher said it was a good-faith gesture to show how sorry they were that Lance had been injured."

"That's a lot of money for an apology," Ali said. "Why would they do something like that?"

"That's what I wondered, too," Sister Anselm said. "It sounded fishy to me. I'm worried that the company is trying to worm its way into the family's good graces for reasons we don't understand. Lance's mother could certainly use the money, but I advised her not to take it."

"Probably a good call," Ali said.

"In the course of the day I asked some pointed questions about the family's financial situation. It sounds as though thirty-seven thousand dollars would be enough to keep them out of foreclosure. Having had her turn down the check, I'm looking into some other avenues to help her out."

Ali had a pretty good idea where Sister Anselm would go looking for help.

"This evening," Sister Anselm continued, "a kid named Andrew, a friend of Lance's, came by to visit. He told us that Lance and his former computer science teacher, a guy named Mr. Jackson, were working on a computer application that would make it easier to access something called the 'dark Web.' Do you know anything about that?"

"Nothing," Ali said. "B. and Stuart Ramey probably do."

"That's why I'm calling. Andrew seems to think that Lance's invention, whatever it is, might be really valuable in the right hands. Mr. Jackson, the guy helping with the project, supposedly committed suicide, and now someone tried to murder Lance. That got me to thinking," Sister Anselm continued. "I'd like someone from High Noon to look into Everett Jackson's alleged suicide."

"Since you used the word 'supposedly,' I take it you don't believe Jackson took his own life?"

"I'd like to know for sure if he did or didn't. The people who frequent this dark Web sound rather dodgy to me — drug dealers and such. For all I know, my patient is as bad as they are, but if the dark Web is at the bottom of all this, maybe whoever targeted Lance targeted the teacher as well."

"Targeted him and got away with it," Ali said. "I'll be glad to check into this, but I can't right now. I'm on the road. The Internet on this side of the pond is currently having a major malfunction, so it may take longer for me to reach either Stuart or B. As soon as I do or as soon as I find out anything, I'll get back to you." By then Ali was past Winchester and on the A34.

"Good enough," Sister Anselm said. "I need to go now. Travel safe."

Ali spent the rest of the trip mulling over everything Sister Anselm had told her. Ali herself had no idea what the dark Web was, but she had an idea that it was something with which both B. Simpson and Stuart

Ramey would be well acquainted.

She made good time. An hour and forty minutes after leaving Bournemouth she arrived in Littlemore and located the Oxford Science Park and the parking lot for the Danby Building. The word "Oxford" had evoked images in Ali's mind of gown-clad dons striding through a campus made up of ancient stone buildings. The buildings of the science park, however, looked more like modern multistory office structures, complete with walls that were more glass than anything else. The contemporary buildings plunked down in the middle of the English countryside made it all more than slightly jarring. Leaving the car downstairs, Ali took the lift up to the main lobby, where a directory sent her to Banshee Group's space on the fourth floor. The firm's light and airy reception area was dominated by large pieces of brightly colored modern art. Other than the presence of a staffed reception desk, the place might have been an art gallery, with a reception desk. Nowhere was there any clue about Banshee's darker reality, the task of identifying war dead from atrocities all over the globe.

The young blond woman seated at the desk greeted Ali with a warm smile. "Ms. Benchley is expecting you, Ms. Reynolds.

She's just through there." She gestured toward a door that led to an inner office.

Once inside Ali found herself facing a huge desk made of some exotic hardwood. Behind it sat a small green-eyed woman with a huge halo of wiry bright red hair. When Kate Benchley stood up, Ali realized that her hostess probably didn't clear five feet. "Ms. Reynolds, I presume?" Kate said, holding out her hand.

Ali nodded.

"Welcome to our little corner of hell." She gestured behind her. Through a floor-to-ceiling double-paned glass barrier Ali saw a well-lit laboratory space filled with banks of expensive-looking equipment, each with its own computer terminal. Six or seven white-coated technicians, all women and all wearing protective caps and latex gloves, bustled around the room.

"I'm sure Marjorie told you what we do here," Kate resumed. "Unfortunately, no matter what the politicians promise, say, or do, we always have a ready supply of bodies in need of identification."

"You bring them here?" Ali asked.

"No," Kate answered. "We have a whole group of people who spend most of their time on the road, flying from one war zone's mass grave sites to another — war zones in

231

parts of the world most of us have never heard of. They go to the graves, collect tissue samples from the remains and from any possible relatives. They then see to it that the remains are stored in an organized fashion so they can be retrieved for reburial once an identification is made. After that the samples from the victims and the survivors are sent here for processing."

"That's what the lab is for?" Ali asked.

Kate nodded. "First we try to create a profile. If that's possible, we hope to get a match. What breaks my heart is when we get a whole collection of samples, ones from a pile of bodies that contain both adults and children. It's clear that they all match each other, but we're unable to connect them to any other survivor. It means that a whole family has been wiped off the face of the earth." She paused but only briefly. "Now tell me, would you care for some tea, or would you rather have coffee instead?"

"Coffee, please," Ali said, taking a seat in one of two black leather guest chairs. "Black."

There was a door to the right of the massive desk. Kate disappeared through that into what sounded like a galley kitchen. She emerged a few moments later, carrying two dainty bone-china cups and saucers. "When my uncle was alive, that was used more as a bar than a kitchen," she said. "He had a seemingly endless supply of Scotch in there. I'm more of a gin-and-tonic girl myself, but not until much later in the day. So tell me about your cold case. It must be something if Madge is willing to lift evidence from an evidence room and hand it over. You must have made quite an impression on her."

"I think what she did has more to do with being annoyed with her coworkers than it was with being impressed by me." Ali set her cup on the desk and retrieved two items from her purse — Margaret Elkins's envelope and the cup she had lifted from the hotel dining room. "This is from the evidence locker," she said, pushing the envelope across the desk. "And the cup contains what I hope will turn out to be comparison DNA. The murder victim, Jonah Brooks, died in the fifties. The victim's vehicle was stolen. Investigators assumed it was a robbery gone bad, and the car thief was never found. Investigators stopped working the case years ago."

Kate slit open the envelope and lifted out two see-through envelopes, each containing a small swatch of white material covered with brown stains. "What you're seeing are pieces of material cut from the victim's shirt, both the collar and the cuffs," Ali explained. "The blood may belong solely to the victim, but since there were defensive wounds on the victim's body, we're hoping some of the killer's might be there, too."

"Are you thinking that whoever stole the car may have gone on to be a career criminal and that his DNA will be found in the criminal database?"

"No," Ali said. I suspect that car theft had nothing to do with it and that the killer was a lot closer to Mr. Brooks than anyone ever suspected."

"Do you have someone in particular in mind?"

"The victim had three sons," Ali explained. "Langston, Lawrence, and my friend Leland, who moved to the States shortly before his father's death. He was out of the country and was never considered a suspect."

"I take it the other two brothers were investigated and ruled out?"

"They may have been investigated," Ali said, "but it sounds to me as though everyone accepted the robbery story at face value and let it go at that. I think it's possible that either one or both brothers were involved."

Kate slipped the evidence bags back into the envelope. "Where are the other brothers now?" she asked.

"Both of them are deceased."

"Then what's the point?"

"The third brother, Leland, is back in the UK for the first time in sixty years. He wants to get to the bottom of this. That cup is the one he used last night at dinner."

"You and the third brother do realize that our findings won't be admissible in a court of law?"

"We do."

"What about the two who are deceased?" Kate asked. "Do the other brothers have surviving children?"

"Both do," Ali answered. "Children and grandchildren."

"What happens to them if after all this time one of their forebears is blamed in absentia for something that happened decades ago? Even if there's no legal conviction, finding out that one's father or grandfather was a cold-blooded killer might make things a bit dicey at the next holiday get-together."

Kate's warning was delivered with a smile, but with the specter of next summer's Jeffrey Brooks's family reunion hanging in the balance, Ali took the remark quite seriously.

"My obligation is to learn what I can and give the information to my friend. What he

235

decides to do with it will be entirely up to him. I can tell you, however, that since he's one of the kindest men I know, I don't see him going around blowing up other people's lives just for the fun of it."

Kate nodded. "Very well," she said. "We may be putting the cart before the horse anyway. Getting a profile from samples this old, especially ones that haven't been stored properly, can be challenging. That's why I invest in all the latest equipment. Samples that were totally useless only a few years ago are yielding positive results." She stood up. "If you don't mind, I'd like one more cup of coffee before we head into the lab."

Kate disappeared into the lab, taking both cups and saucers with her.

"How long have you been running this place?" Ali asked when she returned.

"Almost from the time I graduated from university," Kate said. "My parents died in a car crash when I was little. We were living in the States then. They named my father's brother, Arnold, as my guardian, and I came here to live. Uncle Arnold was a bachelor with no children of his own, so he had some rather outrageous ideas about child rearing. I was barely out of primary school when he took me to Bosnia to deal with mass graves. My father's parents had a fit, but Uncle

Arnold had more money and better lawyers. Eventually, the other grandparents gave up.

"Arnold Benchley was an Oxford man through and through. That's where he wanted me to go, too, but they used some lame excuse to bar me from admission. Uncle Arnold shipped me off to UCLA to get my degree. Three years after I came back to Oxford, he died, leaving me in charge. Now I'm back in Oxford, running his company and living in his house. When it comes time for me to do some hiring, people from Oxford come crawling to me with their little hands out, begging for jobs. Sometimes I take them. Sometimes I don't. When I don't, I chalk it up to the jerks on that admissions board. All of whom were male, by the way."

"Is that why all the people I see in the lab are women?"

Kate nodded, and smiled again. "Payback is a bitch," she said.

"Have you ever met any of Marjorie's fellow detectives?" Ali asked.

"No," Kate said. "I've been lucky enough to avoid that, but I know enough about them from her that I don't need to. And please don't think we're a pair of fire-breathing feminists. I have a perfectly wonderful husband at home. He's an artist.

And Marjorie's husband, Phil, was killed by a drunk driver when their son, Aiden, was eight. Phil was a good guy, too." Kate nodded toward the diamond on Ali's ring finger. "I take it you've found a good one, too?"

"We're getting married over Christmas."

"There you are, then," Kate said. She polished off her coffee and stood up again. "No one's allowed inside the lab in street clothes, so let's get suited up and go deliver your cup and envelope to Donna Sparks. When it comes to degraded samples, she's the best there is."

With that, Kate swept up the envelope and Leland's porcelain cup and headed back out to the reception area with Ali trailing along behind.

15

LeAnne was startled awake at ten o'clock in the morning by a discreet tap on the door and someone saying, "Housekeeping."

LeAnne had been determined to tell Lance about the extent of his injuries, including the loss of his leg, and Sister Anselm had understood. It was only after that difficult conversation, with Lance fading in and out of consciousness, that Sister Anselm had persuaded LeAnne to make use of the sister's currently unoccupied hotel room.

LeAnne had walked the three blocks from the hospital to the hotel, carrying the grocery bag containing the rest of the clean clothes her mother had brought down from San Leandro. Once she undressed and switched off the light, she fell asleep the moment her head touched the pillow and had slept for a solid nine hours. That could have been attributed to sheer exhaustion, but it was probably also due to the fact that Lance now knew the truth about his situation. His mother was no longer bearing that terrible burden alone.

There was a coffeemaker in the room. After taking her second leisurely shower in as many days, LeAnne fixed a cup to take along back to the hospital. Sister Anselm met her in the ICU waiting room.

"How are things?" LeAnne asked.

"They've adjusted his meds. He's sleeping again, really sleeping this time," Sister Anselm added. "Have you had breakfast?"

"No."

"Go to the cafeteria and eat something," Sister Anselm urged. "Man does not live by coffee alone, and woman doesn't, either."

LeAnne made it into the cafeteria just under the wire before they switched over to lunch. She had finished eating her toast and rubbery scrambled eggs when her phone rang. "Hi, Mom," she said. "How are things at home?"

"I was just watching the noon news," Phyllis replied. "What was the name of the guy who came to the hospital yesterday?"

"Which one?" LeAnne asked. "Andrew Garfield showed up last night; Mr. Crutcher stopped by during the afternoon; and Mr. Dunn was the one who was here in the morning when you were."

"Mr. Dunn?" Phyllis asked. "That's the guy from the detention center?"

"Yes."

"Do you remember his first name?"

LeAnne had to think a minute before she was able to dredge it to the surface. Finally, she remembered. "Lowell, I believe," she said. "Why?"

"I was just sitting here watching the noon news," Phyllis replied. "A man identified as Lowell Dunn died in a house fire here in San Leandro last night."

"He what?" LeAnne demanded.

"He died," Phyllis repeated.

"How is that possible?" LeAnne asked. "He offers to help us one day, goes so far as to say he's willing to lose his job, and the very next day he ends up dead? Was it arson?"

"No," Phyllis replied. "According to what the reporter just said, it was an accident with no sign of forced entry; no sign of a struggle. According to her, the fire investigators believe an improperly extinguished cigarette was tossed on top of something combustible. The house was equipped with a smoke alarm that evidently wasn't functioning."

LeAnne cleared her table and hurried

back upstairs. When she reached the door to Lance's room, she waved at Sister Anselm and gestured for her to come out to the waiting room.

"What's wrong?" Sister Anselm asked. "You look upset."

"The man who came by yesterday and offered to help us died in a fire overnight in San Leandro."

"The one who offered you the check?"

"No, the other one. Mr. Dunn. He worked at the juvenile detention center. They're saying his death was accidental, but I don't believe it. He offered to do what he could to help us, and I'm sure what happened to him is related to what happened to Lance."

"I think it's time to call the police department and report your suspicions," Sister Anselm said.

"If I do that, they're going to ask me if Lance is awake so they can come interview him."

"As well they might," Sister Anselm said. "It's about time someone heard Lance's side of the story."

"Talking to him won't do any good," LeAnne said. "I already asked him. The last thing he remembers is being up on the ladder, decorating the tree."

"Still the cops need to talk to him, and

it'll be better to be cooperative than not. The doctor says he may get moved to a regular room as early as tomorrow. When you speak to the detectives, let them know that's the soonest they'll be able to see him."

LeAnne nodded. "All right," she said.

Taking advantage of LeAnne's presence, Sister Anselm headed for the elevator, determined to get some sleep herself. Walking away, she stuck her hand in her pocket. LeAnne Tucker was relieved when the item that appeared in Sister Anselm's hand turned out to be her cell phone rather than her Taser.

16

Marjorie Elkins had said that Kate would make time to see Ali in the morning, but the detective couldn't have predicted how Ali and the head of Banshee Group would hit it off. By the time the samples were handed over to Donna Sparks, it was close to lunchtime, and Kate insisted on taking Ali to her club.

"It used to be a bit more stuffy," Kate said. "All male and all Oxford. Then the economy tanked and they needed more revenue, so they let in some of the riffraff, yours truly included."

The Dons Club turned out to be in town, in one of the old stone buildings that Ali had expected to begin with. They drove into a courtyard, where they were met by a parking attendant. The stately marble and granite lobby would have been at home in any grand hotel.

The properly attired host led them

through a bookshelf-lined library and into a cozy but well-appointed dining room where the service was impeccable and the food was even better. Ali thought the roast pork in mustard sauce with green peas was sinfully good, and the conversation wasn't bad, either. After dessert, followed by more coffee, Ali finally set off on her drive back to Bournemouth far later than she should have, considering the storm visibly bearing down from the north. Sleet started to fall as she pulled into traffic on the Oxford Ring Road.

When her phone rang a few minutes later, she saw it was B. Not wanting to talk on the phone while dealing with dicey weather and an unfamiliar road, she pulled over to the curb to talk to him. "How's the world traveler?" she asked, "and where's the world traveler?"

"On the ground in Zurich," he said with a groan. "I'm in the car on the way to my hotel. Where are you?"

"On my way back from dropping off some blood samples at a private DNA lab in Oxford."

"Whose blood?" B. asked. "If we're talking about a crime, why not a regular crime lab?"

It took a few minutes for Ali to lay out the

details about how her attempt to identify Jonah Brooks's killer had been stymied by the local authorities and how Inspector Elkins and Kate Benchley had come to her aid.

"Too bad we don't have someone like Elkins on our side in Austin," B. grumbled.

"Why?"

"The first call I had once I got off the plane and before I made it through customs was from Sister Anselm. Yesterday a guy named Lowell Dunn, a facilities manager at the detention center, came forward and spoke to Lance Tucker's mother. He was of the opinion that a person or persons unknown inside the facility were responsible for turning off the security monitoring system, as well as being responsible for the attack on Lance. He said he even had some idea who might have been involved."

"Great," Ali said. "We need him to take those suspicions to the cops."

"That's not going to happen," B. said miserably. "He's dead."

"Dead?" Ali asked. "What got him? Car wreck? Heart attack?"

"His house burned down overnight just after he got home from the hospital, where he had offered to help Lance," B. answered. "Lowell Dunn died of smoke inhalation. At least that's what the autopsy said. And the fire is being marked down as accidental. Investigators are saying that it started from a smoldering cigarette dropped on top of something combustible in a trash container. Dunn was a smoker."

"Which is all very fine except he had just offered to help your guy."

"Right," B. replied.

"So Lowell Dunn is dead, and so is Lance's old computer science teacher. If you'll pardon my saying so, it sounds like Lance Tucker's friends and acquaintances are dropping like flies."

"Agreed," B. said. "I have Stu working like crazy to find out everything there is to know about both Lowell Dunn and Everett Jackson."

"What you haven't told me is why we're so deeply involved," Ali interjected. "I'm ready for a straight answer."

For a moment B. didn't reply. "I think High Noon was used to perpetrate a series of injustices on a very talented young man, and I'm trying to right that wrong. Lance has invented something that may well be a game changer in terms of cyber security warfare and there are plenty of people, some of them good and some bad, who might want to gain control of his talents and capabilities."

"I assume you're one of the good guys?" Ali asked.

"Yes," B. admitted, "but he won't have a chance to work for anybody if someone kills him first."

"If High Noon is involved, who else is?"

"Homeland Security for one," B. replied. "And UTI, too. They're about to launch their own security branch."

"You're talking about that fifty-thousand-dollar check that came in yesterday?" Ali asked. "Is this part of that?"

"I think so. They're probably hoping to bring Lance in to help create it."

"This is beginning to sound like some sort of bidding war," Ali said.

"It is, with good guys and bad guys thrown into the mix, some of whom don't draw the line at murder. That's one of the reasons we've been using encrypted files. In case someone is watching, I don't want to tip a hand about our involvement."

"I don't understand," Ali said. "Why is Lance so valuable?"

"Because he's the next generation of hacker," B. explained. "I figured that out when I caught a glimpse of some of the codes he wrote while we were investigating the school district server incident. UTI probably spotted the same thing. Lance made one small error that made it possible for us to catch him, but he's good — very good. Lots of people are working on HOST projects now, but he's at the head of the pack."

"On what?"

"Hide on server technology. Lance calls his GHOST, for 'go hide on server technology.' He's either made or is on the verge of making a real breakthrough in that regard, and any company or governmental agency connected to cyber security is going to want him on their team. They'll want to use his talent to create ways to penetrate cyber security walls so they can think up ways to defend against same. I'll admit it straight out: I'd like him on High Noon's team, but right now my main goal is keeping him alive."

"How did Sister Anselm get pulled into the mix?" Ali asked.

B. sighed. "Bishop Gillespie just got an eye-popping estimate on the job of bringing St. Bernadette's Convent up to current building code compliance with twenty-first-century plumbing and wiring. It was down to either fixing the place or abandoning it. I made the good bishop an offer he couldn't refuse."

"You agreed to take over fixing St. Bernadette's if he'd send Sister Anselm to help
you look after Lance?"

Having had some experience in accepting
charitable donations in lieu of payment for
work done, Ali could hardly throw stones.

"So which is it, then?" she asked. "Is
someone trying to recruit him, or are they
trying to kill him?"

"Maybe a little of both," B. suggested.

"Does any of this have to do with the dark
Web?"

Ali's casual reference to the subject took
B. aback. "You know about that?" he asked.

"Yes," Ali said. "I do."

"Here's the deal: Lance has created a
program that is able to infiltrate dark Web
sites without leaving any cyber footprints.
The place is a nightmare for law enforcement and for any number of other people
as well. That's one of the reasons I'm
prepared to hire Lance right this minute,
and pay him enough to make it worth his
while, medical benefits included."

"Without so much as a high school diploma?"

"I'm hiring a brain, not a framed diploma
slapped on a wall. Look at Stu Ramey and
me. Do you see either one of us walking
around bragging about our respective de-

grees in computer science?"

Caught up in the conversation, Ali had failed to notice that outside her parked car, snow was falling in huge feathery flakes. It was sticking on the roadway and starting to accumulate. It was only a little past four, but already the sky had darkened to the point that nightfall seemed mere minutes away.

"Look," she said, "the weather's turning bad, and I have a two-hour drive ahead of me. I'd better hang up so I can pay attention to the road. If I take a wrong turn, I might end up in London instead of Bournemouth."

After saying their goodbyes, Ali ended the call but put the phone on the seat. Once she started the wipers, she realized she was dealing with a wholesale blizzard. Hunching her shoulders to the task, she eased the Land Rover into what was now rush hour traffic. Two long hours later, when she exited the A34 toward Southampton and Bournemouth, there were far fewer cars on the road. With the snow still tumbling out of the sky, Ali was glad that the vehicle behind her seemed to be maintaining a safe distance.

She took the roundabout at Wessex Road and Cambridge and started south to the hotel. Though she wasn't going fast, when an approaching vehicle veered into her lane, years of right-hand driving overcame recent experience: She instinctively swung the wheel in the wrong direction. The road was slick enough that her next move was an overcorrection. As the approaching vehicle dodged back into its own lane and zoomed past, Ali felt the back left wheel of the Land Rover catch on the lip of the pavement and slip off onto the steep shoulder.

What happened next seemed to be in slow motion. Yes, her vehicle had four-wheel drive, but with two of them in the air and a third digging into the snowy shoulder, the remaining wheel lost traction, too, and the Land Rover began to tip. Somewhere in her distant memory, she recalled something her dad had said about exploding air bags breaking people's arms. At the last moment before impact, she let go of the wheel. After that there was nothing.

"Lady, lady," a voice called out of the darkness. "Are you all right?"

Ali opened her eyes. The interior of the Land Rover, illuminated by a vehicle behind her, was littered with a layer of deflated air bags and tiny pieces of shattered glass. There was so much pressure on her chest that she could barely breathe. "I'm okay, I think," she managed.

"Hang on. I'll help you out of there. There's a tree next to your door. You'll have to come out this way."

That was when she realized that the man was speaking to her through the Land Rover's shattered passenger window, while she, held in place by her seat belt, was hanging upside down. Her rescuer slithered in through the glass, found the release on the belt, and then eased her down and out into the falling snow. "Come sit in my car," her rescuer said. "I've called the police and an ambulance."

Without the seat belt tight around her, Ali could breathe again, but she was shaking all over. Gratefully, she allowed herself to be led to an idling Volvo, parked on the shoulder with its emergency lights flashing.

"I saw the whole thing," the man said, opening the back door and helping her inside. He was mid-thirties, maybe. Dressed in jeans, hiking boots, a ski parka, and a pair of leather driving gloves, he, at least, was properly dressed for the weather. "Lie down here, rest for a moment, and stay warm," he said. "There's a blanket on the floor."

Ali looked down. The blanket was old and ragged and smelled of dog, but her teeth were chattering with a combination of fright and cold, and she was grateful when he spread it out over her.

"That guy was coming straight at you in the wrong lane," he said. "It's a wonder he didn't hit you head-on."

"I know," Ali agreed. She was still shaken by what might have been a very serious accident. "Did you see what kind of car it was?"

The man shook his head. "Something dark and fast. Never had a chance to see the license. I was too worried about you."

"Speaking of license," Ali said, automatically reaching for her purse, "I'm going to need my own. It's back in the Land Rover somewhere."

"You stay put and stay warm," the man told her. "I'll go find your purse."

"And my phone, too, please," Ali said. "It was loose on the seat. And see if you can find the rental papers," she added. "They were in the glove box."

While the man trudged away, Ali lay on the bench seat and shivered. She felt bruised and battered. Her collarbone hurt where the seat belt had grabbed her, but nothing seemed to be broken, which meant she was very lucky. By the time the man came back with her goods, Ali could hear the distant sound of approaching emergency vehicles.

Her iPhone was the last item he handed to her. "It took a while to find the phone," he said. "It had fallen out into the snow. It got wet, but I hope it's all right."

Ali tapped the button to switch it on. To her immense relief, the device lit right up. She wanted to call B. and let him know what had happened and that she was all right, but if he was dealing with some kind of major Internet crisis, he didn't need to hear that she'd been involved in a minor motor vehicle accident. The question of calling him was suddenly rendered moot by the arrival of emergency vehicles with pulsing red lights. A uniformed patrol officer opened the Volvo's door and then stood there, shining the beam of a flashlight in her eyes. "Are you hurt?" he asked.

"Not really," she answered. "Just a little shaken up is all. Shaken up but lucky."

"Mind telling me what happened here, miss?"

"I was driving along when an approaching vehicle veered into my lane," she explained. "When I tried to get out of his way, I overcorrected and crashed."

"You were in that one, then?" he asked, nodding toward the wrecked Land Rover.

"Yes," she said. "It's a rental. I picked it

up in London when I flew in from the States." Putting the phone away, Ali fumbled with the rental agreement as she spoke, but the cop seemed less than interested in it.

"This wrong-way driver — what kind of vehicle was he in?"

"I don't know. It happened too fast, and it was snowing like crazy. All I saw was a pair of headlights coming straight at me."

"How exactly did you come to be sitting in this one?" he asked, tapping the roof of the Volvo.

"The driver must have been right behind me when it happened. He saw the whole thing, but he didn't see what kind of car almost hit me. He was the one who helped me out of the Land Rover, and he let me sit here while he went back to get my stuff for me."

"Any idea where this Good Samaritan is at the moment?" the cop asked. He peered around at the snowy landscape before finally accepting Ali's proffered paperwork.

"He was right here a minute ago," she answered. "The last thing he did was hand me my phone. He must be here some-where."

"You have no idea who he is?"

"No, none at all. I never saw him before. He was right behind me when it happened, and he stopped to help."

"Strange," the cop said.

"What do you mean 'strange'?" Ali asked. "Isn't that what most people would do — stop to help?"

"Most people," the cop said. "But not most car thieves."

"What do you mean?"

"This Volvo was reported stolen from a car park in Oxford earlier this afternoon."

An EMT appeared behind the officer. "Sorry it took so long," she said. "The roads are a nightmare tonight."

The officer ceded his place beside the car, and the medic took over. In a matter of minutes the medic pronounced Ali fit. What followed were three hours of dealing with official matters, including filling out and signing countless forms, then contacting the rental company to get the right towing company to collect the wreckage. She still hadn't managed to place a call to B. Instead, when she called the hotel to let Leland know that she'd been delayed, he took it upon himself to notify B. The tow truck driver was dropping her off at the hotel when B., none too happy, called her. "You should have called me first," he grumbled.

She laughed at that, which made her chest hurt. There were evidently more bruises than just the one on her collarbone.

"What's so funny?"

"You're in Zurich dealing with the world's Internet problems. What could you do about me being run off the road?"

"I could at least worry," B. said. "Tell me what happened."

She sat downstairs in the hotel lobby long enough to tell him.

"So the Volvo was stolen from Oxford where you were earlier, but they never found the Good Samaritan car thief?" B. asked when she'd finished.

"Never. He seemingly disappeared into thin air."

"The cop is right," B. said. "An ordinary car thief wouldn't have stopped to help anyone."

"Are you saying I was deliberately targeted?"

"Maybe," B. replied.

"But why? By whom?"

"My guess is this has something to do with the Lance Tucker situation, unless your messing around in the cold case there in Bournemouth has raised someone's hackles."

"That's not possible," Ali said. "I'm looking into a murder that happened sixty-odd years ago. The two most likely suspects,

Leland's brothers, are both dead."

"Are you still on the good side of that lady detective in Bournemouth?" B. asked.

"As far as I know," Ali said. "And I hit it off with Marjorie's childhood friend, Kate Benchley, in a big way. Why?"

"Get back to her and see what she can tell you about this stolen Volvo: where it was stolen and when."

"All right," Ali said. "I'll get in touch with her first thing in the morning."

She looked up in time to see Leland Brooks step out of the elevator. He was wearing a coat, scarf, and gloves and looked ready to brave the weather.

"There you are," he said. "I was about to hire a taxi and come looking for you."

"Is that Leland?" B. asked.

"Yes, and he looks like he's ready to do battle for me again."

"Great," B. said. "Have him take you into the bar and buy you a hot toddy. Doctor's orders."

"Yes, sir," Ali said, laughing again and enjoying the fact that her phone conversation with B., which dealt with serious issues, had begun and ended with laughter.

"What's so funny?" Leland wanted to know.

She ended the call and then stood up to

hug Leland. "The men in my life," she said. "They're all busy looking after me. B. thinks you should take me into the bar and order me a stiff drink."

"I'll be happy to do so," Leland said with a dignified bow, "but it might be helpful, madam, if you'd consider living in a fashion that doesn't require quite so much looking after."

17

Once inside the wood-paneled bar, they settled on a corner table. Leland ordered a Guinness while Ali had a scotch on the rocks. She had yet to learn to drink her scotch neat and doubted she ever would.

She had to repeat the story for Leland's benefit. He listened to every word with concern lining his face.

"Luckily, I signed on for all the insurance options. That means Hertz is arranging for another car from the local branch to be delivered to the hotel in the morning. Unfortunately, they don't have a Land Rover available. Not that having four-wheel drive did me any good when that guy ran me off the road."

"You're sure it was a guy?" Leland asked.

Ali shrugged. "Sorry," she said. "I just assumed it was a guy. Probably someone who'd had one too many and was trying to get home from the pub. B. is under the impression that it may turn out to be some kind of deliberate attack, but since he spends all his time battling conspiracies of one kind or another, he may be jumping to conclusions."

Leland observed with a frown, "But the guy who tried to run you off the road was coming from the other direction."

"And the one who helped me was driving a stolen vehicle. He had left the scene without a trace by the time the cops got there."

"It was snowing," Leland said. "Wouldn't he have left footprints if nothing else?"

"There were first responders there along with the tow truck driver. I'm sure there were plenty of footprints, so maybe they couldn't sort out his. Or else he called someone to pick him up, and in all the confusion, no one noticed. I told B. that I'll check with Inspector Elkins tomorrow and see if she can tell us anything about the stolen Volvo."

Nodding, as if that settled the subject, Leland leaned back in his chair. "What did you learn about the DNA testing?" he asked. It was typical of Leland that he would wait to address his own concerns until after he had ascertained that Ali was all right.

"Kate Benchley handed our samples over to her best technician," Ali said. "They're so degraded that there's no guarantee that they'll be able to develop a profile."

"How long before we hear?"

"I wasn't given a timetable, but Donna, the technician, said she'd get right on it."

An elderly gentleman, leaning on a cane, appeared in the doorway of the bar. For a moment, he stood peering around the room. Ali noticed that once his eyes settled on their corner table, he squared his shoulders and came purposefully in their direction. Before Ali had a chance to connect the dots in her head, or give Leland a word of warning, the man was standing beside them.

"Good evening," he said to Leland. "I believe the applicable American phrase is 'long time no see.' " He turned to Ali. "How do you do. My name is Thomas Blackfield. Lee and I were friends once a long time ago. Do you mind if I join you?"

Struggling to master her surprise, Ali did her best to be gracious. "Please do," she said.

With a combination of consternation and astonishment on his face, Leland rose to his feet. Thomas held out his hand. Leland hesitated before he returned the gesture and the two men shook.

"Please sit," Thomas said. "We're too old to be jumping up and down like a pair of broken jack-in-the-boxes."

Once they had taken their seats, Thomas turned to Ali. "I presume you would be the lovely Ms. Reynolds whom Daisy Phipps told me about?"

"I'm not sure what my cousin may have told you, but Ms. Reynolds is my employer," Leland said shortly. There was nothing at all welcoming in his demeanor.

The barmaid showed up. Thomas ordered a glass of chardonnay before he spoke again. "Daisy called and reported that you were in town," he said. "I hoped you would call me, but since you didn't, I decided to take the bull by the horns, as it were, and here I am. How long has it been?"

"Almost sixty years," Leland said. His voice was tight.

"Did you ever marry?" Thomas asked. "Daisy implied that you had."

"My marital history is none of Daisy Phipps's business," Leland said, "and it's none of yours, either, but no, I did not. Now, if you'll excuse me, I believe I'll go up to my room."

With that, Leland stood and left the room. Thomas watched him go, shaking his head. "I had hoped that after all this time, we'd be able to put the past behind us and be friends," he said regretfully. "Lee wrote to me after he left town, you know, but I returned his letters unopened. I'm very sorry about that now. I tried writing back to him much later, but my letters came back unopened as well, and I couldn't very well go to his family asking for information."

"He's not exactly himself at the moment," Ali said. "He's had a few shocks to the system since we've been here."

"What kind of shocks?" Thomas asked.

You for one, Ali thought. On the one hand she didn't want to betray any of Leland's confidences. On the other hand, Thomas, Maisie, and Daisy were the only people still standing who had been around at the time of Jonah Brooks's death. Since Leland had charged Ali with getting to the bottom of it, this might be her only chance to ask questions.

"Leland knew that his father had died," Ali said, "but until this week, no one had ever specified that he was murdered."

"What did they tell him?"

"That Jonah Brooks was dead, that Leland had been disowned, and that his mother wanted nothing to do with him ever again."

"I suppose Langston told him all that?" Thomas asked.

Ali nodded, "And Leland took Langston at his word."

"He shouldn't have," Thomas said. "Langston was a liar. He was always a liar. I tried to tell Mr. Brooks as much at the time, and I thought he believed me. He said he did, but nothing came of it because he died before he could do anything about it."

"You thought he believed you about what?" Ali asked.

"That Langston was slandering Leland. I told him there was no way Lee would have betrayed his country. As soon as I got out of hospital and was able to get around on my own, I made it a point to see Mr. Brooks at the print shop here in town to tell him so."

"You were in the hospital?" Ali asked. "Why?"

"Because Langston came by my house and beat me up," Thomas said. "He knocked out a couple of teeth and then kicked me while I was down. My knee hasn't been quite right ever since. Put an end to my cricket days, Langston did."

"Did you report the attack to the police?"

Thomas shook his head. "You know about Lee and me? The truth, I mean?"

"I know that you were attracted to each other."

"That's a diplomatic way of putting it, but

that's what it was. We were very young. I think it was the first real romance for either of us. These days they'd call what Langston did to me 'gay bashing.' They might even refer to it as a hate crime, but back then it was business as usual. If it had been reported to the police, chances are I'd have been laughed out of the police station. Or worse, one of the coppers might well have taken a swing at me, too."

"When was this?" Ali asked.

"The beating? Right after Lee left town. Days after. It was a couple of weeks later when I was up and able to start teaching when I got wind of what Langston and that high-placed pal of his were saying about Lee behind his back. I heard rumors that Mr. Brooks was considering disowning Leland, if he hadn't already done so.

"I was offended by that. I was still on crutches, and I didn't have my own car, but I wanted Mr. Brooks to know the truth. My mother drove me to the print shop. I gave her the excuse that I was thinking about ordering some engraved stationery." He paused and smiled grimly. "My mother was a sweet woman, you see," he added. "She was also incredibly naive. She bought my story in its entirety, just like she believed my telling her that I broke my leg when I fell down the stairs."

"Did you tell Mr. Brooks about the beating?"

Thomas pursed his lips. "No," he said. "I didn't, and I didn't tell him about Lee and me, either. I said that Lee and I were friends and that he would never betray anyone, much less his country."

"Did he believe you?"

"He seemed to. It sounded like he had some idea that Langston was up to no good."

"At the time you saw him, did Jonah say anything to you about changing the will?"

"No, not in so many words. What he did say was that he would get to the bottom of it and that he'd do the right thing. The next thing I heard, he was dead. If he intended to change his will, I have to assume he never got the chance."

"When Jonah was murdered, did you go to the police with any of this?"

"No. They focused on the car-thief angle, and that's where the investigation stayed. If there were any other suspects, that information was never made public."

"It might have if you had come forward."

Thomas nodded. "If I weren't a coward, you mean."

"I never said that," Ali objected.

"You didn't have to," he replied with a tight-lipped smile. "I've said it to myself often enough. Had I come forward it would have complicated my own life. Leland was gone. We were clearly over. Mr. Brooks was dead. I couldn't see any point in endangering my whole future by mucking about in all the mess, so I didn't. I stayed away and left the police to sort things out as best they could. Besides, I'd already met Linda by then."

"Linda?" Ali asked.

"My late wife," Thomas explained. "Linda and I were first-year teachers together, and we hit it off right away. I thought that if Langston had left any rumors floating about concerning my sexual proclivities, having a good-looking girl on my arm might hush the gossip. That's the real reason I sent Lee's letters back unopened. The irony was, Linda was a mirror image of me, using me in the same way I was using her: to camouflage the fact that she was a lesbian.

"On that score, the two of us were made for each other. We both loved kids and teaching and books and cooking and traveling. For a long time we were just an ordinary couple walking out. After a while people started asking about when we'd get around to marrying. Eventually it simply made sense to tie the knot. We were compatible in every way but in bed, and we each allowed the other to have freedom of action on that score with a safe haven to come home to afterward. We were married for over fifty years."

"I know," Ali said quietly. "That was one of the shocks that hit Leland this week. I forget which one mentioned it, Maisie or Daisy. When he heard that you had been married for such a long time, I believe he assumed he was mistaken about what the two of you had together."

"Oh, no," Thomas said. "That was entirely real, but given the times, it was also impossible." He finished his wine, looked around for the barmaid, and reached for his wallet.

"Don't worry about the bill," Ali said, waving him away. "I'm going to charge it to my room."

As she watched Thomas limp back out through the bar and into the lobby, what Ali Reynolds felt in that moment, more than anything, was a seething hatred toward a long-dead bully named Langston Brooks.

18

LeAnne had thought the days at the hospital were endless before they brought Lance out of his drug-induced coma, but this day with him awake was by far the worst. Medication did only so much to relieve his pain. Changing the dressings on the burns was pure agony for Lance, and when he screamed about the pain in his legs, it broke his mother's heart for two reasons: because he was in pain and because there was only one leg left.

Nevertheless, she refused to leave her son's side for anything other than the time it took to visit the restroom down the hall; visitors' use of the facilities in patients' rooms was frowned upon. Glued to her son's bedside, LeAnne's thoughts strayed back and forth between two unwelcome topics: she distinctly remembered reading a newspaper report about a phony nurse who had made her way through a hospital somewhere — Seattle maybe? — stealing pain meds from patients' IV trees. Then there was the fact that Lowell Dunn was dead.

News reports about the house fire made it clear that the authorities were treating Dunn's death as an accident, and LeAnne had no intention of trying to convince anyone otherwise. If the person responsible for Lowell Dunn's death was also involved in the attack on Lance, she didn't want to call a killer's attention to the fact that Lance, although gravely wounded, was still very much alive.

Late in the afternoon, with Lance again asleep, Sister Anselm returned to his room and took LeAnne aside. "Have you been home even to visit your other children since Lance has been here?"

"No," LeAnne began, "but —"

"Go back to San Leandro and have dinner with them tonight," Sister Anselm suggested. "I've just had several hours' worth of rest, and I'll be glad to stay here through the night. Your focus on Lance is commendable, but it's not fair to your other boys. They need to know that you haven't forgotten them, and it'll do you a world of good to sleep in your own bed."

"Still —"

"There's one more thing we need you to

do while you're there," Sister Anselm interrupted.

"What?"

"Track down Mr. Dunn's family. I believe he mentioned having a daughter and grandson living in the area. I want you to stop by and offer your condolences."

"Even if I can find out what his daughter's name is or where she lives, why would she want to hear that from me? I'd only just met her father."

"If there's even the smallest chance that Mr. Dunn died because he offered to help Lance," Sister Anselm said, "then you owe him something, and you owe his family, too."

The nun spoke in a manner that brooked no argument. For a few brief moments, LeAnne was propelled back in time. Long ago, as a first-grader, she briefly attended a parochial school, a Lutheran one rather than a Catholic. Mrs. Grace, the stern teacher in charge, hadn't been a nun, but the rules were the same: What Mrs. Grace said went. She allowed no weaseling or excuses. She issued orders with the confident expectation that they would be obeyed without question.

In this instance, Sister Anselm and Mrs. Grace could have been twins. The nun had couched her remarks about LeAnne's going back home for the night in the light of its being good for all concerned. Even so, LeAnne recognized it as a direct order rather than a suggestion.

"What am I supposed to do when I see his daughter?" LeAnne asked.

"Put yourself in her shoes," Sister Anselm said. "You've been at the hospital all this time with all the reports circulating that Lance was supposedly responsible for his own injuries. Wouldn't it have been nice if someone had come forward who seemed to take Lance's side?"

LeAnne thought about how she had blurted out her story, first to someone on the phone and later to Sister Anselm. She nodded.

"What if Mr. Dunn's daughter is in a similar situation? Maybe it's true that her father's death was an accident. No doubt she will have heard that version of events from the fire marshal, but what if she has another opinion? What if she has some ideas about what happened that the cops aren't willing to consider? What if her concerns have been brushed aside the same way yours were?"

"You're asking me to leave Lance's bedside to go on a recon mission?"

"If that's what you wish to call it, yes," Sister Anselm said. "If I were to show up unannounced, she'd look at me as a stranger and I most likely wouldn't get anywhere, but you as a grieving mother to a grieving daughter? That's going to work like gangbusters."

"How do I find her?"

Sister Anselm handed LeAnne a piece of paper. On it was written the name Susannah Dunn Bissell, with an address on South Seventh Street in San Leandro along with a telephone number. Below it was another San Leandro address, this one on Main Street.

"How did you get this information?" LeAnne asked. "I don't remember seeing the daughter's name or address mentioned in any of the reports."

"Sometimes," Sister Anselm counseled, "it's better not to ask about the origin of one of God's mysterious blessings and simply go with the flow."

"What's the second address?" LeAnne asked.

"That's a gun shop: Jake's Guns and Ammo. It's just off Main and Mountain. A Taser has been purchased in your name. They're holding it for you."

"You bought me a Taser?" LeAnne said.

"Are you kidding?"

"Not at all," Sister Anselm responded. "I'm dead serious. Considering what may have happened to Mr. Dunn, I regard your having a Taser as a wise precautionary measure. I didn't purchase it personally. It went on the expense account."

LeAnne studied the paper. Although she had never ventured inside Jake's, she recognized the name. It was located on the north side of town in a small strip mall that she drove past twice a day. The other address was close to downtown. "All right," she said at last. "I'll do it."

"If you like, I can call ahead and let them know you're coming."

LeAnne glanced at the clock. It was three-thirty. "What time does Jake's close?"

"Nine."

"There should be plenty of time. They'll just give me the Taser and that's it?"

"You'll need to fill out the questionnaire for a background check. The Taser won't be activated until that comes back. In the meantime you can watch the training video."

Capitulating, LeAnne folded the paper and stuffed it into her pocket. Half an hour later, having called to let her mother know that she'd be home for dinner, LeAnne Tucker rode downstairs in the hospital elevator wondering as she went what kind of weird nun Sister Anselm could possibly be.

Don't worry about it, LeAnne told herself. Just go with the flow.

In the parking garage, she had to pay a king's ransom to bail her aging Taurus out of hock. Fortunately, there was enough room left on her one working credit card for the charge to go through. The car had been parked there long enough to be dusty, but there was sufficient charge in the battery that it turned over on the first try, and there was enough fuel in the tank to make it to San Leandro. Thinking about trying to find the money to refill the tank made her wish that she had kept Mr. Crutcher's check rather than giving it back.

Traffic heading for the freeway entrance moved at a snail's pace. Even though it was cold and windy outside, LeAnne had to admit that after close to two weeks of being confined to the hospital's stale atmosphere and artificial light, it felt good to be outdoors in real sunlight and real air. Despite the chill, she drove with her window cracked, savouring the wintery breeze on her face.

LeAnne wasn't exactly lighthearted, but with each passing mile, she felt slightly more hopeful. However Sister Anselm had come into the equation, her reassuring presence made all the difference because LeAnne was no longer alone in the battle. She could leave the hospital for a few hours, knowing that Lance wouldn't be there alone. She'd be able to look Thad and Connor in the eye and tell them honestly and in person that she believed Lance would make it. His life would be altered and so would theirs, but somehow, together, they would make it work.

LeAnne was enough ahead of rush hour that once on the freeway she made good time; it was only five-thirty as she approached the San Leandro exits. Her mother had told her that due to basketball practice, she and the boys wouldn't be home for dinner until close to seven; there was no rush. When LeAnne reached the downtown exit, she hesitated, but in the end, she turned off there and headed for the address Sister Anselm had given her. She wasn't looking forward to meeting Lowell Dunn's daughter, but she had said she would, and LeAnne Tucker liked to think she was a woman of her word.

Susannah Bissell lived in a neighborhood of aging clapboard houses that backed up on an abandoned railroad right of way. The street out front was parked full of cars, so LeAnne had to park several houses away. Walking back, she noticed that the Bissell home was in better shape than some of its neighbors. A boy's bicycle leaned up against a small wooden porch, and a young black kid of eleven or twelve sat on the front porch, cell phone in hand and earbuds dangling from beneath a faded Texas Rangers baseball cap.

LeAnne was only a few feet away before he noticed her and stood up. "Who are you," he asked, "another cop to talk to my mother about what happened to my grandfather?"

"I'm not a cop," Leanne said. "My name is LeAnne Tucker. I'm a friend of your grandfather's — more of an acquaintance than a friend. I wanted to tell you and your mother how sorry I am about what happened."

"She's got people with her right now," the boy said. "Friends and stuff."

"Of course," LeAnne said. "I don't want to intrude, but could you maybe let her know that I'm out here?"

With a shrug, the boy turned and went inside. A few minutes later, the door opened and a woman came out. She was about LeAnne's age. Her dark eyes were bloodshot. She clutched a white hankie in one hand. "You're the mother of the boy Papa went to see in the hospital yesterday?"

Her words sounded more like an accusation than a welcome. LeAnne nodded. "I heard about the accident," she said. "Your father was kind to my son. I wanted to say how sorry I am."

"No matter what the cops say, it wasn't an accident," Susannah Bissell declared.

"But it said on the news —"

"I don't care what it said!" she declared. "After my mother died, I gave my dad strict orders that if he was going to keep on smoking, he was going to have a smoke alarm, like it or not. We had one installed and I made sure the batteries got replaced just like you're supposed to do whenever we switch over to daylight savings time. The fire marshal tried to tell me that the alarm probably started beeping and Papa took the batteries out himself. That didn't happen. My husband is the only one who messes with the smoke alarms or their batteries. The investigator wrote it into his notes, but I don't think he was listening, not really."

"They're saying the same kinds of things about my son," LeAnne offered quietly. "The cops claim he set himself on fire deliberately, even though I've told them that makes no sense. What I wanted you to know is that when your father stopped by to see us at the hospital yesterday, he said the same thing. He didn't believe Lance did it, either. I'm afraid that's why your father's dead — because he was taking our side."

There was an electric moment, and in that instant, the connection Sister Anselm had hinted at between the grieving mother and grieving daughter snapped together.

"Is your son going to be all right?" Susannah asked.

"I think so. They had to amputate one leg, but so far the other one shows no sign of infection. In other words, he's better than he was."

"On the way home from Austin, Papa was talking about Lance," Susannah said. "He thought your son got a raw deal."

"That's the other reason I came to see you," LeAnne said. "Did he say anything specific about that, about his offering to help us?"

"He was more than just offering," Susannah said. "Papa told me he was suspicious about one of the guards. When he was a kid, the guy got sent to juvie for being a firebug. After he got out and had his juvenile record expunged, he pulled enough strings to hire on as a guard at the same detention center where he used to be a prisoner."

"A firebug?" LeAnne asked.

"You know, an arsonist. Papa said that Marvin Cotton was the first person the cops should have looked at, but since they hadn't, he started asking a few questions himself."

"If this Marvin guy's record was expunged, how did your father know anything about it?"

"My father had dyslexia," Susannah explained. "He couldn't read or write. It was supposed to be a big secret. My sister and I figured it out; we just never let on. One of the ways he coped was by having an encyclopedic memory. If he heard something once, he remembered it. He probably could have told you the name of every kid who came through that detention center in the last forty years. He knew what they got sent up for and how long they were in. Most of the kids were way worse off when they got out than when they went in. He told me Lance was an exception to that rule, that he was still a good kid. That's why he wanted to help find out who set your son on fire."

"Did he come right out and say he thought Marvin was responsible?"

"No, but before I dropped him off, he told me that he had been talking to the warden's office to find out what shift Marvin was working that day and whether he had been anywhere near the rec room."

"In other words, your father had already been doing some checking on Marvin before he came to the hospital yesterday?"

"Evidently," Susannah said. "But I have no idea how far he had gotten."

Far enough to step on somebody's toes and get himself killed, LeAnne thought.

Another vehicle stopped out front. As a new family of well-wishers arrived to visit with Susannah, LeAnne took her leave. Back in the car, she called Sister Anselm.

"I talked to Susannah Bissell," LeAnne said. "Her father evidently thought that one of the guards, a guy named Marvin Cotton, might have had something to do with what happened to Lance. What should we do now, give that information to the police?"

"We still don't have any solid information," Sister Anselm said. "We have the unfounded suspicions of a man who's dead."

"So we do nothing?"

"I didn't say that," the nun responded. "Let me run that name by a few people and see what they come up with."

19

Back in the suite, Ali found the sitting room empty. The door to Leland's room was closed, with no light showing in the crack under the door. It was only eleven. She was tempted to call B., but knowing he'd spent a long day on the plane, she decided to let him sleep. Instead, firing up her computer and finding the Wi-Fi connection working properly, Ali sent him a long e-mail, telling in detail about her visit to Banshee Group and her long chat with Thomas Blackfield after Leland's abrupt departure from the bar.

When her phone rang, she was surprised to see Sister Anselm's name in the caller window. "Hey," Ali said, "how's my favorite matron of honor?"

"I'm currently your favorite patient advocate," Sister Anselm said. "Have you had a chance to look into the situation with Lance's former teacher?"

"Not yet. I was busy all day, and someone ran me off the road on the way back to the hotel. Hang on. Let me take a look at my mail."

There were no direct messages from Stu on her e-mail list, but there was one from her mother at High Noon. When she opened it there was another scenic Sedona photo, which no doubt contained an encoded message from Stu. Turning from her computer, Ali reached for her purse and began searching for her thumb drive.

"You were run off the road?" Sister Anselm interjected. "Are you all right? Did you get hurt?"

"Bruised by the seat belt but otherwise fine."

"What happened?"

"A guy swerved into my lane. I managed to avoid hitting him, but my car ended up in a ditch. What makes the case even more interesting is that the Good Samaritan who pulled me out of the wreckage turned out to be a car thief."

"You have the uncanny ability to attract trouble wherever you go," Sister Anselm said with a laugh.

"Thanks for laughing," Ali said. "It didn't seem all that funny when I was hanging upside down in the rental car. Hertz doesn't think it's especially funny, either. What's happening on your end of the world?"

The laughter went out of Sister Anselm's voice. "I ordered Lance's mother to take the night off. She went home to spend some time with Lance's brothers, who have barely seen her since all this happened. She just called, though. On her way through San Leandro, she uncovered something I'd like High Noon to look into. It could be important."

"What?"

"LeAnne stopped off to see a woman named Susannah Bissell. Susannah is the daughter of last night's fire victim."

"Yes," Ali said. "Lowell Dunn. B. told me about him earlier. What happened?"

"According to Susannah, Mr. Dunn mentioned that he thought he knew who might have been involved in what happened to Lance — a guy by the name of Marvin Cotton."

"Who's he and what do we know about him?" Ali asked.

"Not a lot," Sister Anselm said. "I tried Googling him but didn't get anywhere. According to Susannah he's currently a guard at the same juvenile facility where Lance Tucker was incarcerated but a number of years ago, Cotton was also an inmate there."

286

"On what charges?"

"Arson, supposedly, but there's no easy way to verify that. Cotton's record was expunged. With this new case of something that might be arson too, I was hoping High Noon could look into it."

Ali had spent the entire time they'd been on the phone searching for the thumb drive and worrying that it might have tumbled out of her purse in the accident. She finally found it, but just as she inserted it into the computer, Leland's door opened. Wearing his robe, he came out to the sitting room and sat down across from her. Ali trusted herself to be able to do two things at once, but not three.

"Let me get back to you on this once I see what Stu's sent me."

"Whenever is fine," Sister Anselm said. "I'm not going anywhere."

Leland started to rise. "I shouldn't interrupt."

"I'm fine," Ali said, putting down the phone and closing the computer. "Are you all right?"

"I can't sleep," he said. "Guilty conscience. I shouldn't have stomped off like that. It was rude of me to leave you to deal with Thomas. I don't know what came over me."

"What came over you is an unexpected dose of the past," Ali said.

Leland shook his head regretfully. "I should have left it buried. I never should have come back here and stirred things up. I had no idea it would affect me this way."

"Why wouldn't it affect you?" Ali asked. "Finding out your father was murdered had to come as a huge shock, and then being confronted by Thomas with no advance warning? That had to come as a shock, too."

"Why did he even come here tonight?"

"Because he was hoping that after all this time you could still be friends."

Leland shook his head. "I don't think so. Thomas sent my letters back unopened. The words on one of the envelopes, 'Return to Sender,' were written in his own hand." The hurt of that long-ago betrayal was still heavy in Leland's voice. "I got the message. It came through loud and clear."

"A message," Ali said, "but not the whole message. Thomas returned your letters because he was hiding from who and what he was. That's why he took up with Linda, the woman who became his wife. They were both teachers and they were both gay. Yes, they may have been married for fifty years but it was also a lie — a companionable one, but a lie nonetheless. And speaking of letters, what happened to the ones he sent to you?"

"If he wrote letters to me, I never got them," Leland said.

"See there?" Ali said. "I think that's why he came here tonight — to explain all that. I believe he also came with the hope that he could have you back in his life."

"I'm not sure I can do that," Leland said.

"Your brother beat him up," Ali said. "Broke his leg, knocked out some teeth, and got away with it."

"Langston did what?" Leland was aghast.

"After you left town, Thomas heard the rumors that Langston was circulating about you, so he went to your father to plead your case. He said he thought he had convinced your father that you'd been wronged. He believes your father intended to do the right thing but he died before he was able to do anything about it. The cops were all over the car-thief theory, but Thomas may have uncovered a possible motive for your father's murder, one he never mentioned to the authorities. Had your father lived long enough to revise his will, Langston would have been sharing the estate with two brothers rather than with one."

"Greedy bastard," Leland muttered.

"So what happens if this turns out to be

true and we solve your father's homicide?" Ali asked. "What happens if blood evidence places Langston at the scene of the crime? Do we tell his great-grandson Jeffrey the truth, or do we leave that piece of the past safely buried?"

"I don't know," Leland said, rising from his chair. "There's one more thing for me to toss and turn about, although knowing they have a murderer in the family would give Maisie and Daisy plenty to talk about for the rest of their lives." He returned to his room, closing the door behind him.

Ali was copying Stuart's file into her thumb drive when the room's phone rang. She snatched it off the table before the end of the second ring.

"Did I wake you?" B. asked.

"No, but if it's midnight here, it's two hours later in Zurich. Why are you awake, and why are you calling on the hotel phone? Leland's probably awake, too, but if he'd been sleeping, the phone might have disturbed him."

"I'm awake because I'm worrying."

"About me? I told you, I'm fine. I had some Aleve in my purse, and I took some."

"That's not what I'm worrying about. I've been thinking about your traffic incident. Tell me again what happened, in detail, from the moment you saw the oncoming headlights until the cops showed up."

Ali went over it again. B. made no comments until she finished.

"After the guy pulled you out of the Land Rover and went back to get your purse and phone, how long was he gone?"

"I'm not sure. He helped me into his car. I lay down in the backseat, and he covered me with a blanket of some kind. Once he left, it seemed like he was gone a long time, but that may be because I was scared and not thinking straight. The time lines are probably a little disjointed."

"No," B. said. "I think it took a long time because he was doing something else while he was gone."

"What?"

"I'm thinking this was a planned event, and you were deliberately targeted," B. said. "If I'm not mistaken, someone put a tracking device on your vehicle so they would know where you were at all times."

"A tracking device?" Ali echoed. "How would someone have done that?"

"Sometime between when you rented the car and when you were run off the road. I believe whoever staged the accident chose to strike at a time and place when you'd be alone and going slowly enough that they could force you off the road without necessarily killing you."

"You're saying this was a two-man operation?"

"Yes, one in the approaching vehicle and one in the vehicle behind you. The guy in the Volvo who was there as your supposed 'rescuer' was there to lay hands on your phone. You couldn't see anything he was doing when he went back to your car, could you?"

"No, like I told you, I was lying down in the backseat."

"I'm assuming he used that time to remove the tracking device and clone your phone," B. said. "In fact, I'd be willing to bet money on it. So for now, your phone is bricked as far as any sensitive material goes. That includes voice conversations, as well as e-mails and texts. The problem is, whatever's in your document folder is also at risk, since anything that goes on your computer is also available on your phone and iPad."

"Crap," Ali said.

"That's putting it mildly. Who have you talked to on the phone since you got it back?"

Ali had to think before she answered. "Hertz, the tow truck guy, you, and Sister

Anselm."

"What did the two of you talk about?"

"She wanted me to have Stu get some information on a guy, a guard at the detention center named Marvin Cotton. Lowell Dunn seemed to think he might be connected to all of this."

"If Marvin Cotton happens to be part of what happened here, that also means you and Sister Anselm have just given him a huge heads-up."

"Great."

"What about your thumb drive?"

"I still have that."

"Good," B. said. She heard the relief in his voice. "When I put Stuart to work on Marvin Cotton, I'll let him know that we need a whole new encryption protocol ASAP. Fortunately, none of High Noon's official encryption program ever showed up in your phone. Otherwise we'd really be in the soup."

"What do we do about my phone, cancel it?"

"No," B. said. "For the time being, continue using it but only for noncritical communications. For whoever is listening in, it will look as though nothing is wrong. Let's see if we can set a trap with misinformation and find out who's responsible. My money's on UTI."

"The guys who tried to buy off LeAnne Tucker?"

"The very ones."

"I can't believe they cloned my phone," Ali said. "I feel violated."

"You have been violated," B. replied. "That's what cyber security is all about. You feel violated, and I feel pissed. Now let's both get some sleep. We're going to need it."

Without the heart to use any of them, Ali left her collection of compromised electronics in the sitting room. If they were being used to spy on her, she didn't want them anywhere near her. Rather than going straight to bed, she ran a hot bath and then sat in it, still feeling violated.

As the steam rose up around her, she remembered the time in seventh grade when she'd proudly taken her new diary, a Christmas present from Aunt Evelyn, to school with her when classes resumed in January. She'd been in the library, writing in the diary about a sleepover with her best friend, when a boy from their class, a mean kid named Todd Mortimer, had come by and grabbed the diary out of her hands. He'd spent the rest of the day entertaining the boys in her class by reading pieces of it aloud.

This is the same thing, only much worse, Ali realized, and whoever did it isn't going to get away with it.

20

After a grueling day of rehab and bandage changing, Lance Tucker was once again sleeping in the arms of pain meds. Grateful to have her patient resting comfortably, Sister Anselm Becker let the lonely hours tick away by remembering the other time she'd been in Texas. The first time she'd been here.

At the outbreak of World War II, Sister Anselm had been a child when her father, Hans, a recent German immigrant, had been arrested and incarcerated as a suspected spy. While being jailed in Milwaukee for a year, he had come down with TB. By the time he was transferred to the new internment facility in Crystal City, he was desperately ill. Because medical care at the camp was almost nonexistent, Sister Anselm's mother, Sophia, a native-born American, asked to be allowed to join him in order to care for him. She was told by the authorities that permission could be granted but on only one condition: that she relinquish her American citizenship along with that of her two daughters, Rebecca and Judith.

After selling most of the family's worldly possessions, Sophia and her daughters arrived in Crystal City with only what could be carried in three small suitcases. For most of the family, the move to Texas was an unmitigated tragedy. Rebecca hated every minute of it, but for ten-year-old Judith, the camp was an adventure. After living in a basement apartment in Milwaukee and enduring the perpetually gray winter skies, Judith thrived under the bright blue skies. She loved the wide-open spaces. The school system was rudimentary at best, but Judith, already bilingual and with a natural affinity for languages, soon learned to speak the languages of her newfound friends and their parents.

Eventually, the family was shipped to New York and then put on a ship to be "repatriated" to Germany in a prisoner-of-war exchange. During the voyage, Hans Becker died. By then Sophia, too, had developed TB. Dreadfully ill, she and her daughters were set adrift as displaced persons in war-torn Europe. The family was taken under the wing of a convent in France. It was there that Judith's uncanny skill with language came to the attention of a wise mother superior who harnessed those abilities and educated her in nursing. It was a combination of those two things — her nursing skills and fluency in multiple languages — that had brought Sister Anselm to the attention of Bishop Gillespie and eventually, all these years later, had brought her back to Texas.

At four o'clock in the morning, Sister Anselm was drowsing at Lance's bedside when there was a tap on the door. She hurried to answer it before a second knock awakened the patient. Outside, she found a fresh-faced teenage candy striper holding a small bouquet of flowers. "For Mr. Tucker," the girl said.

"He's asleep right now," Sister Anselm explained, moving the girl farther into the waiting room and away from the door. "I'll give them to him when he wakes up."

Sister Anselm stood waiting, flowers in hand, long enough for the young woman to step into the elevator and disappear. The middle of the night was an odd time for flowers to arrive, coming in through the hospital's front entrance, since, after ten o'clock each night, that was the only way in or out. The bouquet first would have been dropped off with a receptionist at the front desk, who would have summoned the candy striper to deliver them. Sister Anselm studied them. There was no price tag on the bottom of the small square vase, nothing to indicate which florist might have provided the collection of bright red rosebuds and tiny white mums. An envelope on a clear plastic prong stood in the middle of the flowers, but there were no identifying marks on that, either. The only thing visible was the handprinted name Lance Tucker.

Taking the flowers back into Lance's room, Sister Anselm set the bouquet down on the bedside table. In the process, she made some small noise that was enough to awaken the patient.

"Could I have some water, please?"

Sister Anselm poured fresh water into a glass and handed it to him.

"Mom said you're not a regular nurse. Who are you again? And where's my mother?"

"I'm your patient advocate," Sister Anselm explained. "Your mother went home to spend the night with your brothers."

"How long have I been here?"

"Almost two weeks," Sister Anselm said. "Your mother's been here the whole time you've been in the burn unit. I encouraged her to go home for one night, at least."

When Lance finished drinking, he handed the glass back. As Sister Anselm returned it to the table, he caught sight of the bouquet. "Somebody sent me flowers? Who?"

"There's a card," Sister Anselm said. "I left it for you to open."

She plucked the envelope out of the arrangement and handed it to Lance. It took a moment for him to tear it open. When he removed the card, a tiny piece of paper fluttered out and drifted down onto the spread of his bed. As Lance read the card, Sister Anselm retrieved the stray bit of paper and handed it back, noticing that it was a photo, printed on ordinary computer paper, and crookedly cut to fit inside the envelope. The subject appeared to be the photo of a small blond-haired boy wearing a backpack. An older woman was helping him into the backseat of a car.

As soon as Lance read the message, Sister Anselm saw from the monitor that his heartbeat sped up. "Oh, God," he said despairingly. "It's bad enough that they came after me. Now they're after my family, too?" Crushing the envelope, the card, and the photo into a single wad of paper in his fist, he flung them across the room, where they bounced off the bathroom door.

"What's wrong?" Sister Anselm asked.

"Who's after you?"

"I can't talk about it right now," Lance said. "I've got to think. Go away and leave me alone. Please."

Sister Anselm complied, but on her way out of the room, she paused long enough to pick up the three discarded pieces of paper. Out in the waiting room, she pulled them apart. The tiny gift card featured a top border gaily emblazoned with the words HAPPY HOLIDAYS. The words below the greeting, printed in the same handwriting as on the outside of the envelope, were of another order entirely: "We know where they live. We'll be in touch."

Sister Anselm read through the message three times, internalizing the implied threat, then studied the photo before pocketing the papers and reentering the room. Lance's eyes were closed, but she could tell from the monitor that he wasn't asleep.

"I read the card," she said quietly, "and I looked at the picture that was in the envelope. I'm assuming the boy is your little brother. Who's the woman?"

"My grandmother," Lance answered. "I already told you, I don't want to talk about this."

"You have to," Sister Anselm urged. "If someone is threatening your family, you must call the police."

"I can't," he croaked. "No police."

"Then let me talk to them," she said.

"No."

"Why not?"

"Because the police are behind it," he said. "They have to be the ones who are doing this."

"Why do you say that?"

"Because whoever tried to burn me up was able to get to me inside the detention center. They didn't have to bother waiting until I got out."

"Clearly, you have something these people want," Sister Anselm said quietly. "It's either something they want for themselves or something they're desperate to suppress. I believe some of the same people killed Mr. Dunn."

Undisguised shock washed across Lance's pale face. "Mr. Dunn is dead, too? That nice old guy? No. What did he ever do to hurt anyone?"

"What he did," Sister Anselm explained, "is come by the hospital and offer to help you. He told your mother as much, and that very night, his house burned down. They're saying the fire was an accident caused by a smoldering cigarette, but I'm not sure I believe that. His daughter doesn't. What about you? What do you think?"

Lance stared at her and didn't answer.

"Doesn't that make what happened to Mr. Dunn sound a lot like what happened to Mr. Jackson?" Sister Anselm continued. "I've been given to understand he committed suicide shortly after you went to jail, but maybe he committed suicide the same way you set yourself on fire."

The room fell silent for a long moment. Lance was the one who finally spoke. "You're right," he said finally. "Mr. Jackson didn't commit suicide. As soon as I found out he was dead, I asked to speak to the detectives and told them so. They insisted that he had died of a drug overdose, even though I tried to tell them that he would never do such a thing. They claimed he was despondent because the school district thought he was behind my stunt of taking down the server and that the school superintendent was looking for a way to fire him. I tried to tell the cops how bogus that was — that I'd done the server gig all on my own — but no one was interested in what I had to say. They wouldn't listen to me then, and they won't listen to me now. Besides, you saw the note. That's what it really means. If I even try going to the police, they'll hurt Connor."

"What's all this about?" Sister Anselm asked. "That dark Web thing? That ghost or spook or whatever it is you invented?"

Lance gave her a searching look. "Developed," he corrected after a pause. "But how do you know about that? Have I been talking in my sleep?"

"A friend of yours from school was talking about it," Sister Anselm said. "Andrew seemed to think whatever you created is going to be the next great thing."

"I wish I'd never even heard of the dark Web or GHOST," Lance Tucker said. "Now leave me alone, please. I don't want to talk about this anymore. And get rid of those flowers, too. I can't stand to look at them."

Without another word, Sister Anselm removed the bouquet from the room and dumped it in the trash. Then she returned to her chair in the room and listened as Lance's breathing gradually steadied. Once he was sleeping again, she was left to struggle with her conscience. When Bishop Gillespie had asked her to take this case, he had told her up front that B. Simpson feared Lance's life might still be in danger. Now she knew that to be true. The danger was real, especially with Lowell Dunn dead and the remains of the note threatening Lance's younger brother in her pocket.

Sister Anselm's problem was with Lance's adamant refusal to involve the police. His belief that there was a law enforcement element sounded like the ravings of an overly active imagination, but what if he was right? She was sure B. Simpson and his associates were fully prepared to work with Lance on whatever difficulties he was facing, but without Lance's cooperation and assent, Sister Anselm couldn't go to High Noon any more than she could go to the police. Her vow of patient confidentiality forbade it. There was no wiggle room. Her primary obligation was her patient's welfare. What was she to do, she wondered, if it turned out that Lance's welfare and his wishes were in direct conflict?

At other times, when faced with some serious dilemma, Sister Anselm had always been able to look to Bishop Gillespie for counsel and advice. This time she felt unable to do so. Instead, she plucked her rosary beads out of her pocket. It was Sister Anselm's firm belief that any time you didn't know which way to turn was a good time to turn to prayer, and before another hour passed, she had her answer.

Much later, when the first nurse came into the room to check Lance's vitals, Sister Anselm left them alone to go to the restroom. On the way, she stopped short at the trash container where she had tossed the discarded flowers. Even as she was digging the bouquet out of the can, she was telling herself she was nothing but a paranoid old woman, but she did it anyway. Once she had retrieved the flowers, vase and all, she took them into the restroom and locked the door behind her.

She placed the flowers on the counter and studied them. They didn't look inherently evil, and despite having been tossed in the trash, the red roses and spidery white mums were in surprisingly good shape. One flower at a time, Sister Anselm removed the blooms from the water-soaked spongelike brick that took up most of the space in the vase. That was where she found it. A tiny microphone in a green plastic waterproof envelope had been tucked in among the stems.

Even though it was exactly what she had been looking for, Sister Anselm was shocked by her discovery. Had Lance not insisted that the flowers be removed from his room, the bug would have allowed the eavesdroppers to be privy to every word said in Lance's presence.

What should she do about it? Put it down on the floor and crush it under her heel? No, she decided, the noise from that might indicate to someone listening that the bug's presence had been discovered. She examined the tiny flute-shaped plastic container that had held the bug in place in the bouquet. The plastic container indicated there had been a need to protect the device from moisture. With that in mind, Sister Anselm plugged the sink and filled it with hot water. Then she dropped the mike into the water and gave it a good long soak. Once it was dry, just to be on the safe side and in case it was working, she didn't put it in her pocket. Instead, she took it downstairs to her locker and dropped it into the purse she left stored there during the day. She hadn't been able to see, much less read, any identifying numbers on the device, but she suspected they were there, and she hoped they would lead back to whoever was behind this.

Feeling quite pleased with herself, Sister Anselm squared her shoulders and returned to her patient. It was almost time to put the rest of her plan into action.

21

When Ali woke up the next morning, her whole body hurt. The seat belt had left a web of bruises. Out in the sitting room, Leland had ordered a breakfast tray with coffee, orange juice, and toast. He was trying valiantly to be his usual chipper self, but his haggard look as he passed her a cup of coffee told a different tale. "I'd say neither one of us got a good night's sleep."

Ali nodded. "B. thinks he's figured out why I was run off the road. While I was resting in that stolen Volvo, the guy who was supposedly helping me cloned my phone. For the time being, any communications on my electronic devices have to be considered compromised. I wanted to tell Marjorie Elkins about what happened yesterday and thank her for her help, but under the circumstances, I don't dare send her an email. I prefer to go see her in person."

"If you don't mind," Leland said, "I'd like

to accompany you on that trip. Regardless of how the results come out, I owe Detective Elkins a debt of gratitude."

An hour later, they took a cab from the hotel to the police station, where Leland had far better luck with the receptionist than Ali had had earlier. In the squad room, Ali led Leland to Marjorie's corner desk. "Well, well," she said, looking up with a smile as they approached. "I hear you had an adventurous night last night. I heard all about it at this morning's briefing. I appreciated that you made no mention of your visit to Banshee Group."

"Yes," Ali said. "A sin of omission, I'm afraid. I told them I was seeing a friend in Oxford and let it go at that."

"Except for the stolen car, it would be easy to consider the incident nothing other than an ordinary traffic accident," Marjorie said. "What do you think?"

"That it wasn't an accident," Ali said.

"Deliberate then," Marjorie said, "but to what purpose."

"Our assumption is that the accident was staged in order to gain access to my phone."

"Your phone?"

Ali nodded. "We think the guy in the stolen car, the one who supposedly stopped to help me, took advantage of the situation to clone my phone."

"Why would that be? Do you believe this alleged attack had something to do with Mr. Brooks's situation, or was it due to something else?"

There was a certain wariness in Marjorie's tone that told Ali they weren't on as good terms as they had been the night before.

"Something else," Ali said. "Something going on in the States."

"Since it's apparently spilled over into my jurisdiction, would you care to tell me what that is?" Marjorie asked. "I was just doing an Internet search on you, Ms. Reynolds, something I probably should have done before I went out on a limb and gave you that sample. You appear to live in interesting times. Both of you do."

Marjorie shoved several computer-generated printouts across the desk. The last one dealt with the shoot-out in northern Arizona, the one in which Leland had saved Ali's life. "So I'm asking," Marjorie continued, "since my neck may be on the line here, what the hell are you up to, and what's on your phone?"

"There's a kid in Texas," Ali said. "His name is Lance Tucker. He was in the process of developing some amazing new software when he pulled a stunt that got him in trouble with the law. He got sent to jail. Two weeks ago, somebody tried to kill him."

"What's your connection to all this?"

"My boyfriend's —" Ali stopped and corrected herself. "My fiancé's company is interested in protecting the kid from further harm and maybe, eventually, hiring him in order to have access to Lance's innovative software."

"And the company in question would be High Noon Enterprises?" Marjorie asked. "The cyber security firm footing the bill for Mr. Brooks's DNA testing?"

Ali nodded. "We think the people behind last night's incident, a start-up cyber security company, are also looking to gain access to Mr. Tucker's software."

"I need the name of that rival company," Marjorie said.

Ali paused before she answered, but only for a moment. "UTI," she said. "That stands for United Tracking Incorporated."

Marjorie stared at her computer for a moment, then typed something into it. She waited as if for a search engine's response. When it came, she sighed, picked up another piece of paper, and passed it over to Ali. "Here," she said, "Meet Edward Fullerton."

Staring back at Ali was a mug shot. She

recognized the image at once. "That's the guy from the Volvo!" she exclaimed.

Marjorie nodded. "I thought as much," she said.

"But this is a mug shot," Ali said. "Who is he? Is he already locked up somewhere?"

"That's an old mug shot," Marjorie countered. "And no, he's not currently locked up anywhere so far as I know."

"How did you get this?"

"I called Kate," Marjorie answered. "She had her building's security people go through their film from yesterday. Right around noon, they spotted an unidentified man tinkering with what appears to be the back bumper of your Land Rover. He arrived and left the Science Park's car park, driving — you guessed it — the stolen Volvo. I had the security guy send me the clip. I extracted a photo of the man's face, processed it through several levels of image enhancement, ran the resulting picture through our facial recognition software, and there you have him, Mr. Fullerton himself, a guy who, over the past twenty years, has accumulated a history of maybe a dozen car thefts. He also has a younger brother named Jonathan, who aspires to follow in Edward's footsteps." Marjorie passed along another sheet of paper. The photo on it was a close likeness to the first, although the man in this photo appeared somewhat younger.

"Meet Edward's most likely accomplice," Marjorie said.

"What are you going to do about this?" Ali asked.

"I can't very well do anything, now can I?" Marjorie Elkins sounded more than slightly provoked. "For one thing, it's not my case. If I bring up any of this with my superiors, questions will be asked, not only about my connections to Kate and to Banshee Group, but to you. In other words, all I'm doing at the moment is giving you the two names. I suspect that high-powered fiancé of yours will find a way to make the necessary connections without my having to lift a finger." There was a pause during which Marjorie Elkins gave Ali an appraising look. "What did Kate say about your sample?" she asked.

"That even though it was old and degraded, she thought it might work. She's put one of her best people on it. Thank you."

"Good," Marjorie said. "You're welcome, but I need you for a favor as well."

"What's that?"

"If you happen to find out anything more about Mr. Brooks's father's murder, leave me out of it, please."

"Yes, ma'am," Ali said. "We'll be only too glad to."

Minutes later, Marjorie ushered them out to the lobby and left them there. The determined manner in which she walked away made it clear that she was washing her hands of the entire situation.

"Being put out on the street like that was unexpected," Leland murmured. "I never had a chance to thank her properly."

"Just as well," Ali said. "The less we have to do with her, the better off she'll be. Let's go back to the hotel and send what she gave us to B."

Out on the street, it took a while to flag down a cab. It was raining, a steady drip, which meant that the temperature had warmed up considerably from the day before.

In the Highcliff's business center, Ali used the hotel fax machine to send B. and Stuart copies of the mug shots as well as the accompanying information. Using Leland's e-mail account, they passed along everything Marjorie Elkins had given them.

Out of habit, Ali had slipped her phone in her jacket pocket. When it rang a few moments later, it startled her. Seeing that it was B. on the line, she answered somewhat warily.

"Good morning," he said. "How are you feeling this morning?"

So this is how it will be, Ali thought. On the phone, we'll stick to the weather and our health.

"Not too bad," she said.

"Your package just showed up," he said. "Thanks. It's exactly what I needed."

In other words, B. had the photos. By now he probably already had assigned people to start a data-mining process on the two Fullerton brothers. If there were any obvious connections between them and UTI, Ali was sure High Noon would uncover them.

They chatted for a few more minutes — inane stuff about the wedding, about when B. planned to leave Zurich, about any number of other things. It sounded so stilted and phony, Ali was sure that anyone listening in was bound to see right through it. When a second call came in, she was relieved to switch over in time to discover that her replacement rental car had been delivered to the hotel. She turned to Leland. "What say we go for a ride before someone has a chance to tamper with it."

Leland nodded. "Now that you mention it, there is somewhere I'd like to go."

"Where's that?"

"To see Thomas Blackfield," he said.

"We'll be going back to London tomorrow. From what you told me, I believe I owe him an apology. I'd like to put things right before I go."

"You know where he lives?"

Leland nodded. "Yes, in Bourne Close, above the Pig and Whistle."

"Do you want me to drop you off and pick you up?"

"No," Leland said. "You said you'd have my back. Since you've been privy to this whole sordid situation, I'd rather have you with me than to go see him alone. I'll call ahead and make sure it's all right if we stop by."

It was only a little past eleven when they arrived at the pub and lucked into a parking place right out front. A collection of wooden benches and tables were stacked and chained together along the outside of the building. In warmer weather, perhaps it was possible to dine outside, but not today.

The interior of the Pig and Whistle was a low-ceilinged affair that, even in the non-smoking present, reeked of previous generations of smokers. A gas log fireplace burned at the far end of the room. Thomas Blackfield sat in the booth closest to the fire with a pint of ale on the table in front of him.

As they approached the booth, Leland was

the first to speak. "I'm sorry," he said, sliding into the opposing booth. "Sorry for what my brother put you through; sorry for thinking ill about you all these years. Clearly, I didn't know the full story."

The barmaid arrived almost before Ali slid into the booth behind Leland. He ordered a pint of ale. Ali stuck with coffee.

"I can recommend the Cornish pasties," Thomas said. "I live upstairs, and I've been smelling them baking all morning."

When the barmaid brought their drinks, they ordered pasties all around. As Leland took his first sip of ale, Thomas reached into the vest pocket of his jacket and pulled out a folded piece of paper. "I brought this with me last night," he said. "I meant to give it to you, to back up my story, but then I never got a chance to tell you."

"I believe Ali here told me most of it," Leland said. "That Langston had everyone in town buying some tale about my being a traitor; that even our parents believed him and wrote me out of the will as a consequence; that Langston beat the crap out of you and put you in the hospital; that you talked to my father and told him Langston was a liar. Thank you for that, by the way, for going to bat for me all those years ago."

Thomas tapped the paper with his finger

but made no effort to move it. "It was a long time ago," he said. "The wonderful thing about being relics like us is that as far as most of the people on the planet are concerned — and even folks here in town — that era is ancient history."

Leland nodded.

"Your father's solicitor was the firm of James, James, and Miller, correct?"

Leland shook his head in wonder. "I had forgotten that completely, but yes. He was always proud to be affiliated with one of the oldest firms in town."

"It was disbanded in the early seventies," Thomas said. "The James brothers were twins and died within days of each other in the early sixties. By the early seventies, Miller was seriously ill. There were no children interested in taking over the firm, so it died on the vine and was disbanded."

"Too bad," Leland said. "From what I knew of them, they were all good men."

"They were that," Thomas agreed.

"I can't imagine what they thought when my father disowned me, but he would have gone through them," Leland said. "He trusted them and wouldn't have used anyone else."

Thomas nodded. "That's what I thought, too. Ali told you about my going to the print shop to talk to your father?"

"Yes, she said you thought you had brought him around to thinking more favorably of me."

"I still do," Thomas said. "As I said, Kevin Miller died in the early seventies, but for years his widow kept his office just as he'd left it, complete with an antique partners' desk, leather-bound appointment books, a collection of ancient and very valuable fountain pens, blotting pads, law books, even a functioning radio console from the thirties. After Mrs. Miller died in the late nineties, she left the whole of her estate, including her long-dead husband's office, to the Bournemouth Historical Society. The first time someone from there ventured inside, she said she felt as though she had stepped into a time capsule, and she had. They dismantled the room, down to the paneling and wainscoting, and moved the whole kit and kaboodle to the museum, where it boasts a display room all its own."

"What does any of this have to do with my father?" Leland asked.

"I'm coming to that," Thomas said. "You see, I belong to the historical society. Linda spent years serving on the board of directors. So when the display opened, I was granted special permission to spend some time in the room on my own. I wasn't sure if this would be there, but I believe it offers firm proof that your father had changed his mind. As soon as I found it, I took the book to the office and copied the applicable page. This is it."

He paused for a moment and then pushed the piece of paper in Leland's direction.

As Leland unfolded it, Ali craned her neck to see what it was. It appeared to be a page taken from an old-fashioned oversize appointment book. The eight-by-eleven copy covered only part of the page, starting at eleven A.M. Each entry showed a name and a notation of purpose. Property sale; property dispute. The third entry showed the name Jonah Brooks. Next to the name was a simple two-word notation: Revise will.

"That was from Stewart James's appointment book for 1954," Thomas explained. "That page is from October 13, three days after your father died. A month earlier, on September 16, weeks after you left town, there's another listing for Jonah Brooks with the same notation. I believe the first appointment was when he wrote you out of his will. I believe the second appointment, the one he died without keeping, was one in which he intended to disavow the first one."

The paper trembled in Leland's fingers. Tears glistened on his cheeks. He turned to Ali. "It's proof, isn't it."

"Circumstantial, perhaps," she said, "but telling nonetheless."

The barmaid came by to deliver their platters of steaming pasties. She looked at Leland's tearful face and saw the same expression mirrored in the face of the man across the table.

"Will that be all now, Thomas?" she asked solicitously, as though demonstrating a willingness to eject Ali and Leland if they were causing her regular customer any difficulty.

"That will be all, Patty," Thomas said quietly. "Thank you for asking."

22

Even before LeAnne went to bed, she had planned on sleeping in the next morning. She awakened at six-thirty to the sounds of her mother getting the boys fed and ready for school. Rather than rushing out of the room to help out, she simply lay there listening, both shocked and grateful that they didn't need her. Still, it hurt her feelings to think that, in her absence, Thad and Connor had learned to function quite well without her.

After Phyllis left to take the boys to school, LeAnne treated herself to a shower. Venturing into the kitchen in her robe, she poured a cup of coffee and then turned to the pile of unopened and unpaid bills that had accumulated on the kitchen counter, many of them stamped with FINAL NOTICE. There was no point in opening any of them. LeAnne had no money, wasn't working, and might not have a job to go back to. As she went to put the stack back down on the counter, a business card hidden among the larger envelopes slipped out and fluttered to the floor. On it was the name detective Richard Hernandez, along with a series of phone numbers. Scribbled on the back in Phyllis Rogers's handwriting were the words: "Contact him for help building a wheelchair ramp."

Suddenly furious, LeAnne flung the card in the trash. How dare he? she wondered. The guy who arrested Lance and sent him to that horrible place is interested in building a wheelchair ramp now that his leg is gone? No way in hell is he getting anywhere near my house. Besides, if I lose the house, who needs a damned wheelchair ramp? It was all too much. LeAnne was verging on tears when her phone rang. "Mom?" Lance said after she said hello.

Just hearing his voice was enough to jar LeAnne out of her momentary funk. Losing the house was nothing. Lance was hurt, and he may have lost a leg, but at least he was alive. He was awake and able to speak. The endless days of sitting at his bedside and wondering if he would awaken were over. "How are you?" she asked.

"The doctor was just here," Lance said. "They're planning to move me out of the burn unit and into a regular room later on today, maybe this afternoon."

You are better, LeAnne thought. You're not just saying it. "That's great," she said aloud. "Your brothers will be thrilled. They've been begging to come see you. Once you're in a regular room, they'll be able to do that. They've missed you terribly."

"It'll be good to see them," Lance said quietly. "I've missed them, too."

That had been an issue the whole time Lance was locked up. Thad and Connor had begged to see him, but Lance had absolutely forbidden it. He hadn't wanted them to see their big brother in his jail jumpsuit; hadn't wanted them to remember him like that. So how could it be okay for the boys to see him lying in a hospital bed, terribly injured and with an amputated leg? What kind of memories would that leave behind? LeAnne wondered. Lost in thought, she came back into the conversation with Lance asking, "Where did you get her?"

"Get who?"

"Sister Anselm. Where did you dig her up? I asked if she's a doctor or a nurse. She says she's a patient something. Advocate, I think is the word she used. That makes it sound like she should be on my side, but it's just the opposite. She just keeps hanging around and pestering me."

"Sister Anselm is there to look out for you, Lance," LeAnne said, "and we're lucky to have her. Knowing she would be there with you was the only reason I could come home last night. I never would have left if she hadn't been there in my place."

"She bothers me," Lance said. "A lot. When are you coming back?"

"As soon as Grandma gets back from driving the boys to school. I'll be there sometime between nine and ten. Is there anything you need?"

He seemed to consider for a long time before answering. "Do you remember my box of Transformers?" he asked.

LeAnne laughed. "Of course I remember your box of Transformers. How could I forget? You were totally addicted to them by the time you were four. I thought when you started with computers, you'd get over that fad, but you never did. The last time you caught Connor trying to play with them, you almost bit his head off. I saved them for you, and I put them up on the top shelf in my closet so he wouldn't be tempted again."

"Would you mind bringing them to the hospital?"

LeAnne blinked in surprise. "You're kidding, right? You're almost eighteen years old, you've spent the better part of the last year in jail, and for the last two weeks you've been in a hospital bed hovering on the verge of death, but now you want to play with your Transformers?"

"Just bring them," Lance insisted. "Please."

"All right," she agreed. "I will."

The back door opened. Phyllis came in from the garage, reeking of cigarette smoke and accompanied by her dogs. Phyllis's smoking was the single bone of contention between LeAnne and her mother. Phyllis wouldn't quit, and LeAnne wouldn't allow cigarettes inside her house. They had hammered out an agreement that Phyllis would smoke out-of-doors or in her car and not around the children. That meant every time she came back into the house, a cloud of smoke came with her.

The two dogs, both pugs, took one look at LeAnne and began barking their heads off. "Sorry to have them barking at you in your own house," Phyllis apologized.

"Why shouldn't they?" LeAnne asked, leaning down to pet them. They sounded fierce but they weren't. "They've hardly seen me the whole time they've been here.

If they didn't bark, they wouldn't be doing their jobs."

"How did you sleep?"

"Like a log," LeAnne answered, stuffing the stack of unpaid bills into the pocket of her robe.

"Did you have breakfast?"

"Not yet."

"While you get dressed, I'll make scrambled eggs and toast."

"Thanks, Mom," LeAnne said. She took her coffee cup into the bedroom and set it on the dresser. Then she went into the closet and retrieved the brightly colored cloth bag that held the Transformers. Originally, the briefcase-shaped bag had contained a collection of wooden tracks and a dozen or so little multicolored train cars that hitched together with magnets. Along with cars and tracks, the set had boasted a supply of bridges, buildings, tiny houses, and trees that could be set up beside the tracks. Now all those wooden pieces were nothing but a distant memory. At first, Lance had been enchanted with the train set, but once Transformers appeared on the scene, he lost interest completely. The wooden pieces had disappeared long ago; all that remained was the cloth bag.

Setting it on the bed, LeAnne unzipped it

and looked at the collection of brightly colored plastic toys that looked like one thing but could be unfolded and turned into something else entirely. They had come to Lance over the years as gifts from friends and family. He had treasured them then and, surprisingly enough, evidently still did. LeAnne remembered that when she was a girl, she had adored her Barbie dolls, but by the time she was eighteen, she was quite sure, she had outgrown them. How could Lance still find these strange pieces of plastic so fascinating? Shaking her head, LeAnne zipped the bag shut and put it next to her purse.

Out in the kitchen, Phyllis had made a sumptuous breakfast: bacon and eggs, toast and jam and orange juice. Seeing the food on the table made LeAnne feel guilty because she knew that the money for all the groceries in the house had come out of her mother's pocket. When LeAnne sat down at her place and picked up her napkin, she discovered a pair of twenty-dollar bills tucked under the napkin. Seeing the money was too much, and she burst into tears.

"What are you crying about?" Phyllis demanded.

"I'm sorry you're having to be here. I'm sorry you're having to use your own money to buy food for my kids. I'm sorry things are so bad."

"Oh, honey," Phyllis said, "don't worry about it. You told me last night that Lance is getting better. That's what matters, so quit your crying and eat your breakfast."

"You shouldn't have to give me money."

"Would you have any money in your purse if I didn't?"

"Well, no, but . . ."

"Of course I should, then," Phyllis replied. "Helping out is what mothers do. Besides, if you don't give that old rust bucket of yours a drink of gasoline occasionally, it's going to stop cold and leave you stranded."

LeAnne left right after breakfast. When she stopped for gas, it took all of her mother's forty dollars to not quite fill the tank. She made the fifty-plus-mile drive from San Leandro to Austin in just over an hour. It was a bit before ten when LeAnne pulled into the hospital garage. She felt silly dragging the bag of Transformers out of the trunk and carrying them toward the building entrance. People brought toys to hospitals all the time, but not usually for kids whose voices had changed and whose chins were starting to sprout whiskers.

LeAnne found Sister Anselm in the burn unit waiting room. "The physical therapist is in there with him," the nun explained. "He was quite firm about not wanting an audience."

LeAnne dropped into a nearby chair. "I'll wait, too," she said.

Sister Anselm was quiet for such a long time that LeAnne stole a glance at her to see if the woman had fallen asleep. She appeared to be staring off into space.

"I have something to show you," Sister Anselm said at last. "I had planned on dropping the items back on the floor the way Lance left them, but it's quiet here right now, and I need you to know what's happening."

"Is it something about Lance?" LeAnne asked anxiously. "Is the other leg infected?"

"No," Sister Anselm said. "It's this." She reached into her pocket and pulled out the three wrinkled scraps of paper: the envelope, the note, and the photo.

LeAnne looked at them one by one. "What is this?" she asked at last. "I mean, I know it's a picture of Connor and my mom, but who took it, and what does the note mean?"

"Your whole family is being threatened," Sister Anselm said grimly. "Most likely by the same people who attacked Lance and who killed Mr. Dunn. They might even be responsible for the death of Lance's teacher months ago."

LeAnne blanched. "Mr. Jackson? Are you serious?"

"Completely."

"Did you call the police?"

"No," Sister Anselm said. "I couldn't do that. Lance expressly forbade it."

"Why?"

"You'll have to ask him. The only reason I could show these to you was because he threw them on the floor. Police officers don't need warrants to search through garbage, and I think my confidentiality requirements can stretch that far, too."

"What should I do?"

"Talk to him about it. Get him to agree to let you go to the police."

"This is serious. Why would he not want to tell the cops?"

"You have to ask him," Sister Anselm insisted. "If he won't talk to the police, you can. You're his mother; your hands aren't tied. I'm his patient advocate; mine are."

"I should tell him I found these on the floor?"

"That would probably be best," Sister Anselm conceded. "I was afraid a nurse or orderly might come in and pick them up before you had a chance to find them."

"How did the note and the photo get here in the first place?"

"They came with a bouquet of flowers that arrived in the middle of the night. Other than the card in your hand, there was nothing to tell us where they came from. Fortunately, Lance tossed those out, too. There was a bug in them."

"What kind?" LeAnne asked. "A ladybug? A bee?"

"An electronic listening device," Sister Anselm said. "Something that would have allowed someone access to everything that was said in Lance's hospital room."

"Somebody bugged his room? They're spying on him? This is nuts."

"It may be nuts," Sister Anselm agreed, "but I urge you to regard it as a serious threat to your family."

"I do," LeAnne said, plucking her phone out of her purse. "I'm going to call the cops right now."

"No, please," Sister Anselm said. "Talk to Lance first. See what he has to say."

At that moment Aurelia Rojas, the physical therapist, exited Lance's room. "It's only day two, but your son did very well, Mrs. Tucker," she said on the way past. "Very well indeed." LeAnne was on her feet and headed into the room before the therapist made it as far as the nurses' station. Sister Anselm followed on her heels.

Halfway to the bed, LeAnne put down what she was carrying — her purse and the Transformers bag — and pretended to pick up something she'd found on the floor. She came toward Lance, uncrumpling the papers. "What are these?" she asked. "Did someone send you something?"

Seeing the scraps of paper in her hand, Lance grimaced. "It's nothing," he said quickly. "Just a joke one of the guys sent me."

"It doesn't sound like a joke," LeAnne continued. "It sounds serious, and what is Connor's picture doing here? Tell me, what's going on?"

"I think you should tell your mother the truth," Sister Anselm said quietly. "Of all people, she has a right to know."

"Tell me!" LeAnne ordered. "What's this about?" She saw him struggle. Maybe if he hadn't just been through a physical therapy ordeal, he might have had the strength to resist.

At last he told her. "It's about GHOST," he said.

"Your software program?"

"Mr. Jackson and I were working on it

together. He was going to help me get a patent."

"If your program is what they want, give it to them," LeAnne said. "Surely your brother's safety is worth more than some stupid computer program."

"I can't just give it away for nothing, because it's not only mine," Lance said. "Mr. Jackson and I developed it together. It's going to be worth a lot of money, and half of it belongs to him. Well, to his family."

"If you can't give whoever it is what they want, then we have to call the police," LeAnne insisted. "They threatened Connor. They took a picture of him. Like it says in the note, these people know where we live."

"I'm telling you, the cops are involved in this thing," Lance argued.

"You don't know that for sure."

"I do. They're the ones who went after me like gangbusters for the server disruption. They're the ones who claim Mr. Jackson committed suicide. And now they're saying that Mr. Dunn died accidentally, but I don't believe any of it. He offered to help me, and the next thing he's dead, right?"

LeAnne nodded.

"We are not going to the cops," Lance insisted stubbornly, folding his arms across his chest. "And I'm not giving up GHOST. We were almost there before I got arrested. Mr. Jackson finished it and used it, too. He sent me a note through my lawyer during the trial. He said he got the last bugs out of it and that it worked perfectly. You've got to believe me, Mom. It's important."

"If you won't let me call the police," LeAnne said, "how do we protect Connor?"

"I think I know someone who would most likely be interested in giving you a hand," Sister Anselm suggested quietly.

Both Lance and LeAnne looked at her in surprise. "Who?" LeAnne asked.

"His name is Simpson," Sister Anselm said. "B. Simpson. He's a good friend of my bishop. He's also the man who suggested that I should come here to help out."

"You mean B. Simpson of High Noon Enterprises?" Lance asked. "That B. Simpson?"

Sister Anselm nodded.

"Wait," LeAnne said. "I remember that name. He was the computer guy who testified against you during the trial, remember?"

Lance didn't acknowledge his mother's question. He was staring at Sister Anselm with the same kind of astonishment and wonder LeAnne had seen when he was four

years old and opening the very first Transformers box that he'd found under the tree
on Christmas morning. "Are you saying
B. Simpson knows about me and my program?"

Sister Anselm nodded. "He heard what
had happened, and he was concerned that
if one attempt had been made on your life,
there might be another. That's why he asked
me to come look after you and bring this
along." She reached into her pocket and
pulled out the Taser. LeAnne had seen it
before, but Lance's eyes widened even
more.

"It sounds to me as though you've been
here under false pretenses all this time,"
LeAnne said, whirling to face the nun.
"You've been acting like you're all concerned about Lance when you've really
been trolling for this Simpson guy. I'm going straight downstairs to file an official
complaint with the hospital. I'll demand
that they bar you from coming back or having anything more to do with my son or
with me."

"Mom, don't," Lance said.

"Don't?" LeAnne demanded. "Didn't you
hear what she just said? She's working for
someone else. She doesn't give a damn
about you."

"B. Simpson is one of the best cyber security guys on the planet," Lance said. "He's also one of the world's best hackers. He can help us."

"You don't want me to call the police, but you think some guy who sent this pretend nun to spy on you and on me is more trustworthy than the cops?" Beside herself, LeAnne was practically screeching. "I've never heard of anything so ridiculous!"

Totally focused on each other, Sister Anselm and Lance seemed to have tuned LeAnne out.

"If I can reach Mr. Simpson," Sister Anselm said, "do I have your permission to speak freely?"

"Yes," said Lance. "Please."

"No," LeAnne said. "Absolutely not."

"Very well," Sister Anselm said. "I'll see what I can do."

"You won't," LeAnne said. "You'll do no such thing!"

"I'm sorry, Mrs. Tucker," Sister Anselm said. "Lance is my patient and my primary responsibility. What he says goes."

She left the room with LeAnne still sputtering, "I can't believe it. Why are you doing this!"

"Of all the people involved in cyber security, B. Simpson is the one guy who will know what GHOST is worth. Maybe he'll even want to buy it," Lance said.

"He's probably underhanded enough that he's going to try to trick you out of it," LeAnne grumbled. "For all we know, he's the one who's targeting Connor. What are you thinking?"

"Look at me, Mom. I'm lying on my back. I've got one leg, a criminal record, no high school diploma, no college degree, and no prospects. If B. Simpson is interested in GHOST, this might be my one opportunity to make a life for all of us: for you and the boys, for me, and even for Grandma."

"Right," LeAnne said sarcastically, dropping the bag of Transformers on the bed beside him. "Now you're all hot to talk about your future? I thought all you wanted to do was play with your damned Transformers!"

Furious, she stalked from the room. She caught up with Sister Anselm halfway across the waiting room, grabbing the nun's arm and pulling her to a stop. "How dare you interfere in our lives this way? Is that why you had me return the check that man tried to give me? Were you just looking out for this B. guy friend of yours?"

"I believe that your son and his teacher succeeded in creating something that has the potential to be very valuable. Your accepting that check might have put Lance in a difficult position and left him unable to negotiate the best possible deal for himself and for Mr. Jackson's family, too. In other words, everything I said before is true: What I've been doing here has been and is looking out for Lance. Now, if you'll excuse me, I need to make a phone call."

LeAnne watched Sister Anselm walk away. Still furious, she returned to Lance's room, hoping to talk some sense into his head.

23

After the emotional beginning, the rest of the Pig and Whistle lunch was far more mundane. From Ali's point of view, it felt like eavesdropping on a class reunion sixty or so years after graduation. While Thomas and Leland talked about jobs and where and how they had lived and traveled, Ali concentrated on her pasty, which more than lived up to its advance billing. It was delectable and huge. Ali and Leland left the pub with leftover servings large enough for another meal.

"So?" Ali asked once they were safely in the car. "What do you think?"

"Thank you for talking me down out of my tree," Leland said. "I'm glad Thomas and I had a chance to spend some time together."

"What now?" Ali asked. "The weather report predicted sun breaks this afternoon. Since it's our last day here, is there anything else you'd like to do before we head back to London tomorrow? Maybe stop by Jordan's-by-the-Sea for a visit?" she added with a grin.

"No, thank you," he said at once. "I don't need any more time with the girls. One visit was more than enough for me. Since the weather is fine, though, there is one place I'd like to go: Stonehenge. It's only forty miles or so from here. When we were kids, my father used to take us there on the summer solstice to watch the sun come up through the stones. I'd like to go one last time."

Ali turned the key in the ignition and put the Jaguar in gear. "Do I need to put in the directions, or do you know the way?"

"I know the way," Leland said.

"When you say one last time, does that mean you won't be coming back for the reunion?"

"I don't think so," he said. "With Thomas's help, I believe I have the answers to the questions that have haunted me all this time. I always thought of my father as a fair man, and I never could reconcile that with his disowning me. I'm sure he did so in the heat of the moment, based on the mistaken assumption that I had betrayed my country. The DNA situation may yet provide definitive proof, but for my money, I believe Thomas's assertion is correct: that Father had reconsidered his first rash decision, and that's why Langston killed him — to prevent Father from keeping the appointment to change his will."

"Will you share any of what you've learned with Jeffrey?"

"Certainly not," Leland said. "I refuse to repay his and Charlie's kindness by passing along the unwelcome news that his grandfather was most likely a murderer."

For the next while they drove at a leisurely pace, through Hum, Ringwood, Fordingbridge, Downton, and Salisbury, with Leland recalling incidents from those long-ago summertime trips with his father and his brothers. Ali realized that was all a gift from Thomas Blackfield. At last Leland could remember the good times the family enjoyed without having long-ago memories colored by the hurt that came later. The drive to Stonehenge was more than a simple trip down memory lane; it was a way to recapture something that had seemed irretrievably lost.

By the time they arrived, a ray of sunlight slanting down through the clouds lit the circle of stone in bright relief against the winter-yellow grass. Astonished by the underground car park, Leland told of his father parking along the shoulder of the road next to open fields and letting his sons scramble ahead in their eagerness to get there. Leland was dismayed to learn that visitors were now forbidden to touch the massive ancient stones, especially the long flat ones fallen to the ground, ones that he and his brothers had clambered over in sheer joy. He led Ali to the spot in the very center of the circle where father and sons had stood to watch the sun come up over the horizon.

"Thank you," he said at last, turning back toward the car. "My father had lived through the Great War. He hoped there would never be another. I had forgotten what an innocent time it was back then, and today has given me back a measure of that."

Even though they had walked in mostly bright sun, they were chilled through by the time they returned to the car. On the trip back to Bournemouth, they stopped for tea at a shop in Salisbury, more to warm up than because they were hungry. Finished with tea, they were just getting back into the car when a text message came in over Leland's phone. "Here," he said, handing it to Ali. "It's from Mr. Simpson."

Leaving Zurich within the hour on a charter. Should be at BOH by six-thirty or so. It'll take an hour to refuel. If you and Leland are there by seven, we should be able to take off again at seven-thirty. We should be in Austin early tomorrow morning.

Ali read through the message twice, then glanced at her watch. In traffic, she estimated, they were at least an hour from the hotel. "What are the call letters for the Bournemouth airport?" she asked.

"I have no idea," Leland said. "Why?"

"Because it sounds like B. has chartered a plane, and we're on our way to Austin."

"To Austin," Leland echoed. "In Texas? What about our flight from London to Phoenix? Mr. Simpson already paid for that, didn't he?"

"It's on his frequent-flier account, so he'll either get the miles back or he won't." Ali turned the key in the ignition, put the Jaguar in gear, and hit the gas pedal. Hard. The drive back to Bournemouth was anything but leisurely. While she drove, Leland used his phone to look up the airport. BOH was indeed the official airport code for Bournemouth International.

"What's in Austin?" Leland asked eventually.

"A boy named Lance Tucker," Ali answered, realizing as she did that Leland had no background whatsoever on the situation in Texas. For the next few minutes, as they tore down the A338, she filled him in. Leland listened without comment until she'd finished.

"I'm sure," he said, "that chartering a jet for a transatlantic flight is a very costly proposition. Mr. Simpson must regard whatever's going on as very serious."

"My thoughts exactly."

They rode in silence for another few moments, then Leland laughed aloud.

"What's so funny?"

"The irony of the whole thing," he said. "The last time I left England, it was by working on board a tramp steamer. I left the country with the clothes on my back and all my worldly goods stuffed in a duffel bag. This time I'm leaving in luxury on board a private jet. That's the other good reason for not coming back. How could I possibly top this?"

"You can't," Ali agreed.

At the Highcliff, it took only fifteen minutes for them to pack up and go. They were at the airport with the car checked in and luggage in hand by the time B.'s jet landed on the tarmac. When the stairs came down, B. stepped off, followed by a flight attendant and two pilots. Ali left Leland with the luggage and ran to greet B. While a tanker truck began the refueling process, Ali led B. into the terminal. Although he was glad to see her, there was no denying the grim set to his jaw.

"What's going on?" she asked.

"Someone threatened Lance's family today, including his grandmother and his six-year-old brother," B. said. "Someone also attempted to plant a listening device in his hospital room. Sister Anselm was smart enough to locate the device and disable it.

"All along my strategy has been to keep High Noon's interest in Lance's work under the radar. Assuming that much of your phone information is somewhere in the public domain, being quiet about it is no longer necessary or even feasible. Our plan now is to go there tomorrow and talk to him. If he's amenable, I want to take High Noon's involvement with him public in the cyber security world. I'm convinced that GHOST is the reason he and his family are being targeted, and I want the world to know that they have some allies in that fight."

"What do I do?"

"If I need one, you're my media babe," B. said with a grin. "We'll make you the public face of High Noon Enterprises. I want the bad guys to know that whatever it is they want from Lance Tucker, they'll have to come through us to get it."

"Am I your fianceé or your lightning rod?"

"A little of both?"

They walked into the airport lounge, where, after B. said hello to Leland, they took seats together on a sofa.

"When did all this happen?" Ali asked. "How do you know about it?"

"The threat was issued overnight. Sister Anselm called me at about ten-thirty Texas time this morning, right after Lance finally gave her permission to talk to me about it. I started figuring out a way to get us there, including arranging this charter. This aircraft, a Legacy, belongs to one of my best customers. It happened to be on the ground in Zurich and ready to go. I was on my way here in under an hour."

Ali thought about that, then said, "If Lance's family is being threatened, why call you for help? Why not go to the police?"

"Sister Anselm is the one who called, but she did so at Lance's behest. His mother wanted to call the cops, something Lance adamantly opposed. Sister Anselm negotiated a mother/son peace treaty and they agreed to call both — local law enforcement and me. Sister Anselm asked me to speak to Lance's mother, LeAnne, to give her my read on the situation. She almost hung up on me because she holds me partly responsible for Lance going to jail in the first place. Even though they're calling the cops, I'm not sure how much good it will do."

"Why?"

"Because I'm not sure law enforcement will take the idea of the threat seriously. The note doesn't come right out and say, 'I'm going to harm your family.' It's more subtle than that. Sister Anselm sent me a copy. Take a look."

Switching on his phone, B. selected an item in his photo gallery and passed the device to Ali. On the screen was a photo of the printed note.

"The first picture is the note that accompanied the bouquet of bugged flowers. The next one is a picture of Connor, Lance's little brother, getting into his grandmother's car. That one was taken in front of the family home in San Leandro. The last one is LeAnne's mother."

"I see what you mean," Ali said. "What's written here — 'We know where they live'

— doesn't constitute an actual threat."

"Especially if the local cop shop is invested in the official versions of the other events we believe are connected to this case: Lowell Dunn's 'accidental' fire or Everett Jackson's 'accidental' overdose."

"To say nothing of Lance's 'self-inflicted' burns," Ali added.

"The note uses the word 'we.' That's plural, that implies more than one person is involved. The targets are plural, too: 'they.' I suggested to LeAnne that she might want to pull Lance's brothers out of school and bring them and their grandmother to Austin with her. If someone truly is targeting the whole family, they'll be harder to find if they're not at home and following their usual routines."

"To say nothing of having three additional people — Leland, you, and I — looking out for them," Ali surmised. "Did you mention to anyone there that we're coming?"

"No. You know that, and I know that," B. said, "but nobody else does, including Sister Anselm. As far as the rest of the world is concerned, you and Leland are scheduled to be in the UK until your return flight on Sunday afternoon. I'm not supposed to leave Zurich until two days after that. Those are the reservations listed on the calendar in your phone. So our arrival in Austin should come as an unwelcome surprise to any number of people. That's why I sent the message on Leland's phone instead of yours."

One of the pilots stopped by. "Okay," he said. "Refueling's complete and luggage and catering have been loaded. All I need now is to check your IDs." As they followed the pilot out the door, Ali grabbed one last piece of luggage, a hanging bag.

"What's that?" B. asked.

"It happens to be my wedding dress," she told him. "It's riding in the cabin with me, and no, you can't see it."

"Wouldn't think of asking," B. said. "Not on a bet."

On board the plane, they settled into cushy leather seats.

"How long is this going to take again?" Ali asked.

"The transatlantic part takes six hours," B. explained. "We'll land in Reykjavík for fuel and again in White Plains to clear customs. That could take as much as several hours, less if we're lucky. We'll be chasing time zones all the way. With the six-hour difference between here and Austin, we could be on the ground in Texas as early as midnight."

By half past seven, the plane was airborne. Once they hit cruising altitude, the flight attendant came around with offers of food and drink. Rather than accepting one of the proffered sandwiches, Leland charmed the woman by dining on his own hand-carried leftover pasty.

"How was your trip home?" B. asked Leland.

"Not altogether what I expected," Leland replied. "I've learned more about my family history than I cared to know, but I very much appreciate your efforts on my behalf."

For the first leg of the trip, that was what they discussed — Ali and Leland's sojourn in Bournemouth. After an hour, though, Leland excused himself to settle down on the couch with the seat belt fastened around him and a blanket spread over him and leaving Ali and B. facing each other across a polished foldout table. "Ready for a major debriefing?" B. asked.

Ali nodded.

"Take a look at this," he said, opening his computer and turning the screen in her direction. The photo was one of an older gentleman whose face seemed vaguely familiar, although she couldn't place him.

"Who's that?" she asked.

"His name is Trevor Fullerton."

"Fullerton? Like the guy in the Volvo?"

"The very same," B. said with a nod. "The guys who ran you off the road are Trevor's nephews. Once we had their names, thanks to Marjorie Elkins, it wasn't difficult for Stuart to access their bank records. Both of them had wire transfers in the amount of two hundred pounds come in yesterday afternoon. The transfers led back to their uncle Trevor."

"Sounds like a generous sort of uncle to have," Ali said.

"Yes," B. said, "but the story gets better. Once Stuart had Trevor's name, he upped his game and found out several telling details. It turns out Trevor lives in New York City. According to his income tax records, he occasionally does fieldwork for UTI."

"You shouldn't have access to those records," Ali pointed out.

"Granted," B. agreed. "But Trevor shouldn't have used his nephews to threaten you. In Stuart's book, that made him fair game."

"Running me off the road was worth four hundred pounds?"

"Not running you off the road; cloning your phone. I'm convinced you weren't the real target; High Noon is. I suspect UTI views me as their new branch's most likely competitor. They're probably hoping to backtrack on communications between us to locate High Noon's servers. The Fullerton boys aren't going to have much time to enjoy their ill-gotten gains. I believe several anonymous tips have already been called in to the Oxford Police Department. They may not have Stuart Ramey on their side, but they'll be able to connect the dots."

"What about UTI?"

"They're lobbying to land Lance Tucker and GHOST for their team. That's why they tried to give money to Lance's mother a couple of days ago: to get her to make sure Lance hooks up with them rather than anyone else, especially me. But that's not going to happen. When it comes to recruiting Lance Tucker, I intend to be very persuasive. As in: Have checkbook, will travel."

"But if UTI wants Lance to work for them, why would they try to knock him off?" Ali asked. "Why threaten to harm his family?"

"I don't think UTI has anything to do with the threats," B. replied. "As far as they're concerned, Lance Tucker is a commodity. They want him for the work he's already done and for whatever work he might do in the future. The threat came from some other players in this game that we have yet to identify. Once we find them, I'm guessing they'll prove to be the ones responsible for the attack on Lance, and maybe on Lowell Dunn and Everett Jackson."

"You're thinking those two deaths are homicides, even though law enforcement says otherwise?"

"I do," B. said. "With a killer savvy enough to make sure they don't look like homicides."

"How do we find this other team?"

"For the next several hours of this flight, you and I are going to use my computer and iPad and the onboard Wi-Fi to create a comprehensive list of every name associated with all of these supposedly separate incidents."

"Starting when?"

"Starting at the beginning — with UTI's tagging project and with Lance's takedown of the school district's server. That's what brought him to my attention. That may be where UTI's interest started and what put our unknown assailants into the mix as well. Once we've created our list, we'll turn it over to Stuart and have him go to work on it. He'll toss our collection of names into a cyber soup and run them through several levels of data-mining and relational programs and see what comes out the other end. If there are connections to be made, I have every confidence he'll make them."

"Aren't you worried about someone being able to tap into our search history and know what we're up to?"

"Not at all," B. replied. "Not on this plane, anyway. I set up the security system for this aircraft myself."

"What exactly are we going to do with all this accumulated info? By the time Stuart finishes running it through his blender, I'm guessing it won't be entirely aboveboard."

"We'll do the same thing we did in Oxford," B. answered. "We'll help local law enforcement along with a few carefully placed anonymous tips."

They spent the next three hours working that way, with B. calling up articles from which Ali compiled a comprehensive list of names that she loaded onto the thumb drive. They looked for anything related to Lance Tucker, Lowell Dunn, Everett Jackson, and Marvin Cotton. It turned out Marvin Cotton's supposedly sealed and expunged juvenile record wasn't at all difficult to find if you knew where to look. At age sixteen, he had been convicted of setting fire to a barn in which three horses had perished.

"That's interesting," B. said after reading that. "You know what they say about arsonists."

"What?"

"Once a firebug, always a firebug. Which gives us something else for Stuart to go looking for: whether Marvin Cotton and Lowell Dunn had any run-ins while they were both working at the detention center."

An e-mail alert sounded. Ali had been working on B.'s computer, and a partial message flashed across the upper-right corner of her screen. "You just got an e-mail from Sister Anselm," she told him. "Do you want me to read it to you?"

"Sure."

Ali read the message:

LeAnne Tucker just called. Her mother's gone missing from the house in San Leandro. The local police say that since the mother is an adult, she can't be declared missing, nor will they do anything to investigate the incident until 48 hours have elapsed. Please advise.

Ali felt her heartbeat speed up. "It's started, hasn't it?"

"Looks that way," B. said. "Do you happen to have any new photos on your phone?"

"I took a few at Stonehenge earlier today. Why?"

"We'll encrypt our list of names and upload it to one of those. You keep working on the list. I'll get back to Sister Anselm and tell her to be on full alert. If somebody has already grabbed the grandma, the ransom demand to Lance is going to come in sooner than later."

"Sooner than we'll be able to get there?" Ali asked.

"I hope not," B. said grimly.

While B. used his iPad to send off a series of purposeful texts, Ali went back to surfing the net but it seemed too much like empty-headed busywork. It reminded her of elementary school teachers asking kids to take whatever words they had missed on a spelling test and rewrite them correctly ten times on a piece of paper. Phyllis Rogers had already gone missing. What was the point of gathering all this information? What could Stuart Ramey, sitting at his computer terminal in Cottonwood, Arizona, possibly do with it to keep something terrible from happening to the poor woman?

Then, remembering what Stuart and B. and Leland had managed to do while she had been imprisoned in the trunk of a speeding vehicle, Ali gave herself a kick in the pants and threw herself into the task at hand. As the plane plunged ever westward through the night, this was all they could do.

As Ali worked through the articles, many from the *San Leandro Lariat* and some she had already seen, Ali noticed that, like small-town papers everywhere, the *Lariat* was big on publishing names: School events, community events, board meetings, and church events all came with full listings of attendees.

As the aircraft began its descent into Reykjavík, an item about that year's homecoming celebration caught Ali's eye. San Leandro High's homecoming king and queen that fall were listed as Andrew Garfield and Jillian Sosa. Ali remembered seeing those names listed together in another article. It took a while for her to track it down, but at last she did. In addition to being homecoming royalty, Andrew Garfield and Jillian Sosa had been co-captains of the team that had walked away with yet another Longhorn computing trophy.

"That's interesting," she muttered.

"What?" B. asked.

"You were a nerd in high school," she said.

"Did anybody ever nominate you as potential royalty for a homecoming dance?"

"Are you kidding?" B. said. "I never got invited to a homecoming dance, to say nothing of being elected royalty."

"Andrew Garfield and Jillian Sosa, the kids who became co-captains of the computer science club after Lance left, not only won the competition, they also were voted king and queen at homecoming."

"I guess times have changed," B. said.

A bell chimed signaling their descent. Ali looked away from the computer screen and rubbed her eyes. "I'm done," she said. "I can't do any more. At least not tonight. Is there anything you want me to add before I encrypt and punch Send?"

"Yes," he said. "Here is a list of phone numbers."

Ali typed them in as he read them off.

"Whose phones are those?" Ali asked. "And what's Stu supposed to do with them once he gets them?"

"That's every phone connected to the Tucker family," B. explained, "including the landline in Lance's current hospital room. Tell Stu I want a tap on every one of them ASAP."

"These are warrantless wiretaps, you know," Ali pointed out. "That means you're coloring outside the lines again."

"Yes, I am," B. agreed. "And I hope to God it works."

24

Angered by what LeAnne saw as Sister Anselm's unwarranted interference, she had stormed back into Lance's room to argue her case. He was lying on the bed amid a scatter of brightly colored transformers and holding one, much smaller than the others, in his hand. "Did you call Grandma?" he asked.

LeAnne recognized it as a teenage ploy of changing the subject. If they talked about LeAnne not calling her mother, then they wouldn't be talking about Lance's opposition to calling the cops.

"I need to talk to her about this in person," LeAnne said. "If I call her up and tell her over the phone that someone may be after Thad or Connor, she'll freak out. I'm going to drive back home and talk to her about it."

"But not to the cops, right?" Lance said.

"Look," LeAnne said, "I agreed to let

Sister Anselm call that High Noon guy. How about if you meet me halfway and let me talk to the cops in San Leandro? Maybe they can put some extra cars in our neighborhood and keep an eye on things."

"No," Lance said.

"Why are you being so stubborn?" she asked. "The cops are supposed to be on our side."

"That's easy for you to say," he said quietly. "You haven't spent the past six months in jail."

LeAnne's phone rang while the nurse was in changing the bandages. Watching the process was so painful that it left LeAnne almost sick to her stomach. When her phone rang with a blocked call, she used the interruption as an excuse to flee the room before she answered.

"Mrs. Tucker?"

"Who's this?"

"B. Simpson with High Noon Enterprises. Sister Anselm gave me your number."

"I don't want to talk to you," she said, poised to hang up. "You're one of the people who helped send my son to prison."

"Wait, Mrs. Tucker," he begged. "Please hear me out. The San Leandro school district is one of my company's customers. When the server disruption happened, it was my job to track down the source, and that led back to your son. So you're right, my company provided some of the evidence used against him, but we're not responsible for the high-handed way the local prosecutor used it. Your son is a bright young man. While my investigators and I were dealing with the case against him, I had the opportunity to see samples of Lance's code writing, and they are nothing short of brilliant. I understand that when he received threats against your family, Lance requested that Sister Anselm contact me and ask for my help. I'm more than happy to give it."

"I can't understand why he thinks you'll be more help to him than the cops will," LeAnne grumbled.

"I don't understand it, either," B. agreed. "With a threat of this kind, you need feet on the ground to counter the bad guys. That means you have to have the local police jurisdictions in your corner."

"What if they won't agree to help?" LeAnne asked. "What happens then?"

"We'll deal with it," B. said. "Until they do, I hope you'll consider bringing the boys and their grandmother to Austin with you. If whoever is targeting you is San Leandro–based, it'll be more difficult for them to succeed if they're dealing with a moving target in a situation where their intended victims are somewhere other than at home, going through very predictable routines."

In spite of herself, LeAnne burst out laughing. "Bring them to Austin?" she said. "Are you serious? I don't know what planet you live on, Mr. Simpson, but I was barely keeping a roof over my children's heads before all this happened. Now with Lance in the hospital and me not working, you expect me to bring the whole family, including my mother's two dogs, to Austin? Where are they supposed to sleep — in my car in the hospital parking garage?"

"I already told you, Mrs. Tucker, I'm prepared to help in whatever way seems necessary. If you would like, have Sister Anselm call over to the Omni and add another room or two to her reservation."

LeAnne thought about the check Sister Anselm had handed back, insisting that there was more money out there to be had. Was this the same thing? "How do I know I can trust you?" she asked.

"You don't," B. conceded, "but actions speak louder than words. Let me show you instead of telling you."

Forty-five minutes later, LeAnne was in her Taurus, headed north on I-35, and cursing herself for letting B. Simpson convince her that he was a good guy. Still, the man had given her the impetus to go against Lance's wishes. After all, nothing in the supposedly threatening note said specifically that the police were not to be notified. Her intention as she approached the second San Leandro exit was that she'd stop by the San Leandro police headquarters and let them know what was going on. As she neared the turnoff, however, she noticed that the energy provided by her mother's breakfast had diminished. Knowing she needed to eat, she changed her mind and stayed on the freeway for one more exit. It would be cheaper to make a lunch at home than it would be to eat at a fast-food joint along the way.

At the house LeAnne found her mother's car was parked in the driveway, and the pugs, Duke and Duchess, were barking like crazy inside the house. When she let herself into the kitchen, she noticed her mother's purse on the counter. The dogs, locked behind a baby gate in the dining room, let loose with another round of racket. "Quiet, you two," LeAnne ordered, then she called out, "Mom, I'm home."

There was no answer.

She ventured as far as the dining room door and opened the gate, allowing the dogs into the kitchen. Just inside the dining room, she almost stepped in a mess that one of the dogs had left on the floor. LeAnne rounded on them. "You bad dogs," she exclaimed. "What have you done!"

Knowing they were both in trouble for what one of them had done, the dogs shut up at once. That was when LeAnne noticed how quiet the house was. Her mother was more than slightly hard of hearing and always had the radio blaring out country music at full volume from one end of the house to the other. There was no music playing.

"Mom," LeAnne called again. She went back to the kitchen and checked Phyllis's purse. Her phone was there, tucked in the outside pocket. So were her car keys. Wherever LeAnne's mother had gone, she was most likely on foot.

Grumbling under her breath, LeAnne armed herself with a fistful of paper towels and returned to the dining room to clean up the mess while the dogs watched her warily from the sidelines. It turned out that pile wasn't the only dog-related problem in the house. In the living room, she found the chewed remains of her beloved jade plant. Grown from leaves from her grandmother's plant, it was the only potted plant of any kind that LeAnne Tucker had managed to keep alive, and she had carefully moved it from Phoenix to Austin when she and the boys left Arizona. Now the plant's stem stood utterly denuded while remains of the chewed leaves lay scattered around the room. "You bad, bad dogs!" she screeched. "Bad, bad, bad!"

Duke and Duchess slunk away together. It was only while LeAnne was cleaning up the second disaster that she began to worry. She remembered her mother telling her that Duke, a rescue, was afflicted with a serious case of separation anxiety; that was why she had brought Duke and Duchess along rather than leaving them in a kennel or with a dog sitter. It was also why the dogs rode in the car with Phyllis when she drove back and forth to the hospital from San Leandro.

If Phyllis had been gone long enough for the two dogs, or even one of them, to get into this amount of mischief, she must have been out of the house for some time. So where was she? What had become of her?

By the time LeAnne had cleaned up the living room, she was no longer thinking about eating a sandwich. She located the dogs' leashes, put them on, and took them out for a walk. Then she loaded the dogs into the Taurus and spent half an hour driving up and down the streets of the neighbor-hood.

When there was no sign of her mother anywhere, she went back to the house, where she pulled her mother's phone out of her purse. There were no clues. The last out-going call on Phyllis's phone was to LeAnne as was the last incoming call. Even more worried, LeAnne phoned the high school and had them call Thad to the office to speak with her, but he was no help, and neither was Connor. Neither of the boys could shed any light on their grandmother's plans or whereabouts.

LeAnne's next call was 911, where the emergency operator was less than helpful. How old was her mother? Seventy-two. Was she in good health? Yes. Did she have any mental deficits? No. Had LeAnne checked with local hospitals to see if she might have been taken to an emergency room and admitted as a patient? No. Right now what she wanted to do was place a missing persons report.

"That's not possible," the operator told her. "You've already told me that your mother is an adult in good mental health. The San Leandro Police Department doesn't accept missing persons reports until after an adult has been out of contact for at

368

least forty-eight hours. You'll need to call back then."

Fighting off panic, LeAnne called all five hospitals in San Leandro. No dice. It was only then, almost three hours after arriving home to find her mother missing, that LeAnne Tucker broke down and called Sister Anselm.

"The cops won't even talk to me about this," she sobbed into the phone. "The emergency dispatcher said it's too soon to try calling them in, so what do I do in the meantime? If this is related to that threat, what are we supposed to do about it if the police won't lift a hand? The card said whoever it was would be in touch. Has anyone tried to contact Lance?"

"Not that I know of," Sister Anselm said. "At least I haven't seen anyone come through here. Let me get in touch with Mr. Simpson and see if he has any suggestions. I'll get right back to you."

While she waited for Sister Anselm to call back, LeAnne took the dogs and went to collect Connor and Thad from school. Thad was annoyed because he didn't want to miss basketball practice while Connor was overjoyed to ride in the backseat with Duke and Duchess. Back at the house, Thad slammed off into his bedroom, while Connor parked himself and the dogs in the family room to watch *Scooby-Doo!*. When Sister Anselm called, seemingly an eternity later, LeAnne took the call in her bedroom.

"Sorry," Sister Anselm said. "For some reason, Mr. Simpson's phone went to straight to voice mail. There's at least a seven-hour time difference between here and Zurich, so he may have turned off his phone overnight. I sent him an e-mail and a text. I'll get back to you as soon as I hear anything." There was a pause. "Wait. I'm hearing from him now."

LeAnne waited. Eventually, Sister Anselm came back on the line. "He can't use his phone right now, but he'll send you a text."

LeAnne sat on the edge of her bed, feeling helpless and clinging to her phone like a lifeline. Soon the text came in.

Sister Anselm says your mother is missing and that the 911 operator wouldn't take the report. Did you speak to anyone about the earlier threat?

LeAnne stared at the screen and flushed with guilty embarrassment before she replied, fumbling with clumsy fingers on the screen.

No. I wanted to have a sandwich before I tried talking to them. That's when I discovered Mom was gone. I got both boys from school. They're here with me. I don't know what to do.

The reply from B. Simpson was almost instantaneous. He was obviously far better at texting than she was.

Is there any sign of a break-in?

No.

Do you have any contacts with the San Leandro Police Department — anyone you could turn to without going through the official dispatch line?

LeAnne thought about that. At last she remembered the business card that had been hidden in among her bills. Detective Richard Hernandez.

Maybe. I'll go check.

Slipping the phone in her pocket, she hurried out to the kitchen. Naturally, her mother had emptied the trash between the time LeAnne had thrown out the business card and the time she had disappeared.

LeAnne went out through the back door and opened the garbage bin. She had to dig past the doggy-bomb layer before she found that morning's trash.

Moments later, she replied:

Got it. Name and phone numbers. Detective Richard Hernandez. But why would he help me? He's the guy who arrested Lance originally.

Again, B. Simpson responded within seconds.

For the same reason I'm helping. Maybe we both think Lance got hosed. Call him, and send me his numbers. I can't call him right now, but I'll be in touch with both of you in an hour or so, once I clear up a few things.

LeAnne sent the detective's three listed numbers. Then she studied the card again. It was late in the day. It was possible the detective was at work, but it seemed more likely that he'd be at home. Squaring her shoulders, she dialed the cell phone number for the detective Phyllis Rogers had called "a nice man."

As the phone started ringing, LeAnne crossed her fingers and hoped.

"Detective Hernandez," he answered.

"I don't know if you remember me," she began. "I'm LeAnne Tucker."

"Lance's mother," he said.

"Yes," she breathed.

"Is something wrong?" the detective asked. "He hasn't taken a turn for the worse, has he?"

"It's something else," she said, feeling her throat constrict. "It's about my mother. She's missing."

"The nice woman who's been bringing Thad to practice?"

Obviously, "nice" was the operant word here.

"Yes," LeAnne said. "That's the one."

"Have you called it in?"

"I tried to, but the person I talked to said no one would take a report because Mom's only been gone a couple of hours. The thing is, she came here to look after my boys, and she never would have missed picking them up after school. She wouldn't have gone off and left her dogs behind, either. We believe that a threat to our family was sent to Lance's room at the hospital in Austin last night. This situation may be related to that."

"What kind of threat?"

"Someone sent Lance a bouquet of flowers without saying who sent them. In the envelope, there was a photo of my mother and of my younger son, Connor, Lance's little brother. They were getting into my mom's car, and the photo was taken on our street here in San Leandro. The message that came with it said, 'We know where they live.' "

"Did you mention any of that to the dispatcher?"

"I tried, but she didn't exactly listen."

"I'll listen," Richard Hernandez said. "I'll be right there."

"Do you need the address?"

"No," he said. "I remember where you live. I've been there before, remember?"

The phone call ended. LeAnne was standing with the phone in one hand and the business card in the other when Connor came into the kitchen. "I'm hungry," he said. "When's dinner?"

She rummaged through the fridge, found bread, butter, and cheese, and whipped out a stack of grilled cheese sandwiches. Connor and Thad were hunched over the table eating when the doorbell rang.

LeAnne had a moment of déjà vu. There was that other time she had opened the front door to find Detective Richard Hernandez standing on her front porch, holding up his badge and ID. That had been the worst day of her life. She had stood in stricken silence as Lance had been handcuffed and hustled into the back of a waiting patrol car.

Taking a deep breath, she pushed the memory aside and swung the door open. This time when she saw Detective Hernandez standing there, she was beyond grateful.

"Any sign of your mother?" he asked.

LeAnne shook her head. "Not yet."

"May I come in?"

"Please," she said. "And thank you for coming."

25

It was snowing when they got to White Plains, not so much that they couldn't leave after clearing customs and refueling, but enough that the aircraft had to be de-iced before takeoff. In the airport lounge, Ali overheard someone tell the pilot that it was a good thing they were scheduled to fly out soon, because the overnight snow was expected to turn into a blizzard by morning.

For most of the time they were on the ground, B. was on his phone. Ali left her phone turned off and in her purse. Her mother would be provoked by her daughter's long silence, but with her cloned phone out there somewhere, that seemed to be the best idea.

"Okay," B. said when they'd reboarded the plane and were waiting for the de-icing. "We'll be flying directly to San Leandro rather than Austin."

"Still no word on the missing grandma?" Ali asked.

"Not so far," B. said. "I've been on the phone with Detective Hernandez of the San Leandro Police Department. He's the guy LeAnne called in to help. He says that since there's no sign of a struggle at the house, and since Phyllis Rogers isn't considered an 'at risk' adult, his hands are tied. San Leandro PD is sticking to their original forty-eight-hour requirement."

"In other words," Ali said, "if it is to be, it's up to us?"

"That's right. Without other feet on the ground, ours had better be."

"What about Sister Anselm?" Ali objected. "If LeAnne isn't in Austin, and if we're not going to Austin, shouldn't we have someone there at the hospital with her?"

"Funny you should ask," B. said. "I put that very question to Bishop Gillespie. He has a friend in Dallas, Father Michael McLaughlin, a retired priest who also happens to be a former Navy SEAL. He's already on his way. I called Sister Anselm and let her know that backup is coming."

Ali laughed. "I guess we can stop worrying about her, but what about Lance? How's he coping with the idea that his grandmother is missing?"

"He's in a state, convinced that whatever happened to her is all his fault."

"No one has contacted him or made any demands for her safe return?"

"Not yet, at least not as far as Sister Anselm knows. She said a boy from San Leandro High who was in Austin today for a conference of some kind came by the hospital and dropped off a gift and a get-well card. The gift was a computer. What makes that interesting is the kid who did it is Andrew Garfield."

"That's intriguing," Ali said, supplying some of the information she'd gleaned from her research. "He's the co-captain of the science team and, as near as I can tell, he's the school superintendent's son."

"That makes sense," B. said. "The card was signed by all the kids in the computer club, and that's who sent the computer."

"I'm not buying that," Ali said. "The computer club exists under the aegis of the school system whose server Lance Tucker hacked. I can't imagine anyone in the district would approve spending that kind of money on someone with Lance's public track record. No faculty adviser in his right mind would let the kids get away with that, certainly not one who wanted to keep his job."

"What makes this even more interesting," B. said, "is that Lance never opened the box. After Andrew left, he had Sister Anselm put the computer in the clothes locker in his room."

"Is that important?" Ali asked.

"I think so," B. said. "After all these months of being offline, why wouldn't Lance jump on the chance to put his fingers on a keyboard? That was one of the terms of his sentence — that he have no computer access. Lance is a kid who grew up living and breathing computers. If it had been me, I'd have torn open that box and been on the hospital Wi-Fi within minutes. Asking Sister Anselm to put it away shows an amazing amount of restraint on his part."

"Maybe restraint is what he doesn't have," Ali suggested. "Maybe that's why he had her put it far enough out of reach so he can't lay hands on it. Maybe he's worried it'll have some kind of bug hidden in it the way the flowers did."

"That's possible," B. agreed, "or even a keystroke logger. Come to think of it, if I wanted to make off with his GHOST program, that would be the best way to capture it: to log the password keystrokes he uses to access it."

"I think we need to know a whole lot more

about the kids in that computer science club," Ali said, "all of them. The fact that they cared enough to send him a computer means that, for good or ill, there's still a connection there."

"Fair enough," B. said. "I'll ask Stu to take a long look at all of them and see if anything pops."

With the de-icing process complete, the plane taxied to the end of the runway and took off. For a while, the world outside Ali's window was a sea of swirling snow. Eventually, they popped out above the cloud cover into a frigid, star-spangled night. Across the aisle from where she and B. were seated, Leland sat with a blanket draped over him and with a paperback book resting forgotten on his lap. He was already asleep.

"Take my advice," B. told Ali. "If we want to have anything on the ball tomorrow, we should make like Leland and grab some sleep."

Leaning back in his seat and unfolding his own blanket, B. was out like a light in under a minute. Ali knew that was part of B.'s ability to deal with jet lag: He could fall asleep on command. She couldn't. She sat there for a long time, staring out into the nighttime sky and wondering how Lance Tucker, a troubled jailbird kid, could be worth this amount of money and effort. And what about GHOST? Everything she had learned about Lance's program bothered her. She wasn't concerned about what B. would do with GHOST if he managed to lay hands on it; he would use it to create defenses against it. But what about those other people, like the ones from UTI who had run her off the road? And what about the people who had taken Lance's grandmother? Had she been kidnapped by someone hoping to gain control of GHOST? What would such people do with that kind of technology?

Ali understood that B.'s whole focus was to keep Lance's program from falling into the wrong hands. Ali's problem right then was that she didn't know if she wanted it in the right hands, either.

It was almost three hours later when the plane bumped onto the tarmac in San Leandro and taxied to a stop. A running Cadillac Escalade was parked beside them. Ali and Leland staggered off the plane and into the waiting rental car while B., disgustingly bright-eyed and bushy-tailed, wrangled luggage and keys.

"Okay," B. said as he sat in the driver's seat keying an address into the GPS. "We've got rooms at the San Leandro Inn. Detective Hernandez and LeAnne Tucker are going to meet us there."

They were leaving the airport and waiting for the security gate to close when B.'s cell rang. "Yeah, Stu, we just landed in San Leandro," he said, switching the phone onto speaker. "What have you got?"

"I've taken a long look at the two dead guys, Lowell Dunn and Everett Jackson. I managed to get the autopsy report on Jackson. Definitely suicide. Try twenty-two Oxycodones and about that many over-the-counter sleep aids, all washed down with a fifth of Jägermeister. That's not an accident, so as far as we're concerned, his death is off the table. I got lucky with the other case, though: Lowell Dunn's daughter made enough of a stink about the missing batteries from the smoke alarm that the cops went back out and took another look. I hate it when crooks are stupid. It takes all the fun out of it."

"Why?"

"He removed the batteries and dropped them in a neighbor's trash can. Unluckily for him, the garbage on that street won't be picked up again until Monday. The cops found them and got a partial print that led back to a guy who works at the detention facility."

"Let me guess," B. said. "That would be Marvin Cotton?"

"That's the one. How did you know?"

"Like I told Ali earlier: Once a firebug, always a firebug. But who is this guy, really? Is he some kind of computer whiz, masquerading as a prison guard?"

"Hardly," Stu said. "He doesn't even have a computer at home. He uses one at work. The cops haven't found the smoking gun yet, because they're probably waiting to get a warrant. Once they do, they'll find the same thing I did, and that's when the official story about Lance's injuries being self-inflicted will be blown out of the water."

"What kind of smoking gun are you talking about?"

"I found a weird message from Cotton to a guy who works for the security monitoring company at the detention center. All that was on it was a list of numbers. At first I thought he was writing in some kind of code, but it's not code at all. A search led me back to the camera-repair work order we found at the very beginning of our investigation. That e-mail went out the day before the attack on Lance, and it gave the accomplice the exact locations of the cameras that needed to be taken offline. Since both Cotton and the camera technician were working from the same set of schematics, the two lists were exactly the same. That's how I was able to make the match."

"What about the technician?"

"He quit his job a week ago and left town. No one knows where he went, and so far, we're the only ones who are interested."

"What are we saying here?" Ali asked from her side of the car. "Does this mean the attack on Lance was some kind of beef between him and the guard?"

"I'd say not," Stuart said. "Last week Marvin Cotton paid off a car loan for thirty-eight hundred bucks. He also cleared up an almost-two-thousand-dollar credit card bill. The guy got a windfall, and I'm guessing it was a payday for attacking Lance. That missing technician probably picked up a fistful of cash for that as well."

"Sounds like attacking Lance was worth about the same amount of money as cloning my phone," Ali observed. "The only question is, who paid the freight: the people who attacked me or someone else?"

"My money's on UTI," B. muttered.

"What if it's someone else completely?" Ali asked. "What if the people we're looking for aren't the ones who want to defend against GHOST? What if they want to use it? Who all knew about GHOST?"

"Most of the kids in the computer science club knew something about it," B. said. "At least that's the impression I'm under."

"Have you been able to take a closer look at any of those kids, Stu?" Ali asked.

"Not yet," he answered, "but I found a roster online. I'll get on it right away."

"Any idea when's their next meeting?" Ali persisted.

"Tomorrow afternoon," Stuart answered. "Actually, later today — two o'clock at the school. Why?"

"Lance may have been out of the picture for the school year, but they remember him fondly enough that they chipped in to give him a computer. I think we need to talk to them. One of them might know something without being aware of it."

As B. turned in to the hotel entrance, they ended the call. Ali and Leland clambered out to check in, again leaving B. to deal with the luggage and the car. While Ali stood waiting for room keys, a couple who looked to be in their forties came through the sliding door. Ali pegged the guy for a cop the moment she saw him. The woman, a brunette with gray roots showing, was thin to the point of being scrawny. Her face, which might have been pretty once, was marred by the dark circles under her eyes and the downward turn of her mouth. Ali recognized the look all too well: Days of standing vigil at a hospital bed will do that.

Ali handed Leland his room key and stepped forward to greet the new arrivals. "You must be LeAnne Tucker," she said, holding out her hand. "I'm Ali Reynolds, with High Noon. Nice to meet you."

"I'm LeAnne," the woman confirmed with a notable lack of enthusiasm. She ignored Ali's proffered handshake.

Undeterred, Ali turned to the man. "You must be Detective Hernandez."

"We were looking for Mr. Simpson," Hernandez said.

"He'll be right here."

As B. finished with the bellman, his phone rang again. While he was answering it, the ring of someone else's cell phone echoed through the granite-lined lobby. LeAnne immediately dove for her purse. When she extracted the phone and looked at the caller readout, her already pale face went another shade lighter. "Hello?" she asked anxiously. "Thad? What's going on?" There was a momentary pause, but then her face brightened. "Oh my God. She is? Really? Is she okay?"

LeAnne held the phone away from her face. "It's my son," she explained to Ali and the detective. "It's about my mother. She just turned up at the house on foot." Into the phone, she said, "Did she say where's she'd been? What do you mean she doesn't know? How can that be? Okay, tell her we're coming right now. I'll have Detective Hernandez bring me right back to the house."

LeAnne ended the call and turned to the detective. "We've got to go," she said. "Now."

They were out the door before B. had time to finish his conversation. When he did, his face was grim. "Crap," he said. "We're too late."

"What do you mean, too late?" Ali asked. "Lance's brother just called. His grandmother is home. She's safe."

"She's safe because Lance gave up GHOST. That was Sister Anselm on the phone. She said the ransom call came in on the phone in Lance's room a few minutes ago. After he answered, he listened for a few moments, then he reeled off a long list of letters and numbers."

"A password, do you think?"

"No doubt, and Sister Anselm wasn't quick enough to catch it."

"What do we do now?"

"We follow LeAnne Tucker and Detective Hernandez back to her house and find out what, if anything, Phyllis Rogers can tell us about what went on today."

26

"What the hell was Lance thinking?" B. grumbled as he drove. "Why would he give away the farm?"

"To save his grandmother's life?" Ali offered. "That seems like a good enough reason to me, especially since it seems to have worked."

"I still think he screwed up. Whoever has it will be able to sell it to the highest bidder, and Lance will be cut out of the deal. It never occurred to me that he'd be so stupid. Call Stu back and put him on speaker," B. said, handing Ali his phone. "Let's find out if he got any kind of a lock on the ransom call to the hospital."

"The answer is no," Stu replied when Ali repeated B.'s question to him. "I have a recording. The caller was definitely female, and she used one of those voice-modifying programs. I'm working on decoding it right now. The call didn't last long enough to establish a trace, but if we ever find the right number, it'll show up in the billing. Has the FBI been called in?"

"Not so far," Ali answered, "but since there's been a ransom demand, paid or not, Detective Hernandez will have to report it. He's a sworn police officer. He won't have a choice."

"Which means that High Noon's involvement is going to be a lot more high-profile than I intended, and GHOST will be, too," B. said. "It's one thing to make GHOST an issue in the cyber security world. Once the FBI is involved, it won't be good for anyone. We need to try to get ahead of the media curve."

"How?"

"First I get Ali back to the hotel, then I'll drive to Austin and see if I can get Lance to sign on the dotted line, complete with an up-front bonus that should solve his family's looming foreclosure problem."

"Even without GHOST, you want him?" Ali asked.

"Absolutely," B. said. "Someone else may have his original program, but if he wrote it once, he can write it again, and it'll be a close enough approximation that we'll be able to create defenses against it."

They were pulling up in front of LeAnne's

house at 4034 Twin Oaks Drive. The windows were ablaze with light. Illuminated under the porch light, Detective Hernandez stood smoking a cigarette. When B. turned off the ignition, Hernandez ground out his smoke and strode toward them.

"How is she?" Ali asked.

"Mostly unharmed," Hernandez said. "Cold through from being left outside, and some bruising on her arms and legs from being loaded in and out of the trunk of a car, but otherwise okay. The last thing she remembers, she was cleaning house this morning after LeAnne left for the hospital. After that everything's blank."

"I know how that works," Ali said. "Somebody gave her a dose of scopolamine."

Detective Hernandez gave Ali a searching look. "That was my first thought, too. What made you think of it?"

"Somebody hit me a lungful of scopolamine not long ago," Ali said. "It wasn't a pleasant experience, and I still don't remember everything that happened."

"Can you tell what went on here?" B. asked.

"Mrs. Rogers remembers coming to on the sidewalk a few blocks from here. When she woke up, she had a pillowcase over her head and duct tape around her hands and legs. She's a tough old bird, I'll give her that. She managed to get loose and find her way home. I went back and collected the duct tape and the pillowcase."

"She didn't see who was responsible or remember what kind of vehicle dropped her off?"

"No."

"And there aren't any witnesses?"

"Not so far," Hernandez answered. "If anyone saw anything out of line around here yesterday morning, they have yet to come forward. LeAnne asked me to wait until after you got here before calling the incident in. With Mrs. Rogers safe at home, I didn't have a problem with that. Besides, I wanted to see if the two of you had any clue as to what's going on. What can you tell me?"

"Somebody took her," B. said. "And then they let her go."

"What's this all about, really?" Hernandez asked. "Look around. This isn't the kind of neighborhood where someone can visit the nearest ATM to meet a ransom demand."

"It's not about money," B. said. "At least not directly. Before Lance got sent to prison, he and his computer science teacher invented a cutting-edge program called GHOST. It's a program my company would like to have in our bag of tricks, and I was prepared to pay good money for it. We're pretty sure there are a number of other entities interested in GHOST, including whoever grabbed Mrs. Rogers."

"Why did they let her go?"

"Because they got what they wanted," B. replied. "The ransom demand was called in to Lance's hospital room in Austin. He gave them the access codes. Whoever took Mrs. Rogers has the program."

"I've been with LeAnne Tucker for the past several hours," Richard Hernandez said. "If she knows about this, she hasn't mentioned any of it to me. So how is it that you two are privy to so much information?"

"We were worried about Lance, so I stationed an operative in the hospital to look out for him," B. answered. "There's already been one attempt on his life, and we were afraid there'd be another. Unfortunately for us, the bad guys went for Mrs. Rogers instead of Lance, and we didn't see that coming."

"It sounds like you were expecting someone to make a move long before the threatening note showed up."

"Yes," B. said, "and I believe we've been proved right."

They were still standing on the sidewalk outside LeAnne's house. Ali shivered involuntarily. "It's cold out here," she said. "How about if we go inside for the rest of this discussion?"

B. wasn't ready to move. "What brought you here, Detective?" he asked. "Why here on this street in the middle of the night?"

"Mrs. Tucker called me."

"You're the guy who arrested Lance in the first place. Why would she call you?"

"She had my number."

"Why?"

Hernandez paused before he answered. "After I heard what happened to him, I stopped by and talked to Phyllis, the grandmother. I offered to organize a crew to install a wheelchair ramp." He shrugged. "I guess I've always felt a little guilty about the part I played in what happened to Lance. Yes, he was a hacker, but he also seemed like a good kid. It looks to me like they threw the book at him when they didn't need to."

"You arrested him," B. said, "and High Noon supplied the evidence that made the arrest warrant possible. We're on the same page, Detective Hernandez: You and I both think Lance and his family got a bum deal, and maybe, if we work together, we can do something about it."

"Work together how?"

"Does the name Lowell Dunn mean anything to you?" B. asked.

Hernandez shrugged. "The name sounds familiar, but I'm not sure why."

"Mr. Dunn was head of maintenance at the detention center. He was someone who liked Lance and was in his corner. Hours after coming to the hospital and telling LeAnne that he didn't buy the official version of what supposedly happened to Lance and after offering to help, Mr. Dunn died in a house fire."

"Okay," Richard Hernandez said. "I remember now. That incident happened earlier this week. I believe the guy was smoking in his La-Z-Boy."

"That's what initial reports said," B. told him, "but you should check with your department."

"Why?"

"Because the Dunn case is now being treated as a homicide."

"Since when?"

"Since this afternoon," B. said. "A guy by the name of Marvin Cotton, a guard from the detention center, is currently in custody. Cotton has a history of arson offenses. You might want to check with the scheduling records at the center and see if he had the opportunity to ignite the cloud of aerosol

395

glue that set Lance Tucker on fire. There's also a good chance that if you happened to take a look at Marvin Cotton's e-mail history at work, you'd find a communication from him to a technician who disabled certain security cameras inside the detention center, cameras that made it possible for whoever set the fire to come and go without being caught on video."

"Does this technician have a name?"

"No," B. said, "but you should be able to find that out with a minimum of difficulty."

"Should I bother to ask how you came to know all of this?" Hernandez asked.

"Probably not," B. said, "but if you pass along any of these suggestions to the detectives assigned to the case, just call it gut instinct. That'll be better for you, and it'll definitely be better for us."

"Fair enough," Detective Hernandez said with a laugh. "How about we go inside before your friend here freezes to death?"

He led the way. Ali turned back to B. "When you said we needed an Inspector Elkins on the ground in Texas, I thought you were kidding."

"Hardly," B. said. "That's one of the tricks I've learned from our old friend Stuart Ramey. With him, it's standard procedure."

"What's that?" Ali asked.

"Make friends with the locals. Come on, let's go in. You are freezing."

27

As soon as Ali stepped into the living room, two small dogs catapulted out of a shabby easy chair where they had been cuddled next to a wan older woman swathed in a layer of blankets. The dogs raced toward the door in a frenzy of high-pitched barking; after ascertaining that Ali and B. represented no immediate threat, they returned to the chair and resumed their previous positions.

"You must be Mrs. Rogers. I'm Ali, and this is B.," Ali said. "We're with High Noon. We wanted to talk to you about what happened today."

"There's no point," Phyllis Rogers said. "I don't remember any of it. Well, maybe some. I remember waking up a time or two in the trunk of a car. That's all. I've heard that there are supposed to be levers or buttons or something in cars to let people out of trunks these days, but I was in no condition to find one."

"You probably were dosed with scopola-mine," Ali said. "It's one of the date-rape drugs. There's an airborne version called Devil's Breath. Someone used some of it on me once. I was out for hours."

"It happened to you, too?" Phyllis asked. "Did you ever remember anything?"

"Eventually, I remembered bits and pieces from just before it happened. And that's what I wanted to ask you about. Do you remember anything at all?"

Phyllis frowned. "I took the boys to school. LeAnne was here for breakfast. I was clean-ing up the house when the doorbell rang. I remember walking toward the door. I looked out the peephole, and I seem to remember there was a woman standing outside, but that's all. I don't remember anything else until I woke up outside on the ground a little while ago."

"We'll see if there are any prints on the doorbell," Detective Hernandez put in, "but I'm guessing that's going to come up empty."

"What about the dogs?" Ali asked. "Where were they? Wouldn't they raise hell about a stranger showing up and doing something like that to you?"

"I was vacuuming," Phyllis explained. "Duchess is petrified of the vacuum cleaner.

She goes into a blind panic if a vacuum cleaner comes too close to her, so whenever I vacuum, I lock them in the dining room."

"You mentioned that you saw a woman on the front porch," Ali said. "Did you get a look at her?"

"Not really. She was looking back toward the street. All I saw through the peephole was the back of her head. She had long dark hair pulled back in a ponytail."

"Young or old?"

"I couldn't tell. Young, maybe, but I'm not sure."

"You said she was looking back toward the street. Did you see a vehicle there?"

"No, not that I remember." Phyllis paused and frowned. "Wait, there was something about the garage. I remember being in the garage, but I don't know why. My car was parked in the driveway."

All through the conversation, LeAnne had been sitting on a sofa near her mother. Ali turned to her. "Can you show me the garage?"

When they reached the door that led from the kitchen to the garage, Ali used the eraser end of a pencil to press the door opener. When the light came on, it revealed a two-car garage. In one bay sat an eighties-vintage Taurus with faded blue paint. The other bay was stacked full of boxes, bikes, skateboards, and an accumulation of stuff that most likely was deposited on moving day and never unpacked.

"That explains why no neighbors noticed what happened," Ali said. "Whoever did this put their own vehicle in the garage so no one would see your mother being loaded into the trunk."

"I understand that someone took her, but I don't understand why they let her go," LeAnne said.

"Your son paid the ransom demand," Ali said quietly.

"But how?"

"He gave the kidnappers what they wanted: his program."

Shaking her head, LeAnne leaned against the doorjamb and began to sob. "Now he's lost that, too? Poor Lance. That was the one thing he had left — his precious program. He thought if High Noon wanted that, he'd at least have a chance of getting somewhere, but if GHOST is gone . . ."

Ali reached out and touched the woman's shoulder. "Give your son credit," she said. "He did what he did in hopes of saving his grandmother, and it appears to have worked."

There was a single step leading from the

kitchen down into the garage. LeAnne sank down on it as though she no longer had the strength to stand. "You don't know Lance. He was always such a good kid. Until that hacking thing, I don't think he was ever sent to the principal's office. All because of that, his life is ruined, and so is ours. Before this happened, he was headed to college; he had a girlfriend; he was going somewhere. All of that is gone. He's got nothing. My boss called this afternoon: I've missed so much work the past two weeks that I've lost my job. That means we'll lose the house and be on the street. How can I be such a failure?"

"You're not a failure," Ali said. "You're a single mom doing the best you can. And if Lance was willing to give up something as important to him as GHOST in order to save his grandmother's life, that means you've done something right."

"I was furious with him this morning when he insisted on having that full-of-business nun call Mr. Simpson instead of the police. That made no sense to me."

"Your son must have figured out that everything going on had something to do with his GHOST program. He probably also realized that someone like B., someone who's part of the cyber security world, would know a whole lot more about cyber crime and how to deal with it than anyone in a small-town police department."

LeAnne shook her head. "Cyber this and cyber that. I wish Lance had never had anything to do with computers. His father's father bought Lance an old laptop for his eighth birthday. By the time he was ten, he was figuring out how to do programming. He was entering his freshman year when we moved here. I was a little worried when Mr. Jackson started taking such an interest in him. You hear things these days about teachers exploiting kids or molesting them or something. When I realized there were girls in Mr. Jackson's club, too, I didn't worry as much, but he and Lance did spend huge amounts of time together after school and on weekends. I know that."

"As I recall from what happened at the trial," Ali said, "there were surprisingly few e-mails going between them, and there was nothing at all linking Mr. Jackson to the hacking situation."

"Mr. Jackson was one of the few teachers who spoke out publicly against the tagging system, but nobody was able to prove that he had any hand in the actual hacking. Believe me, they tried. They searched through all of Lance's e-mail accounts and our phone records, trying to establish that there was a direct connection. After poor Mr. Jackson took his own life, there was even more gossip about it, but nothing ever came of it."

"You just mentioned that Lance had a girlfriend."

LeAnne nodded. "Jillian."

"Jillian Sosa?" Ali asked. "The co-captain of the computer science team?"

"That's the one, and that's where they met, in the computer club. She's a sweet girl, and smart. I liked her a lot, even though I worried that it was like a reverse-Cinderella thing."

"Meaning?"

"Her parents both died — in a car wreck, I think. She met Lance when she came to San Leandro to live with her aunt and uncle a year or so ago. They have plenty of money, and obviously, we don't. I worried that she and Lance were getting too serious, especially when I came home from work one night and figured out that she had spent the night. I was worried that she'd get pregnant. When the hacking thing came along, that was the only good thing: Lance broke up with her. He claimed he did it for her own good because he was afraid she'd get sucked down the drain right along with him. He said he had done the hacking on his own, and he was going to pay for it on his own without taking anyone — not Mr. Jackson or Jillian — along with him. He was afraid she'd be considered guilty by association."

Ali thought about what she had learned about Jillian Sosa. While Lance was in the slammer, Jillian was busy being homecoming queen and co-captain of the computer science club. She hadn't exactly been pining away since their split.

"One of the kids from school dropped by to see Lance at the hospital tonight," Ali said. "Andrew Garfield. He brought Lance a card and a new computer, both of which were compliments of the computer science club."

"Really?" LeAnne asked. "Andrew stopped by again?"

"He'd been to the hospital before?"

"A day or so ago," LeAnne said. "I was glad to see him. It felt to me like all my son's old friends from school just abandoned him. As for the computer? Lance will be overjoyed. The cops confiscated his old one, and they're holding it as evidence. I knew Lance would be asking for a new one, and I had no idea how I'd pay for it." That little bit of good news seemed to help revive LeAnne. She stood up and straightened her shoulders. "I'd better get back inside and see if Mom needs any help. This has been a very tough day in a series of tough days. She should probably go to bed, and I should, too. But what about tomorrow? Do I let Thad and Connor go to school?"

Ali thought about that. "With your mother back home safely, it would seem, on the surface at least, that the danger is past. Still, I don't think it would hurt to err on the side of caution. I'd keep the two younger boys with me if I were you. Your mother, too, for that matter. For the next several days, while the police are investigating this latest incident, I'd keep the whole family close to me and as far from their regular schedules as possible."

LeAnne nodded. "All right," she said. "I'll see what I can do."

Just then the garage door opened. Wrapped in a blanket and clutching a pack of cigarettes, Phyllis Rogers appeared in the doorway.

"Mother," LeAnne exclaimed. "Where are you going?"

"Out to the car to have a smoke," Phyllis replied.

"After all you've been through today, you can smoke inside if you want."

"No," Phyllis said. "Don't break down your own conditions." She pressed the button to open the garage door and stepped out into the winter night.

LeAnne shook her head. "She's a stubborn old bat," she said, "and tough as nails."

Leaving Phyllis to smoke in privacy, LeAnne and Ali returned to a living room full of police officers, in uniform and out. When Phyllis finished her cigarette and came back inside, a detective with a notebook in hand sat on a footstool in front of her, asking questions that sounded similar to the ones Ali had been asking a few minutes earlier. A crime scene technician on her knees was carefully sweeping up whatever was to be found by the front door, searching for minute traces of the substance that had been used to incapacitate Phyllis. Detective Hernandez had done enough to explain Ali and B.'s presence that they were free to go as soon as Ali and LeAnne returned to the living room.

Outside in the car, B. put the key in the ignition and turned to Ali. "Where would you like to go?" he asked. "I can take you back to the hotel and drop you, or you can come with me to Austin. What's your choice?"

"Austin," Ali said. "We've both had way too little sleep. You're not driving there on your own."

"Thanks," B. said. "I was hoping you'd say that."

It was almost one in the morning when they headed south on I-35. When B.'s phone rang a few minutes later, Ali answered with a laugh, putting the phone on speaker. "What a surprise to hear from you at this hour," she told Stuart Ramey. "Do you ever sleep?"

She already knew that the answer was "very little." Stuart kept his very capable hand on the company's tiller from a pizza-box-strewn office in High Noon's Cottonwood headquarters. There was a rumpled cot in the back corner where he slept, and a shower in a bathroom down the hall. When B. was on the road, Stuart generally kept the same hours, matching B.'s many time-zone shifts in spirit if not in body.

"Not when I've got stuff to do," Stuart said. "I've got a handle on the camera technician who went off the grid. His name is Arturo Miejas. He's a naturalized citizen, but he's originally from Monterrey, and he has family members mixed up in the Cabrillo cartel."

"Wait," B. said. "You're telling us that the Cabrillo drug cartel may be involved?"

"I'm not saying they are or aren't, but I am saying that someone close to some Cabrillo associates was involved in the attack on Lance. I think we'll be able to trace back to Arturo's computer the keystrokes that took those cameras out of service. By the way, he and his wife and two kids crossed back into Mexico at Juárez late last week. None of them has been heard from since."

"Sounds like somebody helped him stage a quick exit before the authorities started looking for him," Ali observed. "How come nobody helped Marvin Cotton?"

"Cotton's stupid," B. replied. "He screwed up on the Lowell Dunn fire. But if the Cabrillo cartel is involved in this, he'd know better than to rat them out. If he tries to turn state's evidence to dodge the death penalty, he's a dead man. The cartel will take him out no matter where he is."

"What else do you have for us?" Ali asked.

"Slave driver," Stu said, "but I do have an additional item or two. For one thing, you were right about the computer, and so was Lance."

"The gift computer?" B. asked.

"That's right. I had Sister Anselm dig it out of the box and hook it up to the hospital Wi-Fi. Sure as hell, I ran a diagnostic on it and found a keystroke logger. Whoever installed it taped the box back up so it looked like it came fresh from the factory."

"Did you disable the logger?"

"No, I didn't," Stu said. "I had Sister Anselm give me the serial number. I'm tracking the sales information. Then I had her put the computer back in the box, tape it up, and put it away. If Lance tries to use it, he needs to know that someone — most likely from the computer science club — is watching his every move. I've taken a cursory look at everyone on the club roster. As far as I can tell, the kids are a nerdy bunch: good grades; no criminal records; no extracurricular activities other than computer science. They remind me of someone else I used to know back in the day — sort of like looking in the mirror fifteen years later."

"I think you need to take a really close look at the club's two co-captains," Ali suggested.

"Andrew Garfield and Jillian Sosa?" Stu asked. "Makes sense, since Andrew's the one who delivered that computer to Lance's room. What's the deal with Jillian?"

"LeAnne Tucker just told me that Jillian and Lance were an item before he got shipped off to jail. Now it looks as though Andrew has taken up where Lance left off."

"I'll look into it," Stu said. "I promise. But not tonight. I don't know about the two

of you, but if I don't get some shut-eye
pretty soon, I'm going to fall over onto my
keyboard."

"Morning is fine," B. said. "We're on our
way to Austin to talk to Lance."

"That would be the great middle-of-the-
night recruiting gamble?" Stu asked.

"None other."

"Good. Tell me how it went later on in
the morning," Stu said. "Right now I'm going to go lie down."

"I wish I could go lie down," Ali said. "I'm
dead on my feet, too."

"We've got rooms at the Omni," B. said.
"I made the reservations when we were supposed to fly into Austin, and I forgot to
cancel them when we changed the itinerary.
We'll go there once we square away things
with Lance."

"We're going to rent a room without luggage?" Ali asked. "Won't people talk?"

"Let 'em," B. said.

They pulled into the hospital parking
garage just after two; they had to walk
around the building to the main entrance.
A security guard let them into the elevator
and directed them to the fifth floor. The
burn unit waiting room held one person, a
fit-looking man in his sixties, wearing a
clerical collar. Wide awake and with his

arms crossed on his chest, he sat next to a closed door, daring anyone to try to gain entrance.

"You must be Father McLaughlin," B. said. "I'm B. Simpson. This is my fianceé, Ali Reynolds."

"I'm sure you are who you say," Father McLaughlin said, "but if it's all the same with you, I'd still like to check those IDs. Sister Anselm went back to her hotel to get a couple of hours of sleep, but she gave me my marching orders. She said the nurses could come and go, but as far as visitors are concerned, the two of you are it."

When Ali opened her purse to get out her ID, she was surprised to see a Taser lying on top of her wallet. She knew that B. usually carried one in his checked luggage and was surprised that he had slipped it into her purse without her noticing. Still, she was glad to have it.

Once Father McLaughlin had checked their IDs, he nodded them toward the door. It was the middle of the night, so Ali expected to find Lance Tucker asleep. He was lying with his hospital bed propped up, facing a television set, but the sound was muted and he didn't seem to be watching the weight-loss infomercial.

He looked toward them as the door

opened, and an unexpectedly impish grin crossed his face. Lance Tucker had suffered major, life-changing burns and had lost a leg, but his expression said he had everything he wanted in life and more. "Mr. Simpson?" he asked, holding out his hand.

"With High Noon Enterprises," B. answered. "And this is my fianceé."

Ali offered her hand. "I'm Ali Reynolds."

"Sister Anselm told me you were willing to help, but I never expected that you'd drop everything and come here. She says you were in Austin when they dropped Grandma off at the house in San Leandro? Is she all right? They didn't hurt her?"

"A little banged up is all," Ali said. "She's lucky, and so are you. In kidnapping cases, even when the ransom demands are met, the outcome isn't always good."

"The kidnappers only think the demands have been met," Lance said. "They're wrong."

"What do you mean?" B. asked.

"They wanted GHOST. As far as they know, they got it. They have access to a GHOST file on a cloud along with the fifteen-digit code needed to activate it. What they don't know is that they'll have only twenty-four hours of access before the whole thing blows sky-high."

B. said, "I came here because I'm interested in GHOST. I was hoping to purchase it outright or license its use, but it sounds as though you've installed some sort of failsafe protocol so the program will self-destruct."

"It's better than that," Lance said with a grin. "As soon as they log on, that computer and every IP address the first computer is networked to or has been sent worm-contaminated files that will begin uploading the contents of their hard drives to my cloud storage. The data-dump process will take four to six hours, depending on the Internet connection and the amount of material. That's the reason for the six-hour delay before the second set of confirming passwords is applied. If they don't appear, then the worm goes back to that whole flock of computers and reformats the hard drives. It's dead simple. I'll have collected all the information on their computers. Unless they've got current backups, they'll have nothing."

"You installed a Trojan in your own program?" B. asked.

"Designed it in along with everything else," Lance said. "Are you still interested?"

"I suppose," B. said. "But now that GHOST has fallen into someone else's hands . . ."

"It hasn't," Lance said. "Not really. I gave them a file that they thought was GHOST. It's called GHOST; it's just not the real thing. Mr. Jackson and I were afraid that something like this might happen — that someone would try to gain unauthorized access, so we created a dummy file with a few critical pieces missing. They've had it for what . . ." He looked up at the clock on the wall. ". . . almost three hours now. They'll be able to use it for another three. At that point, they'll get an error message and the computer will shut down. When they try to reinitiate, they'll need another fifteen-character password. After three tries with an incorrect password, reformatting initiates. Even if they power down the computer, the worm will resume the moment power comes back on." Lance paused, looked at B. and Ali before adding, "Sweet, huh?"

"If you gave the kidnapper a worm-infected version of GHOST, where's the real one?" B. asked.

Lance reached under his pillow and pulled out a tiny object. It was made of red, white, and blue plastic. As it began to unfold, Ali recognized it for what it was: a Transformer. When her son, Chris, was a preteen, he had been a big fan of Transformers.

When the tiny robot was fully deployed, Lance handed it over to B.

"A thumb drive disguised as a Transformer?" B. asked.

Lance nodded. "When the cops went through the house, they searched everywhere for anything computer-related. I kept this in a box with the rest of my Transformers. They never bothered to unfold any of them. They looked in the box, decided it was just a bunch of old toys, and walked away, which is just what Mr. Jackson said they'd do. He kept one like it in a box of toys at his house."

"What's on the thumb drive?"

"A beta version of GHOST. That's the one I used to disable the school server. If I'd been able to use the finished version, you might not have caught me. The cops tried like crazy to link the attack to Mr. Jackson, but they couldn't because he didn't do it. They could only trace it back to my computer."

"Where's the final copy of GHOST?"

"On the cloud. Mr. Jackson finished the design work after I was arrested."

"This is where you did the programming for GHOST?" B. asked, holding up the thumb drive.

Lance nodded. "All of it. We kept the finished files in a shared cloud account with another fifteen-digit password and a second password required six hours later. That's how Mr. Jackson and I worked together. We could go to the shared account and compare notes without having any of our GHOST work resident on either of our computers and without any e-mail trails back and forth."

"It sounds like you and Mr. Jackson were serious about security."

Lance nodded. "We were. He told me GHOST was far enough ahead of the curve that it would be worth a lot of money." He looked at B. "Is that still true?"

"Maybe," B. answered. "Since you and Mr. Jackson created this together, what was your arrangement?"

"Fifty-fifty. It's Texas," Lance said in answer to B.'s questioning look. "We operated on a handshake."

"Nothing in writing?"

"No, he didn't want to feel like he was taking advantage of me, so we agreed that once I was eighteen and old enough to sign a binding contract, we'd sell GHOST to the highest bidder. Mr. Jackson was hoping he'd have enough money to be able to stop teaching and do some traveling with his

417

wife. I thought maybe I'd have my college education paid for in full." Lance's grin faded. "Except now Mr. Jackson is dead, and I'm not going to college. I'm hoping you're still interested."

"Oh, I'm interested, all right," B. said, "but I have some questions. Mr. Jackson committed suicide on the day you were sentenced. Do you have any idea why?"

"People said it was because he blamed himself for what happened to me. That wasn't his fault. Like I told you, I did that on my own. He objected to the school district buying into the tagging program, and so did I. I didn't think they had any business knowing where I was every moment of the day."

"Did I understand you to say that you still haven't seen the final version of GHOST?" Ali asked.

"Not yet. Like I said, Mr. Jackson uploaded the last tweaks to the cloud after I was in jail. I won't even try to access them until I can use a secure computer and a secure server."

"What about the computer Andrew Garfield gave you tonight?" Ali asked.

"I'm worried it might not be so secure," Lance said, "and I don't trust the hospital Wi-Fi."

"You were right to be worried," B. said. "We were worried, too. I had High Noon run a diagnostic. We found a keystroke logger on it. Would Andrew Garfield have done that?"

Lance shook his head. "Maybe," he said. "Andrew and I used to be friends, but I've been gone a long time. Maybe things changed."

"You know he's taken up with your former girlfriend in your absence?" Ali asked. "Andrew and Jillian were elected homecoming king and queen."

"Jillian's a wonderful girl," Lance said. "She's had a tough life. Her parents died. She had to come here to live with her aunt and uncle. When I realized I was going to jail, I broke up with her. I didn't want her to waste her senior year on the sidelines, waiting for me to get out. As for homecoming, Mom probably didn't tell me about it because she thought it would hurt my feelings, but good for them. That's something Andrew was working on last year. I'm delighted they pulled it off."

"What do you mean working on?"

"Jocks and cheerleaders usually win those elections. Andrew was trying to fix it so someone else could win."

"To rig the election, you mean?"

"I may be the best hacker at San Leandro High School, but I'm not the only one," Lance said. "I'm just the one who happened to get caught." When he turned back to B., all semblance of joking had fled. "Are you still interested in GHOST, Mr. Simpson?"

"Not sight unseen," B. said. "And I'll want a finished version, not a beta. If you give me one that has a Trojan in it, you can kiss your computer science ass goodbye. Understand?"

"Yes, sir."

"If I decide to make an offer, I'll see to it that Mr. Jackson's survivors are fairly compensated for his part in the development. Fair enough?"

In answer, Lance held out his hand. A shadow of Lance's grin returned. "Remember," he said, "this is Texas. A handshake works." He and B. shook. "Now," Lance added, "I need a piece of paper."

Ali produced paper and a pen from her purse. Frowning in concentration, Lance spent some time working on the paper. When he handed it back, it contained two long lines of numbers and letters. "You'll need the thumb drive to access the cloud account," he said. "When you get there, choose the last GHOST file listed and open that — that'll be the finished version. Once

you open it, you'll need both passwords —
one initially, and one six hours later, when
you get the error message. After that you're
good to go."

Ali looked down at the two strings of
numbers. "You remember all these?" she
said.

"Sure," Lance said. "Passwords are easy
to remember."

"Not for me," Ali said.

It was a family joke that her original
password, sugarloaf#1, was still her password. After the phone cloning, she knew
she was destined to lose the password war.

With the sheet of paper tucked in her
purse, Ali and B. left Lance's room. Father
McLaughlin was still at his post. He nodded to them as they passed.

"Are you really going to try opening
GHOST on your computer?" Ali asked B.
as they headed down the hallway for the
elevator.

"Hardly," B. said. "Do I look stupid? Trust
but verify. I'll have somebody in the High
Noon world send a new computer to our
hotel room first thing in the morning. I'll
use the thumb drive on that."

"What do you mean, first thing in the
morning?" Ali asked wearily. "It's already
morning here and sometime in the after-

noon where we were yesterday. I don't know about you, but I'm done for."

"I take that to mean that checking in with no visible luggage is no longer a problem for you?"

"Don't be cute," Ali grumbled. "I'm too damned tired for cute."

28

In their room, Ali fell into bed stark naked and slept without moving or dreaming. When she awakened hours later, B., backlit by sun shining in through the windows, was standing beside the bed, holding out his phone.

"It's your mother," he said. "Apparently, she's on the warpath. I'm on my way to the shower."

Ali tried to clear the sleep out of her throat before she answered. "Hi, Mom."

"Where in the world are you?" Edie Larson demanded. "I called off and on all day yesterday. You never answered and you never called me back."

Ali's phone, still turned off and most likely totally discharged, lay in the bottom of her purse. She hadn't remembered to turn it back on. "Someone hacked in to it," Ali said. "I don't feel comfortable talking on it when someone else might be listening in on the conversation."

"Someone hacked your phone?" Edie repeated. "Can't B. do something about that? Isn't that what he does for a living, for Pete's sake?"

"He's been quite busy," Ali said.

"I'm calling about tomorrow," Edie said. "You probably booked a shuttle to get back home to Sedona after your flight from London, but if you want, Dad and I will be glad to drive down to Phoenix to pick you up. Those shuttle rides aren't very comfortable, especially if you're already tired."

"Thank you, Mom," Ali said. "That's kind of you, but we won't be on that flight. We're in Austin right now."

"Austin?" Edie exclaimed. "As in Texas? How did you get there? What's going on?"

Call waiting buzzed. "Mom," Ali said, "it's a long story. I'll tell you about it later. There was a sudden change in plans, and I didn't have time to let you know. Right now, I'm on B.'s phone and he's got another call coming in. I'll have to get back to you."

She caught a glimpse of the time as she switched over to the other call. It was after nine in the morning. She had slept for more than six hours.

"I'm looking for Mr. Simpson."

The voice was familiar, but Ali couldn't

immediately identify it. "He's in the shower," she said. "This is Ali Reynolds. Who's this?"

"Detective Hernandez, San Leandro PD."

"What's up?"

"Marvin Cotton is dead."

"The arson suspect?" Ali asked. "How did that happen? I thought he was in police custody."

"He was," Detective Hernandez said. "He was in an interrogation room out at the jail. The detectives had been talking to him, but then he lawyered up. A guard was taking him back to a holding cell when some kind of altercation broke out. When the scuffle was over, Cotton was unconscious. He was taken by ambulance from the jail to the hospital, where he was pronounced dead. The guard is currently out on administrative leave. The sheriff's department says the investigation is ongoing. I got a sneak preview of the tapes. No doubt the guard will claim self-defense, but if it were my call, I wouldn't be buying it. The guard used lethal force when he punched Cotton in the throat. I think it was deliberate."

"Are you sure you should be telling us this?" Ali put in.

"I'm sure I shouldn't, but from where I'm standing, I know there's a puppet master out there somewhere, pulling strings, and those strings may reach deep inside the law enforcement community. So far it seems to be confined to lower-level folks — guards and the surveillance technician, for instance — but what if it's more widespread than that? What if it goes higher? I'm not a crooked cop, and I sure as hell don't want to work with crooked cops. Cotton's death means that all the urgency to investigate Lowell Dunn's homicide just went out the window. Why clear a case that's already closed? Ditto for the attack on Lance. Cotton is responsible, one and done. In the long run, the only people still asking questions about those incidents will be you."

"What about the attack on Phyllis Rogers?" Ali asked.

"Traces of scopolamine were found in LeAnne's front entry. That's been declared a kidnapping and the investigation is in the hands of the FBI. If somebody local has been pushing things under the rug, it won't go away quite as easily with the feds involved, and that's a good thing."

The bathroom door opened. B. emerged through a cloud of steam wearing the previous day's rumpled shirt. That was when Ali remembered that their clean clothes and luggage were still in San Leandro. So was

Leland Brooks.

Ali shoved B.'s phone in his direction and dug in her purse for her own phone.

"Who is it?" B. asked.

"Detective Hernandez," she said.

While B. took over his phone, Ali located her own along with the charger. Once she had it plugged in, she dialed the San Leandro Inn.

"Good morning," Leland said cordially. "I came down to breakfast without you. I hope you don't mind. I thought you needed your beauty sleep."

Ali flushed with embarrassment. "Leland, I'm sorry. We're not there. We're in Austin. Right after you went upstairs with the luggage last night, everything went nuts. We never went to our room. We came to the hospital to talk to Lance Tucker. By the time we were finished, we were too tired to drive all the way back to San Leandro. Once I get dressed, I'll come back for you."

"That's all right," Leland said reassuringly. "Please don't stress yourself. Come when it's convenient. The hotel here is comfortable enough. After the day we had yesterday, I'm finding it rather pleasant to be in a room that isn't moving."

Ali hung up. With B. still on the phone in the living room of the three-room suite, Ali

427

took her turn in the shower. She came out a few minutes later, grateful for the terry-cloth robe she had found in the closet. B. was on the sofa with a computer on his lap. On the floor was a scatter of used packaging materials. The low coffee table held a carafe of coffee and two cups. Ali stopped long enough to pour one for herself before sitting down on the couch beside him. By then the Transformer-shaped thumb drive was already plugged in and lit up. "Find anything?" she asked.

"GHOST is here," B. said. "I'm assuming it's the completed version, since it's one of the last files Everett Jackson added to the cloud. I haven't tried opening it yet. But there were a couple of much smaller files added after that. Take a look at this." He moved the computer screen in Ali's direction.

" 'Sorry'?" she read. "A one-word message? What does that mean?"

"I think it means that Everett Jackson was being blackmailed." With a click, B. switched to a video entitled "Teacher's Pet." It was poorly lit and grainy but clear enough. The only prop in the picture was an old-fashioned teacher's desk with a green blackboard in the background. What was happening on the desk may have been educational, but it was also X-rated. A naked young woman lay on her back with her legs clamped around the bare rump of the man moving on top of her. He was much older and almost entirely bald. Looking directly into the camera, she was smiling as though she knew the lens was there while he had no idea.

"Mr. Bare Butt is Everett Jackson?" Ali asked.

"It's got to be. Why else would he have it? The porn video was posted one day prior to the day of Mr. Jackson's overdose."

"Is there a way to tell where the file came from?"

"It was probably e-mailed to him. With his livelihood at stake, he wouldn't have left it on his computer any longer than it took to copy it and post it here. He probably erased the original in a hell of a hurry. I know I would have."

"It might still be on the server," Ali suggested.

"You're getting good at this stuff," B. said, "and you're right. It might be, but someone would need to know to go looking. Luckily I happen to know just such a guy."

"Was a suicide note found at the time?" Ali asked.

"No," B. said. "I checked. So maybe that's

what 'sorry' means. The message on the cloud may be a suicide note intended specifically for Lance. Unfortunately, there's also another possibility."

"Which is?"

"That the blackmail demand to Everett Jackson was the same as the ransom demand sent to Lance in exchange for his grandmother's safe return."

"GHOST?"

"Maybe he gave it up, and that's what he's saying sorry about."

"If he did knuckle under to a blackmailer's demands, which copy would he hand over?" Ali asked. "The one with the working passwords or the one with the exploding cigar?"

"Maybe neither," B. muttered. "What if Jackson decided to end it all instead of giving up the program? With him gone, the blackmailer might have decided there was no point in releasing the video. Had it been made public, that video would have gone viral in minutes."

"I'm assuming our next step is to try to identify the girl and figure out if she played a part in what happened to Phyllis Rogers yesterday."

"I'm calling Stuart," B. said, picking up his phone. "If the video was sent to Jackson's school address, a file with the words 'Teacher's Pet' shouldn't be at all difficult to find, especially since the San Leandro school district was and is one of our clients. If it's on Jackson's personal e-mail account, that'll be a little more difficult."

"What if it isn't there at all?"

"We'll figure out something else."

As B. went to dial Stu's number, Ali stood up. "You do that," she said, kissing him goodbye. "I'm going to get dressed and drive to San Leandro. I'll pick up Leland and our luggage and be back in time for lunch."

"I'll be at the hospital," B. told her. "Detective Hernandez says the FBI will be paying Lance a call. I told Sister Anselm to let me know when they get there."

It was ten past ten when Ali collected the car from the parking valet and headed north on I-35 with her half-charged phone on the car seat next to her. As she drove the long straight stretch of highway through the wide expanse of Texas landscape, she couldn't get the images from the video out of her mind. There was no question that it had been consensual sex. Rather than looking as though she had been forced into the act, the girl had looked downright gleeful. Triumphant.

431

"She targeted him," Ali said aloud, "nailed him, and now he's dead. Now we need to nail her." She picked up the phone, dialed Stu, and punched speaker. "Did B. send the video?" she asked.

"Yes, ma'am," Stu said. "Hot stuff."

"Was it on the server?"

"Nope. Not on the school's, but from correspondence there, I was able to locate Jackson's personal account. It'll take me a while to get into that server, but I'm sure I'll manage."

"What if you don't find it there?"

"I'm already putting it out in the world of FR," Stu said.

"FR?" Ali repeated. "What's that?"

"My favorite new science: facial recognition. A search like that takes time, and I have to go through certain channels, but if our hot little number happens to have a Facebook page, we'll be able to find her."

When Ali arrived at the hotel in San Leandro, Leland Brooks was waiting for her in the lobby, suitcase at the ready. Seeing the car, he came outside to greet her. "I thought about prevailing on the doorman to let me check you out of your room," he said, "but then it occurred to me that you might want to change into fresh clothing."

"To say nothing of having a chance to put

on some makeup," she said. "I promise I won't take long."

"No rush," Leland said. "No rush at all."

Grateful for his understanding, Ali went up to their otherwise unused room, where she showered for a second time and changed into the last of her clean clothes. She was putting the finishing touches on her face when B. called. "How are things?" he asked.

"After the past several days, nothing can top the pleasure of showering and putting on clean underwear," she said. "How are things with you?"

"Lance evidently had a bad night after we left. They took him somewhere for PT as soon as he woke up."

"Does he know about the video?"

"Not yet. I didn't want to drop that on him until after the FBI finishes up with him. Everett Jackson's widow still lives in this town. If we can prevent that video from becoming a public circus, we will. I was afraid if Lance knew about it before the interview, he might be tempted to lie about it. Lying to the feds is always a bad idea."

"Are they there now?"

"They stopped by just after the therapist wheeled Lance downstairs. Sister Anselm told them to take a number and wait. Instead of sitting here in the waiting room, they went downstairs for coffee. Sister Anselm and I were a little surprised that Lance's mother hasn't shown up and that we haven't heard from her. We've tried calling LeAnne's numbers, both her cell and her landline, as well as her mother's cell phone. The calls go straight to voice mail."

"That seems odd," Ali said. "Leland and I will be leaving the hotel in a few minutes. We'll stop by the house on our way out of town. It'll only take a few extra minutes."

"Good thinking," B. said.

Twenty minutes later, driving B.'s rented Cadillac, Ali turned onto Twin Oaks Drive. Nearby yards were dotted with Christmas decorations — plastic manger scenes and some deflated blow-up snowmen — that looked forlorn rather than cheerful on the winter-dry grass. An older-model Honda with Oregon plates was parked in the driveway. Ali stopped the Escalade next to it. "I'll be right back," she told Leland.

She got out. The door to the garage had a row of small windows along the top. Peeking through, she saw the silhouette of a parked car. When she punched the doorbell, the sound was greeted by a chorus of barking and the scrabbling of paws on tile as two dogs, no doubt Phyllis Rogers's pugs, raced to the door. The dogs came, but no one else did. Ali rang the bell again, and the dogs went nuts. Giving up, she was walking back to the car when she heard a cell phone ring.

The sound seemed to be coming from inside the garage; after several rings, it stopped. She looked at the garage door. It was closed and locked. She was almost back to the Escalade when she glanced at the Honda. The passenger door was unlocked. On a whim and remembering Phyllis's cigarette break from the night before, Ali leaned over and looked inside. Sure enough, there were two garage door openers perched on the driver's visor. When she opened the car door, the air inside the vehicle was thick with cigarette smoke. Reaching across the seat, Ali punched the button on the first opener. Nothing happened, but when she punched the button on the second one, the door clattered, shivered slightly, and then rose.

Ali was just closing the door on the Honda when two dogs, no longer barking, came racing through the garage. They dashed past Ali without a glance, making a purposeful beeline for the dead grass in the front yard.

"Mom?" It was a child's voice, wary and uncertain. "Are you home? Where were you?"

"It's not your mother," Ali said. "My name is Ali Reynolds. You must be Connor, Lance's younger brother. I'm a friend of your mother's."

The wooden door slammed shut in Ali's face. "I'm not supposed to let anyone into the house when I'm home alone," the boy said from the other side. "Where's my mom?"

"I don't know," Ali said, turning back to the parked Taurus. "I heard a phone ringing in here a moment ago. Let me see if I can find it."

She opened the car door and looked inside for the phone. That was when she saw what was in the backseat. Who was in the backseat. The girl from the video lay faceup on the cloth bench seat. With her eyes wide open and a bullet hole in the middle of her forehead, there was no doubt she was dead.

The phone rang again. This time Ali was able to follow the sound. On the far side of the car, lined up on a workbench, were three cell phones and two purses. The caller ID readout on the ringing phone said, "Oakwood Lutheran Church." Leaving that phone and the others where they were, Ali backed away from the car, reaching for her own phone and dialing as she went.

"Nine-one-one. What are you reporting?"

"A homicide," Ali said. "At 4034 Twin Oaks Drive."

"Who's calling?" the operator wanted to know. "Do you know the victim? Are you sure the victim is deceased?"

They went through the standard list of questions. By then, Ali had reversed course and was back at the kitchen door. So were the dogs. "Connor," she said. "Please. You need to let me in. What happened here?"

Slowly, the door inched open. A child wearing a pair of faded Spider-Man pajamas peered out at her through teary eyes. He had a mop of long blond hair. Several missing baby teeth gave him a wry look. He was probably six years old. Maybe seven.

"I don't know what happened," he said in a rush. "When I woke up and climbed down from the top bunk, everybody was gone — Mommy, Grandma, and Thad. I thought they'd be right back, because Grandma hardly goes anywhere without her dogs. I thought maybe they took Thad to a basketball game or something. So I had breakfast and watched cartoons. I even put the milk away. When one of the dogs made a mess in the house, I tried to clean it up. I hope I'm not in trouble. But then I started to get worried. I was going to call Mom's cell phone and ask her when she'd be home, but the phone in the house isn't working. I don't know what's wrong with it."

The words spilled out of him in a torrent. When he finally paused for breath, Ali heard the sounds of approaching sirens. Connor must have heard them, too. "Are they coming here?" he demanded, his eyes wild. "Did something happen to my mom?"

Ali let the kitchen door close behind her. "Let's go wait in the living room," she said, taking him by the hand.

"Wait for what? What's happened?"

"The police will be here in a little while," she said. "They're going to need to talk to you."

"But I don't know anything," he insisted with stark terror on his face. "If the police are coming, they might take me away like they did Lance. Don't let them, please. I want my mommy."

Ali wanted to hold the boy and comfort him, but he slipped out of her hand, darted across the living room, and threw himself, sobbing inconsolably, on the couch.

There was a hard rap on the front door, the distinctive knock of an arriving cop. "Police," someone said. "Open up."

At once the dogs set off on another barking rampage. "Help me with the dogs, Connor," she begged. "Please."

Still sniffling, the boy straightened up, scrambled off the couch and grabbed one of the milling dogs while Ali caught hold of the other. With a struggling dog gripped in one hand, she swung the front door open.

"We had a call about a homicide?" A uniformed officer loomed in the doorway. He didn't have his weapon out of its holster, but his hand was poised an inch above the handle. He peered warily into the room, assessing the threat. Seeing only a woman, a child, and two very frantic dogs, he relaxed some but not completely.

"She's in the garage," Ali answered. "In the car. The garage door's open."

"Anyone else in the residence?"

"No," Ali said. "Just the boy and me."

Nodding, the cop backed away from the door.

"You said homicide," Connor said accusingly. "I know what that is. It means someone is dead. Is it my mommy?"

"No," Ali said evenly, "it's not your mommy."

"Who is it, then?"

"I don't know."

Her phone rang. B. sounded exuberant. "Stu just called. That most recent facial recognition program works like a charm. He's identified the girl in the photo. It's

Jillian Sosa."

"Lance's ex?" Ali asked. "Are you kid-ding?"

"Not kidding," he said. "That girl must be something else to be dating Lance and screwing around with his teacher at the same time."

"She was something else," Ali said.

"What?"

"Past tense, B. If Jillian Sosa is the girl in the photo, she's dead. I'm back at LeAnne's house. I just found the girl from the video out in the garage. Someone put a bullet through her head."

29

There was a moment of stark silence while B. internalized what had been said. "What about everybody else?" he asked finally.

"Connor's here. The dogs are here. Everybody else — LeAnne, Phyllis, and Thad — are gone."

"Crap," B. said.

Ali had a far stronger term in mind, but with Connor in the room and hanging on her every word, she didn't dare use it. "You can say that again," she said.

"Is LeAnne the shooter? Maybe she figures out that Jillian betrayed Lance. The two of them have some kind of confrontation. LeAnne shoots Jillian, and afterward she goes on the run."

"No," Ali said. "That can't be what happened. LeAnne didn't leave under her own power. She wouldn't have left Connor here alone all morning. He's only six. If she'd left willingly, she would have taken her purse and phone. She didn't. That's why I looked in the garage. Leland and I were about to drive away when I heard the phone ringing."

"Any sign of a struggle?"

"Not inside the house, and not in the garage, either, except for that single gunshot."

"Someone came into the house and marched them out at gunpoint," B. theorized. "This sounds like a rerun of what happened to Phyllis yesterday, probably by the same people. They're pissed because they discovered Lance screwed them over with his worm. Now they've upped the ante and taken three people instead of one. You've called the cops?"

"They just got here. What's going on there?"

"Lance is downstairs for PT, and Sister Anselm went for breakfast. I'll give him all this bad news when he gets back up here. It's going to hit him hard."

"He's not the only one," Ali said, looking across the room at Connor. He sat on the sofa, hugging the dog with what was close to a death grip. He looked so lost and alone that it broke her heart. "I've got to go," she told B. Ending the call, she turned her full attention to the boy. She sat down next to him on the couch and joined him in patting the dog. He wasn't comforted.

"I heard what you said," he declared accusingly. "Jillian's dead. How can that be? I liked her. I don't understand how she can be dead. And what if the same thing happens to my mom and Thad? What if they're dead, too? What will happen to me?"

With no acceptable responses to the distraught child's barrage of unanswerable questions, Ali was relieved to hear a light tap on the door. At once, both dogs set off a clamor. Ali was struggling to hang on to her squirming pug and to help Connor contain his when Leland Brooks let himself into the house.

"There's a crime scene out there," she said. "How'd you manage to talk your way past all those cops?"

He grinned back at her. "Charm is good," he said, "but being old helps. All I told them was that I needed to use the facilities. They let me right through." Coming across the room, Leland stopped in front of Ali and patted her dog on top of the head. It quieted immediately, allowing Leland to turn to Connor and the second dog. "My name is Mr. Brooks," he said, holding out his hand. "I'm a friend of Ms. Reynolds here. Who are you?"

The boy gravely accepted the proffered handshake. "I'm Connor," he said. "I'm scared. Jillian is dead and my mom is gone and I don't know if she's ever coming back."

"My," Leland said. "This all sounds rather serious. We'll have to see if there's something to be done about it. Do you mind if I sit down here with you and your dog?"

Connor said nothing as Leland joined them on the long sofa. When there was yet another knock on the door, Ali handed her pug to Leland and went to answer. She found Detective Richard Hernandez standing on the porch.

"This isn't my case," he said quickly. "I heard the radio transmission and knew it was LeAnne's house. I was afraid it was her. I'm glad it isn't. What's going on?"

"My mom is gone," Connor answered first. "She says my friend Jillian is dead." He nodded toward Ali as tears flooded his eyes. "I liked Jillian," he added. "She used to bring me jawbreakers and sneak them to me sometimes when Mom wasn't looking."

"Wait," Detective Hernandez said, looking from one face to another. "How do you know the victim's name? The guys outside told me they hadn't made an ID yet."

"Her name is Jillian Sosa," Ali explained. "She used to be Lance's girlfriend. I didn't

444

know her name when I found the body, but I do now."

"How?" Detective Hernandez asked.

"I still want to know what happened to Jillian," Connor insisted, looking at Ali. "Why won't you tell me?"

Before Ali could to respond to either question, Leland inserted himself into the conversation, asking Connor, "Did you say these dogs have been here with you all morning?"

Connor's questioning eyes swiveled from Ali's face to Leland's. He nodded.

"Have they had anything to eat?" Leland asked.

Connor shrugged. "I don't know," he said.

"I'll bet they're hungry." Leland rose from the couch and beckoned for the boy to follow. "How about the two of us take those dogs of yours out to the kitchen and see if we can find them some food?" he suggested. "What are their names again?"

"Duke and Duchess," Connor answered. "Duchess is the black one. Duke is brown. Grandma says he's apricot."

"I suppose, with a name like Duchess, she's a girl dog, right?" Leland asked.

"Right," Connor told him. Obligingly allowing himself to be diverted, Connor led Leland out of the room.

Ali turned to Detective Hernandez. "Here's the short version of what happened. Connor woke up this morning and found everyone — his mother, his grandmother, and his brother — gone. He was left here alone."

"Gone?" Detective Hernandez asked. "As in taken? Isn't this where we started yesterday with what happened to LeAnne's mother?"

"It sounds like it," Ali agreed, "and it may be the same people. We've learned that the program Lance used for the ransom demand was bogus, and it came with some serious strings attached. The bad guys may have decided to try again in hopes of getting the real program."

Another knock on the door announced the arrival of two plain-clothes detectives.

"Look," Ali said. "I'm going to be stuck here giving a statement. Call B. You still have his number?"

Hernandez nodded.

"He'll be able to bring you up to speed."

The two new arrivals looked first at Ali and then at Detective Hernandez. "Hey, Rich," one of them said. "What are you doing here? You're property; we're homicide. Isn't this supposed to be Mike's and my case?"

"I happened to be in the neighborhood when the call went out," Hernandez said. "Thought I'd stop by and lend a hand."

"We've got it."

Biting his lip, Detective Hernandez turned and was gone. The lead detective introduced himself as Michael Hopper and his partner as Alvin Harris. They got straight to business. Ali gave them her information as succinctly as she could, losing patience as they went over and over the same ground. Hopper's questions seemed to focus on the idea that LeAnne was the fleeing perpetrator of a homicide rather than the victim of some other crime. He rejected Ali's assertion that no mother would willingly leave a six-year-old child at home alone. He also took exception to what he referred to disparagingly as Ali's "tentative" identification of the victim. The more he asked, the less she wanted to tell him. As the interminable interview drew to an end, Detective Harris summoned a crime scene tech, who swabbed Ali's hands to check for gunfire residue.

"You'll make yourself available in case we have any more questions?" Detective Hopper asked when the technician left.

"Of course," Ali said.

Hopper nodded to his partner. "All right,

Alvin," he said. "I'm thinking our next call should be to social services. Have them come by and pick up the kid."

Ali remembered the stark dread that had flashed across Connor's face at the idea of being hauled away by the cops. It was understandable: After Lance was arrested, he had disappeared from this little boy's life for the better part of a year. The last thing Ali wanted to happen was for Connor to be exiled into some form of foster care.

"Look," she said, "Connor's older brother Lance is in Austin. We'll be going there as soon as we finish here. If you leave him with me, I'll see to it that he's with family rather than being dumped with complete strangers."

"Didn't you already tell us that the brother is in a hospital?" Hopper replied. "And let's not forget, Lance's ex-girlfriend is the one who's dead in the garage. This doesn't sound like a good call to me."

"By all means," Ali agreed. "Let's not forget that someone has been murdered. And let's not forget that Phyllis Rogers, the grandmother who is missing again, was taken and held hostage for a number of hours yesterday. No wonder he's scared."

"Ms. Reynolds —" Hopper began, but Ali continued. "Until you're able to determine if the rest of the boy's family has been kidnapped, don't you think we should at least regard Connor as a potential target? What happens if you put him into the system and he gets shipped off to some unsuspecting foster family? What are the chances that you'll be endangering them as well? My fiancé's company, High Noon, has engaged a former SEAL to provide beefed-up security for Lance. He would also be looking out for Connor."

Obviously unconvinced, the two detectives exchanged glances. Hopper stood up. He went over to the swinging door that led into the kitchen, pushed it open, and peered into the other room. Looking over the detective's shoulder, Ali caught a glimpse of the peaceful scene in the kitchen. Leland and Connor sat huddled over the kitchen table, intently focused on a game of checkers. Under Leland's chair, the two pugs lay back to back, sleeping.

Hopper sighed and let the door swing shut.

"Please," Ali said, pressing what she felt to be a slight advantage. "If you'd like me to, I'd be happy to discuss this matter with your captain."

She knew she was skating on the edge of truth in any number of ways. Father

449

McLaughlin was a retired SEAL, all right, but he had come into the picture the same way Sister Anselm had: through the efforts of Bishop Gillespie rather than through High Noon Enterprises. As for Connor's big brother? Lance was in no position to assume custody of anyone. For one thing, for the next week and a half anyway, he was a minor. He was also still officially an inmate at the San Leandro Juvenile Detention Center. Ali knew that if she were forced to follow through on her threat to go to Hopper's superiors, she would probably lose.

Much to her amazement, Detective Hopper caved. Maybe he didn't like dealing with social services. Maybe filling out their forms would have been one piece of paper too many. Maybe he just wanted to finish up this day's work at a decent enough hour to have Saturday dinner with his wife and kids.

"So we can state in our report that you'll be transporting him . . . What's his name again?"

"Connor."

"You'll be transporting Connor to Austin and handing him into the custody of a family member?"

"That's correct. His brother Lance."

"All right," he said. "I guess we're done here."

Once the two detectives were out the door, Ali grabbed her phone and dialed B.

"Took you long enough," he said.

"The detectives just now left. What's going on?"

"You remember that worm Lance was so proud of?"

"Yes, what about it?"

"It worked like a charm — even better than a charm. Stu has more broadband connection than anyone down here, so he's processing the data that the worm sent to Lance's cloud from four different computers. Data-dump analysis takes time. Stu's still working on the first batch. That one has an IP address that leads back to the computer lab at San Leandro High School. The user ID is Zorro. I've rented another car. I'm on my way to San Leandro right now. I'm hoping to get there before the computer club meeting is over."

"Why?"

"Because according to Stu, the stuff stored on that computer is dynamite. It's full of all kinds of information about the Cabrillo cartel's dealings with drug contacts and clients that stretch from Monterrey, Mexico, to Denver, Colorado. I want to talk to the new club adviser and find out who exactly uses that computer. My first guess is

Jillian, but I need to be sure."

"You're saying she used Lance's program to hack in to a drug cartel's computer system?"

"Either Jillian did it or it was someone else. That's what they were trying to do when the worm wiped out their computer capability."

"B.," Ali said, "this all sounds really dangerous."

"It is dangerous. For everybody involved, High Noon included. These are very bad guys. Stu says that his preliminary analysis indicates there's enough detail in the files to blow the inner workings of the cartel sky-high."

"Maybe they should have hired some cyber security," Ali said.

Her bit of gallows humor fell flat. B. didn't respond.

"But why would a high school computer club mix it up with a Mexican drug cartel?" Ali asked.

"That's what I'm hoping to find out by talking to the rest of the kids in the club."

"They have no way of knowing Jillian is dead, do they?"

"They shouldn't," B. said. "As far as I know, the victim's name has yet to be released."

"Shouldn't you call in someone to go with you?" Ali asked. "Detective Hernandez, maybe?"

"I already told him some of it," B. replied, "but I'm worried about bringing law enforcement any deeper into all of this than they already are. For one thing, the information the worm captured constitutes an illegal wiretap. If that comes to light, High Noon will be in big trouble. What's more, without warrants in place, none of what we have could be used in court, although if I were a crook who called myself El Cabrillo, I'd be looking for somebody with blood in my eye."

"Which means," Ali said, "that we have vital information about the bad guys, none of which we can use, but which has the potential of putting us in the middle of a shooting war?"

"That's about it," B. answered. "Lance's GHOST poked a very sharp stick into a hive of killer bees, and they may be swarming after us."

Ali thought about that. "Look," she said finally, "why don't I drop Leland and Connor off someplace so they can eat lunch? Then I'll come meet you at the school. How far away are you?"

"According to the GPS, I'm about fifteen

minutes out."

"I'll see you there."

There was a slight hiccup in the phone. "Hold on," B. said. "Stu's on the other line. I'll call you back."

Ali stood in the kitchen doorway silently watching the checkers game. Moments later, her e-mail alert sounded. She had two messages, both containing a photo. One looked like Jillian Sosa in a senior photo. The other appeared to be a school photo of the same girl taken several years earlier. The caption under that one said: Serafina Miguel.

A minute or so later, B. called back. "You've seen the photos?"

"Either Serafina and Jillian are the same person, or they're twins. What's the story?"

"Stu's looking into it. The second photo comes from the *Los Angeles Times* five years ago, when she graduated from UCLA with a master's degree in computer science at age sixteen. That picture was part of a story celebrating the success of immigrants from Mexico."

"Five years ago?" Ali asked. "What's she doing posing as a senior at San Leandro High School? How did she even get admitted?"

"Good question," B. said. "Something else

for Stu to work on when he has a free moment."

"Think about this," Ali said. "We're about to enter a high school building where someone in the computer club has been gathering information on a drug cartel," Ali said. "At least one member of that club has been shot to death. Is it a good idea to go there when the only weapon we have between us is a single Taser?"

"You could always bring along our secret weapon," B. said.

"What secret weapon?" she asked.

"Leland Brooks."

Even over the phone, Ali could tell B. was smiling. "Don't even joke about that."

"These are kids," B. argued. "Geeky kids. How dangerous can they be?"

"One of their former star members happens to be both geeky and dead," Ali pointed out.

There was a momentary silence. "All right," B. said at last. "This probably isn't something we should do on our own, so you make the call. We have a choice here. We can bring in the homicide cops you talked to, the ones who just left; we can call in the feds, who may already be tracking this because of what happened to Phyllis yesterday; or we can contact Detective Hernandez, the local guy, who, for one reason or another, seems to give a damn about what happens to Lance Tucker and his family. What's your poison?"

"Definitely the local guy," Ali said. "You call him while I get Connor and Leland gathered up and out of the house. I want them gone before the CSIs who are outside in the garage come inside to start tearing the house apart for evidence."

Punching the off button on her phone, Ali entered the kitchen. As she approached the table, Connor looked up at her with concern. "Are the cops coming for me now?" he asked.

"No," Ali answered. "They're not. How would you like to go to Austin to see your brother?"

Connor's eyes widened. "To see Lance? Really?"

"Yes, so maybe you'd better put on something besides those Spider-Man pj's. If you happen to have a backpack, throw some extra clothes in that: some jeans, socks, underwear, shirts, and a jacket."

"What about a toothbrush?"

"That, too."

"Will I be able to stay at the hospital with him like Mom does?"

"That remains to be seen," Ali said.

With that, Connor scampered off to his room. Clearly Leland had kept him so completely occupied with the game that he'd forgotten to miss his mother.

"What about the dogs?" Leland asked. "We can't very well leave them here, can we?"

By the time Connor emerged from his room with his loaded backpack, Ali and Leland had located two leashes and filled a grocery bag with Duke and Duchess necessities: dog dishes and cans of food.

"You'd better gather up the board and the checkers and put them in your backpack, too," Leland directed Connor. "We'll want to have those along to help pass the time."

As Connor hurried to comply, the dogs, aware that something was up, were on their feet and milling around the kitchen. Leland called them, and they came at once, standing docile and calm as he fastened leashes to collars.

They left the house with Leland holding the dog leashes in one hand and Connor's sturdy little hand in the other. Walking behind them, Ali couldn't help but marvel: Leland Brooks was not a grandfather and would never be a grandfather, but he would have been a great one.

As they climbed into the Escalade, it was

clear they weren't leaving a moment too soon. The CSI techs were preparing to enter the house. Ali knew that she, Leland, and Connor would all need to be fingerprinted eventually; their prints, hers especially, would be found in any number of places, both in the house and in the garage. The dogs eagerly clambered into the car and plunged all the way to the far back.

"Wait," Connor wailed once he was in the car. "We can't leave."

"Why not?" Ali expected him to offer some kind of objection about leaving his mother behind. He didn't.

"I need a car seat," Connor announced in all seriousness. "A booster."

Ali had a momentary vision of the blood-and-brain-spattered mess that covered the booster seat in the back of LeAnne Tucker's Taurus. "Just a minute," she said.

Climbing out of the driver's seat, she hurried over to the Honda, where she was relieved to see that Phyllis kept an extra booster seat in her vehicle. Ali grabbed it. The cloth seat reeked of stale smoke. In the Escalade, the foul odor quickly obliterated the spotless rental's cheery new-car smell, but the presence of the stinky car seat was enough to overcome Connor's objections.

"Okay," he said, snapping his seat belt. "Now we can go."

30

Ali dropped Leland and Connor at a nearby McDonald's that came complete with an indoor playground. She kept Duke and Duchess with her as she drove to the school.

San Leandro High was a sprawling campus with an immense parking lot and a cluster of buildings. The part of the lot closest to the athletic field was full of vehicles. From the bleachers a throng of fans cheered the opposing sides in an afternoon soccer match. Much closer to the buildings was a far smaller grouping of cars. She pulled up to that group of vehicles just as B. opened the door of one of them, unfolded his long frame, and climbed out. Naturally, the dogs went into full bark mode.

"I didn't know that was you," she said, climbing out and glancing at the unfamiliar vehicle, a Ford Focus.

"It's the only car I could get delivered to the hotel in a hurry," he said. "Maybe we can trade later. You can drive that one. The Escalade has more leg room."

"Fine with me," she said. "But you may want to stick with the car you've got until I get Phyllis Rogers's pugs out of this one."

True to form, the two dogs were on their hind legs in the driver's seat, barking like crazy. "You're right," B. agreed with a laugh. "Given that, maybe my need for additional leg room is overrated."

"Do you know where we're going?" Ali asked.

He pointed to a group of four smaller, squarish buildings that stood at some distance from the main part of the school. "I asked," B. said, "and was told they're out here in one of the portables."

Ali looked at the nondescript buildings, all of which had seen better days. "They're no more portable than Chris and Athena's mobile home is mobile," she said. "Why do they call them that?"

"No idea." They walked toward the building. "How should we play this?" B. asked.

"We don't tell them about Jillian, that's for sure," Ali said. "Let's try for something a little less inflammatory."

The doors they tried on the first two buildings were locked. The third one opened. The room was filled with ten or so

461

library-type tables, each holding a series of three old-fashioned PCs that might have been considered state of the art in the 1990s. They came complete with a jumble of cables that led down to electrical floor outlets and old-fashioned Ethernet connections. The fifteen or so kids sitting in the room had mostly pushed aside the keyboards on the aging school-owned computers and were engrossed in their own devices, leaving the taxpayer-purchased equipment to sit untouched in useless splendor.

A man in the front of the room glanced at the door as Ali and B. entered. "May I help you?" he asked, stepping forward to greet them. "I'm Martin Warren, the computer club adviser."

"I'm B. Simpson with High Noon Enterprises. This is my associate Ali Reynolds. My company handles cyber security for the San Leandro school district," B. continued. "We have some concerns that one or more of the computers here might be involved in unauthorized activity — by that I mean criminal activity."

Mr. Warren grinned as he shook his head. "I doubt that. As you can see, most of the kids bring their own equipment these days. Only the ones who can't afford laptops utilize these tired old PCs. They're so low on memory that I finally gave up bothering to upgrade them. It was too time-consuming, and they'd crash again a day or so later. They're mostly useless. We keep them here for show because no one in the administration is willing to take the heat for throwing them away."

"They're all still connected," Ali pointed out, looking down at the cable connections and electrical outlets under each table.

"Just because they're connected doesn't mean they work," Mr. Warren insisted.

"If you don't mind," B. said, "we'd like to take a look at the serial numbers."

"Sure," Mr. Warren said with a shrug. "Help yourselves."

They found the offending machine a few minutes later in the far corner of the room. Mr. Warren was correct. It was no longer working, but that wasn't due to missing updates. When B. tried to turn it on, the words "Fatal Error" flashed across the screen before it went completely dark.

"Lance's worm," he said to Ali, and she nodded.

"Did you find what you were looking for?" Mr. Warren asked. He rejoined them just as the dying computer went dark and shut down for good. "That's odd," he said. "These machines are all old, but I've never seen one of them do that before."

"Does anyone in particular use this machine?" Ali asked.

Mr. Warren looked mystified. "No one," he said. "This is a holdover from the district's first generation of computer purchases. It's not exactly steam-driven but close. That's why it's stuck back here in the corner."

"It may become evidence in a criminal case at some point and a fingerprint tech will need to dust it for prints," B. said. "If you don't mind, please cover it with something and tell your students that it's entirely off limits."

Mr. Warren frowned. "This sounds serious," he said. "May I ask what this is all about? Should I have asked for a warrant?"

"We're not at liberty to say what this is about," Ali said, "but I do have one question. How many kids are involved in this organization?"

"Twenty or so."

"Did the group send someone to a hospital in Austin yesterday?"

Mr. Warren frowned. "Not that I know of."

"The person brought a brand-new computer to a patient there, someone who used to belong to this organization. We were told it was a gift to him from the club."

"What student?" Warren asked.

"Lance Tucker."

Mr. Warren seemed to bristle. "Absolutely not," he said. "I've never met Mr. Tucker, but I know him by reputation. Considering his record, I wouldn't give that kid the time of day, much less condone my students giving him a computer."

"What can you tell us about Jillian Sosa?"

Mr. Warren shrugged. "What's to tell? She's brilliant and an absolute treasure to have around, both in class and in the club. After Lance left and Mr. Jackson, the previous adviser died, the club was in danger of being disbanded. Jillian and Andrew Garfield worked like crazy to keep it from going under."

"What can you tell us about Mr. Jackson?" Ali asked.

"Not much. I was his replacement, so I never met him. My understanding is that he took his own life," Mr. Warren continued. "As far as I can tell, it was terribly unfortunate and unnecessary, and it was all over this." He rolled up his shirtsleeve to reveal a blue plastic band that looked like one of those colorful bracelets people wear to show their affiliation with various kinds of charitable causes. "These stupid ID bracelets are just a way of keeping track of students and

465

teachers. Jackson was offended and got some of the kids in the group up in arms about it, which resulted in that whole server disruption controversy. I agree the tracking system is a bit intrusive, but it's nothing to get that excited about."

Unless you happened to be a teacher who was screwing a student, Ali thought. In that case, that student/teacher locating program might present a very real threat.

"Getting back to Jillian," Mr. Warren continued. "Some of the work she's done this year would be what you'd expect from a graduate in computer science rather than a high school senior. Even without Lance's help, she and Andrew walked away with the statewide competition. Considering the school district almost disbanded the club, that was a real coup."

"Andrew would be Andrew Garfield?" Ali asked. "The school superintendent's son?"

"Yes, he is that," Mr. Warren agreed, "but Andrew doesn't expect any special treatment. In this group, he's just one of the kids."

"Does he happen to be here today?" B. asked.

"Sure," Mr. Warren said. "He's the red-haired kid in the front row. Since Jillian isn't here this afternoon, I asked him to work with some of the kids who are struggling. He's smart enough in his own right, just not in Jillian's league."

"Could we talk to him?" B. asked.

"Sure," Mr. Warren said, "I don't see why not. Hey, Andrew, mind coming over here for a minute?"

A lanky young man extricated himself from a group of girls and sauntered over to where Ali and B. stood with his teacher. Ali knew the boy was a senior, which made him the same age as Lance, but he looked younger. Remembering that Andrew had been homecoming king to Jillian's homecoming queen, Ali couldn't help wondering if Jillian and Andrew had engaged in more intimate kinds of behavior, not unlike what the girl had been doing with the unfortunate Mr. Jackson.

"This is Mr. Simpson," Mr. Warren said. "With . . . Who did you say again?"

"High Noon Enterprises," B. supplied.

Ali noticed that the boy's face paled. "You've heard of us?" she asked.

Andrew nodded.

"We understand you came to visit Lance Tucker in Austin the other day and that you brought him a computer, purportedly from the club," B. said. "The problem is, Mr. Warren here says that the club wasn't the source of the gift, so I'm curious: Where exactly did the computer come from?"

"Jillian," Andrew said. "She said it was sort of an early birthday present. She was afraid that if Lance thought she was the one giving it to him, he might not accept it. His family is kind of poor, you know. That's why she said to tell him it was from everybody."

"Did you know it had a keystroke logger loaded on it?"

"A keystroke logger," Andrew repeated. "How could it? It was brand-new, still in the box."

"We traced the serial number," B. said. "It was part of a shipment of computers that went missing between the factory and the suppliers months ago. I've seen this kind of thing before: Someone buys the stolen computers, adds a few unwelcome components, and resells them as new. Most of the time, the buyer is a soon-to-be-divorced spouse trying to get the goods on a partner suspected of catting around."

Two red splotches of anger appeared on Andrew's pale face. "That bitch!" he exclaimed. "She's after GHOST, isn't she? She used me to deliver the computer, and all the while she was trying to cut me out of the deal. We're done! That's it! I'm never speaking to her again. Ever!"

Ali and B. exchanged glances. Andrew Garfield was right. He wouldn't be speaking to Jillian Sosa ever again. She was dead, and Andrew clearly had no clue.

Ali sat down on a nearby chair and pulled Andrew down beside her. "The two of you were close?" she asked.

"I thought so," he said.

"Tell us about her," Ali said. "Tell us what you know."

"Her parents died," Andrew said. "I don't know the whole story on that, because she didn't like to talk about it. I think they died in a car wreck. She came to live with her aunt and uncle at the beginning of her sophomore year."

"Do you know anything about the aunt and uncle?"

Andrew shrugged. "Not much. Their name is Barnes. I think her uncle's name is Howard. He's from here. Her aunt is Katrina or Katerina or something that starts with a K. She came from Mexico. They're loaded, I guess. They live on Par Five Drive in San Leandro Country Club Estates. They drive fancy cars. Jillian has a new BMW, and they let her do whatever she wants. She can come and go at all hours while the rest of us have to deal with curfews."

"Why did Jillian want GHOST?"

"Do you know what GHOST is?"

Ali nodded. "Just the basics."

"Well," Andrew said, "we all want it. Everyone does. GHOST is supposed to be the cyber version of Harry Potter's invisibility cloak. You can go to any website or domain name and no one can tell you've been there. That's why we were all so surprised when Lance got caught doing that server attack. If he'd used GHOST, he would have gotten away with it."

"When's the last time you saw Jillian?" Ali asked.

"The other day when she gave me the computer to take to Lance. I wanted her to come with me, but she said she'd be busy all weekend. Something about relatives from Mexico."

"Did she mention which relatives?"

"No."

"Have you spoken to her by phone?"

"I tried calling her," Andrew admitted, "but I got a weird message that her number was out of order. Probably a problem with billing. That happened to me once when my mom forgot to pay the bill."

More likely a problem with GHOST, Ali thought. Lance's worm had disabled Jillian's phone at the same time it shut down her computer. "So you and Lance Tucker were friends?" Ali asked.

Andrew nodded. "Are," he corrected. "We're still friends."

"What about you and Jillian?" Ali asked. "I may be old-fashioned, but in my world, friends don't date other friends' exes."

"It wasn't that big a deal," Andrew replied. "Lance had broken up with her long before she asked me out."

"She asked you?"

Andrew nodded, but then he squared his shoulders. "But if she's been going after GHOST behind my back, it's all over between us."

It certainly is, Ali thought. She was tempted to tell him the truth, but she didn't.

"How did she get along with Mr. Jackson?" B. asked.

"Great," Andrew said. "The teachers all love her."

I'll bet, Ali thought.

"Did she ever mention to you that she had some connections to a Mexican drug cartel?"

Andrew laughed outright. "A drug cartel? You're kidding. Why would Jillian Sosa have anything to do with people like that?"

B.'s distinctive ringtone sounded, and he left the room to take the call. He came back moments later, gesturing for Ali to follow him and mouthing the words "We have to go" all the while holding his hand over the speaker.

Mystified, Ali did as he asked. "What?" she asked, once they were outdoors.

He shook his head to silence her. With his phone on speaker and his hand over the microphone, he held it up for Ali to listen. The first voice she heard was Sister Anselm's.

"He's my patient," the nun was saying. "If you're taking him, you're taking me. As the doctor already explained, it's much too soon for him to leave the hospital. He's barely out of the ICU and in no condition to leave the hospital without proper medical assistance, which I'm prepared to provide."

"Please," a second voice said. "She said there'll be a doctor there and attendants in the ambulance waiting downstairs. If I don't bring him to Felix, she says she'll kill my mother and Thad, just like she did Jillian."

Ali turned questioningly to B. "LeAnne?"

He nodded. Giving her the phone, he took out his iPad and began typing a message to Stuart Ramey, which he showed to Ali as soon as he pressed Send.

Activate the GPS on Sister Anselm's phone. She'll be on the move. We need to know where she's going. And see if you can find anything on someone named Felix.

"I've got to go." Lance was speaking. "I want to go. This is all my fault and my responsibility."

"And you're my responsibility," Sister Anselm said firmly. "You still need constant medical care. You may leave this hospital against the doctors' orders, but you won't be leaving it without me. If you're getting in that ambulance, so am I. Is that clear?"

With his iPad in hand, B. was typing again, this time to Father McLaughlin.

Sister Anselm and Lance leaving. Ambulance waiting downstairs. Try to get tab info. Follow if possible. Stay out of sight. We'll be tracking them remotely.

"It's too dangerous," LeAnne was insisting to Sister Anselm. "I can't possibly allow it."

"Sorry," the nun replied forcefully. "Unless you're prepared to resort to violence — something I don't recommend — I don't see how you can stop me, so let's stop arguing and get things under way."

The phone beeped, indicating that the call

had ended.

Ali turned to B. Standing by his elbow, she read what he had written. "You're sending Father McLaughlin into the fray? Is that a good idea?"

"I understand from Bishop Gillespie that Father McLaughlin has spent the last thirty years serving as either chaplain or priest in some of the hottest hot spots on the planet. He'll be fine."

The reply from Stuart Ramey showed up seconds later.

Got her. Still at the hospital. I'll keep you posted once they start moving. I asked Father McLaughlin to send photos of the ambulance as well as any of the people associated with it. Facial recognition already worked once on this case. Maybe it'll work again. I'll search what I can for Felix.

Ali frowned. "How did he do that so fast?"

"Do what?"

"Get a location for Sister Anselm's phone."

"After what happened a few months ago?" B. asked. "Stu has every High Noon–connected phone programmed into our computer system. He types in the number, and the program tells us where that person is. Or at least where that person's phone is. It gives us a starting point, which was more than we had for you when they slapped you into the back of that speeding Mercedes."

"Sister Anselm's phone, too?" Ali asked.

"And Father McLaughlin and Bishop Gillespie."

"So mine, too," Ali said. "What about yours?"

"Sauce for the goose," B. said. His phone rang. "Hello, Detective Hernandez," he answered. "Apparently we have a new ransom demand that LeAnne Tucker came to the hospital in person to deliver." He paused and then added, "Yes, at least she was all right a few minutes ago, when we overheard her speaking to Sister Anselm. She claims that both her mother and her son Thad are being held hostage to ensure her safe return. LeAnne referred to the kidnapper as a woman, and what the woman wants is Lance Tucker. They're having his mother spring him from the hospital and take him to an undisclosed location."

There was another pause.

"That's a fair assumption. With Jillian out of the picture, whoever is after Lance's GHOST program probably needs someone with enough computer savvy to run it. Who better than one of the guys who wrote it?"

Ali could hear Detective Hernandez's voice rumbling in the background. The sound was enough to let her know that he was speaking, without allowing her to overhear any of the content.

"You're right," B. said in reply. "We'll bring in the local authorities once we know which ones those should be. Until Sister Anselm's phone starts moving on the map, we won't know where they're headed. I'll let you know when we do. In the meantime, get me whatever you can on Jillian's auntie. Right, Katerina Barnes. If you could come up with a driver's license photo and send it to Stu, that would be a big help. Thanks."

B. ended the call. By then Ali had glanced at her watch and was edging away from him toward the Escalade. "Hernandez is a good guy. Let's hear it for making friends with at least one of the locals," he said. Noticing she was slipping away, he added, "Where are you going?"

"I left Leland and Connor at McDonald's just up the street. They've been there for over an hour. I need to bail them out. I was going to take Connor to Austin, but that's not going to work."

"No," B. said. "It won't. We'll see if we

can check them back in to the hotel here. I hope to hell they take dogs."

31

Duke and Duchess met Ali's return to the car with an ecstatic chorus of greeting, and they did the same when Connor scrambled into the booster chair in the backseat and fastened his belt. Preoccupied with the dogs, the boy looked up when he realized Ali was pulling in to a hotel parking lot.

"Hey," he said. "I thought you told me we were going to Austin. To the hospital. I thought you said I'd get to see Lance."

"Sorry," Ali replied. "There's been a slight change of plans. It turns out Lance is in the process of leaving the hospital. Until we know for sure where he's going, you, Mr. Brooks, and your grandmother's dogs will have to hang out here."

Glancing in the rearview mirror, she could see that Connor was screwing up his face in preparation for turning on the waterworks. Leland quickly jumped into the rapidly deteriorating situation and steered things in a more constructive direction. "How would you like to go swimming?" he asked.

"Swimming?" Connor asked. "It's too cold to go swimming."

"The hotel has an indoor pool," Leland told him. "I saw it this morning, and the sign says it's heated."

"I didn't bring a swimming suit," Connor objected.

"That's why hotels have gift shops," Leland said. "That allows you to purchase whatever you may have forgotten to bring along. Now, while Ms. Reynolds and Mr. Simpson get us checked in, how about if you take the dogs for a walk on that strip of grass over there. Do you have the plastic bag I gave you?"

Grudgingly, Connor produced a brand-new poop bag from the pocket of his jeans.

"Be sure to use it," Leland admonished.

"I know how," Connor said. "I've done it with Grandma lots of times."

"Sorry to stick you with kid and dog duty," Ali said to Leland as they watched the boy march across the drive with the dogs strutting obediently at his heels.

"Don't worry about me," Leland said. "I can tell that you and Mr. Simpson have your hands full. I'm glad to be able to make some small contribution, but try not to forget me the way you did this morning," he added with a twinkle in his eye. "That was a bit hard on the ego."

By the time the dogs had finished and they were all in the lobby, B. had completed the registration process and handled the luggage issues. "Ali and I will take the Escalade," he said, handing Leland the keys to the Focus. "This way, if you need a vehicle, you won't be stranded."

"I expect we'll be fine right here," Leland said.

B.'s phone rang, and he handed it to Ali. "I'll drive," he said. "They're headed north, we're headed south. You're in charge of communications."

"Okay," Stuart said over the speaker. "Detective Hernandez sent me a driver's license photo for Katerina Barnes, and Father McLaughlin sent me a photo of a woman standing next to the waiting ambulance, smoking a cigarette. We have a match. Sister Anselm's phone is moving north on I-35, and so is LeAnne Tucker's, presumably in the same vehicle. Katerina is driving a red Cadillac STS that left the hospital right after the ambulance. Now that they're out on the open road, Father McLaughlin is staying behind both vehicles by a mile or so, far enough back so they won't realize they're being followed."

"Let's hope," Ali said.

"According to the information on Katerina Barnes's license, her place of birth is Monterrey, Mexico, and her maiden name was Cabrillo."

"Cabrillo as in Cabrillo cartel?" B. asked.

"That's right. Ernesto Cabrillo is listed as Katerina's father. At least he used to be."

"Are you saying he's dead?" Ali asked.

"No, I'm saying he disowned her. Sent her packing six years ago without so much as a peso to her name. Fortunately for her, she landed on her feet a few months later when she found Mr. Barnes, first name Howard. He's a wealthy native of San Leandro. He was a recent widower when he ran into Katerina, three decades his junior, at a party in Acapulco. After a fun-filled whirlwind courtship, they married in Las Vegas three weeks later."

"What's Katerina's connection to Jillian?" Ali asked.

"They're not blood relations," Stu said, "at least not so far as I can tell. Because of our ongoing relationship with the San Leandro school district, it wasn't hard to get into their records. Ms. Sosa was enrolled as a sophomore in San Leandro High in September two years ago, which would be three years after she got her master's in computer science from UCLA. Ms. Barnes, claiming to be Jillian's aunt and legal guardian, enrolled her in school, but I got a look at the documents she used. They're definitely forgeries. That goes for Jillian's birth certificate and her shot record as well."

"All of which means Lance's GHOST was the target of the operation from the beginning," B. concluded. "That's why she went to San Leandro High in the first place and why she posed as a student there when she was already a college graduate."

"How would Serafina even know about GHOST?" Ali asked.

"Ghost technology has been a topic of continuing discussion in the geek world for years," B. explained. "If there were rumors floating around in the blogosphere that someone was getting close to making it work, it would have been hot news."

"What about Serafina's parents?" Ali asked. "LeAnne mentioned that Jillian's parents died in a car wreck."

"Close but no cigar," Stu said. "They're both dead, but not in an MVA. Francisco and Luisa Miguel were living in San Diego six years ago when they were murdered in a still-open-and-unsolved home invasion case. At the time, Serafina was at UCLA. She came home for a weekend break and found her parents' bodies several days after the murders. A few rumors surfaced that Cisco Miguel, a CPA, may have worked for the Cabrillo cartel. Those rumors were never confirmed, and no solid evidence linking the cartel to the crime has ever been found."

"In other words, the only thing Serafina and Katerina seem to have in common is a shared grudge against a single enemy: Ernesto Cabrillo, the head of the cartel. Somehow they joined forces and decided to target Ernesto's operation."

"You're on the money there," Stu said. "I can tell from the files that Jillian stored on the school computer that she was totally focused on amassing as much information as possible about the cartel's internal workings. She had put together impressive lists of contacts — dealers, bankers, drivers, traffickers, whatever it takes to keep a complex distribution network moving. She has files that contain lists of bank account numbers, complete with passwords and balances."

"Are there any names on those lists that you recognized?"

"The one that jumped right out at me is the firebug, Marvin Cotton. He's done odd jobs for the cartel for years."

"So who was he working for at the time

he attacked Lance and went after Lowell Dunn — for the cartel or for Jillian and Katerina?"

"Can't say for sure," Stu answered, "but I wouldn't be surprised if Jillian and Katerina made use of some of the Cabrillo worker bees uncovered by Jillian's research and had them do some odd jobs on the side."

"She was tapping into their files and using some of their resources?" Ali asked.

"If she did all that without having GHOST capability and without getting caught," B. mused, "then she was an amazing hacker in her own right."

"A dead hacker now," Ali reminded him. "But how was she planning on using the information she was gathering on the cartel? Did she intend to hand it over to law enforcement or do something else with it?"

"It looks to me," Stu said, "like Jillian was all about disrupting Cabrillo's operation. That's not true about Katerina. Her e-mail correspondence indicates that she has a surprisingly cozy relationship with a guy named Alonzo Diaz. Ever heard of him?"

"Never," B. said. "Who's he?"

"Alonzo Diaz is Ernesto Cabrillo's closest competitor in terms of geographical proximity and relative power. Alonzo is to Juárez what Ernesto is to Monterrey."

"It looks like we have two women, joined at the hip as far as targeting Ernesto is concerned, but maybe not on the same page on how to go about it."

"Which may also explain why one of them is dead and the other one isn't."

"What's Mr. Barnes's role in all this?" B. asked. "Is he an active participant or an innocent bystander?"

"I haven't gotten to any of the data off his computer yet," Stu said. "Stay tuned."

"What's going on with those vehicles?" Ali asked.

"Still northbound," Stu said. "Maintaining a steady pace. If it looks like they're starting to slow down, I'll let you know."

"Have you gone looking for Felix yet?" B. asked.

"That's on my list," Stu said. "There's only one of me, you know. Maybe it's time we talk about getting me an intern after all. I'll check on Felix next."

"Fair enough," B. said. "Call from Hernandez coming in. Gotta go." He switched over to the other call. "What's up?"

"Detectives Hopper and Harris just went by the Barneses' place on Par Five Drive to do a next-of-kin notification. They found more than they bargained for."

"Don't tell me."

"Yup. No one answered the front door, but they found the back door ajar. Detective Hopper decided to dot I's and cross T's. He got himself a warrant before he and Detective Harris went inside. When they did, they found Howard Barnes dead in his bathroom, shot in the back while taking a shower. The house has one of those new-fangled constant-supply hot water heaters, and the water was still running. By the time Hopper turned the water off, the victim was mostly parboiled. I'll keep after the CSI folks. If the weapon here turns out to be the same gun that killed Jillian, I'll let you know. Any news on the ambulance?"

"According to Stu, it's still headed north on I-35."

"Fair enough," Hernandez said. "I've made a few calls. If this goes down in San Leandro County, our rapid-response team will be at the ready. They're calling it an exercise, but they'll be on duty and ready to deploy as needed. The problem is, do we want them? If it turns into a siege situation, the hostages will die. Believe me, people around here still remember Waco."

"Right," B. said. "We need to extricate the hostages without provoking a firefight."

A message alert came in from Stu, and Ali read it aloud. "Felix's Auto Recycling," it said. "Saucedo. It's on Jillian's list. Checking satellite photos now."

"Where's Saucedo?" B. asked.

Ali checked her phone. "Just inside the San Leandro County line, but we don't know for sure that's where they're headed," she said. "If we have Detective Hernandez call in a strike on what turns out to be a legitimate business . . ."

Just then, Stu called back. "Okay. I've got a current satellite feed."

"From where?" B. asked.

"Better you don't know. It turns out that the only businesses at the Saucedo exit are two truck stops and the junkyard. Felix's Auto Recycling is a Texas-sized place with what's supposedly the largest selection of Corvair parts in the country. There's a long building at the front of the property. I'm assuming that's where the sales counter would be. There are several other structures on the property. The hostages could be in any of them. From what I'm seeing, there's a lot inside that salvage yard that doesn't look like junk. In the middle of the storage place, away from the outside fence and surrounded by a fort of stacked wrecked cars, is an interesting collection of vehicles that appear to be in perfect working order.

"I saw a couple of vans, a brown one with

UPS markings and a white one with FedEx markings. How often do you see competing vehicles garaged on the same lot? Beyond that, we've got a duke's mixture of rolling stock: several moving vans with company logos, a hearse, two more ambulances, a tanker truck, and a fire truck. None of those look like junkers, and they can't be seen from outside the yard."

"It sounds like we're dealing with a major transportation hub."

"Yes, with one additional detail: There's a helicopter pad in the very center of the yard. That is, the spot is marked for a helicopter, but there isn't one parked there now."

"If Katerina's making a run for it and planning to take Lance with her, the chopper's probably already on its way."

"What do you want me to do?" Stu asked. "Call Hernandez?"

"And start a gunfight? No," B. said. "What if they have as many drivers hanging around as they have vehicles, and what if all of them are armed because they're used to provide extra security?"

"That could be bad," Stu said.

"Right, so let's level the playing field and get rid of the extra hands. Did Jillian happen to have Ernesto Cabrillo's e-mail address in her collection of intel?"

"Yes, she did," Stu replied. I've got it right here."

"I want you to use our copy of GHOST. Hack in to Ernesto's e-mail account and send a spoof message to whatever e-mail address you have for the junkyard. Say, 'DEA on way. Get out! Now!' After you do that, since what you're watching probably is DEA satellite feed, you'd best shut it down. A lot will be happening in the next little while, and I'd like to have as few eyes watching as possible."

Somewhere out of reach, Ali's phone rang. She remembered dropping it in her purse much earlier, but the purse was currently stowed on the floorboard behind the passenger seat. She had to unfasten her seat belt and clamber half onto the seat with her knees in order to reach it. By the time she retrieved her phone, it had stopped ringing; a call from an unknown number showed in the screen. Thirty seconds later, the phone vibrated in her hand, this time with a voice mail.

"Kate Benchley here," said a cheery Brit voice when Ali punched the Play button. "Thought you'd want to know. The samples weren't all that degraded after all. Donna was able to work her magic. The bloodstains from the collar, presumably from the victim, belong to a male who is almost certainly the father of both whoever left the stains on the shirtsleeves as well as the sample taken from the coffee cup, which I'll return to the Highcliff the next time I go to spend some time with Marjorie.

"You know the odds on DNA," Kate continued. "These three individuals are definitely related, with a 99.99777 percent certainty, but without some other corroborating evidence, Donna's findings won't be enough to carry the day in a court of law. Give me a call to let me know what, if anything, you want me to do with these results. Cheerio."

"Who was that?" B. asked.

"Kate Benchley from Oxford," Ali said. "She just told me who murdered Leland's father."

"What are you going to do about it?"

"Tell him, I suppose," Ali said. "What happens after that will be up to him."

32

The Saucedo exit sign appeared overhead, along with another sign on the shoulder announcing gas and food. No lodging. B. slowed and switched on his turn signal. "I'll fill up with gas," he said. "You keep an eye out and tell me if you see anything."

While Ali watched, an odd assortment of vehicles — vans, trucks, and pickups — came streaming out of a business across the freeway from the gas station. Some entered the freeway northbound and sped away. A few crossed over and continued westbound on the surface road, while the remainder entered the freeway headed south. The last vehicle to leave, a pickup, stopped just outside the junkyard's razor wire–topped fence. The driver got out, closed the gate, and then locked it with a length of chain and a padlock.

Done filling the tank, B. climbed into the car. "I counted fifteen vehicles in all," Ali told him. "The last guy to leave locked the gate."

"Okay, Stu," B. said. "Whatever you told them worked. They all bailed. Great job. Now where's that northbound ambulance?"

"They're only ten miles out, but they've pulled off into a rest area. I directed Father McLaughlin to drive past them and take the next exit, five miles ahead, then wait to see what they do. I'm guessing that someone from the junkyard called to warn them of the impending raid. They may be considering going elsewhere."

"If they're all gone," Ali wondered, "what are the chances that the only people left inside are Phyllis Rogers and her grandson, two hostages who are completely expendable now that Katerina has Lance?"

"If they're not dead already," B. replied.

"So what do we do? Call Hernandez and tell him to bring on the strike force?"

"It'll take those guys at least fifteen minutes to get here," B. said. "We may not have fifteen minutes. Let's see if we can get them out ourselves."

"Alone? Without backup?" Ali responded. "Cops call that Lone Rangering, and it's a bad idea. Especially since we have no weapons and no Kevlar vests."

"You'd be surprised," B. told Ali as he

punched buttons on his phone. "You might be very surprised."

A moment later, Father McLaughlin's voice boomed over the speaker.

"Hey, it's B. and Ali."

"Good to hear from you. What's up?"

"I know Stuart directed you to hold up, but we're parked across the highway from the junkyard, and we have an issue. We believe — or rather, we hope — that we've sent most of the bad guys packing. Right now, before that ambulance shows up, we have a tiny window of opportunity."

"To extract the other two hostages?"

"How did you guess? I know you offered to help out by lending us weapons and vests earlier. Stupidly, I turned you down. At this point, I've changed my mind, and I'm ready to accept same."

"Where are you?"

"At the 76 station on the west side of the Saucedo exit, but we're headed for the gate to the junkyard right now. We're in a red Cadillac Escalade. If you're northbound, the gate to the junkyard is on the east side of the freeway along the frontage road just beyond the exit."

"I'm on my way," Father McLaughlin said. "I should be there in a jiff."

"Tell him there's a chain with a padlock

on the gate," Ali warned. "The only way we'll be able to get inside is to drive through."

Father McLaughlin said with a laugh, "I may be a man of God, but I'm also a man of action. I believe in being prepared because it turns out most people aren't, including, presumably, the two of you. Along with a few extra weapons and a spare Kevlar vest or two, I always carry a pair of bolt cutters in the back of my car. Doesn't everybody?"

"Point taken," B. muttered.

He was preparing to drive away from the gas station when Ali stopped him. "Wait," she said. "I want to go buy some jerky. We're going to a junkyard. If there happens to be a junkyard dog, I want to be prepared, too."

Father McLaughlin pulled up in a dusty, disreputable, and very unpriestly-looking Isuzu Trooper moments after B. and Ali stopped in front of the locked gate. He got out, wrestled a large bolt cutter out of a locked tool chest in the Trooper's cargo hold, and made short work of the padlock.

"Ambulance is still stationary," Stu reported. "If you're going to do this, get in and get out in a hurry."

The good father seemed to be in no rush at all. Once they had driven the Isuzu and the Escalade through the opening, he took his time closing the gate and replacing the chain and the lock, positioning them so the lock appeared to be engaged. "It might be enough to slow them down," he explained in response to Ali's clear exasperation. "Now, I believe I promised you vests and weapons?"

First he hauled out two Kevlar vests that they put on immediately. B.'s was slightly too small, and Ali's was too big, but they were for protection rather than a fashion statement, and Ali was glad to have them.

Father McLaughlin reached back into the Trooper, opened a metal case, and retrieved two handguns. "I trust you both know how to operate these," he said. "They're loaded: six in the magazine, and that red pop on the slide shows there's one in the chamber."

He handed over a pair of Kahr P380s. Ali hefted her weapon and then expertly stripped it down. The Kahr was unfamiliar to her, and if there was a chance that her life would depend on it, she needed more than a relative stranger's word that the P380 was in good working condition. She checked the rounds in the magazine. They were .380ACP hollow-point bullets. Hoping the Kahr had been properly lubed and cleaned, she put it back together and passed it to B.

Once she had checked out the second weapon, she dropped it into the pocket of her vest. After a moment's consideration, she took it out of the pocket and tucked it into the waistband of her underwear. She had the jerky unwrapped and at the ready, but so far there was no sign of any dogs.

Father McLaughlin looked around. "Seems like a big place. Do we have any idea where to look for those hostages?"

"Best guess, they're in one of the metal buildings," B. said. "I doubt there's any sense in trying the front door."

"Let's try it anyway," Ali suggested. "The hostages may not be there, but this way we'll know for sure if someone is minding the store."

"Okay, you take the front. We'll try the back. If somebody does come to the door and asks what you want, tell them you're looking for body parts for your husband's 1962 Corvair Monza," B. said. "That's something almost no one will have on hand."

Ali drove the Escalade to the front entrance while B. and Father McLaughlin, in the Isuzu, drove to the back. Peering in through grimy windows, she saw a grubby linoleum-covered counter with a pair of dilapidated stools parked in front of it. At

496

the far end of the counter stood an old-fashioned cash register with the drawer wide open. No, Ali told herself. The guy who left isn't coming back.

Her phone rang.

"Trouble," B. said. "The ambulance is on the move."

"We need to go, then."

"We can't. We think we've located the hostages. They're in a locked shed with some kind of motor running inside. The doors are metal. One has a deadbolt and the other is barred on the inside. Father McLaughlin is hooking a chain up to the back of his Trooper and hoping to pull the slider loose, but it's taking time. Once we get to them, we'll need to get them out. If they've been in there long enough to have suffered carbon monoxide poisoning, that may not be easy."

Ali looked at the northbound lanes of the freeway. There were cars visible but no sign of the ambulance. "Somebody needs to stall them, then," she said. "How long before they get here?"

"Stu says five minutes, no more."

Ali turned and looked at the junkyard's front entrance, at a gate that looked locked but wasn't. The padlock was all bluff. Squaring her shoulders, Ali decided she would be, too. "I'll do it," she said. "At least I'll try. You guys do whatever you can to rescue the hostages. I'll go back to the gate and use the Escalade to block it shut. The only way for Katerina and her henchmen to get to you or the hostages will be through me. If you have to, use Father McLaughlin's bolt cutter and make a hole in the back fence big enough to drive his Trooper out."

"Wait," B. objected. "I didn't mean for you to —"

"Too late," Ali said. "I'm already on my way. I'll leave my phone on speaker so you'll know what's happening."

"I can't let you do this," B. argued. "I never should have put you in this position."

"We got into this position together," Ali told him. "We'll get out of it the same way."

From the far side of the building, she heard a boom that sounded like a mini-explosion followed by the clattering of metal. She hoped that meant Father McLaughlin had succeeded in popping the door off the shed. In the Escalade, she drove back to the gate and parallel-parked on the far side of it.

With the vehicle in park, she took a deep breath. In the stillness, even with the phone in her pocket, she could hear urgent shouting, ragged coughing, clattering, and banging — all of them the welcome sounds of living. She let out her breath and then sat there, trying to relax and calm her nerves; trying to summon the courage it would take to face down someone she already knew to be a cold-blooded killer. Having wandered into the thick of what might be a dispute between two warring drug cartels, she had come to the fight armed with a single pistol and seven hollow-point bullets. Her only hope was to try to deescalate a shooting war into a war of words. Was that even remotely possible?

"I'm in position," she said. Her phone, on speaker, was in the left pocket of her vest. She shifted the pistol from her waistband to the right-hand pocket. Ali was a trained shot, a capable shot, but would that give her enough of an edge against two armed guards and a killer? Probably not. And if a hail of bullets came speeding at her, bent on mowing her down, would the paltry vest be any kind of help? Unbidden Ali recalled Jillian Sosa's wide-open eyes as she lay dead in the back of LeAnne Tucker's Taurus. Jillian had been shot in the head. Bullet-resistant materials could help with body shots, but no Kevlar vest in existence would protect against a headshot. None at all.

"Got 'em," B. said breathlessly. "They

need to be checked out in a hospital. Should we try coming out through the gate?"

"No," Ali said decisively. "There's not enough time. Use the bolt cutter and go out through the back."

"All right," B. agreed, "but once the hole is made, it'll only take one of us to get them to the hospital. The other one should stay here with you for backup. You pick."

"You go; Father McLaughlin stays," Ali said. "He's a better shot."

If B.'s feelings were hurt by her unflinching assessment of his combat capabilities, he let it pass without a word.

Out on the freeway, Ali caught a glimpse of a tiny speck of red speeding north. "They're coming now," she said. "Still on the freeway, approaching the exit. Go now. Get Phyllis and Thad to safety."

"Ali, I —"

"Don't talk," she urged. "Go! Please."

She opened the car door and got out. In order to pull off this colossal bluff, she would need to look perfectly at ease, as though she didn't have a care in the world and wasn't scared to death. Her knees still shook as she walked up to the front fender of the Escalade and leaned against it. With the back of one foot propped against the tire and with her hands stuffed casually in her pockets, Ali hoped she looked relaxed even though every nerve in her body was strung tight. If need be, she was fully prepared to use the poised foot to kick off from the vehicle and propel herself forward.

The ambulance slowed as it approached the stop sign at the top of the exit. She tried to prepare herself. She knew that four lives hung in the balance: Lance's, LeAnne's, Sister Anselm's, and her own. What could she possibly say that would be powerful enough to win this war of words? A moment later, she knew. "I'll lie," Ali Reynolds said aloud. "I'll lie like crazy."

The ambulance turned right at the top of the overpass and then, after a few short yards, turned left onto the two-way frontage road. In a block or so, it slowed again and prepared to turn in to the junkyard. Having prepared herself to face down the two guards, Ali was astonished to see LeAnne Tucker behind the wheel of the rumbling ambulance. In the passenger seat was a woman. Although Ali had never seen her before, she realized this had to be Katerina Barnes.

The passenger door swung open. The dark-haired woman with shoulder-length locks who swung to the ground from the cab of the ambulance was probably a decade younger than Ali. Her figure was nothing short of spectacular. She was dressed in a smart knit pantsuit that spoke of money and power. Almost as an afterthought, Ali noticed the weapon in Katerina's left hand, pointed directly at Ali's chest.

Automatically, Ali tried to assess the weapon's capabilities. It was most likely a semiautomatic. There would be lots more shots in the clip than Ali's paltry seven. Forcefully, she pushed that self-defeating thought out of her head. If you started comparing numbers of potential shots, you had already lost.

"Who are you?" Katerina Barnes demanded. "You don't look like DEA. No letters on your vest. Besides, they don't drive Escalades, and they wouldn't show up with a search warrant in hand and leave the gates locked."

Years earlier, when Ali was starting out as a television news reporter, she had suffered dreadful cases of nerves before those first few stand-up live reports. Over time, she had learned to look at the camera and focus. In this case, the weapon pointed in her direction served the same function, giving her focus and purpose.

"And you don't look like an ambulance attendant," Ali said with a toss of her head.

"I guess that makes us even."

"Move your vehicle. Now."

"No," Ali said.

"Move it, or I'll shoot."

"If you do, you'll be very sorry."

Katerina frowned as though she didn't quite grasp what had been said. Maybe it had been spoken in a foreign language. "What do you want?" she asked.

"I want the people you're holding prisoner," Ali said. "Lance, his mother, and Sister Anselm."

Katerina laughed. "You can't be serious. You think I'm just going to hand them over?"

"I am and I do," Ali said calmly. Inside the pocket of her vest, her hand felt steady on the firm grip of her pistol.

"Why would I do that?"

"Because I have GHOST and you don't," Ali said. "You need GHOST, too, but you shot the person you hired to run it. The only other person who can do that for you is the person in the back of that ambulance. If something happens to Lance Tucker, you're screwed."

"He'll do what I say," Katerina said. "Otherwise his family dies, starting with his mother." She turned back to the ambulance and waved the gun in LeAnne's direction.

"Out," she ordered. "Now."

LeAnne opened her door and stumbled to the ground. The open plea for help in her expression came close to disrupting Ali's concentration.

"Move your vehicle," Katerina repeated. "I have a helicopter to catch."

"It's not coming," Ali said, hoping that was true. If Katerina had been playing both ends against the middle, she suspected Felix's Auto Recycling was fully stocked with operatives on either side of the Cabrillo/Diaz line. Word of the DEA raid would have gotten back to her friend Alonzo. Surely he wouldn't risk losing a helicopter.

"Of course it's coming," Katerina said. "Why wouldn't it?"

"Because Alonzo Diaz knows you betrayed him — that you set up this meeting for the sole purpose of allowing the DEA to confiscate his aircraft," Ali said.

"But I didn't," Katerina objected. "I wouldn't do that. Ever. Besides, you're not the DEA."

"Believe me," Ali said, "there will be plenty of proof to show you did," Ali said. "As for your father? Ernesto will receive a flurry of e-mails containing a sampling of the documents that you and Jillian stole from his organization. He'll also have copies of e-mails that spell out the mutually beneficial relationship you've established with his most dangerous competitor."

Katerina's olive skin paled in the harsh afternoon sun. "Those files don't exist anymore," she hissed. "Jillian told me they were gone, that we couldn't get them back."

"That's because Jillian thought she knew how to use GHOST when she didn't. I have it, I know how to use it, and I'm fully prepared to unleash it on you."

Father McLaughlin appeared as if out of nowhere, rising up from the far shoulder of the frontage road and strolling into Ali's line of vision, then disappearing at the back of the ambulance. Behind him came a second figure. It took Ali a moment to realize who it was: Detective Hernandez. How had he gotten here?

If there were any sounds as the back doors of the ambulance swung open or as Father McLaughlin and Detective Hernandez hefted the gurney out of the vehicle, they were masked by the roar of traffic speeding by on the freeway. Moments later, Ali caught a glimpse of the two men rolling the gurney to the far side of the road and out of immediate danger. They were followed by the spare, hurrying figure of Sister Anselm.

Ali felt a moment of pure joy. She was winning. Four of the people in the line of fire were now in safety. Two remained: LeAnne Tucker and Ali.

Totally focused on her opponent, Katerina saw none of this. She had no idea she was losing. No matter what happened, based on numbers alone, she had lost and Ali had won.

"This is ridiculous," Katerina said. "You can't hurt me."

"I won't have to," Ali said with a smile. "Once I send those e-mails, the men in your life — the remaining men in your life, since poor Howard is no longer with us — will join forces to take you down. One or the other of them will be able to get to you no matter where you are. More likely, they'll hire someone to do it for them, just like you hired Marvin Cotton to set Lance on fire and burn down Lowell Dunn's house. Being burned is a particularly tough way to go, by the way, but I'm sure there's more than one firebug imprisoned in the state of Texas who will be happy to earn some extra cash on the side."

Katerina's weapon wavered slightly. Ali knew that she had landed a blow.

"If you tell them I've betrayed them,

they'll kill me," she said. "Especially my father."

"Yes," Ali said. "I thought as much."

"You don't understand," Katerina said. "He never wanted me. He wanted a son to carry on his name and his business. He had picked out someone for me to marry, someone he thought would be a suitable heir. When I refused, he threw me out."

"And you've been trying to even the score ever since. Sorry, Katerina. Game's over."

"Why are you doing this?" Katerina asked. "What do you want? Is it money? I have plenty of money."

"I want you to put down your weapon and turn yourself in. If you get yourself a good enough lawyer, maybe he can wrangle you a deal. That way, if you plead guilty to the three murders I already know you're responsible for, maybe the state of Texas will agree to take the death penalty off the table. If you're in prison for life without parole, I can live with that."

"And if I don't plead guilty?" Katerina asked.

"The e-mails I mentioned before get sent. They'll go through GHOST. We'll be able to manipulate them so they'll look like they came directly from you. We'll also be able to fix the time stamps."

That was where the bluff came in. Ali wasn't the least bit sure it was possible, but she understood that if she spoke the words with enough authority, they might seem feasible.

"Will those doctored e-mails stand up to legal scrutiny in a court of law?" Ali shrugged. "Who knows? Besides, it doesn't really matter; they're not going to law enforcement. They're going to your father and to Alonzo Diaz. The cartels can afford to have some top-notch cyber folks on their payrolls, but based on everything I've seen so far, they don't. Our GHOST-authored material will be accepted as gospel by what passes as cyber security for both cartels."

"They won't believe any of it," Katerina declared. "They'll figure out it's all a lie." She said the words, but Ali could see that the woman's confidence was slipping. The tool she had planned to loose on others was being turned on her. Instead of giving her power, GHOST had transformed her into a target.

"The way I see it, Katerina," Ali continued calmly, "is that you have two choices. You either lay down your weapon or take your shot, your choice. You may put a bullet through me, but I promise you this: If the state of Texas doesn't find a way to execute you for your crimes, somebody else will do the job."

Detective Hernandez reappeared on the passenger side of the ambulance. He carried a drawn weapon in one hand and a pair of cuffs in the other. "I believe it's over, Mrs. Barnes," he said. "You're outnumbered and outgunned. Now drop your weapon and get on the ground."

Katerina stiffened when she heard his voice. After a long pause, she dropped to the ground, but she didn't relinquish her weapon. Instead, she swung it around and took a wild shot at Hernandez before rolling under the ambulance. She fired again. Bullets pinged off the ground where Hernandez had been standing, but he was no longer there. He had leaped onto the vehicle's running board and clung there. Ali couldn't tell if he was wounded or not. On the far side of the ambulance, LeAnne had bounded to relative safety in the driver's seat.

As the scene unfolded, Ali knew she had mere moments before Katerina's deadly weapon would be turned on her. She dropped to the ground, landing on her belly with the Kahr in hand. Over the years, she had spent days on the target range with her Glock, practicing and honing her skills, but range work was always done with a stationary target — a paper target. This was a live woman, a human being, who was armed, dangerous, and beyond desperate.

Holding her breath, Ali sighted down the barrel of the unfamiliar weapon. Katerina was on the ground. LeAnne and Hernandez had taken cover with the ambulance, leaving Ali a relatively clear shot.

Katerina was focused on Hernandez and firing blindly at him. Ali knew she needed to make her first shot be her last shot. Shooting through the chain-link fence left her at risk of being hit by shrapnel. She had to make sure that her aim was true. Taking one last steadying breath, Ali pulled the trigger. The sound of the shot was reverberating in her head when Ali heard Katerina scream. That was when she knew it was over.

She scrambled to her feet and pushed open the gate. The chain and the broken padlock scattered uselessly to the ground. By the time Ali reached the passenger side of the ambulance, Detective Hernandez was pocketing Katerina's weapon, which had come spinning out from under the vehicle when the hollow point slammed into her arm.

"Thanks," he said with a smile. "That was some shooting! Now cover me while I pull her out from under there."

Hernandez grabbed one of Katerina's kicking legs and pulled her toward them. Screaming in pain, the wounded woman cradled her mangled arm as she emerged. The hollow point had entered just below her elbow and exploded out the far side of her forearm.

Seeing the damage and the blood and knowing she was responsible for it, Ali went all wobbly. As the adrenaline rush left her, the quaking returned to her knees. She felt sick to her stomach. She turned away from Hernandez and staggered over to the side of the road, where she bent over and heaved into the weeds. It was only when the retching stopped that Ali heard the thump of helicopter blades. The craft came close, but it didn't land. Instead, it circled far above as if trying to determine what had happened. Then it headed west, going back the way it had come.

When Ali returned to the ambulance, Sister Anselm and Detective Hernandez were tending to Katerina. While the detective kept them covered, Sister Anselm used his belt as a makeshift tourniquet around Katerina's upper arm. Katerina was sobbing but no longer screaming as the departing helicopter passed overhead. She turned on Ali. "You said it wouldn't come," she said accusingly. "That's what you said."

"Too bad," Ali told her. "I lied."

33

What happened next was a form of controlled chaos. The ambulance that B. had summoned to pick up Lance arrived first and had to be diverted to take Katerina to the same ER where Thad and Phyllis had been dropped off a little earlier. B., driving Father McLaughlin's Isuzu, arrived in time to see the two attendants, overseen by a hovering Sister Anselm, load a gurney into the back. Frantic, he raced forward and almost collapsed with relief when he caught sight of Ali standing on the far side of the ambulance.

"Who was that?" he asked, nodding toward the departing vehicle as it squawked once and the engine grumbled to life.

"Katerina," Ali answered.

"What happened to her?" B. asked.

"I shot her," Ali said simply. Then she leaned into his chest, breathing in the warmth of his body and reveling in the strength of his encircling arms.

"Are you okay?" he murmured into her hair.

"I am," she said, "but I don't think your plan of using me as High Noon's media babe is going to work out very well. This one's going to be a PR nightmare."

"Screw the PR problems," B. said. "I'm just glad you're all right."

At some point in the action, LeAnne had gone across the frontage road to look after Lance. Now she returned with Detective Hernandez at her heels. She went straight to B. and pulled him into a hug. "Richard and Father McLaughlin told me what you guys did. I can't thank you enough."

The first cops arrived in a cacophony of sirens. "The detectives will be here soon," a uniformed deputy told Hernandez. "They've gone to get a warrant. They said that anyone who isn't injured or in need of medical care should stick around to give statements."

When the second ambulance arrived to collect Lance, LeAnne went with him. Everyone else stayed where they were. By the time the detectives started asking questions, Father McLaughlin had collected B.'s Kahr and stowed it, along with his own weapon, in the locked chest in the back of the Trooper. The weapon Ali had used would be taken into evidence and most likely lost to him. He was philosophical about it: "That's all right. My kid brother runs a gun shop in Pecos. He can get me another one without any trouble."

Three hours later, the statements were given and signed. Since lives had been threatened, the detective assured Ali that he doubted any charges would be forthcoming, but she should probably plan to stay around for the next several days, until all questions had been answered.

At last, B. and Ali set off to collect Connor from the San Leandro Inn and take him to the hospital to rejoin his family. They found Leland and the boy in the business center. Leland was working on an e-mail while Connor was caught up in a game of solitaire. Duke and Duchess, both on leashes, were tethered to the back of Leland's chair.

Connor sprang to his feet when he caught sight of Ali. "Is my mom okay?" he asked.

"She's fine. Your brothers are fine. Your grandmother is fine. Now, if you'll give me a couple of minutes to change out of these clothes, we'll take you to see them."

"But where are they?"

"They're at the hospital."

515

"I thought you said they were okay."

"They are. Lance still needs hospital care. Thad and your grandmother were taken there to be checked out. They probably won't have to stay."

"Come on, Connor," Leland said. "Let's go walk the dogs while Mrs. Reynolds changes her clothes."

By the time they reached San Leandro Community Hospital, Phyllis and Thad had both been treated and released. Phyllis's emotional reunion with her dogs in the parking lot was almost as touching as Connor's waiting room reunion with his mother and Thad.

"We've been booted out of Lance's room," LeAnne explained. "Two detectives, Hopper and Harris, are in with him, probably asking him the same questions they asked me: about Lance's relationship with Jillian and if he had ever mentioned that her name was really Serafina. They also asked if I had any idea why Jillian would have come to our house last night. They said her BMW was found parked three blocks away. It was loaded with packed suitcases, as if she was getting ready to leave town."

"What did you say?" Ali asked.

"I told him I had no idea why she came there. I hadn't seen her since Lance broke up with her early last year. Since Lance has been either in jail or the hospital this whole time, I can't see how he'd know anything about her, either."

Detective Hopper emerged unannounced from Lance's room and looked around. "Well now," he said, "now that Ms. Reynolds has finished playing Wyatt Earp in the shoot-out at the O.K. Corral, perhaps she'd care to enlighten us as to how she knew who our victim was before we did."

"FR," Ali said without hesitation.

"FR?" he asked.

"Facial recognition technology," she replied. "Our company, High Noon Enterprises, uses it all the time."

"You seem to know more about this case than seems reasonable for an innocent bystander," Hopper said. "Tell me this. The M.E. says the autopsy revealed that Jillian Sosa, aka Serafina Miguel, was pregnant at the time of her death. Would you care to hazard a guess about who might be the father?"

"Maybe you should talk to Andrew Garfield," B. suggested. "He would be a good place to start."

It was only by chance that Thad Tucker was sitting on a waiting room chair that was behind and slightly to the side of Detective

Hopper when that exchange took place. Because Ali was looking at the detective, Thad's face was in the background. She saw the stricken look that crossed his face. In that instant, Ali knew.

Over the next few minutes, Hopper let LeAnne know that since her home was still an active crime scene, the family would have to stay someplace else until it was released. Eventually, the detectives left. B. was on the phone with the hotel, making additional room arrangements, when Thad Tucker stuffed his hands in his pockets and made for the door. "I'm going outside for a while," he said. "I need some air."

Ali followed him down the hall. Instead of going out through the lobby and into the parking lot, he slipped into a room that turned out to be a chapel. Ali paused for only a moment before following him inside. The chapel was tiny, with three wooden pews in the dimly lit room. Several votive candles set in colorful glass vases burned on a stone hearth in front of a small statue of the Virgin Mary.

Thad sat in the front pew, hunched over and sobbing. Ali slipped into the pew beside him. "How long had you and Jillian been dating?" she asked.

Thad turned his tearstained face in her

518

direction. "How did you know?"

"I knew because Duke and Duchess didn't bark," she said. "If they had, they would have awakened the whole family. I realized when I saw your face in there that they didn't bark because Jillian was someone they knew well."

Thad bit his lip and nodded. "They knew her," he said. "After Grandma went to bed at night, I'd leave the garage door open so Jillian could come in and out."

"She spent the night?"

Thad swallowed and nodded. "Sometimes."

"How often?"

"Often. Do you think I'm the father?"

"Do you?"

Thad nodded again. "Probably," he said. "It was all her aunt," he added. "She wanted Lance's program. She's the one who took Grandma the other day. When Lance gave them the program, Jillian talked her aunt into letting Grandma go. Then something went wrong with the program. Jillian came to the house to warn us that her aunt was upset. Somehow we ended up sitting in the backseat, necking. The next thing I knew, there was a woman standing in the garage. She had a gun pointed at us. She told me that I needed to go get my mother and grandmother and make them come down to the garage. If I didn't, she would shoot Jillian. I did what she said. I got them both. I thought she'd let Jillian go. She didn't. She pulled the trigger and Jillian was gone."

Overcome, Thad stopped talking and sobbed some more. Recalling the terrible scene in the back of LeAnne's Taurus, Ali understood why. She let him cry. At last he quieted.

"You're not going to tell Lance about Jillian and me, are you?" he asked.

"No," Ali said. "I'm not telling. You are. Did Detective Hopper ask you about any of this?"

"I told him I couldn't sleep. That I was outside just walking around when Jillian and her aunt showed up. I didn't want to say what was really going on."

"This is a homicide investigation," Ali said. "You have to. You can't withhold material evidence."

She paused, thinking about the white lie she had told about recognizing Jillian's face without ever mentioning the damning video of Jillian with Everett Jackson.

Okay, you're a hypocrite, Ali told herself. What else is new?

"Jillian was such a sweet girl," Thad continued. "I can't believe she's gone. I can't believe that awful woman killed her."

Ali took a deep breath. "Let's get a couple of things straight. The girl you knew as Jillian Sosa was not sweet, and she wasn't seventeen years old. She was at least twenty-two, a college graduate, and the woman she was working with, Katerina Barnes, wasn't her aunt. They were working together to get control of Lance's GHOST program. I'm sure that's why she went out with him, and it's probably why she went out with you, too. She was stringing you along because she thought you might have some idea of what Lance had done with the program or where he had hidden it. She probably even went through your house searching for it when you weren't home. This week she and Katerina had a serious fight. I think Jillian was trying to make a run for it. She might have made it if she hadn't stopped by to see you."

Thad was aghast. "You're kidding me! She was twenty-two? Are you sure?"

Ali nodded. "I'm sure," she said. "How old are you?"

"Fifteen."

"Which makes what she did to you, and probably to Andrew Garfield, too, statutory rape. Come on," she added, standing up. "First we have to tell your mother and

521

Lance about this. Then you have to talk to Detective Hopper."

For a long moment, Thad didn't move. Finally, he nodded. "All right," he said reluctantly. "Let's go."

34

It was after midnight when Ali and B. finished arranging car rentals and getting back to the hotel so they could crawl into bed. When Ali awakened the next morning, she had no idea where she was. When she looked at the clock radio next to the bed, she was astonished to see that it was ten o'clock in the morning. B. was in the shower. He'd had coffee delivered to the room. Dreading the idea of having to shower and put on yesterday's clothing, Ali went to the closet, hoping to find a hotel robe. What she found instead, hanging next to the bag with her wedding dress, was a closet full of clean clothes, not just for her but for B. as well.

Ali stood in front of the closet and marveled. Then she noticed that the paper bag containing B.'s underwear and socks had been opened; obviously, he had discovered the surprise. Sure enough, when B. emerged from the shower minutes later, he was half dressed.

"Either you need to give Leland Brooks a raise or I will," he said. "That man is a wonder."

Ali slipped into the shower. She came out dressed in the pantsuit she had worn on the day she drove to Oxford to see Kate Benchley. In the course of the evening, she had told B. about the voice mail from Banshee Group, but by the time they returned to the hotel, they had assumed that Leland was in bed asleep and hadn't wanted to disturb him.

"I need to tell him about the message from Kate," Ali said. "Do you want to come along?"

"No," B. said. "I'm working on something with Stu. Besides, that was yours and Leland's case. You can do that on your own. By the way," he added. "I've ordered a new phone, iPad, and computer for you. They're on rush delivery. They'll be here tomorrow."

"Is that necessary?" Ali asked. "Couldn't it have waited until we got home?"

"No," B. said. "Until the investigation winds down, there's no telling how long we'll be stuck here, and as we move forward with Lance on the purchase or whatever, I don't want to risk any more electronic eavesdropping."

"I'm not sure I want us to have anything to do with GHOST," Ali said. "You may think that talking on your cell phone or sending an e-mail is private, but programs like GHOST mean those transactions aren't private at all."

"Unfortunately," B. said, "that is absolutely true, but who do you want in charge of GHOST — somebody like Katerina Barnes? The drug cartel guys? Or Stu Ramey and yours truly?"

Shaking her head, Ali went to finish getting dressed. When she went looking for Leland a little while later, he wasn't in his room, the dining room, or the lobby. She found him in the business center, plugging away on a computer. He had an e-mail screen open, but he closed it immediately and almost guiltily when she entered the room.

"We were at the Highcliff for days," she said. "I never saw you in the business center once."

"I've been corresponding with Thomas," he admitted, looking abashed. "We were only together for a few weeks back then, but it would appear that I made as big an impression on him as he did on me. We've a lot of ground to make up. He says he's always wanted to visit the States. I'm hoping we can work something out. I've told him I can pay his way. I've plenty of money set aside for my old age. As they say, you can't take it with you."

"That's partly what I wanted to talk to you about," Ali said. "What Thomas helped us with."

"My father?"

Ali nodded. "Kate Benchley called yesterday and left a voice mail. I saved it. Would you like to hear it?"

Leland shook his head. "Just tell me."

"The blood on the collar of the homicide victim's shirt belongs to a male. The blood on the cuff of the shirtsleeve belongs to a man who was the victim's son. I sent along another sample as well: yours. The analysis shows that you are the brother of the man who left the bloodstain on the shirtsleeve. That means, unless there's another brother we don't know about, the killer was either Lawrence or Langston."

Leland was silent for a moment, then nodded. "Langston," he concluded at last. "That bloody bastard! At least we know now."

"Yes," Ali agreed. "At least we know, and what are you going to do about it?"

"Nothing," Leland said. "We've proved it,

as far as I'm concerned. I don't need to involve anyone else. It's too late for that."

On Monday morning, Ali and B. were waiting outside Lance's hospital room in San Leandro when a new physical therapist wheeled him back into his room.

"I don't know how to thank you," Lance said as tears welled in his eyes. "If I'd lost them all, I don't know what I would have done."

"The point is, you didn't lose them all," B. said with a smile, "but there is a way you can thank me."

"How?"

"By going to work for High Noon," B. said.

"You'd consider hiring me?" Lance asked. "Why? I'm still an inmate. I don't have a degree. I don't even have a high school diploma."

"What you have is a brain," B. said, "and a top-of-the-line product."

"GHOST?"

"Yes." B. nodded. "GHOST. For right now I'd like to offer you a lease/purchase agreement for the rights. High Noon will give you a large enough down payment that you'll be able to help your mother keep her house. A similar amount will go to Everett

Jackson's widow, Irene."

A frown creased Lance's face. "You just offered to hire me. What would I be doing?"

"Your first assignment will be to enroll in college. As long as you're there, you'll be paid a monthly stipend that should cover all your expenses. Again, Irene Jackson will receive an equal amount."

"What happens when I graduate?"

"We'll draw up an agreement that says if you wish to end the relationship at that point, High Noon can purchase the program outright at a predetermined price. If you want to stay on, you can buy your way into partial ownership of High Noon using the same predetermined amount as part of the buy-in. In the meantime, High Noon has first rights of refusal on any software you develop."

Ali had been watching Lance. When B. finished, the boy sat there for a moment as if transfixed. Finally he shook his head.

"I take it your answer's no?" B. asked.

"Not at all," Lance replied. "I mean, I can hardly believe it. This is too good to be true. There's only one problem. None of what you're offering will come in time to save the house."

"What do you mean?"

"I'm not eighteen yet. If I signed something, would it even be legal?"

The grin that returned to B.'s face was suddenly a mile wide. "What do you mean, would it be legal? You don't have to sign anything."

"Why not?"

"This is still Texas, isn't it?" B. asked. "How about a handshake?"

When Ali and B. emerged from Lance's room, a man in a suit was standing by the windows, talking discreetly into his telephone. B. said nothing as they walked through the waiting room, but when the elevator doors closed behind them, he burst out laughing.

"What's so funny?" Ali demanded.

"Did you see that guy in the waiting room?"

She nodded.

"I've never seen him in the flesh, but Sister Anselm sent me his photo. That's Daniel Crutcher, the local representative to UTI."

"The one who offered Lance's mother fifty thousand dollars?"

"That's the one," B. said. "I'm sure he's here to sign Lance up. How do you spell 'too little, too late'?"

Ali thought about that. She hadn't been entirely convinced that she wanted High

Noon to have GHOST, but if it meant beating out the people who had run her off the road? "Great, then," she said. "Good for us."

On Tuesday, Detective Hopper declared that the house on Twin Oaks Drive was no longer a crime scene and the Tuckers were allowed to go home. In their absence, the blood-spattered Taurus had been towed away. Detective Hernandez recommended a crew of people who went through the house cleaning up all the fingerprint dust that had been left behind by the crime scene techs. Armed with the initial deposit from the sale of GHOST, B. was able to escort LeAnne to the bank, where she was able to bail the house out of foreclosure. Then he accompanied her to the local Ford dealer and helped LeAnne negotiate the purchase of a replacement Taurus, one that turned out to be the first brand-new, off-the-showroom-floor vehicle that LeAnne Tucker had ever owned.

Late on Tuesday evening, B. and Ali went to the home of Irene Jackson. When they rang the doorbell of the modest tract home in a less than stellar neighborhood, the woman who answered the door did so cautiously, peering at them through the peephole first.

Seeing the need for a woman's touch, Ali took the lead. "I'm Ali Reynolds," she explained through the closed door. "And this is B. Simpson of High Noon Enterprises. We're friends of Lance Tucker's. We came by to tell you that Lance has negotiated a lease/purchase agreement for the program he and your late husband created. We're here to deliver your share of the down payment."

The door opened a little wider. "Lance sold GHOST?" Irene asked. "Really?"

In answer, B. held up the cashier's check with her name printed on the payee line. "Yes, really," he said. "This represents your share of the down payment. You'll be receiving a monthly stipend until Lance decides to terminate his agreement and sell the program to us or to someone else. At that time, you or your heirs will receive the remainder of your share of the purchase price."

Irene Jackson took the check. She stared at it wonderingly, as if not quite believing it was real. Then she shook her head. "Everett always said it would be worth money someday, but I never believed him. Thank you. Thank you so much."

Ali and B. didn't stay long. As they walked

back to the car, Ali took B.'s hand and squeezed it. "You're sure that video of Jillian and her late husband is gone?"

"Completely," B. said. "It'll never see the light of day. Stu made certain of that."

On Wednesday morning, when they went back to Twin Oaks Drive to say goodbye to the Tuckers, B. and Ali were surprised to find a busy construction crew working at the front door. Richard Hernandez, wearing jeans and a cowboy shirt and carrying a hammer, sauntered down the sidewalk to meet them. "These are some of the dads from the JV basketball team," he explained. "We're here to install the wheelchair ramp. We want to have it done in time for him to come home. He may not be here in time for his birthday, but he should be here by Christmas."

Glancing at B., Ali knew he understood. Richard Hernandez had come here to help right a wrong. That was part of the reason she and B. had come as well.

"LeAnne's inside, by the way," Detective Hernandez added. "She and her mother are busy putting up a Christmas tree, a live one. We just brought it home from the store."

Someone in the crew called for Rich's help. As he walked away, Ali turned to B. "I notice he's been hanging around a lot," she observed. "What do we really know about Detective Richard Hernandez?"

"For one thing," B. replied, "he's a fifteen-year veteran of San Leandro PD. He's divorced; owns his own home; his car is paid for; and he has full custody of his son, who's Thad's age."

"You did a credit check on the guy?" Ali asked.

"I did," B. said.

"Why?"

"Because I'm thinking that he's showing more than a professional interest in LeAnne Tucker, and I wanted to know what kind of guy he is."

Ali shook her head. "You're hopeless," she said.

They made their way into the house through the construction zone. When the doorbell rang, Duke and Duchess came scrambling to the door, barking as usual. It could have been the joyful sound of the barking dogs that made Ali smile just then, or it might have been her belief that life was about to get a whole lot better for LeAnne Tucker and her little family.

When it was time to head home, B. didn't attempt to make connections to Sedona through Austin. Instead, they took a charter directly from San Leandro. They landed at the Sedona airport as the sun was going down behind mountains to the west and while rays of sunlight were still glinting off the red rocks to the east.

As they taxied toward the plane's scheduled Fixed Base Operator, Leland leaned back in his seat and smiled. "It's good to be home," he said.

"It would be better if I had more than ten days to get ready for the wedding," Ali said. The closer they came to home, the more she worried about that.

"You'll be fine," B. said. "We'll be fine." He glanced over at Leland. "I noticed you were using the Wi-Fi earlier. Did you hear back from Thomas?"

Leland Brooks nodded happily. "He already has a passport, and he's working on getting a plane reservation. He says he's honored to be invited. He's always wanted to see Las Vegas, and I told him this would be a perfect time."

"You invited Thomas to the wedding?" Ali asked B.

"I did," B. admitted. "My gratitude for those clean clothes in the hotel closet that morning knows no bounds. I gave Leland a choice. I told him it was either invite Thomas or accept a raise. He opted for this.

You don't mind, do you?"

"Not at all," Ali said. As the plane came to a stop, she unfastened her seat belt and then went back to the closet in the rear of the plane to collect her hanging bag. Before exiting the plane, she stopped at the top of the stairs and squared her shoulders. "Okay," she said. "I have the groom, I have the dress, and I even have a few guests. Now it's time to go face my mother."

"Good luck with that," B. said, grinning. "Good luck to both of us."

ABOUT THE AUTHOR

J.A. Jance is the *New York Times* bestselling author of the Ali Reynolds series, the J.P. Beaumont series, the Joanna Brady series, and four interrelated southwestern thrillers featuring the Walker family. Born in South Dakota and brought up in Bisbee, Arizona, Jance lives with her husband in Seattle, Washington, and Tucson, Arizona. Visit her at www.JAJance.com.

The employees of Thorndike Press hope you have enjoyed this Large Print book. All our Thorndike, Wheeler, and Kennebec Large Print titles are designed for easy reading, and all our books are made to last. Other Thorndike Press Large Print books are available at your library, through selected bookstores, or directly from us.

For information about titles, please call:
(800) 223-1244

or visit our Web site at:
http://gale.cengage.com/thorndike

To share your comments, please write:
Publisher
Thorndike Press
10 Water St., Suite 310
Waterville, ME 04901